I0614807

Bring the Curious Midwife

d.a. gregory

.

For Roxie

Chapter One
The Girl's Curious

November 1957

On May 3, 1941, I walked across the stage at Emma Sansom High School in Gadsden, Alabama—me and a hundred and twenty-seven other educated, handsome, beautiful, know-it-all graduates. The world was ours for the taking, or so Mayor Williams said during his speech. I was the first in my family to graduate high school. Ida and Dewey St. Clair, my Mama and Daddy, finished the ninth grade and my older brother Bill made it to the tenth before dropping out when he turned sixteen. Some of those I graduated with I'd known since first grade. We'd come from a small feeder school out in the county called High Point that only went to the ninth grade, the same school my parents had attended. I'd even had some of the same teachers there. No one seemed to know for sure why the school was called High Point because it wasn't on a mountain or even a hill. Mama said it was named for a Cherokee Indian chief whose name sounded something like High Point. I guess she should know because she's part Indian, like a lot of people around here. There was no doubt though where the name of our high school came from.

Emma Sansom had been a real person and in school we learned the story of her helping General Forrest find a shallow spot to cross Black Creek during the War Between the States. My great-great-grandfather Yates fought in that war as a major in the 12th Regiment of the Alabama Cavalry and he's buried in the Pine Bluff Baptist Church cemetery. We still put flowers on his and his wife's graves every third Sunday in May at decoration. Decoration Days are as important as Easter for members of the churches in the area. They're on different Sundays during the month of May so people can visit and put flowers on the graves of distant relatives buried in all the local cemeteries. Her maiden name had been Mary Otha Nunn and that's where my name came from. I've only ever known one other Otha, but Mama says it was an everyday name when she was a little girl. My middle name's really Maybelle, but I shortened it as soon as I knew what it was. Daddy picked that name and Mama said that it was the name of one of his old girlfriends, even though he denied it whenever the matter came up.

For as far back as I can remember, Daddy worked at the Goodyear plant in Gadsden. He was there when it was built, working as a carpenter and when it was finished, he took a job in maintenance. My brother went to work there as soon as he turned sixteen and I rode to school and back every day with them. I had to wait around until they got off work, but it still beat riding the school bus for an hour and a half each way.

Mama told me once that Daddy tried farming for a while right after they got married; he was no good at it though and they nearly starved to death. When Bill was born, they needed a more steady income so Daddy tried carpentry and decided he liked it. After work and on the weekends, he and two of his friends, L.J. and Roy Lee, built the house Mama still lives in. Daddy then helped them build their houses. The lumber for all three came from land that Daddy's dad owned. I barely remember my grandparents on Mama's side, Grandpa and Grandma Yates; they died of tuberculosis when I was little. Daddy's parents though, Grandpa and Grandma St. Clair, lived to be an old couple and sat in the front row at my graduation. For a graduation present, they gave me ten acres of land. I knew the value of land even then and tried to talk them out of it but they insisted. "Free people own land," Grandpa told me, "and I want you to always be free." I didn't exactly understand what he meant by that, but Mama told me that Great-Great Grandfather St. Clair came to America from Ireland not much more than a slave. He worked his whole life for a hundred acres of land, never getting paid in money and depending on the Yankee landowner for everything it took to keep his family fed. That land's still owned by his descendants and now I own ten acres of it. Bill got his ten acres when he turned twenty-one and his land joins mine. That's about the only thing Bill and I have in common, other than a birthday. I was born exactly a year after him, on December 8. He was born in '21 and I was born in '22.

I guess it's human nature for all parents to tell their little girls they're special and mine told me that as far back as I can remember. Mama said I favored her youngest sister Jolene a little with my long blonde hair, but that I was always a lot taller than she'd been when she was my age. I figure my height came from Daddy's side of the family. Everyone else in the community thought I was special too. It wasn't because I was really smart or really talented, because I wasn't. I was pretty, far and away the prettiest girl around, and—the word everyone used was—curious. They didn't mean curious like asking a lot of questions either. Down here in the south it means odd. I was odd. Not that I had two heads or anything, but I wasn't much like the other girls of any age around where we lived.

My earliest photograph is of me kissing my cousin Rosalind—not Roslyn as she would make clear to anybody she met for the first time. All the relatives called her Rosa and she said she was nicknamed that because she was born with a twist of red hair on the very top of her head. I thought it was just short for Rosalind. That kiss wasn't one of those "on the cheek" kind that everybody thinks is so precious either; we were too old for that. It was a real kiss, even if no one but the two of us knew.

Nobody back then had a camera and when traveling photographers would come through in the summers and set up at the school, families who could afford it got their pictures taken. We'd never done that before, but Mama had saved back a little money that year and declared it was time we had a family photograph. As it happened, her cousin Marjorie and Rosa, her daughter, were visiting for a few days and they came along with us for the picture taking that Saturday morning. After the photographer took about a dozen pictures of our family, he asked who the pretty redheaded girl with us was. After saying what a shame it would be not to get her in a picture, Mama had to tell him she didn't have enough money for anything but the family photograph. Rosa was a charmer though, and within a few minutes, the photographer agreed to take a few pictures of the two of us for free. It was his idea that we kiss in one of them and everyone thought it was cute. I was six, she was seven; too old to be doing baby kisses like everyone thought we'd do, so we didn't. I still have that picture.

What made me curious, more than anything else, was that I liked girls more than boys—always had, even when I was little. Everybody knew it, and as I grew up it was plain to see if you bothered getting to know me. People said it ran in our family; Aunt Jolene was curious too, according to Mama. She ran off up north to join the Shakers when she was sixteen and never married. We heard from her from time to time when I was growing up, usually around Christmastime.

That picture of Rosa and me kissing was my most prized possession through my childhood and I told people she was my girlfriend. All the other girls had boyfriends, but I had a girlfriend. Some said it was a terrible waste, me being as pretty as I was and not wanting anything to do with boys. I heard that for the first time in fifth grade and it was the eighth-grade teacher, Mrs. Dobbins who said it to another teacher. I hadn't overheard it myself, but Bill had and he took all manner of delight in telling me, and adding that she also said I was just like Jolene, who'd been in her class years before. When I told Mama, she sat us both down and wanted to know exactly what was said and which teacher had said it. She didn't tolerate anyone saying things about her kids they ought to keep to themselves and Mrs. Dobbins mentioning Mama's sister in her gossiping was something she really shouldn't've done. The next morning, Mama got dressed up in her church clothes, made an extra lunch and rode the bus to school with us.

Whenever a parent came to school, it was for something important and everybody noticed. She stayed all day and rode the bus back home with us. I found out later that Mama had spent most of the day in Mr. Hudgins's office and that several teachers had been called in. I was too afraid to ask her what was said, and she wouldn't have told me anyway, but I'm sure she cleared the air. Mr. Hudgins had only been principal a year and hadn't yet had the pleasure of meeting Mama. He remembered her after that though, and anytime later on when the two met, sugar wouldn't melt in his mouth.

Mama always said she was ordinary as dried beans and that I got all the good looks the Yates family had been saving up for generations waiting for me to come along. Uncles and aunts on Daddy's side were tall and good looking, so I think some of mine came from that side of the family too. She might've thought she was plain, but my daddy loved my mama, and me too. When he would say, "Otha Maybelle, you could have your pick of any boy in the county," Mama would always add, "or girl." They knew I liked girls and I guess Mama having a sister who was the same way made things a little easier on me.

What was hard, though, was finding a girl who liked me. I didn't have my pick of any girl in the county even if Mama thought I should. I was pretty, everybody agreed, but I was pretty the way boys saw it, and girls my age saw pretty a whole different way. To girls, another girl was only pretty if she wasn't prettier than her. If she was, then she was either stuck up or a floozy. They had a hard time figuring out exactly which one I was. I wasn't stuck up. Nobody could say that about me. There was nothing for me to be stuck up about. During the Depression, we were just as poor as the next family, my clothes were no better than anyone else's, and if there was field work or anything else that had to be done, I wasn't too good to help. We had no crops to look after, but a lot of my classmate's families had acres planted and every able-bodied person helped their neighbors. Still do. It was just expected. A lot of what I know about life I learned picking cotton or pulling corn. You singled out a row between people you wanted to talk to because if you didn't the day went awfully slow. The first colored person I ever talked to was a girl in the row next to mine. She was twelve and I was ten. In the field, we didn't seem so very different but anywhere else, we wouldn't've been seen talking.

As for the floozy part—boys talked about kissing girls and girls talked about kissing boys, but girls didn't talk about kissing other girls. I'd kissed half the girls in the sixth and seventh grade classes by the end of that school year, but the other half didn't know and I wasn't about to tell them. It was a sort of understood thing that if I got a kiss from one of them, I wouldn't spread it around and they sure wouldn't either. Who was I going to tell anyway? Those girls were all alike; they liked boys and wanted to get married and have babies someday, but to them it was all right if they kissed me. It wasn't like they were cheating and I for certain had no intentions of stealing their boyfriends. They all said that kissing me was only practice, except some of them sure seemed to like it. I wasn't a threat to anybody and most girls liked being seen with me;

I think because I was pretty and not stuck up. Some saw me as a kind of bodyguard who could keep away boys they didn't care for. The boys all knew I wanted nothing to do with them and they couldn't imagine their girlfriends ever doing anything out of the ordinary with me. Maybe I did things with other girls, not with their girlfriends though. Most had only kissed their boyfriends once or twice anyway and couldn't have imagined what I might have in mind for them. The problem was, I was all right for kissing, but when it came to other things—and thanks to Cousin Rosa, I learned what those other things were—they held back. They were nice enough about it and I understood. They weren't like me and there was nothing I could do about it. By the time I was sixteen I was fit to explode and wondering exactly where up north the Shakers lived.

So I wasn't stuck-up and I wasn't a floozy. What I was most of all, was lonely—just deep down lonely. I liked being a girl and I liked being a pretty girl, but what I was looking for was a girlfriend and there wasn't one to be found. More than that, I wanted a girl to want me for her girlfriend; someone who would ask me out on dates and someone to do all the other things with that girls my age were doing. Dates were never anything special, usually a ball game of some kind or a church social, but I wanted to be asked all the same. There didn't seem to be anyone out there in our little community like me. I was curious, and I didn't know anyone else who was. I thought Rosa was— maybe a little bit. She lived in Eufaula down in South Alabama and we didn't get to see each other but maybe for a day once or twice a year. Right after I finished sixth grade though, her mama and daddy let her come up for a week in the summer and that was about the biggest week of my life up to then. She came on a bus all by herself and we picked her up at the depot in Gadsden. It'd been a year since I'd seen her and she'd grown up a lot since then, although I could've picked her out of a crowd with her long wavy red hair and freckles. She was a year older than me and would be the first girl close to my age to understand me and the way I was.

We took our baths together, mainly because Mama said it was a waste of hot water to fill up the tub again, and in the heat of the summer we didn't like being in the kitchen with fire in the stove any longer than we had to. We didn't get power in the house until long after I'd already moved out on my own and then it was only for lights and the radio. Up until then we'd had coal oil lamps and a battery powered radio we could only listen to for half an hour on weeknights and an hour on the weekends. Batteries were hard to come by. We didn't have running water and a hot water heater until the Christmas after the war. It was a present to the family from Daddy and about the best one I ever remember. Mama still talks about that Christmas.

Before Rosa arrived, I'd wondered if Mama would let us have our baths together with her knowing how partial I was to girls. There was never any mention of it. I guess she figured whatever was going to happen would happen sooner or later anyway and besides, her cousin Marjorie knew I was curious and she'd let her daughter visit for a whole week. Maybe everyone just imagined I was too young to have any carnal thoughts or that Rosa would put me straight if I got too interested in things I shouldn't. It was a mystery to me, but questioning Mama's thinking on the matter never would've crossed my mind.

Wednesdays and Saturdays were my normal bath nights. I got two baths a week; Bill usually only took one, on Friday nights. Mama and Daddy got theirs whenever they could. In the summers, we all took our baths in a big galvanized steel tub on the screened-in back porch that ran the full width of the house. The nearest family to ours lived half a mile away and there were trees all around our back yard, so we had our privacy. In the winters, we had to drag the tub into the kitchen after supper and then back out into the yard to empty it. In the summer, we just turned it up and let the water run through the cracks between the boards on the back porch. In the coldest part of the winter, we couldn't do that. It would freeze before the planks dried and make the porch so slippery we couldn't go out the back door for days. I loved my baths in the summer. After washing, I would sit out there on the back porch and wait for my hair to dry; fewer towels for Mama to have to wash, I thought, and I liked that time alone out in the open air. Mama said when I was little she couldn't keep clothes on me whenever I was outside and I guess I never got over it.

Before we got undressed that Saturday night for our first bath together, I went to my room and found the picture of us.

"Remember this?"

"Of course I do. It was my first kiss. How sweet; you kept the picture. I've been kissed lots of times since then." I hadn't really thought that ours was her only kiss, but it was nice of her to say that it was her first.

"But have you kissed another girl?"

"Nope, you were my first and last."

I was glad she hadn't kissed another girl after me. I don't know why, but it didn't matter to me how many boys she'd kissed, so long as I was the only girl.

"Can you help me get my dress off over my head, Otha May? It's too little, but I think it's pretty and I'm going to wear it as long as I can get in it. Mama says I'm growing so fast she can't keep me in clothes."

In the dead of summer no one wore a lot of clothes around the house. The men and boys mostly wore overalls with or without a shirt and the women and girls usually just shift dresses and a pair of panties.

She pulled her dress up over her waist as far as she could get it. I stood in front of her, pulled it over her head and was thankful for the lamp on our back porch. I knew she had breasts already. I'd noticed them filling out that tight print dress she was wearing, but I couldn't've guessed how much that dress was holding back. I tried not to stare but it was the first time I'd ever seen real breasts other than Mama's. Rosa's were pretty as June apples and just about the same size—and there were freckles on them too. I didn't need any help getting my dress off over my head; I asked her to help me just the same. Even though she was a year older than me, we were almost the same height, but without our dresses, standing that close, it was plain to see which of us was older. My breasts hadn't even started to round out, but I could see signs they would soon. My nipples were bigger and sometimes they would shrivel up and absolutely ache. Rosa's were big as quarters and a pretty pink color. Getting to see her breasts up close like that was something I'd thought about ever since Mama told me she was coming for a visit.

For our first bath, Mama let me use some of her lilac bath salts she saved for special occasions. The water was slippery to the touch and it smelled nice too. Rosa pulled her panties down, stepped out of them and into the warm water. That's when I first caught a glimpse of the little tassel of red hair between her legs. It was as red as the hair on her head and the shape looked a little like the long chin whiskers some teenage boys would try to grow to make themselves look older. I knew girls and boys got hair down there—girls did talk about that, especially if they were pretty sure the girl they were talking to was still slick as a peeled onion like me. I looked between my legs after every bath, but I saw no sign of any hair sprouting. I slipped out of my panties and into the water before Rosa could see how baldheaded I was down there.

The water was warm and the bath salts made my skin feel smooth. It was a nice slippery feeling. Before Rosa arrived, Mama had given me a new cake of Palmolive bath soap we could use. She said young girls shouldn't use hand soap on anything but their hands. She had a cake of

Cashmere Bouquet on her dressing table, but I wouldn't dare ask to use it. Rosa sat across from me in the tub and anytime a breeze would come through the screen wire, her nipples would scrunch up and stand out like the earliest little red blackberries before they fill out and turn. She saw me looking so I thought I ought to say something.

"I hope my breasts start looking more like yours soon. I'm tired of being flat as a fritter."

"They're budding already; that's clear as day, and if you really want them to grow fast, you have to pinch your nipples real hard every morning when you get up and again every night before you go to bed."

As soon as she said that, she reached over, pinched both of mine and busted out laughing.

"Then you must've been pinching yours a lot." And with that, I pinched both of hers—not hard, but hard enough to make her jump. Pinching them wasn't at all what I wanted to do, but it gave me an excuse to touch them, and since she'd touched mine, I figured it was all right.

The Palmolive smelled like vanilla flavoring and we got good and soapy with it. We didn't normally have shampoo soap at home so the Palmolive would have to do. I knew what I wanted to ask her, but she made the offer first.

"Turn around and I'll wash your hair, then you can wash mine."

Nobody had washed my hair for me since I was a little girl. When I got turned around, she slid up close behind me and slipped her legs alongside mine. I'd had no idea before how good it could feel having someone wash my hair, and Rosa's legs touching mine under the warm water stirred up something inside me. When she finished, I leaned over the side of the tub so she could rinse my hair with the pitcher of water we always kept on the back porch just for that. Then it was my turn to wash her hair. We turned around and I slid myself up close with my legs squeezed between hers and the tub. While I washed her hair, I thought what I really wanted to do was reach around and pull her back close to me, but I couldn't bring myself to do more than think about it.

She leaned over the tub for me to rinse her hair, but she'd used all the water in the pitcher on mine. There was nothing to do but go around the side of the house to the well and draw a fresh bucket so that's what we did, both of us naked as Jay birds and laughing the whole time. She bent over and I poured the bucket of cold water over her head. That was enough to make her shiver and run for the house. On my way back to the porch, I saw the curtain move in Bill's window.

Back up on the porch, Bill couldn't see us, and I didn't say anything to Rosa about what I'd noticed. It was dark on that side of the house anyway, except for the moonlight, so he probably hadn't gotten an eyeful. We sat out on the porch and brushed each other's hair until it dried. I checked to make sure there was nobody in the kitchen before we walked through naked to my room with our dirty clothes. It was still early, but we didn't want to get dressed and go out to the living room and listen to the radio with the rest of the family, so we put on our thin cotton gowns, sat cross-legged facing each other on my bed and talked about everything from school to boys. She knew a lot more about boys than I did. She had the most beautiful blue eyes and pale white skin she said never tanned but would sure blister easy enough.

I reached over to my nightstand for the old photo of us kissing and held it at arm's length.

"Yeah, this is my favorite picture in the whole world," I told her. "I think it's perfect and I look at it all the time."

"We should get another one made just like it now that we're practically grown up."

"But then you'd have to kiss me again."

"What makes you think I'd mind that?"

She took my face in her hands and leaned forward. It was a kiss I'll never forget as long as I live, and I didn't want it to end. She must've learned a lot about kissing from somebody. All the kisses from the girls in my class were like play acting compared to how that one made me feel. This was a kiss from somebody who understood what kissing was all about, and I didn't have to ask her for it. For the first time, I wasn't a stand-in for a boy. I was a girl being kissed by a girl who really wanted to kiss me, or that's what I imagined anyway. She didn't just quick-kiss me either; she sort of brushed my lips with hers, barely touching them and it was the most wonderful feeling in the world. This was the way I'd wanted to be kissed and the way I'd tried to kiss other girls—before they backed away. I didn't back away from Rosa; I wanted more. I took her face in my hands, the way she'd held mine, and kissed her the way I'd always wanted to kiss a girl. Then, like I knew what I was doing, I pulled her toward me without breaking the kiss and lay back on my bed. When I finally let her breathe again, she leaned over to my nightstand and blew out the lamp. That's when we did things I'd only dreamed about and a lot of things I hadn't imagined. We were like two snakes in a gallon jug and there were a couple of times when I thought she would scream out loud.

It was late when she finally curled up next to me; like two spoons in a silverware drawer I thought. As I lay there with Rosa's arm across my stomach, a lot of thoughts I'd had for years started to make sense. I knew then why I like girls. I liked how it felt being that close to another girl and I couldn't have even imagined Rosa being a boy. So, that's just the way I was and there was no reason to have to explain it to anybody. All the people I cared about already knew how I was anyway.

The sun was up Sunday morning when I felt Rosa's hand move. That woke me and for a second, I wondered who was in my bed. I don't know why, but I pretended to be asleep. When I opened my eyes, she was leaning over my shoulder smiling.

"Good morning Otha May," she whispered. "I thought I would wake you up with a kiss."

I rolled over onto my back and she kissed me slowly, her lips hardly touching mine. I grabbed her face with both hands and pulled it down to mine. When she opened her mouth a little, our tongues touched. Things were working out just fine that morning and I liked having Rosa right where she was.

I wasn't expecting what came next, but when her lips moved from mine down my neck, it was the most thrilling feeling in the world. I thought I would positively lose my breath. How could any girl ever stand this for very long? It was a feeling like there was something ticklish growing inside me that had to be pushed out and it got so powerful I had to make her stop even if I didn't really want her to.

"Otha May, are you and Rosa awake? Breakfast's on the table and you have to get ready for church. Get up now and get dressed; we're running late."

Making me crazy would have to wait and thank goodness Mama didn't open the door. We jumped out of bed, put on clean panties and got into our church dresses. I'd heard voices from the kitchen earlier, so I knew everyone was up, but I hadn't realized how late it was. We made the bed together and when Rosa pointed to the wet spot on the sheet we'd slept on, we started to laugh, accusing each other of being the cause of it.

Everybody had already eaten, so Rosa and I had the kitchen to ourselves. That was good because I didn't want to have to explain what we were still laughing about and why the smile on my face wouldn't go away. We brushed our teeth at the sink on the back porch after we finished eating and brushed out each other's hair. We were ready to go by the time Daddy got the truck started. That always took some time. It was old and cantankerous and usually required pouring a shot of gas down the carburetor to get going. Mama and Daddy rode in the cab and the rest of us stood up in the bed. I didn't like the way Bill looked at Rosa, who was doing her best to hold her dress down in the wind. Maybe he'd seen more the night before than I thought.

Rosa and I sat with my friends while Reverend Jessop preached on the sin of lust. Years later, in a letter, I would remind Rosa of that sermon and how fitting it had been. After church, I introduced her to everybody. They were all girls who went to my school, but I didn't see them much in the summers except at church. I think a couple of them I'd kissed were a little jealous and nothing could've made me happier. Rosa was prettier and she had real breasts too. When Mary Alice Wester had the chance without anyone hearing, she asked if Rosa was curious like me.

"A little bit," was all I would say. She'd had her chance months before. I'd tried to kiss her in the cloakroom after school and she wouldn't let me. Then she found out I'd kissed Susan Stancil and had a change of heart. It was too late though; I wasn't a floozy.

When we got home it was so hot we couldn't stay in the house, so as soon as Rosa and I got changed, I mentioned something about going swimming in the creek that ran through the woods behind our house. She was all for it. We didn't have swimming suits, so a couple of Daddy's old shirts and our panties had to do. That part of the creek with the swimming hole was on our land, but sometimes boys from the community would swim there anyway. When Bill said he might come with us, I was glad Mama told him he could wait until we got back.

"You know there's a water moccasin in that creek. I've seen it," he warned as we ran out of the house with

Daddy's shirts and a couple of quilts. I'd rather have fought off the snakes than have him staring at Rosa the whole time.

"He's just a horny boy," Rosa said when we were away from the house, "and I know how to handle horny boys."

"But how do you handle horny girls?" I said with a laugh. I knew what horny meant—sort of.

"When I told you that I've never kissed a girl except you, Otha May, I was telling the truth."

"So last night and this morning, with everything we did, you didn't know what you were doing either?"

"I was scared to death, but I knew you liked girls and I hoped you'd like me."

"I like you Rosa; I like you a lot."

When we got to the creek there was no one else around. We went back into the woods a little way, got out of our dresses and into our do-it-yourself swimming clothes. The water was cold and my nipples felt like they were being twisted with a pair of wire pliers. When we had as much of the cold water as we could stand, we got out, took off our wet clothes and lay on our quilts in the sun. There still wasn't anybody around as far as we could tell. When she lay back on the quilt, I got my first long look at her in the daylight. She was a pretty girl all over and just looking at her made me glad I was curious. She turned to me and smiled. I didn't mind at all that she caught me looking.

"I begged Mama and Daddy for a month to let me come and visit. I just had to get to know you better. You're the only girl I know who's…"

"Curious?"

"Yeah, that's what Mama calls Cousin Jolene too. I've never met her, but she gets letters from her sometimes. She writes that she's happy living up north with the Shakers, or are they Quakers. All the women live together and all the men live together in different buildings. I've thought it might be nice living without boys around and having a girlfriend. I've been kissed by boys, but I always wanted to be the one doing the kissing, not just getting kissed. I don't want to be some boy's girlfriend; maybe I want a girlfriend of my own."

"It's like you can read my mind, Rosa. I've always wanted to be the one getting kissed, but none of the girls I know would ever do that. They used to let me kiss them sometimes, though they'd never try to kiss me. I thought maybe I wasn't good enough to be kissed and that they were only using me for practice. I guess I've always wanted to be a girl's girlfriend too, if that makes any sense."

We stayed at that swimming hole talking until it began getting dark and we learned a lot about each other. She'd just started having her monthly cycle and I had to ask all about that. They hadn't been much of a bother for her so far which made me feel better. I hoped that ran in the family too. They didn't seem to cause Mama much grief either. We'd talked some about things like that, but she only answered the questions I could figure out how to ask and there weren't very many of them. Rosa answered other questions, though, that I'd never have thought to ask Mama and we were so talkative that afternoon that neither of us noticed we hadn't had dinner before we left the house. It was best not to swim right after eating anyway. She admitted to me that she would probably get married someday because she didn't hate boys—some she liked a lot—and she wanted to have babies. She laughed when I said boys would probably be needed for that. On the way back to the house, she said something that I'd never thought of.

"Whoever I marry has to let me have a girlfriend though, or I won't be spreading my legs for him—simple as that."

After we quit giggling, what she said got me to thinking.

Supper that night was leftovers from dinner. In the country, the noontime meal is usually called dinner, hardly ever lunch, and the evening meal is always supper. We didn't mind leftovers; since we hadn't eaten earlier it was new to us. Mama would often fry a chicken for Sunday dinner if we had one to spare and I was glad they'd saved us some. We helped with the dishes and Mama gave me a kiss on the cheek after the last dish was dried and put away.

"It's nice having another young woman in the house, don't you think Otha May?"

"Yes Ma'am, it's real nice. Rosa and I have more in common than I could've imagined."

Mama smiled that smile that I always liked to see and one I never saw her give anybody else. "Then I guess she'll love helping with the washing tomorrow about as much as you do."

I hated Mondays for that very reason, but with Rosa around, it would be a lot better.

"Now that there's three of us and only two men in the house, we'll get to pick what we listen to on the radio tonight. Otha May and I usually have to listen to some ball game or the fights, but tonight we can choose. What do you want to listen to Rosa?"

"I like *Amos 'n' Andy* on Sunday nights. It's mine and Mama's favorite. Daddy grumbles about it, but I think he likes it too. He always picks *The Jack Benny Program* if he gets to the radio first; either one would be all right with me."

We listened to *Amos 'n' Andy* and Daddy didn't complain much. I was wanting the program to be over, because the sooner it was over, the sooner I would be in bed with Rosa again. It was sweltering hot that night even with the windows raised. We didn't bother with our gowns and I lay back on my bed waiting to see what she had in mind for our second night together. There were things I had in mind for her too. She threw one leg over me, sat on my hips, and then leaned over and kissed me. When I pulled her close and made my way down her neck with kisses, she started shaking and I was afraid I'd already done something wrong.

"Okay, you have to stop a minute, Otha May. I always thought having someone do that would be the greatest thing in the world, but it's making my heart skip a beat."

"Rosa, there's something I want to ask you and I don't know how to. I've been thinking of what to say all day. It's none of my business, but there was something you did last night—twice, while we were... you know. I thought you were gonna scream."

There was a sort of gleam in her eye as she reached over and turned the lamp way down. "You were about to find out this morning if your Mama hadn't called us to breakfast when she did. I call it boiling over because that's what it feels like, and I learned just last night how much better it is doing it with somebody."

"You can do it by yourself, whatever it is? How'd you figure that out?" I had to ask.

"Remember, I have an older brother too. I think boys do it all the time. At least my brother does, every time he takes a bath I think. He doesn't know I've watched, and the first time was an accident. Our back porch is right outside my bedroom window and one night I walked into my room for something and didn't light the lamp. Through the window I could see that the back-porch lamp was burning, and I didn't know why that should be, so I looked out, and there he was, standing up in the tub, doing it. I watched him more than a few times after that and decided whatever boys could do girls could do too, and I was right."

"Okay, you have to tell me everything now and don't leave out the good parts either." If she'd told me I'd have to jump off Noccalula Falls naked the next day to get her to talk, I would've made that promise. I learned a lot that night and I might've learned a little more the next morning if Mama hadn't knocked on the door again when she did.

"Time to get up girls; that wash won't get done by itself."

After we ate breakfast, we stripped our bed and then the others. Bedclothes got washed first. Mama liked for them to hang out the longest because she said the more air they got, the better they smelled. She was right about that. I loved sleeping on clean sheets. While they were washing, Rosa and I collected all the other dirty clothes and hauled them out to the back porch. I noticed that Mama was doing something in the kitchen out of the ordinary.

"You never mind," she said when she saw I was paying attention. "We have a guest in the house and I'm making something special for dinner. It'll be done by the time you girls get them clothes hung out."

It took all morning long to do the washing and get the clothes on the line, but the time passed tolerably with Rosa helping. Twice I got a kiss between the hanging sheets. On our trips between the back porch and the clothesline, I could smell something good coming from the kitchen. Mama was baking. She was just taking the last layer of the cake out of the oven when we came in the house and I could smell the chocolate in the double boiler on the oven next to the frying potatoes. She only made chocolate cake on special occasions and I guess having some extra help with the washing was special enough. Mama was an artist frosting a cake and some of my earliest memories are of sitting at the kitchen table watching her. She had one special big spoon with a wooden handle she always used, but that day she used two and I soon found out why. Rosa and I sat patiently watching her and when she had the swirls just the way she wanted them, she handed us the spoons. I always got to lick the spoon. I watched Rosa and she watched me. I knew very well what she was thinking about and she knew very well what I was thinking too. I'm glad Mama didn't ask what the two of us were laughing about.

We didn't wait for the cake to cool before it was sliced. "Nothing wrong with having dessert first," Mama said.

"Or licking the spoon," Rosa added with a grin in my direction.

That week with Rosa was about the best of my life, but the most important thing I learned from her was that I wasn't the only curious girl in the world. If Rosa was partly curious, there had to be others, maybe some as curious as me.

We didn't get to see each other much after that summer, but I got letters from her regularly. Right after my graduation, she wrote that she and her boyfriend were getting married. His name was Dallas—or was it Denver? She'd written to me about him some before and I got the idea things could get serious between them. His daddy owned a cotton gin in Eufaula and Rosa said they were pretty well off. I didn't ask if he was going to let her have a girlfriend, although one word from her and, in a heartbeat, I would've been on a southbound bus.

Chapter Two
Hazel

After graduation there were only two choices: get a job or get married and I didn't care much for either one. There were jobs in Gadsden and I could catch a ride with Daddy and Bill every day, or I thought maybe I could find a place of my own in town. There were boarding houses, though Mama wouldn't think of me living with strangers. She was happy having me at home and I made myself useful helping her with work around the house, but she could see how lonesome I was. I even thought about writing Rosa and inviting myself for a visit, and then talked myself out of it. She had a new husband and he might not appreciate the company. The only time I saw anybody other than the family was at church. My friends from high school had paired up and were planning weddings and that was all they talked about. We did have a new family move into the community late that summer though, the Leeths, Emmitt and Uldean. Their oldest was Hazel Ruth. She was a little older than me and married to a boy in the army. Then there was James and Glenda. James would be a senior at Emma Sansom and Glenda would be in fifth grade at High Point when school started. Mama said they moved up from Montgomery County after several years of bad crops, looking to try something else. Daddy got Mr. Leeth a job at the Goodyear and the two of them became good friends. The Leeths lived in one of the Yother's rental houses less than a half-hour's walk toward their homeplace from us.

Hazel was a tall, skinny, sad-looking girl with sunken eyes and dark hair. I was sure she had a story. She showed up one afternoon, just out walking she said, and I invited her to come sit with me on the front porch. We did that with anybody who happened to be walking by, just to be neighborly and have somebody to talk to. I'd seen her at church but hadn't talked to her other than to be introduced by her mother. She had a kind nature and I never turned down a conversation with anybody close to my own age because there weren't many in our little community.

Her visits became regular whenever she walked by and I happened to be sitting out on the porch in the afternoon, which was about every afternoon. Neither of us had too much to say the first few times she stopped by, but that soon changed. We'd only talked for a few minutes that afternoon, about nothing in particular, before I guess she decided to clear her conscience. It was like she'd been working her way up to it for a while. Maybe she thought she could talk to me.

"Let's get this over and done with. There ain't no husband in the army. We moved here because I'm nearly four months pregnant and the boy that got me pregnant wouldn't marry me. It's as plain as that. If the rest of them want to keep up the story they've been telling everybody, I don't care, but that's the God's truth. I guess if there's a war, they'll have my make-believe husband killed off in some faraway place to make everything look right. This wedding ring belonged to Mama's mama and I was supposed to get it when I got married. Daddy says I have to wear it for appearances. I used to try it on when I was little and now I just hate it."

I didn't know what to say to all that, but she said it with such honesty, I couldn't help but believe every word. I was glad we had the front porch to ourselves. Daddy and Bill were still at work and Mama was at Widow Campbell's helping her make blackberry jam. There was no reason for me to have done it, but I took Hazel's hand in mine and then kissed her on the cheek. That was the sort of thing we did; it didn't mean anything, but it seemed to've meant a lot to her.

"They say you're curious, that you won't have anything to do with boys. I wish I'd never let one touch me. I wouldn't be in the shape I'm in now. Of course he said he loved me and that we'd be getting married soon anyway. I think they're supposed to say that after they get your panties off."

"How'd you ever tell your mama? That must've been hard."

"She just came out and asked me a month and a half ago and when I started crying, she knew. I don't know why she suspected. She told Daddy for me and also told him that she wouldn't be able to bear the shame if the news got out. There was nothing to do but move. It's not like we had much to leave behind. The bank took our farm when I was little and we've been sharecroppers ever since, living in a house a lot worse than the one we're living in now."

"What about the boy. Will he say anything?"

"My daddy and his daddy had a long talk. Donnie, that's the boy's name, was made to sit and listen. His daddy first said that he would have to marry me, but Daddy wouldn't hear of it. He might not have been so hardheaded if Donnie's family wasn't just as poor as us. We would've had to move in with one of them and I think that had a lot to do with it. Donnie's daddy told him that if he ever heard anyone in the community say we'd moved because I was pregnant, then he'd have no choice but to marry me anyway and my daddy agreed. So, I don't think he'll be talking; he never wanted to marry me in the first place. I know that now. Girls at school were forever saying it's as easy to spread your legs for a rich boy as a poor one, but I guess I didn't listen. We did it exactly four times and if anyone had ever told me how little there was to it, I would've kept my knees together. It was over and done with before I had time to notice anything—except for the first time and that just hurt. Maybe you have to practice a lot, but as far as I'm concerned, I can take it or leave it. I'm sorry Otha May for talking your ear off; I haven't had anyone to talk to about what happened. We barely know each other and here I've told you everything and a lot more than I should've. Lord, I hope you don't think I'm some kind of hussy. I've only ever done anything with one boy and you see what that got me."

"I don't think any such thing, Hazel and I'm glad you decided to talk to me. I don't know much about boys and I'm not all that interested in learning, but it sounds to me like Donnie did you wrong."

"Oh, he's not a bad boy. I was his first real girlfriend and the first girl he ever did anything with. It's just as much my fault as his. I got to see him the night before we left to move here. It was wrong of me, but I sneaked out of the house at midnight and met him in one of the empty rental houses next to ours. It was my idea that we do it one last time. I was already pregnant, so I figured what could it hurt. What I was hoping was that it would last a little longer. That sounds terrible, hearing myself say it now; I just knew there had to be more to it than what I'd felt the other three times. I was wrong about that too."

I don't know why she opened up to me the way she did, but we talked until Mama got back and I told Hazel a lot about me that I'd never told anybody. She didn't look pregnant; who could tell with the dresses we wore. Mama tried to get her to stay for supper, but she said she had to get home. She didn't make me promise I wouldn't tell anybody what she'd told me; she didn't have to. I wanted a friend and she did too. She was the first girl I knew for sure that had done it with a boy and I was the first girl she'd known that had done it with a girl. She was the only living soul I ever told about Cousin Rosa and I told her everything, only leaving out the things I didn't know how to describe. I guess I left out a lot. She wasn't at all curious like me, but I talked to her like she was. I'd never had anybody I could talk to about things like that and whether she was interested or not, she listened.

Her brother James became a bother though. He'd surely heard I had no interest in boys, but he flirted with me all the same and made a point of walking by the house when he thought I might be sitting on the front porch. Of course I would invite him up to sit for a spell. I didn't want to be stuck-up. Mama wouldn't stand for that way of treating a neighbor. We never talked about anything worth remembering, but he always had something to say. He was good looking for a boy, and I sort of liked the attention; then I heard he'd told everyone at church that he was going to ask me to the next social and that was enough. I barely knew him, and besides that, he was a boy. Hazel thought it was funny and took delight in telling me how much her brother loved me.

"You're the prettiest girl around here whether you like it or not and James's never had a girlfriend before, so be nice to him. He talks about you all the time and you don't have to kiss him or anything."

"I'm not going to be his girlfriend and you know for sure I'd rather kiss you anyway." I hadn't said anything like that to her before and I didn't mean to say it then. She'd already told me she couldn't imagine herself doing anything with another girl and I was satisfied just being her friend. I don't know why I opened my big mouth at that moment.

"Be nice to my brother, but not too nice, and you never know what might happen."

With her saying that and the smile she had on her face when she said it, I would be as nice to her brother as I had to be.

Everybody knew Hazel was married, so boys didn't pay her much attention and I think that bothered her. The two of us had been seen sitting together at church, but that didn't start any gossip. After all, she was married and pregnant, so she couldn't be curious like me. Word got out she was pregnant soon after they moved into the community. She said her mother had told a few of the women and that's all it took. According to Hazel, they thought it was right Christian of me to be a friend to her. She'd become a different girl in the few weeks I'd known her and I like to think I had something to do with that. The sad face and eyes were gone. She had begun to put on some weight and she simply looked healthier. Mama said it was her glow; that all pregnant women got it. Whatever it was, she was happier and looked it.

The highlight of our week was Saturday nights when she would come over after I finished my bath and we'd curl each other's hair for church the next day. It was a tedious thing trying to curl my own but doing hers was easy and it gave us a chance to talk—some would say gossip. Mama had exactly twenty-two bobby pins and she counted them before and after letting us use them to make sure we hadn't lost any. I'd already lost two and felt bad about it.

Sure enough, one Monday afternoon when James came walking by and I invited him up on the porch to sit, he asked me to go to the social the next Sunday with him. Depending on the weather, it could have been the last one of the year. It took him an hour to get around to it and when he finally got the words out, I couldn't bear to turn him down. I got the idea Hazel had told him that if he asked, I might say yes. She knew very well I'd say yes.

That Saturday night before the social, Hazel came over as usual, but she got there a little early and I was still in the tub. Mama and the rest of the family were sitting on the front porch enjoying the cooler air and she told Hazel to go on through the house, that she'd find me on the back porch. When I heard someone open the screen door, I grabbed a towel and covered up. I didn't know who might be wandering through. She stopped at the door when she saw I was in the tub and started to turn around.

"Hazel, come on out. I'm just about to wash my hair. You're early."

"Yeah, I thought if you didn't mind, I'd wash my hair over here. Mama says the curling takes better if you do it right after washing your hair and mine's usually about dry by the time I get here if I wash it at home. She let me borrow her shampoo soap and it smells real nice. I thought if I got here a little early, and you wanted to, we could both try it." I threw the towel back on the rack and finished washing as we talked.

"That's awfully sweet of you Hazel. I guess you've heard about the big date tomorrow afternoon."

"It's all that boy can talk about. He's going to the Sunday social with the prettiest girl in these parts and he wants everyone to know it. Even if he asks, I won't tell him how much prettier you are without your clothes." I saw the grin on her face. "And I don't think your good looks are a waste just because you don't like boys. I'm sorry, Otha May, I didn't mean to say any of that. It's none of anybody's business and it sure ain't none of mine, but people do say that about you—that your good looks are wasted."

"You've heard that too, have you? Well, you know how people are; they're gonna talk no matter what. After I'm seen with a handsome young man tomorrow, they'll really have something to talk about. They might think I've finally seen the light."

I stood up, stepped out of the tub and reached for my towel. I took my time drying off and looked a few times to see if she was watching; she was and she didn't try to hide it. I made sure she got an eyeful.

"What would be a terrible waste," she said with a bigger grin that went from ear to ear, "would be letting some pecker-head boy get his hands on what I'm looking at. I swear Otha May, you're the prettiest thing I've ever laid eyes on—not that I've ever seen another girl naked, but there can't be any as pretty as you."

"So I can break your brother's arm if he tries anything tomorrow?"

"If he so much as touches you, I'll break it—and a lot more."

I didn't bother putting any clothes on. I just let her look. It was awkward with her on her knees leaning over the tub while I soaped up her hair, but there was no other way if we were going to use the warm water we had. The shampoo was heavenly. It made a lot more bubbles than ordinary soap and it smelled so much nicer. There was no warm water for rinsing our hair after she finished mine and the bucketful from the well she dumped over my head in the back yard made my nipples ache. I was more careful and didn't even get her dress wet. Back up on the porch, we combed out each other's hair. She had nice hair and it looked especially good curled. It was about the same length as mine but dark and thick and I loved working my fingers through it.

I'd brought the bobby pins out after heating my bath water, so they were ready for us. We took turns sitting and standing, wrapping strands of hair around our fingers and then pinning it in place. When I finished her last curl, a thought came to me.

"I hear you don't get your period when you're pregnant. Is that right?"

"That's about the only good thing about it so far. I've always had terrible cramps and Mama says after the baby comes I won't have that problem anymore."

"Do you feel any different? I've heard some have morning sickness and all kinds of cravings."

"The only thing I've noticed is that my breasts ache all the time and my belly's starting to round out. You want to see?"

I had only to nod and she stood up, turned around facing me and lifted her dress up over her stomach. She held it there with her chin and pulled her panties down a little. I couldn't really see what she meant. I still wouldn't have known she was pregnant. Her belly was maybe a little round, although I didn't think it was noticeable. I don't know why but I reached out to touch it, then caught myself.

"It's okay, you can touch it and someday I'll tell my baby you were the first person I introduced him or her to."

"Do you have names picked out yet?

"Abigail if it's a girl and Nathaniel if it's a boy. I don't want my baby to have a plain name like everybody else in my family."

I didn't just touch her. It had been a long time since I'd touched another girl anywhere that couldn't be seen. With both hands I felt her stomach as long as she let me. She backed away right after I felt a little tremor run through her. She wasn't the only one getting little tremors. I stood up fully intending to kiss her, but I thought better of it at the last minute. She was the closest friend I had and I didn't want her to think less of me.

"My hair'll be dry by the time I get home, but I'm gonna sleep in these curls tonight anyway. I'm afraid if I take the pins out, they'll go away by morning."

I pulled my dress on and walked her through the house to the front porch where everyone was sitting.

"Looks like we'll have a couple of movie stars at church tomorrow," Mama said when she got a look at us.

I dumped the water out of the tub and went to bed, but I didn't go to sleep right away. If Hazel wasn't curious like me, she wouldn't have to do anything; just letting me touch her would be enough. She hadn't really promised to kiss me if I went to the social with her brother, so I had no reason to think the thoughts I did that night. I don't know if it's possible to boil over in your sleep, but I swear I did; I don't know how many times. I imagined telling her someday what she'd put me through that night.

At church I sat with Hazel as usual. Her hair was beautiful and then her brother came and sat next to me. She just smiled while I fidgeted and imagined everyone was staring. He was well behaved though and didn't try to sit too close or even talk to me. After the service, he walked out with Hazel and me and tried to strike up a conversation, complimenting me on my hair and dress. My hair did turn out nice that day, but the dress was older than both of us put together. It had been Mama's and I wanted more than anything to have a new one for Sundays. Nobody had money for such things, though that didn't keep me from dreaming. I was also sure I could work miracles with a curling iron if I had one.

"I'll pick you up around four if that's all right," he finally got around to saying. Socials usually ran from three to six unless there was something special going on. They were held under a big tent the men put up next to the church right after the Sunday service.

"Daddy's going to let James drive you to the social in the truck this afternoon," Hazel whispered after he was out of hearing distance. "I don't want you sitting too close to him now and I expect you to keep your hands to yourself." That got her a look that would've turned milk.

"You're coming too aren't you?"

"I don't think so. I felt so out of place at the one last month. The boys won't talk to me and I don't want to talk to any of the younger married girls. I don't like lying to them about my husband and they always want to know where he's at, what he's doing and when he'll be coming home."

"What've you told them, just in case I have to back up your story sometime?"

"I never thought about that. His name is Ted, Ted Campbell and whenever I have to describe him, I tell them what my history teacher in tenth grade looked like. We were crazy about him until he got a senior girl pregnant and had to marry her. Ted's three years older than me, six-foot-tall with blond hair and blue eyes. We got married right after I graduated. He's from Vicksburg and was already in the army, stationed at Maxwell, when I met him. I must have gotten pregnant on my wedding night. He's at Fort Dix in New Jersey right now learning how to drive tanks and jump out of airplanes. I figured that if there's a war, he'd be the first to ship out and one of the first killed. With things the way they are overseas, no soldier with his training is getting leave, so that takes care of questions about when he's coming home."

Hazel didn't come to the social, even with my begging, so I had to ride alone with James in his daddy's truck. When he reached for my hand between gear shifts, I didn't pull away. What could it hurt to hold hands with him, I figured. There was a good crowd when we arrived and I could hear music playing. That meant there would be dancing, which was frowned on by some of the older members of the community, but when we had music, there was no stopping what naturally happened. Mostly it was square dancing, which was seen as respectable fun by everybody except the Hardshell Baptists, but sometimes a Virginia Reel was called and that was couples dancing. A few brave souls, all young married couples, danced to it. Of course they were talked about the next week something terrible. There was one Yankee couple, the Brashers from somewhere up north, who knew how to do the waltz and they were forever trying to get us to learn, but most of the music our fiddlers and banjo pickers knew how to play wouldn't do for that kind of dancing. We were pretty sure it was a sin all the same, with the couple being that close. I didn't recognize any of the musicians, although the music was familiar to everybody. James and I square danced to two songs before we even looked for a place to sit. It was something to do and I wouldn't have to make conversation with anybody while doing it.

When the fiddle player announced they were going to play something new they'd just learned, we all sat down and listened. It was beautiful. The Brashers must've recognized it right away because they were up and dancing the waltz after only a few chords were played. I don't know what possessed me, but I grabbed James's hand and dragged him out of his seat. When Mrs. Brasher saw they had company, she took James as her student and Mr. Brasher took me as his. They taught us a few steps then put us back together. One other couple got up their courage and joined us. After they got a quick lesson, they were on their own like us. I made myself a promise that afternoon that I would learn how to do this new dance right if it took me a year. After the dance was over, the Brashers came and sat with James and me. They weren't so bad, for Yankees, and when Mr. Brasher convinced our musicians to play that waltz again for their last song, he asked me to dance. I felt funny dancing with another woman's husband—again—but she didn't seem to mind. She tried to get James to dance with her again, but he wouldn't have any part of it. I figured he was already pretty sure we were going to Hell and dancing with a married woman a second time would make it a conviction for him no amount of repenting would help.

It was after dark when we pulled up to my house. That was the time I was dreading. Everyone had seen us together at the social and I'd even danced a waltz with him. I was expecting him to try to kiss me, since all that I'd already done had sort of made me his girlfriend in everybody's eyes. If he'd tried to kiss me in the truck, I would've left him sitting there by himself, but instead, he got out, opened my door for me and walked me toward the front porch steps holding my hand. When he stopped, he sort-of twirled me half around and kissed me. I wasn't ready for that and didn't have a chance to back away; not that I'd already decided one way or the other. It was over and he was saying goodnight and thanking me for my company before I knew what was happening. It wasn't much of a kiss, but it was my first kiss from a boy and it was on the lips.

Boys talk, and James talked a lot after that date. Hazel didn't come over all week, so on Saturday I walked over to her house. James was in the yard and was surprised to see me; even more surprised when I told him I'd come to see his sister. When he brought her out of the house, I asked her if she would like to walk with me over to the Platt's and watch them make sorghum. That was always a big event. Everyone in the community who raised syrup cane brought theirs to the Platt's in the fall. They had the machinery to squeeze the juice out and cook it down and would do it for part of the syrup. She didn't act like she wanted to go, but I convinced her. When we were half a mile from her house, she stepped in front of me and turned to face me almost nose to nose. She let me have it. I'd never heard her upset about anything and she was just about screaming at me.

"You held hands with my brother, you danced the waltz with my brother, and you kissed my brother. You gonna marry him now? It's all over that he's turned you into a proper girl, that all you ever needed was the right boy to pay you some attention."

"I didn't kiss him, he kissed me," I screamed back.

"What's the damn difference?"

"There's a big damn difference." We were both screaming at the top of our lungs by that time and staring at each other like two cats about to fight. I let her stare me down after she finished having her say and then we continued walking toward the Platt farm. We didn't say anything to each other until we were nearly there. I felt like the biggest hussy in Alabama.

"You didn't let him kiss you?" Her voice was a lot calmer.

"No."

"And you didn't kiss him back?"

"No, I promise. He did it before I knew what his intentions were. It wasn't a kiss, more of a peck that was over and done with before it started."

"And you're not gonna marry him?"

"Lord, no. Marrying any boy's the furthest thing from my mind."

"You mean you still like girls?"

"I like this one girl, but I don't know if she likes me. She talked me into going out with her brother by making me think I might get a kiss from her, but that didn't work out. I don't know if she just playing me along or what."

"Maybe she's been through a lot lately and can't figure out why a girl as pretty as you would be interested in her. Maybe you should just kiss her and see what happens."

In the middle of that dirt road, where anyone could have come driving by, and in broad daylight, I took her face in my hands and kissed her better than any boy could have. I made it a long, slow, drawn out kiss because I didn't know if I'd ever get another. Her arms went around my waist and it was the very best feeling, being held by another girl after so long. When our lips parted, I looked into her eyes as she took a deep breath. Eyes are windows to the soul, Mama always said, and I liked what I saw. Hazel didn't say anything, but as we walked on toward the Platt farm, she held my hand.

The gossipers had their fun with the story that James had made me see the light and Bill kept asking when he was going to have a new brother-in-law. He and James weren't really friends and I was glad of that. Bill had a good job at the Goodyear and he said he had a girlfriend in Gadsden, although none of us had ever seen her. Daddy said he was sweet on one of the girls at the lunch counter near the plant, but that he hadn't seen Bill even talking to her. Now and then he talked about moving out of the house and into a boarding room in town. That was just talk; he liked Mama's cooking too much.

Chapter Three
A Regular Job

The rest of that fall, James still came calling from time to time and until it got too cold, we would sit on the front porch and talk. There was no more kissing and there were no more dates, although he asked me twice to go into Gadsden with him to the picture show. I wasn't hateful toward him and I didn't mind that he sat next to me at church every Sunday. The rumors of our forthcoming engagement soon died down, but the rumors about Hazel and me started up. Some said I was trying to break up her happy marriage and others repeated the first story, that I was doing the Lord's work in being a friend to her. Mama generally ignored rumors whichever way they went, but one Saturday morning we talked about things. Daddy and Bill had left before daylight to deer hunt with some of the other men in the community. It was the first day of the season and as much a tradition as Christmas in our house. Mama and I had the day to ourselves and we talked as we did the ordinary chores of any other Saturday, like mopping floors and splitting wood for the stove. Daddy and Bill split wood for the fireplace, but we had to keep the stove wood box full. It wasn't quite fair because that was a year-round job and the fireplace was only lit in the winter. It was a lot easier splitting the small logs though.

"Otha," she almost never called me Otha May, "I know you and Hazel have gotten to be good friends and I think it's a considerate thing you're doing, helping her. She's going to need your help a lot more in the coming months, but there's talk going around that you might have something else in mind. It's worrying your Daddy more than me. He's never understood why you're curious the way you are and he probably never will. Even growing up with Jolene I didn't understand it too well, though when I was a few years younger than you, Mama tried her best to explain it to me one morning. It was a morning a lot like this one and there were only the two of us in the house. We'd never come right out and talked about how she was and we didn't that time either. For an hour we talked around things that neither of us knew how to put into words and what I remember best was when she told me the Lord doesn't have to tell us what He's doing when He gives us life. At the time, that cleared things up for me. It was heartbreaking for us when she left home and I don't ever want you to feel like you have to. She's happy now. I miss her every day, but she knew people around here would never accept her the way she was. Times aren't much different now and anytime you show an interest in another girl, the talking starts. I can live with that, but Otha, Hazel's a married woman who's about to have a baby and I'd hate to think of you coming between her and her husband."

"There's something I need to tell you Mama, something no one else knows. It's about Hazel, and I've been meaning for us to have a talk about her for a long time. The truth is, she's not married. Her mama and daddy made up that story and told her she has to go along with it if they want to live respectably around here. If word gets out, she'll have to marry the boy that got her pregnant and she doesn't want that. She didn't make me promise I wouldn't tell anybody, but I haven't said a word and I think she'll understand me telling you. I do like her. I like her a lot and I think she likes me and I know she needs me. She wants me to be there when the baby's born, although I don't know what help I'll be."

It was like the weight of the world had been lifted from her shoulders. She hugged me and kissed me like I was her little girl all over again.

"Well if you're gonna deliver that baby, you'd better learn how."

"Deliver the baby? She just said she wanted me to be there."

"Well, you're smart; you could learn and you could do it. I've had two healthy babies, and though I couldn't tell you much about what has to be done, I know someone who can. Grandma Yother delivered you and your brother and she taught her daughter-in-law, Mrs. Yother, everything there is to know about it. She was there with Grandma Yother when my time came both times and she's delivered dozens of babies on her own since then. I think it would be a fine thing for you to learn how to do that yourself. Mrs. Yother doesn't have a daughter to pass her training down to and I bet she would love to have somebody help her. We'll go up to see her this afternoon. Mr. Yother and Elton have gone hunting with your daddy and brother and I know she'd like some company." This wasn't at all what I had in mind, but Mama was so thrilled with the idea, I couldn't say no.

Everybody said Mrs. Yother was what you might call an independent woman. Mama said it was her family, the Luthers, who had the money and that Mr. Yother just married into it. Even during the worst part of the depression, they got by pretty well. They had cattle and land like no one else in the community, but they weren't uppity at all. If it hadn't been for them, a lot of families would've lost their homes and gone hungry. The Yothers had a car and a truck and Mrs. Yother knew how to drive both. You could probably fit five or six of our houses in the Yother's and there were only two people living there. I loved going up there when I was little and playing with Elton, their boy, who was a year older than me. He always had the best toys and a beautiful yard to play in. He started engineering college up in Knoxville the fall after he graduated and didn't come home often, but he wouldn't miss the first day of deer season. I'd never truly talked to Mrs. Yother. I saw her and Mr. Yother at church every Sunday, but that was about it, so I was a little nervous about our visit. I shouldn't've been.

Mama had been right; Mrs. Yother was happy as she could be that we came by. We stayed all afternoon and had some of the best apple pie I've ever eaten. Mrs. Yother seemed especially happy that I'd come along. When Mama got around to telling her that I wanted to learn how to deliver babies, which was stretching the truth, Mrs. Yother's eyes lit up.

"It's not something most young girls are interested in these days. They think a doctor's going to be there when their time comes, but unless the woman moves to town when she's about due, it's usually not possible. That's when they come for me. Some just want their babies delivered by a woman and that makes sense. My Elton was delivered by Grandma Yother and I never thought of having a baby any other way. I always say the man gets his job done in a few minutes nine months earlier and that a woman doesn't need him anymore after that. Take Mrs. Watts for example. Her baby's due soon. It's her first and she was scared to death the first time I examined her. In an hour I had her calmed down and looking forward to the birth. Do you think a man doctor would have taken the time to explain to her exactly what she could expect? The doctors I know don't even like delivering babies and would just as soon someone like me did it. It seems they don't want to see the woman until she's in labor and then they try to rush things along. That's not the way a baby's supposed to come into this world."

Mrs. Watts was Virginia, or Ginny as some called her. I didn't know her well. She and her husband, Evan had just moved into the community from Birmingham a few months earlier. She seemed a little old to me for this to be her first baby. Mama and Mrs. Yother talked mostly like I wasn't there and it was a while before the conversation eventually drifted back around to me.

"If you think you might be interested in learning something about delivering babies, come by Monday around ten. I won't be seeing anyone in the morning as far as I know and the two of us can talk. It's not a calling for every woman and I want you to know what you're getting into first thing."

All the way home Mama talked about how fortunate I was that Mrs. Yother had agreed to talk to me about being her helper. I thought it would be an easy job. After all, women had babies long before there was anyone to help them. I had it figured that Mrs. Yother mostly watched and that I would just be helping her watch.

I had a lot to tell Hazel about that evening when she came over. While we pin-curled each other's hair in the kitchen, we talked.

"Mama's already told me I have to make an appointment with Mrs. Yother. I was dreading it, but with you working there, it won't be so bad. Do you think you'll know enough about delivering babies to help with mine?"

"Mama says I should learn, but I don't know if I'm cut out for it. I don't even know if she's going to hire me. I have to go back Monday and talk with her. Mrs. Yother's nice enough and I've known her for as long as I can remember, but the work she does isn't like a regular job and it sounds like it would be pretty monotonous."

"Watching babies be born? Yeah, it can't be that hard and you'll probably just help with the office stuff, you know, filling out birth certificates and things like that."

"That's what I figure too; it can't be that hard."

What I wanted more than anything that night was to kiss her again, but that didn't happen and there was no mention of our first one. I guess neither of us could figure out how to bring it up, I was afraid maybe she thought it had been an accident or something.

***

Mama got me up early Monday morning after insisting I take a bath the night before even though it wasn't my regular bath night and I'd just had one Saturday. She said I had to be clean and dressed in clean clothes if I was going to get into the baby delivering business. I'd never thought about getting paid to deliver a baby, but doctors did and, according to Mama, they got paid well. It was a forty-five-minute walk to the Yothers' and I left in plenty of time. When I arrived, Mrs. Yother met me at the door. She was a completely different woman from two days before. Her whole personality had changed. She wasn't the sweet neighborly older lady I'd known all my life; she was all business. Even her way of talking had changed and she continued talking as she led me through the house to her office.

"You will listen carefully to everything I say this morning, Miss St. Clair. This is not a job any random woman can do, and to be honest, I doubt you can either. I don't have time to waste with a girl who isn't cut out for it. You're young and bright, but you need the hands, skills, and attitude. In this office and in the examination room, I don't mince words and I expect you to listen and answer my questions truthfully. Do you understand?"

"Yes, Mrs. Yother," was all I could manage. I was shaking so hard I could barely stand.

"They say you like girls and in this business, you have to. Some women can't stand the thoughts of touching another woman the way we do. You don't have a problem with that, do you Miss St. Clair?"

"No, Mrs. Yother."

"Neither do I. A woman's body is a beautiful and wondrous organism, but it's infinitely complex and it takes years to learn even the basics. A man is simple in comparison. Everything is out in the open, but a woman has marvels hidden from everyone except us. We see things that are never seen, and we know their purpose. God was a magnificent creator, don't you agree, Miss St. Clair?"

"Yes, Mrs. Yother."

We entered her office and I was offered a seat in front of her huge oak desk.

"The coffee I put on should be perked by now. Can I offer you a cup?"

"No, thank you, Mrs. Yother."

When she left the room, I looked around and stood up to read the framed papers hanging on the walls: a state of Alabama license to practice midwifery, a diploma from Vanderbilt University School of Medicine for a Bachelor of Science degree in human physiology, a certificate stating she was qualified to teach midwifery in Alabama, all granted to Lois Arie Yother. This was no ordinary woman who happened to have learned how to deliver babies. She was educated and a teacher. I'd never known any of this about her and I don't think many in the community realized who she really was either, and I'd never heard anyone call her Lois, even people her own age. When she returned, she sat behind the desk, sipped her coffee, and looked me straight in the eye.

"Can you hold a baby as it takes its first and last breath? Can you cut a dead woman's belly open and deliver a live baby, then walk out of the room with that baby, hand it to its father and tell him his wife's dead?"

I couldn't answer. I couldn't breathe.

"You have precious minutes to make the decision and perform the surgery. If you don't, the baby's dead too."

I wanted to run out of the room and maybe throw up.

"Can you push your hand up into a screaming woman's vagina halfway to your elbow to turn a baby so that it can come down the birth canal straight and alive? Can you tell a woman you've known all your life that the baby she's carried for months is dead and will have to be surgically removed? Can you tell a thirteen-year-old colored girl she's pregnant and deliver a healthy baby through a vagina that was so small a few months earlier you couldn't get your fingers inside to do a proper examination?"

Didn't the colored have their own doctors? Vagina? Is that what it's called?

"Can you put your fingers inside the vagina of a total stranger? Can you put your fingers inside the vagina of a girl you've grown up with? Have you ever had your finger inside a woman's vagina at all—even your own? That's what this business is about Miss St. Clair. Everyone alive on this planet got here through a vagina if they got here naturally."

"Yes, Mrs. Yother."

"Yes what, Miss St. Clair?"

"Yes, I've had my finger inside another girl's vagina—and my own."

Finally, the woman smiled. I thought she was going to finish tearing my head off.

"Well, you've already passed two of the tests. You're still here and you've at least had your finger in a vagina that's not your own. Congratulations."

She wasn't hollering at me anymore.

"They're not all beautiful young girls like those you dream about waking up next to, Miss St. Clair. Some are fat and ugly, but they all deserve our best. They want a child and it is our responsibility to make sure they have every chance to give birth to a healthy one. Our job doesn't end when the baby's born either. The mother and baby get regular checkups for six months. You're the prettiest girl in this godforsaken place and that'll help you. Older grown women would rather be touched by a pretty young woman than an old ugly one and very young girls would rather be touched by someone closer to their own age, but when it comes to the delivery they want experience, or I'd be out of a job. Girls like girls. It's as simple as that. Some might not like them as much or in the way you do, but they all like pretty girls. It's the way we are and there's nothing unnatural about it."

I started breathing again. She talked for two solid hours and the most I said was "Yes, Mrs. Yother" or "No, Mrs. Yother," but I was able to say that I didn't think she was old or ugly. I got more of an education that morning than I'd gotten in all my years at school. She knew the whole story of babies, from how they were conceived to how they were born. Most of what I thought I knew was dead wrong. When the clock struck twelve, she stopped lecturing, as if she were in a classroom and had another group of students waiting to come in.

"Now I want you to go home and think about the things I've said, Miss St. Clair, and don't come back tomorrow if you have any doubts—and I mean any. I don't want to waste my time with you if you aren't strong enough to make it. You have to be as hard and as cold as steel one minute and more compassionate than a Latin lover the next. That is who you have to be, Miss St. Clair. It's the best career in the world if you're the right person, but I've only met a few and none from around here. You have to do your job through blood and tears. Life will be in your hands and you won't sleep well when it slips away, but seeing that baby's face and hearing that first cry puts you closer to God than any jackleg preacher will ever get. Now go home and give your mother my best; I have work to do. Mrs. Clark will be in with her baby at one and I have to review her file."

I don't remember anything after that, not until I was already halfway home, past Hazel's house. Mrs. Yother was the scariest and most wonderful woman I'd ever met.

I'd known her all my life and didn't know her at all. I ran the rest of the way home and couldn't stop talking to Mama when I got there. Yes, I would be at Mrs. Yother's the next day and I would be early.

***

I was awake when I heard Mama in the kitchen, so I got up and helped her with breakfast. She made me eat something even though I was so nervous I could hardly hold a spoon. She also decided that I would have a bath every night with my new nursing job, that it was expected of me to always be clean and well dressed. I wished I'd had a better dress to wear that day, but the one I chose was clean. I left a little before nine and tried to remember some of the other things Mrs. Yother had said the day before. She didn't only talk about delivering babies; she seemed just as interested in me and what kind of person I was.

It was about nine-thirty when I knocked. Mr. Yother opened the door and he was wearing an apron. I pretended not to notice when he quickly took it off as he showed me back to Mrs. Yother's office.

"Mrs. Yother says you're going to be her new assistant. You don't know how glad I am she's finally found someone she's willing to train. The others didn't last through the interview. Don't tell her I told you, but she had nothing but good things to say about you last night. She hasn't been in this happy a mood in years and anything I can do to help keep that up, you let me know."

He knocked on Mrs. Yother's office door and she gave permission to enter; we didn't walk in as if it were any other room in the house. Mrs. Yother was writing something and didn't look up until she was finished.

"Thank you, Mr. Yother. Miss St. Clair and I have a great deal to do today and if you could see to it that we're not disturbed, I would be grateful."

They spoke to each other like they were hardly acquainted, much less husband and wife. Mr. Yother turned and left without saying a word.

"Please be seated Miss St. Clair. I knew you'd be back. You have that hunger about you; the same hunger I had at your age. Any doctor or midwife can tell you what's involved in delivering a baby, but you don't know anything until you see it yourself. Before that though, you need to learn about the routine examinations I do every month, usually after the fourth month and every two weeks after the seventh. They're called routine examinations, but every one is different. This job is never the same from one day to the next and I never stop learning. Mrs. Redmon will be here at ten-thirty and I'd like you to observe. This is her first visit and you can learn the basics and what I check to make sure she's healthy and that the pregnancy is progressing as it should. She's young and healthy, so I don't expect anything out of the ordinary, but this being her first visit, she will be nervous, and you need to learn how to make her feel comfortable talking to us."

It wasn't so much a request as an order. Mrs. Redmon was Janice Pinkerton, or that was her name when I knew her in school. She was a year older than me and married Darryl Redmon right after graduation. Darryl was Mr. Yother's youngest sister's son. Janice and I weren't really friends, but we talked from time to time in school and at church. She and Darryl sat at the table next to ours at the social when I had my famous first date with Hazel's brother.

Mrs. Yother's examining room next door to her office was an amazing place, with windows in the ceiling for light and she had electric lights on the walls and all kinds of flashlights. The Yothers were the first in our community to get power in their house, but only for lights. Daddy said it must have cost them a fortune. She showed me where everything was and told me what some of the instruments were used for. We wouldn't be needing any of them for Janice since it was her first examination. She also had running water from two tanks on the back porch that Mr. Yother filled every morning and she showed me how to wash my hands all the way up to my elbows with some sort of soap that stung my skin. One water tank had a firebox under it so we could have hot water in the examining room and it would be my job to build the fire in the morning if we had patients coming in. She looked closely at the job I'd done washing my hands and approved. We would wash again before examining the patient. The table in the center of the room caught my attention when we first went in. It was a strange looking contraption with movable additions at the bottom where it looked like the woman's legs and feet should go. Mrs. Yother sat at a little desk in the corner and gave me further instructions.

"All right Miss St. Clair, I would like for you to go into that little room to your right. You turn the light on with the switch on the wall. You will find a stack of white gowns in the cupboard. Change into one, wearing nothing underneath. It's time for your examination. You won't be doing anything to anyone that you haven't experienced yourself. You need to be the patient first and feel what they will feel. My own mother-in-law did my examinations. You can imagine what that was like." She smiled, whether she intended to or not.

I'd come this far and I wasn't going to let a little examination chase me away. From talking with her the day before I had a good idea what I was in for and nothing about it seemed so terrible, but I was still nervous and shaking so hard I couldn't get the gown tied in the back. There was a short stool in the room so I sat on it and tried again before giving up. When I walked out, she was still seated at the small desk. I stood next to the table and didn't move a muscle—except for the shaking. She didn't say a word, just turned and looked at me for several minutes and wrote things on a pad of paper. When she stood up, she walked over and stopped directly in front of me, reached behind my neck to untie the gown, which I'd never gotten tied, and then pulled the sleeves. The gown fell to the floor. I stood there as she looked me over again and went back to the desk to write some more.

"I won't be talking to you during this examination the way I would if you were a normal patient, Miss St. Clair. The talking is mostly to take the patient's mind off what I'm doing. I want your eyes to see and your mind to focus on every detail."

She didn't have to worry about that.

She took my temperature first and showed me how to read the thin red line in the glass thermometer. Next, I was asked to step on a set of scales which also had an attachment that she slid up to measure my height. The breast examination was meticulous. I felt every motion she made with her fingers and she squeezed so hard sometimes I was sure I'd have a bruise. When she lowered the examination table and spread a clean sheet over it, I was pretty sure what I was supposed to do. I lay down and put my feet in the metal loops, which put my knees in the air. The extensions holding those loops were movable and she spread them apart and locked them in position. She then raised the table back up and stood between my knees. If she couldn't get a look at things from that angle, then it just wasn't possible. With a lever under the table, she raised my back up, which put me in an even more uncomfortable position, although I could see better. Still she didn't speak, but I watched and felt everything she did. She spread my vulva—a word I'd already memorized—open and had a look, then covered her fingers in some sort of clear grease from a tube. I watched as she slipped a single finger inside me. If she'd waited a minute for the stuff to warm up, I might not have jumped. The whole examination, beginning to end, was over in about twenty minutes.

"You're a virgin, so I only used one finger and stopped the examination before rupturing your hymen. That will come if you ever decide to have intercourse with a man." I had no idea what a hymen was, and I didn't want to seem stupid, so I didn't ask. By the end of the day, though, I learned not to hold back asking any questions that came to mind.

Janice arrived promptly at ten-thirty and she was surprised to see me when I answered the door. I directed her back to the office and let Mrs. Yother explain that I was her new assistant. She called me Miss St. Clair. I liked that. In the office there were forms to fill out and after asking Janice a dozen general questions about her health, Mrs. Yother showed her into the examination room and gave me my instructions. I was to help Janice undress and put on a gown in the changing room. She didn't need any help and didn't seem to be very pleased that Mrs. Yother had me as her new assistant. When she asked me to turn around while she got undressed I didn't say anything and handed her a hanger for her dress. Back in the examining room, I watched Mrs. Yother and learned how to operate the scales and the extension on top that measured height and then I was given a pad of paper and a pencil. I was to sit and observe and write down everything that was said.

"When was your first missed period, Mrs. Redmon?"

"They've always been irregular. I didn't have one in April, but I did have one in May and that was the last one."

"Miss St. Clair, you can learn a great deal by just looking," Mrs. Yother began after sticking a thermometer in Janice's mouth. "Look at her complexion. Is it of good color? Are her eyes bright and clear? Does she stand erect?" She then walked in front of Janice, took out the thermometer and read it out to me. When she untied the gown, pulled the sleeves down and let it drop to the floor, Janice turned away. "Come now, Mrs. Redmon, we're all girls here and you don't have to be shy."

"It's Otha May. You know she's curious. She likes girls... if you know what I mean."

She talked as if I were in the next room, not sitting four feet from her.

"So do I Mrs. Redmon. I wouldn't be in this profession if I didn't. Would you rather be examined by someone who doesn't like girls? There are plenty of men doctors I'm convinced don't like girls in the least, particularly pregnant ones, who would be happy to examine you for a substantial fee I'm sure your husband can't afford. Or maybe you'd rather have a girl examine you who has never touched another girl in her life and knows no more about a woman's body than you do."

"No, I don't want a man doctor. I couldn't bear that."

"Your husband is the son of my husband's sister, and my husband's mother delivered both your mother and me. Grandma Yother taught me more than I ever learned in school and now I'm teaching someone else so that someday your daughter, if you have one, won't have to endure a strange man doctor putting his hands all over her when it comes time for your grandchild to be born. Nothing that happens in this room will ever be talked about by anyone but you, and if I didn't believe Miss St. Clair was an upright woman with the integrity this profession demands, she wouldn't be here." As she'd promised, Mrs. Yother didn't mince words in the examination room, with me or our patients.

Janice slowly turned back around and faced me. "I'm sorry Otha May. I apologize for being so childish and I hope you can forgive me. There's no excuse for my behavior. It's just that..."

Before I could smile and nod, Mrs. Yother continued her visual examination. "Look at her breasts. Are they symmetrical? Are the areolas and nipples well formed? Are the nipples inverted or erect? Do the areolas protrude? Her body has begun to change and you have to notice those changes even if she doesn't. You will write down everything you see. Make sketches of anything out of the ordinary and the next time we see her, compare what she looks like to what you wrote and drew. That's how things are done. We don't go off into the bushes to squat and have our babies, hoping they live. We care for our mothers-to-be. Please raise both your arms Mrs. Redmon. Now look at both breasts again. Do they maintain their shape? Are they still symmetrical?"

Her breasts looked perfect to me; I didn't stare though. Mrs. Yother then stepped forward and began examining them, one at a time, just as she had mine. I'd felt a little peculiar having my breasts touched by her, and even more peculiar watching her touch someone else's.

"You feel for tone and consistency. There shouldn't be any lumps. Don't be afraid to squeeze the tissue between your fingers, particularly underneath the breast. Also look for any discharge from the nipples. There shouldn't be any at this stage, but if there is, it should be clear and watery."

I could tell by the expression on Janice's face that she was getting the same hard squeezes I'd gotten.

"What should I write down, Mrs. Yother?"

"That's up to you Miss St. Clair. It's your turn. Look at her, walk around her, write down what you see and by all means, don't be shy about asking questions, either of you."

Mrs. Yother took my seat when I got up and I think she observed me more than Janice. I wrote what I saw. I also took a cue from her in the way I addressed Janice.

"Mrs. Redmon has your left nipple always been inverted?"

"Until a week ago, they both were, except when…"

"Except when they're touched, or a cool breeze or cold water causes them to become erect?" I was glad I'd remembered some of the right words for things.

"Yes, but last week the right one turned out and it's stayed out. Is there something wrong with it?"

"That's completely normal, Mrs. Redmon" Mrs. Yother interrupted. "It's likely the other one will do the same thing in a few weeks."

"Slightly protruding areolas," I said aloud, not really sure at the time what the areolas were. From the way Mrs. Yother had described them, I guessed it was the pink area around the nipple. Before then I didn't know it had a name.

"When her breasts grow in the coming months, that condition will likely take care of itself."

"Please raise your arms, Mrs. Redmon," I continued. I looked at her again and made some crude sketches. I was pleased with how easily I could look at a very pretty and very naked girl standing right in front of me and be so removed from her at the same time.

I continued to talk to myself, "Slightly rounded belly."

"And make note of the navel. It's inverted now, but later on they sometimes pop out. That's not usually a problem and you should tell the patient to expect it, especially if she is of a thin build like Mrs. Redmon."

Mrs. Yother hadn't said anything about Janice's belly and I was proud of myself for noticing. Then came the hard part. I stood in front of her and took my index finger and middle finger, the way Mrs. Yother had, and began examining her breasts. It had been a long time since I'd even seen another woman's breasts and I was touching hers. Immediately her left nipple turned itself right side out. That hadn't happened earlier, and I pretended not to notice.

I finished the breast examination and turned back to Mrs. Yother.

"Very good Miss St. Clair; have a seat and finish your notes on what you've observed and felt. Now, Mrs. Redmon, I would like for you to lie down here and put your feet in these stirrup looking gadgets. This is the most unpleasant part of the examination and I apologize for the awkward position. I've always thought a man must have designed these tables. As for you Miss St. Clair, this is the most important part of the examination. Write down everything I say."

I looked up and Janice had her legs spread wide and her knees in the air. I could see things she never would. I had no idea everything down there had a name, some I remembered from my earlier examination, and I did my best to sketch what I saw and label my drawings while Mrs. Yother talked nonstop.

"At this stage, everything will appear normal, but later on, there will be significant changes. Spread the labia majora with your fingers like this and look for anything unusual, like a rash, swollen tissue, or a discharge that isn't milky to clear. What you are looking at is normal lubrication secretion from the vagina—if the patient has followed my instructions not to have relations with her husband for at least twenty-four hours before her examination. Otherwise this could be something else. It should have the consistency of saliva and feel slippery."

She then ran her forefinger the length of Janice's labia majora and held her thumb and forefinger for me to see.

"As a point of interest—and you won't read this in any medical book—if you can stretch the secretion more than an inch between your fingers, it means the woman is ovulating. That obviously isn't the case here. Specifically, you should also ask the patient if she has had any bleeding. Then spread the labia minora and again observe. As you can see Mrs. Redmon has no visible abnormalities. Everything looks just as it should."

Janice squirmed a little and said that she hadn't noticed any bleeding and hadn't had relations with her husband in the past two days. She didn't say anything as I repeated what Mrs. Yother had done. It was peculiar touching another woman like that, one that I wasn't naked in bed with anyway. With my fingers holding things apart, her little pearl, as Cousin Rosa had called it, stood out and I waited for Mrs. Yother to mention its proper name. She didn't. I ran my finger the length of her labia majora, exactly as Mrs. Yother had done, being careful to avoid that curious bump, and then stretched the secretion between my fingers. It broke at less than half an inch.

"Now with that lever under the table, raise the back up to the forty-five-degree mark."

I did as I was told which put Janice in that awkward position I'd been in—and she could see me. That made things even more uncomfortable for me, but it didn't seem to bother her. I watched as Mrs. Yother squirted the clear gooey stuff she'd used with me on her fingers and then mine. I could read what was written on the tube this time: K-Y Surgical Lubricant. It was slippery as motor oil. Later I wrote in my notes that we should put the tube in warm water a while before using it.

"Okay Mrs. Redmon, I'm going to insert two fingers into your vagina to get a feel of your cervix. This won't be very comfortable, but it'll only last a second."

Mrs. Yother leaned forward with her forearm across Janice's lower belly and pushed down. At the same time, she slipped her fingers inside her vagina. I couldn't tell what she was doing with her fingers, but it was over with quickly.

"What you are feeling for, Miss St. Clair is a firm fleshy extension. That's the cervix. Feel it with your fingers as far up as you can reach and notice anything unusual. It should be smooth to the touch. In the lower part of the cervix, feel for the opening. It's oval shaped and at this stage, still quite small."

My fingers went inside her easily and when I pushed down on her lower belly, I could feel what Mrs. Yother was talking about. I ran my fingers over as much of it as I could, several times, and didn't feel anything bumpy, and I found the opening she was talking about. I didn't finish in a few seconds though. I wanted to make sure I touched everything I was supposed to. I had no idea there were things like that inside us. When I removed my fingers, Mrs. Yother wiped the K-Y off Janice and herself, then handed me the towel.

"All right, Mrs. Redmon, it's all over and everything's perfectly fine. Miss St. Clair will help you get dressed and I want to talk to you a moment before you leave."

Mrs. Yother left the room and Janice didn't hesitate to let me help getting her dressed.

"I should never have had any concerns with you helping Mrs. Yother. You're a natural at this Otha May. Your touch is gentle, and I won't ever have a problem with you examining me again. I never thought I'd say it, but I'm glad you like girls. I might not tell Darryl about Mrs. Yother's new assistant though, and how well my first visit went. Men don't understand things like that, you know."

"Mrs. Redmon, I'm happy you have confidence in our services… and I look forward to seeing you naked again real soon."

That caught her by surprise, then she started laughing and I started laughing. We hugged, and she gave me a kiss on the cheek. In her office, Mrs. Yother read Janice a summary of the examination and told her she was doing well. I made her an appointment for a month later and walked her to out to the front porch.

"Thank you again Otha May. I was scared to death over what would be done and what the exam might show, but you have the gift and the touch to make any woman relax, even naked with her knees up in the air."

I was feeling pretty proud of myself when I walked back into the house, but while I was gone Mrs. Yother had made her own notes on my performance and we went over every detail. After she finished raking me over the coals about everything from how I was dressed to the sloppiness of my handwriting and sketches, she gave a slight grin of approval.

"You're good, Otha May. You have the right attitude and good hands. Those are the things that matter in this business. I saw how you made a woman your own age, one you've known most of your life, feel comfortable letting you touch her and see things her husband doesn't even know exists. I may have found my new assistant." And then she became my teacher again. "All right, Miss St. Clair, the interesting part of this job is over. I want everything typed up right now before you forget any details and placed in a file folder you will create for Mrs. Redmon. Have a look at others in the file drawer marked 'current' to see how it's done."

For the first time ever, I was glad I'd taken typing in school. I wasn't very good at it, but I could manage. I was finished by noon and Mr. Yother made ham sandwiches for us. I thanked him for my dinner and thought I would be leaving, but that had only been the beginning of my class; I was then to learn the book details of what I'd seen and done earlier. It was late by the time we finished for the day and Mrs. Yother insisted on driving me home. When we pulled up at my house, she handed me a sizeable package.

"You'll find some things in there you can use, Miss St. Clair. I will pick you up tomorrow at ten. We have to drive out and check on Mrs. Watts. She's due anytime now and I want to see her. Remember, we can be called upon day or night. If I'm sent for, you'll be going with me, so if you hear a knock on the door in the middle of the night, it's me and I expect you to be dressed in five minutes ready to leave, seven days a week."

"Yes, Mrs. Yother."

"Also, I understand you're good friends with Mrs. Campbell. She is past due for her first visit. See if you can arrange it. I want her in the office as soon as possible."

I was lost for a second until I realized who she was talking about.

"Yes, Mrs. Yother; I'll see to it myself."

I took the package and went inside. I was dead tired, but I had to tell Mama about my day—I was careful not to mention any names though or give any details. I also told Daddy not to be too worried if there was a knock on the door in the middle of the night. He wanted to know how much I was getting paid and I had to admit we hadn't talked about money at all. My day had been much too exciting and busy to worry about things like that. I took the package back to my room and opened it. Inside I found three identical dresses and an envelope. The dresses were white with broad blue panels on the front and back. These were real dresses with waists and sleeves made from good material that was thick and stiff. Mrs. Yother must've been saving them for an assistant she hoped to have someday. I had to try one on and show Mama.

"Otha, you're the prettiest nurse in the state." I'd never thought of being a nurse, but if that's what Mama wanted to call me, that was all right. Before getting undressed, I opened the envelope. There was a check for thirty dollars inside and a note saying this was my first week's pay in advance. I had to go back out and show everybody. That was more money than Bill made at the Goodyear, but he was quick to point out that he had a regular eight hour a day job and that mine might be seven days a week for who knows how many hours a day. He was right about that, but I didn't care. I told him and everybody else that I had the best kind of job in the world; I was being paid to learn. I woke up twice that night and rearranged one of my new dresses and the rest of my clothes so I could be fully dressed in two minutes, not five. When Mrs. Watts's time came I would be ready.

Chapter Four
A New World Every Day

"Mrs. Watts is having a hard time," Mrs. Yother told me first thing when I climbed into her car. "Last week when I saw her I made it clear that she was to stay in bed as much as possible. She and her husband have been trying to have a baby for years and I know she will do everything she can to make sure this child is born. The baby hasn't turned the way it should and sometimes bed rest will help. If it's still breech, we'll try turning it and if that doesn't work, we're taking her to the hospital in Gadsden when her time comes. Breech deliveries usually don't go well. I haven't said anything to Mrs. Watts about the position the baby's in because until now I wasn't too concerned and there was no reason to alarm her. I want you to look at my notes from her last examination while we're driving out to her place and you are to take good notes today. If we have to take her to the hospital when she goes into labor, the doctor will want to know her history."

Mrs. Yother had told me what a breech birth was and that it could be dangerous to the mother and baby. One of Mama's friends in Collinsville had a breech birth and the baby died. She was in the hospital too, so I prayed Virginia would be okay and that her baby would be turned right. Mr. Watts was standing on the front porch when we arrived and even from a distance, I could see the worried look on his face. He spoke directly to Mrs. Yother and ignored me standing there with her medical bag.

"Ginny's in bed, but she's not been resting. I think she's ready for this baby to be born. He kicks and keeps her awake at night, so she hasn't slept much the past week. I stayed home from work today, but I have to go in tomorrow afternoon. Isn't there something you can give her to make the baby come?"

"Now Mr. Watts, babies are born when they want to be born, not when we want them to be, and who says it's a boy? I believe you know my new assistant, Miss St. Clair. She'll be helping me take care of Mrs. Watts." Mrs. Yother's voice became that of the plain, kindhearted woman I'd known her to be before I started working for her. She knew how to calm down people by speaking to them the way they spoke, turning her southern accent off and on at the drop of a hat. It was like she was two different women. Mr. Watts showed us into the bedroom and Virginia looked like she'd been through a rough night.

"You can wait out on the porch, Mr. Watts. I want to examine Mrs. Watts and maybe I'll be able to tell you better when the baby might come. You could put some water on to boil so Miss St. Clair and I can wash our hands."

That was what he wanted to hear, an excuse to leave the room.

"Mrs. Watts, this is Miss Otha May St. Clair, my new assistant and she'll be helping me with your examination today. She's learning all I can teach her about delivering babies, but there's no better way to learn than by doing and you're going to be delivering any day now."

"You're Ida and Dewey's girl, aren't you? I've seen you at church; I haven't been able to go much lately."

"Yes, Ma'am and I remember you."

Mrs. Yother and I helped Virginia to her feet and Mrs. Yother removed her gown for her. I sat in the only chair in the room and wrote down everything said and made some notes of my own. It was the first time I'd ever seen a naked pregnant woman that far along. My first thought was about those who say pregnant women are beautiful; they've never seen one naked in her final days before delivery. Everything is all out of shape. Virginia's breasts hung down low and her nipples were almost underneath them. Her navel had popped out and her belly was big enough for twins.

Back in bed with her knees in the air, I got a good look at her vaginal opening and made a sketch. It looked like I could've put my whole hand inside. Everything about her was big and Virginia was not a fat woman. I kept my thoughts to myself and didn't write that part down.

"All right Miss St. Clair come over here and you'll learn something. Put both hands on her belly right where mine are and tell me what you feel."

She had one hand on the side of Virginia's belly and the other down near her vulva. I could almost see through her skin what I was supposed to feel down there. It was a foot. The other side of her belly had a bump in it about the size of a water gourd.

"The baby's feet are under one of your hands and the head is under the other, and you should be able to tell which is which; no wonder Mrs. Watts hasn't been able to rest. If you'll move your hand around her belly, you can feel the baby's bottom. There's been some movement since I was here last, but we're going to help Mother Nature out a little."

I watched as she pushed and kneaded and worked the head down toward the vagina and the butt up; sort of like unscrewing the top on a really big Mason jar, I thought. She went slow and, in a few minutes, the baby's head was pointed in the right direction.

"Now put your fingers here and tell me what you feel."

It was just a little bump and I guess the confused look on my face wasn't hard to read.

"The nose; the baby will be born face up. That's not a problem at all. You were the first baby I saw born face up, Miss St. Clair." Then she smiled. "Grandma Yother always said babies born face up were curious and wanted a look at the world first thing. We just have to make sure, now that the baby's been turned, that the umbilical cord isn't wrapped around the neck. If it is, then the baby will turn back to where it was in a few minutes. Babies are smart. You remember what the cervix you examined yesterday felt like? We're now going to examine Mrs. Watts's and I want you to notice the difference."

We went out to the kitchen where the kettle of water had just begun to boil. Mrs. Yother poured some into the wash basin and rinsed it out, then poured in the rest. We brought our own soap and towels and as soon as the water cooled enough, we washed our hands. Cleanliness was next to godliness for Mrs. Yother. Back in the bedroom, I noticed the baby hadn't turned sideways again and said a silent prayer of thanks.

The vaginal examination was a whole different learning experience. Virginia's cervix was nothing like Janice's. It was broad and flat and situated just inside the vagina. The opening was easy to find. It was wider than my two fingers. Mrs. Yother produced a flashlight and held the vaginal lips—I mean the labia majora and minora—open so I could see. I didn't say anything. I didn't know what to say.

"Everything looks fine, Mrs. Watts. Have you had any contractions?"

"I felt a few quick ones in the past week, but they soon went away."

"Well, you're partially dilated and partially effaced. It won't be long now." I knew those words from Mrs. Yother's lessons, even if the woman she was saying them to didn't.

On the way home, Mrs. Yother reminded again me to be ready for her knock on our door. I would be.

The rest of the week, we only had one other appointment. Mrs. Hancock came in on Thursday morning, and we didn't hear anything from Mrs. Watts. I did make an appointment for Hazel though for the following Tuesday at ten-thirty.

Mrs. Hancock was Mama's age, or pretty close and her pregnancy was a surprise to everyone. Her daughter, Sadie was my age and we'd gone to school together all the way from first grade. I'd kissed her a lot when we were younger, and she was one of the girls I thought liked me, but then she got herself a boyfriend. She had bigger breasts than any girl in fifth grade and she got some teasing because of it. I touched them once through her dress when I kissed her, and she didn't seem to mind.

Mrs. Hancock said she never thought she could have any more children and she hadn't even thought about getting pregnant again. She'd started through the change when she got the surprise of her life. I learned the real word for that was menopause and I learned it on my own from another one of Mrs. Yother's books I happened to be looking through. I don't believe I'll ever see a woman happier about being pregnant than Mrs. Hancock was. Mrs. Yother told me her due date was early December and it looked to me like it could be any day. She also warned me that women her age are usually not pleased about becoming pregnant, but Mrs. Hancock was absolutely thrilled. Maybe that was her glow Mama said pregnant women got. The examination procedure was different again since she was so far along, and Mrs. Yother had me pay special attention, but we didn't find anything unusual.

This examination had been a little worrisome for me because I thought maybe Mrs. Hancock would want me to leave the room; but then when Mrs. Yother explained about how I wanted to learn to deliver babies, she treated me as if I was already qualified to do what I was doing.

Mrs. Yother used the free time the rest of the week to teach me a lot more about what goes on during childbirth. She had wonderful books with colored pictures that made things I'd seen more understandable. On Friday I got up my nerve to ask her something I'd been thinking about.

"Mrs. Yother, I noticed the certificate on your office wall that says you're licensed by the state to train midwives. Have you ever trained anyone?"

"No, not fully. When I was younger, I took on a few girls, but none of them were serious about learning and none ever took the test."

"There's a test?"

"Oh yes, Miss St. Clair, and it's in front of a panel of doctors. They ask you all sorts of questions and you have to do a complete examination of a woman while they watch. The regional test for Alabama, Tennessee, Mississippi, and Georgia is given at Vanderbilt University twice a year."

"That's where you went to school."

"Yes, it is, and you're required to have the recommendation of a licensed midwife to even take the examination."

That's what I wanted to talk about—how I could get a license—but that's as far as the conversation went that day.

Chapter Five
Dora May

That Saturday Mama and Daddy drove into Gadsden to buy tires for the truck and Mama a few things for the house. Bill left early, going fishing. We had a local store, but mostly they just sold gas and a few groceries. Mama wanted some plate glass to fix a window in Bill's bedroom that had been broken out for a year, and a new skillet. The one she made cornbread in had a crack that kept growing and would soon split it in two, and Daddy would not be happy without cornbread for supper. Mrs. Yother said I could have the day off and I wanted to go with them to town and get more uniforms, long sleeved ones for the winter. Now that I was getting paid, I was expected to buy things for myself. I also wanted to get Mama a new dress. The problem was Mrs. Watts. I couldn't leave the house: sure as I did, she would go into labor and I wasn't going to miss that, so I decided to stay home. I ended up sending one of my uniforms and some money with Mama. She could match the size and style. I told her to use the rest of the money for her a new dress; I knew she wouldn't.

I wanted to tell Hazel about my week, but she didn't know I had the day off and that I couldn't leave the house. It would take most of an hour to walk to Hazel's and back and Mrs. Yother wouldn't know where I was. Anything could happen in an hour. If I ran, I could make it in half that time—and if she came back with me, we'd have the house to ourselves most of the day. It'd been a long time since we'd any time alone and I wanted to know if the kiss on the road to the Platt's farm was something that had just happened or if she really did like me. I started to leave for

Hazel's a couple of times but wouldn't take the chance. It would be a lonely day at home by myself.

Saturdays were for floor mopping and I could at least get that taken care of for Mama while she was gone, and Hazel would be by later, since it was Saturday, but probably after everybody got back. Mopping floors always makes me think and I thought a lot about Hazel that morning. I'm pretty sure I mopped the kitchen floor twice. My bedroom was the last floor to be done and after I finished it, I decided I deserved a break. It was past noon and I should have been hungry, but I wasn't. There was something I wanted to do more than make dinner. With all that thinking about Hazel, I got in a hurry to throw out the bucket of dirty water and wring out the mop. There was a section in one of the books, only a paragraph that mentioned "female masturbation"—the real term for Rosa's "polishing the pearl" I guessed after looking up what masturbation meant. When I said it out loud, it sounded like it should have something to do with farming, like "masturbate the soil fully before planting" or something you'd read in a recipe book, like "masturbate ingredients well before pouring into a baking pan."

I had wondered that week, if I took my new job seriously and made a living out of it, would I ever touch myself or another woman the same way again, or would I think of it as another examination. That concern went away as soon as I lay down on my bed and let my mind, and fingers, wander. In Mrs. Yother's medical books I had also looked for what boiling over was really called. I didn't find anything, but all the books were written by men. For them, I read, it was called ejaculation—I had to look that up in the dictionary—but I didn't ejaculate anything when I boiled over. I still liked that word for it though.

Did Hazel ever do what I was doing? I don't know why, but I brought my fingers to my face and stretched the lubricating secretion, as Mrs. Yother had called it, between my fingers. It went almost two inches. I was ovulating. Maybe that's why I felt so… horny. I smiled and wondered if there was a medical word for that too, then decided that the men who wrote medical books probably never thought women got horny. In a few minutes I was at the point of boiling over, but since I was alone and had some time, I slowed things down a lot, making the most of my time alone. It was a long while that afternoon before I forced myself to get up and put my clothes back on.

Sitting on the porch reliving the past hour, I was glad I hadn't been able to go with Mama and Daddy. I guess it was then that I made up my mind to at least try and kiss Hazel again. Whatever happened, I couldn't keep pretending I wasn't interested in being something more than friends. When she came over later so we could curl our hair, it was hard standing behind her trying to get the bobby pins in right while thinking about letting my hand slip down to get a feel of her breasts. The dress she wore was cut a little low in the neck and I tried all evening to get a look. I would get a good look the next Tuesday when she came in for her examination, but Mrs. Yother would be there and besides, she would be our patient then. I was worried about how I was going to touch her the way I would have to without making a fool out of myself. She brought it up after we were finished with our hair.

"On Tuesday, what am I supposed to do? I don't mind telling you I'm a little bit scared."

"I've thought about that too and if you want me out of the room and to have Mrs. Yother do the examination, I'll understand."

"Don't you dare, Otha May; I couldn't stand the thought of going through this without you there. I just wouldn't do it."

"Do you know what's involved with your first examination? It's pretty simple and I can tell you everything that'll be done if you want me to."

"Can you? I thought maybe it was some sort of doctor secret. Mama couldn't tell me anything about her examinations. She says she doesn't remember, but I think she won't tell me because if she did, I might not go. I've had bad dreams about all kinds of awful looking doctor things being stuck up inside me."

"I've got a couple of those awful things with me if you want to see them."

When I held up two fingers, she didn't know what to say and then she smiled.

"The only things that will be going inside you are two fingers. Mrs. Yother says one of the reasons she hired me was because I have small hands and long fingers." Hazel's smile turned into a laugh. Things would be all right.

The next hour was spent talking about her examination and by the time I was finished, she was a lot less nervous. She should've asked me before, but I should've brought it up too.

After Hazel left, I arranged my uniform like I did every night so I could be in it, ready to go in two minutes. Mr. and Mrs. Watts were ready for their baby to be born and so was I.

At church the next day, I sat with Hazel on one side of me and James on the other, just like every other Sunday. I'd gotten used to her brother and since his moment of glory with me, he'd behaved pretty well, although he still asked me to any little social thing that came up.

Pastor Bouldin had just started leading us in my favorite song, "I'll Fly Away," when the church side door opened and Mr. Watts came in looking like someone had been chasing him with a gun. He looked around for Mrs. Yother but found me first and came running up the aisle.

"You've got to come now, Otha May. Ginny says it's time."

Mrs. Yother must have spied Mr. Watts coming in because she was right behind him. I turned and told Hazel goodbye and leaned over the pew to tell Mama what was happening. Everyone kept singing, but they knew why we were leaving in such a hurry. I got in Mrs. Yother's car with her and we followed Mr. Watts as he drove like a bat out of Hell toward his house.

"That damn fool needs to slow down or he'll be in the hospital when his child's born." Mrs. Yother wasn't screaming; she raised her voice from time to time, but she never screamed, although anyone walking on the side of the road that day would've heard her clearly. On the way, she went over everything she'd taught me so far. "If the baby's breech, we'll have to deliver it anyway. There's no time to get her to a hospital now. I saw her yesterday evening and the baby was still turned correctly, but babies have a mind of their own. Are you ready for this Otha May? It might not be anything like you're expecting, and it could be completely different from what I've told you. I can only teach you so much from a book. Remember this always: no one will ever say it out loud, but the life of the mother is more important than the baby's. Mrs. Watts is our patient and we will do everything possible to save her life and if that means we lose the baby, then that's the way it is."

By the time we got there, I was scared to death. Mrs. Yother was cool as a cucumber and spoke to Mr. Watts as if she knew already that everything was going to be all right. Mrs. Watts was having a hard contraction when we walked in and you could have heard her screaming a mile away. As soon as she saw us, it was like we'd brought the Lord Almighty. The screaming stopped and she began telling us what had been happening that night and morning. Mrs. Yother's calmness spread to everyone, even me. Mr. Watts was sent to fetch clean towels and put a kettle on to boil.

"I always send the husband to find clean towels and boil some water. It gives them something to do while the women take care of the important business."

When Mrs. Yother pushed Mrs. Watts's dress up over her belly, I could see the changes in her vagina since I'd last seen it. Swelled and inside out is about the best way to describe things, and there was dried blood on the sheet under her. From the way Mrs. Yother described where it came from, it sounded like a normal part of labor. She was certain she'd covered the "bloody show," as she called it, in one of my classes after work, but I didn't remember.

"Now Miss St. Clair, I would like your assessment of the position of the baby. Tell me what you feel. Mrs. Watts, you're in the middle stages of labor and everything's just fine. Don't push right now. We have to get a look at things first." Southern accent off and on like a light, depending on which of us she was talking to.

As soon as I touched her, another contraction started. I could feel muscles all around her belly making a sort of wavy motion, like the ripples made by a rock thrown in a pond. She didn't scream, but I could tell she wanted to. She held her breath and Mrs. Yother told her that was the worst thing she could do, that she should take short deep breaths as fast as she could. The contraction lasted for a full minute according to Mrs. Yother's watch and it had been ten minutes since her last one. When things calmed down, I felt of her belly carefully and found the baby's nose right where I wanted it to be and the location of the kicking told me for sure where the knees were. A silent prayer of thanks went through my mind that minute.

"Mrs. Yother, I believe the baby is well positioned and face up." I couldn't really turn off my accent, but I tried.

"Very good Miss St. Clair. Now, as soon as that water is boiling, we'll wash up and you can do a vaginal examination and tell me your findings."

I wished I hadn't been wearing my very best church dress.

We washed our hands and I scooted the clean towels under Virginia, then took a warm damp washcloth and wiped her vulva area. The examination took only a few seconds. Everything was right there for me to touch and see. Slightly prolapsed was how Mrs. Yother described her cervix; she didn't seem concerned. She was fully effaced and I guessed the cervical opening was about three inches across at its widest point; with a flashlight I could already see the top of the baby's head.

"This is when our mothers-to-be want to push and get things over with, but with a first birth, that's going to cause tearing and we would rather wait and let things stretch naturally until the cervical opening is about four inches across. She's already been in labor for some time, but this phase can last for many hours. Mrs. Watts, I want you to relax now as much as you can. When the contractions come, don't push through them. Everything's coming along as nature intended and we mustn't hurry it. I can tell you now that it's good we don't remember the pain and suffering of the first birth or none of us would ever have more than one child."

"Everything will be all right now that you and Miss St. Clair are here. Poor Evan's scared to death. I was there when my sister's baby girl was born. I was only thirteen, but I remember what she went through, so I know a little about what to expect. Evan has no idea. If you would, go out and tell him from time to time that I'm all right; it would put his mind at ease."

I volunteered to be the messenger and about every half hour, I gave him some news even if there wasn't any. Her contractions were strong and coming more often, although she didn't seem to be in too much pain and talked to us about anything that came to her mind; some things she probably would never have talked about under other circumstances. We learned that her sister wasn't married when she got pregnant and that after the baby was born, she left with her newborn and no one heard from either of them for four long years. Her father wouldn't let them live at home with a bastard child. He said she would bring shame on the whole family and be a bad influence on the other children. I let everything she said go in one ear and out the other. It was her nerves talking.

At about midnight, Mrs. Yother asked me to go out into the kitchen and see if I could find something Virginia might like to eat. She hadn't had a bite all day. Mr. Watts told me he'd killed a chicken Sunday morning, intending to have it for dinner, so I decided to make something with it. I found a can of vegetable soup and opened it, drained off some of the tomato juice and dumped it in with the cut-up chicken. In an hour, it smelled good enough to eat and everyone was hungry. Some leftover cornbread made for a pretty good meal. Virginia didn't eat much, but she needed something to keep her strength up. She looked tired and her hair was a mess. I could do something about that and found her comb on their back porch. It seemed to make all the difference in the world to her to not look like she'd just come in from the field. During one of the contractions while I was combing her hair, her water broke. I'd been told to expect this but seeing all that liquid gush from her vagina was something I won't ever forget. The towels under her were soaked so I replaced them with fresh ones. Virginia knew what had happened and seemed relieved that things were finally starting to move along.

At two o'clock, I had some news for Mr. Watts that I didn't make up. It was time for her to start pushing. Her cervical opening was a good four inches across and the thing I thought was the baby's head started to look like a head.

"Now Mrs. Watts, we're not in any hurry for this baby to be born. Just push when you feel you need to and let your muscles relax between contractions. Remember me telling you your baby's going to be born face up? If it's a boy, that's so he can pee in Miss St. Clair's face first thing. She's going to be delivering your baby, but I'll be right here, don't you worry."

I wasn't expecting that news.

"Miss St. Clair, I would like for you to get on the bed and sit between Mrs. Watts's knees. Find a comfortable spot because you may be there for some time."

There was no graceful way for me to do what she wanted wearing a dress, so I hiked it up above my waist and climbed onto the bed. Mrs. Yother handed me more towels to put under Virginia until I could get my hands under her bottom easily. I felt like the quarterback in a football game waiting to get the ball. Mrs. Yother handed me the tube of K-Y and told me to smear some everywhere I could reach. With my slim, long fingers, I could reach pretty far. I covered the opening of her cervix and looked at Mrs. Yother for instructions.

"Take your fingers and spread it between her cervix and labia and into her vagina as far as possible; we want to make it easy for things to stretch when she pushes."

I hadn't asked about her pearl, although I wanted to. In the last hour it had swelled to the size of my thumb, but everything else was swelled too, so I didn't ask. When my slippery fingers touched it, Virginia jumped.

"Mind her clitoris, Miss St. Clair or you'll have a baby in your hands before you're ready. In difficult births, we make good use of that little button. Massaging it causes strong vaginal spasms which can aid the other contractions."

So that's what it was called. I liked the sound of it—and I already knew about the spasms.

"You won't see it described in any of my medical books, but every woman knows it exists and what it's good for."

"It's a shame that men don't know what it's for," Virginia said with a grin just before another contraction started. I would forget she said that too.

With that contraction and her push, the baby's head came part way through her labia minora and I smeared more K-Y everywhere. My fingers could even fit between the baby's head and the labia, so I spread the slippery lubricant in there too and felt an ear. The baby's neck was bent so I couldn't see eyes or a nose, but it was surely an ear I felt.

"All right, Miss St. Clair, since this baby is arriving face up, we have to straighten the neck during the next contraction. Slip your fingers inside and gently tilt the head down until you can see the eyes. Then things should proceed like a baby being born face down. The shoulders have to come out one at a time, not both at once and you may have to help with that."

It was a tight fit getting the fingers of both hands alongside the baby's ears, but with the K-Y, I managed. During the next contraction, I tilted the baby's head down and the eyes and nose slipped out. Mrs. Yother had a look and smiled.

"Now Mrs. Watts, we will wait for you to do the rest. You can push as hard as you want. We're almost home."

It seemed like forever before the head was out and I held it in my hands while Mrs. Yother swabbed the baby's mouth with a piece of gauze on a wooden stick. I watched as the baby took a breath at the next contraction. Someday I would tell this new person that I was there when he, or she, took a first breath. I don't know if the baby was moving around or if it was Virginia, but it seemed the little thing was trying to crawl out. I remembered what Mrs. Yother said about the shoulders and reached back inside Virginia to move the one on my left sideways. Just as I did that, there was another contraction. Virginia pushed and groaned and in about three seconds, I had a whole baby in my hands. It all came out at once. It was a real living squirming thing I had in my hands and I wasn't sure what to do with it. Mrs. Yother was ready with another towel and wiped the baby from head to foot.

"It's a little girl, Mrs. Watts and she's got ten fingers, ten toes, two eyes, and a nose."

"She's not crying. I thought all babies cried when they were born." It was a stupid thing for me to say, but I really did think all babies cried when they were born.

"No, not the curious ones. This little girl is just happy to be here. There's no reason for her to cry. Her mother made her birthday easy. Hold her up, Miss St. Clair so she can see her mother."

I picked up the wiggling little baby girl and held her the way Mrs. Yother had taught me, with my hands under her head and bottom, and let Virginia have a look at her new daughter. I wanted to cry, but I knew better; there were things to do. Mrs. Yother took some special twine from her bag and tied the umbilical cord near the baby's stomach and again a couple of inches away. Then with a sharp blade on a steel handle, she cut the cord between the knots.

"Now Miss St. Clair, you can place the baby on Mrs. Watts's stomach so they can get to know one another."

Virginia leaned up and Mrs. Yother helped her get her gown over her head and off. I placed the baby on her stomach with her head between Virginia's breasts and took a moment to take in everything. It was a picture no photographer took, but I would have it forever.

With one more small contraction, the afterbirth, or placenta as I'd been taught, was pushed from the cervix and vagina. Mrs. Yother removed it and wrapped it in a towel to be given to Mr. Watts later for burial. It was time to invite him in to have a look at his new daughter. That baby never did cry the whole time we were there.

It was just about sunup Monday morning when we left the new parents with their new baby girl. On the way home, I got questioned on every detail of the birth of little Dora May Watts. They hadn't thought of a middle name and when Mr. Watts asked what mine was, everyone said it was a good fit. I sort of liked having someone named after me. According to Mrs. Yother, we were lucky—meaning everybody concerned—in that the baby didn't cause any more problems than she did. She then told me all the things that could've gone wrong. I wanted to listen, but I was dog tired and wanted nothing more than to sleep for the rest of the day. When she drove right past my house, I held my tongue.

"If Mr. Yother is as efficient and caring a husband as I know him to be, Miss St. Clair, we'll have breakfast waiting for us and I'm predicting he couldn't resist cooking some of that cured ham Mr. Walker left for us last week. He always makes something special when I'm out for a delivery. You remember back last spring when little Evelyn was born? Well, that ham is the Walker's last payment for her delivery. I'll always take payment in something good to eat and Evelyn cost exactly a side of beef and a cured ham. The way I see it, anything the farmers around here have that I would normally buy anyway is fair payment. Sometimes I feel a little guilty because they always pay me more that way. After we eat breakfast, I'll show you how to fill out a birth certificate. When we go back out tomorrow afternoon, we'll get it signed and I can mail it in to Montgomery."

I wasn't nearly as tired as I thought I was after getting a smell of ham frying in the kitchen. It was a breakfast fit for the governor and I had all I could eat. Then I really wanted a nap, but I paid attention watching Mrs. Yother write little Dora May's information on the birth certificate with a special fountain pen she said was only used for that purpose. Her birth date was September 29 and

Mrs. Yother had me check the calendar twice to be positive. When she offered to drive me home, I politely refused, but didn't complain when she insisted. If it had been much farther to my house, I would've been asleep when we got there.

"Get some good sleep today and tonight, Miss St. Clair. We have Mrs. Campbell coming in tomorrow morning and a visit back to the Watts's tomorrow afternoon."

I don't remember if I answered her or not. Mama was waiting for me and wanted to know all about my first delivery, though she understood when I told her I had to have some sleep first. I didn't bother getting undressed before crawling under the quilts and sleeping like a baby until suppertime. It was the first time in my life I'd stayed up all night, but if I intended to get into the baby delivering business for a living, it wouldn't be the last. It had been a good day and I felt proud of how I'd done. Being the first to hold a new life in your hands would make anyone want to do this job for free. Getting paid for something I would do for nothing, I never thought there were such jobs—and the next day I would get to see Hazel again. This job was too good to be true, or to last.

Mama woke me after everyone else had eaten supper that Monday, asking if I was hungry. Mostly she wanted to talk. It was probably the first time I ever talked to her woman to woman, and the first time I felt like an adult. I had a job, a well-paying one, and I was doing something that needed doing. She already had water on the stove for my bath and helped me fill the tub after I ate. When she handed me her bar of Cashmere Bouquet and gave me a hug, angels in heaven rejoiced. It was a bath I didn't want to end, and I would smell extra nice for Hazel the next morning. Every muscle in my body ached like I'd split wood all day and the warm water worked miracles. We stayed up too late talking, but it was like she had a new best friend to talk to. When I went back to bed, I wasn't very sleepy. My uniform was laid out even if I didn't expect a knock on the door in the middle of the night. My thoughts drifted between looking forward to Hazel's appointment and dreading it just the same. Above all, I had to treat her as a patient and forget everything else while she was there. Hazel knew what the exam involved. I had explained it as well as I could, but what if she had second thoughts and wanted Mrs. Yother to do it? I would have to respect her wishes; that's all there was to it.

I thought I was dreaming when the smell of something frying woke me up. I stumbled out into the kitchen in my gown to find everyone enjoying a breakfast we never had except on Christmas mornings. Mama was smiling like a mule eating blackberry briars.

"Mr. Yother came by before sunup to deliver us this mess of ground steak. He said it was your overtime pay for yesterday and if you don't sit down with us, I'm afraid your daddy and brother'll eat it all."

Steak and gravy, like only Mama could make, with biscuits hot out of the oven, grape jelly and butter—it was a breakfast worth double the overtime.

I left for the Yother's a little earlier than usual. I wanted to thank Mr. Yother for his visit earlier that morning. Maybe I acted different when I went back to Mrs. Yother's office because she figured out right away that I was uneasy about Hazel's appointment.

"I know Mrs. Campbell is a good friend of yours, Miss St. Clair. I see the two of you sitting together at church, but in the examination room, she's not only your friend, she's your patient in need of the services we provide. I've seen most of the women in this county naked and I admit that when I first started, it was a little peculiar. In your mind though, what you feel when you touch her during the examination has to be separated by a mile from your feelings for her outside this office. I watched you with

Mrs. Redmon. She's a pretty girl too, but she never thought you were somehow deriving pleasure from what you were doing and neither did I. That was a critical test for you, Miss St. Clair, whether you know it or not, and you passed. If you hadn't, I would have had no choice but to send you home. It's a part of what's called professional ethics and everyone in our business is held to a higher standard than ordinary doctors. I will be watching you today, but someday I won't be around and you'll be alone with a patient you might have feelings for. When that happens, I'm confident you will remember this talk we had and do your job. Of course, that's not to say we aren't human; we're just trained to be in control of our natural instincts better than most people. We are not animals and our first priority is our patients. We care for every one of them as much or maybe more than their husbands do. Their husbands are men and they will never understand what it means to bring a new life into this world. Their pitiful contribution in a moment of orgasm means little to them, but for the present, it is what we need to create life. Our duty is to that life-bringer. Do I make myself clear, Miss St. Clair?"

"Yes, Mrs. Yother."

Orgasm. If that was the word, it was perfect; rhymed with spasm and I tried not to smile when I thought of that during Mrs. Yother's lecture. I wanted to hear myself say it and then look it up in the office medical dictionary, but she wasn't finished.

"It's also about time you learned something about who you are, and I can think of no one better than myself to tell you. Lesbians have been around since we stopped walking on all fours and swinging in the trees. It is a relatively new invention to label such women as abnormal or curious as you might have heard them described. History gives us a very different picture and if you care to observe the human race—as I have, you might decide that it is your kind who are the normal ones and that those who prefer to be impaled by an erect penis are the aberrations. This kind of talk would get me thrown out of the High Point Baptist Church, although it would be the men of the church who decided to do that, not the women. They know the truth; we all do. Things will be different someday, Miss St. Clair. I won't live to see it, and maybe you won't either, but evolution happens whether we notice or turn a blind eye."

I loved that woman. She had the clearest mind of anyone I'd ever met and every day I wanted to be more like her. I wanted to see the things that were all around that no one else noticed because they never took the time or weren't smart enough to look. After our talk—it was more listening than talking on my part—I decided I wanted to learn everything she knew. There had to be a way and I would find it.

Promptly at ten-thirty there was a knock on the front door and I heard Mr. Yother talking to Hazel. I wasn't nervous anymore. I knew what was expected of me and I knew who I was. I never knew there was a name for it. Lesbian—I liked the sound of that word almost as much as orgasm and was sure it'd been invented by a woman. Were there also men who liked men? I decided probably not, and I should've asked Mrs. Yother. The idea just seemed unnatural to me for some reason. Maybe men thought the same thing about girls like me. All these thoughts ran through my mind in the span of time it took Mr. Yother to escort Hazel back to the office. She was dressed in the navy blue skirt and light blue blouse she wears to church most Sundays.

"Mrs. Campbell, Miss St. Clair and I are so glad you have entrusted us with your care and I can promise you our full attention. Now, how far along are you? Do you remember the date of your first missed period?"

"The middle of June."

"Good, then we'll assume conception occurred near the first of June, so now you're in your twentieth week, sixteen more to go. You can expect to deliver toward the end of February or the first of March."

Mrs. Yother asked all the usual questions and I filled out the forms that would become part of our file on her.

"Now, Miss St. Clair will get you ready for the examination and she can answer any other questions you might have regarding the procedures. I know you're friends and that you hardly know me, so ask her anything you would ask a friend."

Hazel and I had talked a lot about the examination, but now that it was time, she was nervous all over again. She didn't say anything, and she couldn't get her blouse unbuttoned. She gave me a sort of helpless look that got a smile from me. I could do this.

"Let me help with that Mrs. Campbell. It's part of my job after all."

I'd decided I would address her as Mrs. Campbell, to start things off in a professional way, and I unbuttoned her blouse with steady hands. It was a good thing she wasn't asking any questions because I wouldn't have been able to answer them just then. I took one of the hangers and carefully draped her blouse on it as if I'd undressed a dozen girls already that morning. I didn't stare, but my first sight of her breasts would be something else about her to keep me awake at night.

Her skirt had buttons on the side and I had some trouble with them, so I sat on the stool and used both hands.

"This skirt's getting too small. I guess I'll have to start looking for some maternity clothes soon. Mama kept some of hers I can borrow, but I haven't got up the nerve to ask her yet."

Her skirt dropped to the floor and with her hand on my shoulder she stepped out of it.

"It'll be another couple of months before you have to worry about that, Mrs. Campbell. You can wear normal loose-fitting dresses as long as you feel comfortable in them."

She didn't flinch when I reached up and pulled her panties down so she could step out of them. After helping with getting her gown on, the two of us stepped into the examination room to find Mrs. Yother waiting for us.

"Miss St. Clair will be doing your examination today, Mrs. Campbell, if that's all right with you. She's learning and I will be observing her technique. You're in good hands, I assure you."

"Yes, Mrs. Yother, that's perfectly fine with me," Hazel replied. I learned early on that Mrs. Yother was used to everyone saying "Yes, Mrs. Yother" to her.

"Very well. Miss St. Clair, I will be taking notes based on what you find."

I walked around Hazel and looked at her, put her on the scales, and then stuck a thermometer in her mouth. She was normal to above average height and her weight was only a couple of pounds more than mine. Her temperature was 98.9 degrees.

"Patient has good color and clear eyes. She stands erect with no effort and appears to be healthy." I chose my words carefully and tried to speak the way Mrs. Yother spoke when trying to teach me something.

I walked forward and reached behind her neck to untie the string I'd just tied a few minutes earlier. The gown fell to the floor with only a little help from me and I walked around her again.

"Patient's breasts are full and symmetrical; nipples are erect, areolas normal and of light pink color."

"Please raise your arms as high as you can reach, Mrs. Campbell."

"Breast muscle tone is good. Breasts remain symmetrical and well-shaped. Patient has slightly rounded belly and inverted navel. Visual examination reveals no abnormalities. You can put your arms down now Mrs. Campbell."

I did the breast examination by the book. Touching her was what I'd dreamed about, but somehow it wasn't me touching her at that moment. She shuddered a little when I touched her nipples lightly with my fingers the first time and her areolas scrunched up.

"Nipples have normal response to stimulus." I learned that word from one of Mrs. Yother's books and decided on the spot to use it.

Her breasts were soft, and I didn't feel anything unusual when I squeezed the underside of each breast or when I took two fingers and circled each breast from the nipple out while pressing inward, just as the book said.

"Breasts show nothing unusual in physical examination; no discharge from the nipples and no abnormal tissue masses." I surprised myself in how fast I was learning to speak clearly like Mrs. Yother.

"But sometimes they hurt and my nipples ache, like right now."

"That is perfectly normal, Mrs. Campbell," Mrs. Yother interrupted. "Lie down and place a warm damp cloth across them if the pain becomes unbearable. You should also consider buying a brassiere to help support them, particularly in the later months when they will double in size."

"Now Mrs. Campbell, if you would have a seat on the examination table and lie back, we'll do a cervical check and you'll be all done."

I helped her put her feet in the stirrups, spread them apart and went to the sink to wash my hands.

"I do apologize for the unnatural and uncomfortable position you find yourself in, Mrs. Campbell, but it is necessary so that we can have a good look." It was just the way Mrs. Yother would have said it.

Mrs. Yother raised the table for me and I began my examination.

"Labia majora moist and smooth; no irregularities. Have you experienced any bleeding, Mrs. Campbell?"

"No, not since my last period."

I then spread her labia minora with the thumb and forefinger of my left hand and ran two fingers of my right hand the full length of her labia majora.

"Abundant vaginal secretion; tissue is smooth and pink; no irregularities noticed."

I didn't see the point in mentioning her swollen clitoris, but it was standing up like a fencepost in a snowstorm. I was afraid to let the thought of accidentally touching it cross my mind, so I kept talking.

"Everything looks fine, Mrs. Campbell. Mrs. Yother is now going to raise the back of the table and I'm going to insert two fingers into your vagina to examine your cervix."

The K-Y wasn't necessary, but I took some when Mrs. Yother squeezed the tube for me. She had warmed the tube in a cup of hot water, just like I'd suggested. When I leaned forward with my forearm across her lower belly and inserted my two fingers, I expected Hazel to jump back a little; she didn't. Was it the warmed K-Y that made a difference? Her cervix was completely normal, and I took extra time to make sure. I wanted to look at her face, but I didn't dare.

"Cervix is well formed and smooth."

Mrs. Yother handed me a warm wet cloth and I carefully wiped the K-Y from Hazel and then wiped it off my hands. She seemed calm as I helped her sit up on the table and began reciting my findings for her and Mrs. Yother. The examination was by the book and everything had looked and felt normal to me. Mrs. Yother hardly said a word until I was finished. "Very good Miss St. Clair. Now if you will help Mrs. Campbell dress and then bring her into my office, I would like to talk to her a moment.

I helped Hazel with the gown, but I didn't tie it. I didn't see the purpose of putting the gown back on at all, but it was Mrs. Yother's procedure. In the dressing room, I removed the gown, sat on the stool and held her panties for her to step into, but she didn't move.

"I don't like to think about being pregnant. I don't want to be pregnant, Otha May. I'm scared."

I looked up and there were tears streaming down her face.

"Now Mrs. Campbell, childbirth is a perfectly..."

"And stop calling me Mrs. Campbell. Mrs. Yother's not here now. I'm Hazel, remember? I'm the girl you kissed and the girl who kissed you back, or have you forgotten that already."

I stood up, wrapped my arms around her and held her tight. She might be my patient, but she was also my best friend and at that moment she needed a friend more than a beginner midwife. I could have taken advantage of her fear and kissed her. She would've kissed me back, but it wouldn't have been right. Mrs. Yother's lecture on ethics in the examination room was permanently stuck in my mind. I held her until she stopped crying and wiped her tears away with a towel. When I finished dressing her, we stepped into Mrs. Yother's office to hear what she had to say. It was all good news, as I knew it would be, and I made an appointment for her for the next month.

When I walked Hazel to the front door, she turned and gave me a hug.

"Thank you Otha May. Thank you for everything. You're the best friend and the best nurse any girl could ever hope for. I'd like it very much if you'd have supper at our house this evening. We'll eat about sundown. I've already told Mama I was going to ask you and she thinks it would be nice to have you over. Please say you'll come. James and Glenda are going to the High Point basketball game and Daddy will have to take them. Mama will go to bed long before they get home, so we'll have some time alone. Please say you'll come."

"Why, Mrs. Campbell, are you asking me for a date?"

"Yes I am, and if you call me Mrs. Campbell one more time today, I'll never speak to you again."

"Then I'll be there. We only have to go check on Mrs. Watts and her new baby this afternoon and as far as I know, that's it. See you at sundown."

I had wondered how I would ask to see her sometime and she'd asked me. I was on top of the world when I went back to Mrs. Yother's office and I guess I didn't hide it very well.

"Miss St. Clair, I am pleased with your examination of Mrs. Campbell. Even though she's your good friend, you treated her with all the respect we give any other patient. I hate to spoil your obvious good mood, but you have to type up my notes and make a file for Mrs. Campbell, but I'll make lunch for us if you'll do that now while everything's fresh in your mind. Then we can go out to see Mrs. Watts. Don't let me forget the paperwork. We have to get signatures on the birth certificate."

"Yes, Mrs. Yother," I answered with a smile I'm glad she didn't ask me about.

The endless paperwork was what I hated about my new job, but it had to get done and while I was typing in the information, I noticed that Mrs. Yother had scribbled in her notes that Hazel's due date was probably close to Janice's. I hadn't thought about that.

Knowing I would get to spend some time alone with Hazel made the typing go faster, and then I looked up orgasm when I finished. What the books had to say was pretty disappointing. No one seemed to think it applied to women at all, but then again, they were all written by men. I still liked the word anyway. I didn't find lesbian. Lunch was scrambled egg sandwiches with lots of dill pickles and tomato slices. Mr. Yother had made the bread fresh early that morning and I think I could have eaten it without anything else. Things sure were backward in the Yother house, but it worked well for them.

***

"What we are looking for in this visit is any signs of post-partum infection and we want to make sure the baby is nursing properly," Mrs. Yother explained on our way to the Watts house. "Mrs. Watts is a new mother and even though nursing is a natural instinct, sometimes there are problems and I forgot to check yesterday to see if her milk has come in."

"How do you do that?"

"I'll show you when we get there."

Everyone was all smiles at the Watts place. Virginia was up and walking around and little Dora May looked pink and healthy.

"We just need to do a quick follow-up examination Mrs. Watts if you can trust Mr. Watts to watch the baby for a few minutes and put a kettle on to boil."

I followed Virginia and Mrs. Yother into the bedroom, which had been cleaned up by Mr. Watts, according to Virginia. I helped her get her dress off over her head and stacked up pillows on the bed for her back. When she spread her legs, I was dumbfounded at how much the swelling had already gone down. Her vulva still didn't look normal, but it looked a lot better than it had when we left the morning of the day before. Everything else seemed to be back inside her where it belonged.

"I'm really sore down there, but it's not a constant pain, just when I move a certain way."

"That's to be expected," Mrs. Yother assured her. "After all, you've used muscles that have never been used before. Has the baby breastfed?"

"We tried several times before I could relax enough for my milk to drop. It's a funny feeling that's hard to get used to. When she latched on that first time, I peed the bed, but she got all she wanted the next time we tried. I don't think my right breast is working yet, but the left one is fine."

"All right Miss St. Clair, I want you to pay attention. With your permission Mrs. Watts, I would like to use you to show her how to express milk from a breast. With some luck we can get your right one going too. Either of you ever milk a cow?"

Neither of us had, but we'd both seen it done. The Yothers were the only ones around with cows.

"Well that's good because it's nothing like that unless your nipples happen to be two inches long. Milk has to be coaxed from a mother's breast. It can't be forced out without bruising and making it painful to nurse later on. The best way to show you is for me to sit behind you, Mrs. Watts, and it happens to be the only way I've ever been successful in trying."

With that, Mrs. Yother hiked up her dress, crawled into bed behind Virginia and sat with her legs spread around her. It would have been funny under any other circumstance, but I was there to learn. Mrs. Yother reached under Virginia's left arm and took her breast in her hand, gripping it like she was holding a water glass, with her thumb on top and her fingers underneath. She began squeezing her fingers sort of together and down, starting from underneath the breast and working her way to the nipple, over and over again.

"Do you see what I'm doing, Miss St. Clair?"

I bent down close just in time to get a spray in my face. I was so surprised; I just froze and then got another spray. When I started to say something, the milk ran into my mouth. I wanted to spit but I didn't. It had a sweet taste and when I covered my face with a towel to wipe it off, I licked more from my lips. After the two women stopped laughing, Mrs. Yother went to work on the right breast and within a few minutes, had it spraying as well as the left one. It was like the milk was coming from three or four little holes in her nipple. None of the books I'd read mentioned that. I thought there was just one hole in each nipple.

"All right, Miss St. Clair, it's your turn, if Mrs. Watts doesn't mind. You need to know how to do this. I guarantee it's something you'll have to do sooner or later."

I took Mrs. Yother's place behind Virginia. It was sort of comical, holding another woman's breast like that, but I got over it and began squeezing the way Mrs. Yother had. Nothing came out.

"You have to imagine it's your own breast, Miss St. Clair. That's the only way it works for me."

I couldn't do that with her watching so I closed my eyes and began squeezing together and down, working my way toward her nipple. The first spray got a little applause from Mrs. Yother. I opened my eyes and watched as I made it happen again. Once I figured out how, it was easy and before long, I could do both breasts at the same time. Maybe I wasn't supposed to be, but I was pretty proud of what I'd learned to do. Virginia then took a turn and she had both breasts spraying in no time.

Mr. Watts knocked on the door and announced he had successfully boiled water once again. Mrs. Yother and I washed our hands as soon as the water cooled a little and returned to the bedroom for the rest of our examination. Her cervix still felt five times too big and the opening hadn't closed up completely, but Mrs. Yother said that was normal. As I was helping Virginia get her panties and dress back on, Mrs. Yother left her with one last word of advice.

"Keep your knees together until I say so, Mrs. Watts, if you know what I mean. I want things back to normal before your husband pokes anything in there."

She had a way of talking to anyone about anything.

Out in their living room, Mrs. Yother got their signatures on the birth certificate and we said our goodbyes.

On the way back, Mrs. Yother seemed more relaxed than I'd seen her since starting my new job.

"That's what I like to see, Miss St. Clair; a happy mother and father and a healthy baby. Hopefully we won't be seeing them again except at church and for checkups. Who knows, you could be delivering that baby's baby someday."

I hadn't thought about that, but she'd certainly done it before. When she offered to take me home, I didn't argue. It had been a long day without a break and I was plenty tired; lots of time for a short nap before going to Hazel's for supper. *Wait, she'd said I might be delivering Dora May's baby someday. Was she thinking I could learn to be something more than a midwife's assistant?* Thoughts like that kept me from getting much of a nap.

Chapter Six
Someone's Girlfriend

Tuesday suppers weren't special for any family, but it looked like Hazel and her mama had cooked all afternoon. There was fried chicken, mashed potatoes, gravy, fresh turnip greens, blackeye peas, and a peach cobbler for dessert. I arrived at the Leeth place only a few minutes before Mr. Leeth and when he saw the spread on the table, he said I was welcome in their house anytime. James behaved himself, although he insisted on sitting next to me at the table.

Hazel's little sister, Glenda, was a pretty girl and old enough to have heard and understood the rumors about her big sister's friend being curious, but smart enough not to say anything. If I didn't know better, I would swear she was flirting with me a couple of times during supper. I remembered being her age. Mr. Leeth said the blessing and he asked the Lord to watch over our soldiers and to keep us out of the war in Europe. With everything that had been going on in my life, I hadn't kept up much with the rest of the world.

Mr. Leeth, James, and Glenda left for the basketball game right after supper. Hazel and I insisted on cleaning up the table and washing the dishes. Mrs. Leeth didn't complain too much when we sent her into the living room to find us a radio program to listen to. It was nice doing the kitchen work with Hazel. I could imagine us doing that together in our own house someday. I knew she liked me— she hadn't forgotten our kiss, and she had invited me to supper after all—but I wasn't exactly sure what that meant. By the time we finished, *Amos 'n' Andy* was almost over.

Mrs. Leeth was in a good mood and had a special treat planned for us.

"Since you girls were nice enough to clean up the kitchen for me and Mr. Leeth isn't here, why don't you pick what you want to listen to. I'm going to have a nice long bath and go to bed early. It's not often I have that luxury during the week. Otha May, I can't tell you how glad I am you came to supper. It's not every day we have a nurse in the house. Do give your mother my best and tell her I said you're always welcome."

"Thank you for having me. Supper was about the finest I've ever had, and I'll be sure to tell Mama of your kind hospitality."

"I know just the station I want to listen to, WLS out of Chicago. You have to hear this music they're playing, Otha May. Glenda and all the girls at her school are crazy about it. I know she's only in fifth grade, but it's really good."

She fiddled with the radio dial and the strangest music I'd ever heard came on. It was fast, much too fast for a waltz and nothing like square dance music. We sat on the floor in front of the radio and the music seemed to take us both far away from where we were, in the middle of nowhere, Alabama.

"It's called swing and there's a dance that goes with it too. I don't know how to do it, but Glenda says one of the girls that just started her school this year knows. She's supposed to be from Chicago, so maybe she does. I would love to learn. This song they're playing now's called "In the Mood" and it's my favorite. Can't you just imagine being on a huge dance floor, wearing a long flowing dress, with that music playing so loud you can't think? I'm sorry Otha May, I sound like Glenda, but I do dream of such things."

After half an hour or so, Mrs. Leeth stuck her head in the door and told us goodnight. Hazel turned the radio down low and invited me to sit on the couch with her. It was a big couch and she sat closer to me than she had to. There was a lot I wanted to say and even more I wanted to do. Even though I'd seen her completely naked a few hours earlier and touched her in all the places I'd dreamed of, this was different. Just when I'd made up my mind to put my arm around her, she turned sideways on the couch and pulled her legs up under her. I turned the same way to face her and she took both my hands in hers. When I looked into her eyes, she dropped her head low.

"There's something I'm going to say to you. I'll die if I don't and I hope you don't take it the wrong way, so just let me say it, okay? Otha May... I don't like girls, not the way you like girls, and I won't ever, but I want you to like me the way you like girls. Damn, that's not the way I practiced it. I don't like girls the way you do, but I like you the same way you like girls."

"But I'm a girl."

"Don't confuse me. I'm not saying it right. I don't like girls. I like just one girl. I like you. What I'm trying to say is that if you'll have me, I'd like to be your girlfriend. I know you could do a lot better. You're beautiful and I'm plain as dishwater, but I thought maybe I would do until someone you like more comes along. I've never been kissed the way you kissed me... like I was special, and I thought then that maybe you might want me, you know, for a girlfriend someday. I've tried to put the thought out of my mind, but you did kiss me and you didn't have to do that. I'm sorry if I sound like a fool, but I just wanted you to know that if you do want to like me as a girlfriend, it would be all right. Not all right; that's not what I mean. I mean I'd like that very much. I'm going to shut up now before you think I'm dumber than I sound."

"What if I wanted to kiss you again?"

"Then I would let you."

"And what if I wanted you to kiss me?"

"Then…"

"Then I want you to kiss me Hazel. I want to be your girlfriend first—and you're not plain as dishwater either. You're a pretty girl, with or without your clothes. I've wanted lots of girls as a girlfriend, but none of them wanted me, so I just quit trying."

I sat there motionless. She hadn't expected the conversation to go that way, but I wanted to be kissed, to be pushed back onto the couch, my clothes ripped off, and my body taken. I wanted to be the girlfriend, her girlfriend.

"I want you more than anything to be my girlfriend and I promise there'll never be anyone else. You don't have to ask me for a kiss ever again—because I love you, Otha May. With all my heart, I love you. And you won't ever have to ask me…"

She raised her head and took my face in her hands. Her kiss melted into my mouth and when I leaned back a little, she slowly pushed me the rest of the way. I pulled her body into mine, wrapped my legs around hers and slipped my arms around her waist. It was like she let go of everything she'd been holding back for the past months. She forced her hips down into mine and I met her halfway, easing mine upward into hers. A few minutes of that and I was ready to boil over, or whatever it's called. All the things I'd imagined in my bed late at night or early in the morning when I would think about being with her were coming true. Everything was perfect and it all came together in something that probably had Hazel thinking I was possessed, but I couldn't help it. I lifted us both off the couch when I pushed up into her as hard as I could, took a deep breath, and squeezed her legs between mine. Sounds came from me I know I'd never made before; groans and grunts as I tried to breathe so I wouldn't pass out cold. My hands flew over my head when I collapsed back onto the couch and strained to collect my senses. My head was spinning when I opened my eyes. They wouldn't focus.

"Are you all right, Otha May?" she whispered. "Are you having a seizure or something?"

"Yes, several of them, the most wonderful seizures of my life and they're all because of you. You're the one, Hazel; the one I always knew was out there."

I brought her lips to mine and kissed her. It was a kiss I hoped would say more than the words that wouldn't come to me. Holding her that close, I felt secure, like that was where I belonged. Yes, I would be her girlfriend and her lover. We would figure out what that meant later. At the moment, all that mattered was that she was in my arms.

If it had been another hour before we both heard the truck turn up the hill to her house, the evening could have been even better. If we hadn't heard the truck though, we might have given her father a heart attack that night. We were sitting a respectable distance apart when everyone came in and we got to hear all about the basketball game. In the dim light no one could see how flushed our faces were. It was late when I left, and Hazel walked me part of the way home. When we got to the little bridge over the creek that separated my land from the Yother's, I stopped. It was a full moon and I pointed to a hill I'd always thought I would build a house on someday.

"Can you imagine a house over there? It could be our house. When I turn twenty-one it'll be mine all legal and proper and I can do with it what I please." I saw the smile on her face.

"Would you be my wife, or would I be yours?"

"I'm your girlfriend, so I'd be your wife," I answered with a grin, "but I'll be a working wife if that's all right with you, and I promise not to call you my husband."

"Glenda knows how I feel about you. I guess I'm not very good at hiding when I'm happy and I've been a happy girl lately. Last week she asked if you'd kissed me and she didn't seem upset when I told her yes. She'll keep our secret. You should have seen her smile when she said that if I liked girls, at least I liked the prettiest girl in the county. Now I can tell her that the prettiest girl in the county likes me too."

"You can tell her more than that. I love you Hazel Leeth and I'm going to make you the happiest girl in the state. We're going to be something someday; you wait and see."

She took me in her arms and gave me another kiss that made my knees weak. I was finally someone's girlfriend and all that night I dreamed of what our lives together might be like. It was wonderful to plan again. I hadn't done that since I was a little girl, but with her by my side, I would attempt anything. The only problem at the time was that we had practically no chance to be alone together. My birthday was coming up though and I promised myself we would do something together, just the two of us.

**

Thanksgiving was never a big day for our family. Mama would usually fix something special for dinner, but that was it. When I suggested to her that we invite the Leeths and Yothers, it was as if I'd thought of something that had never been thought of before. At work, when I mentioned in conversation with Mrs. Yother what we were planning and that she and her family were invited, she insisted on having the dinner at her house. Things got out of hand from that point and the dinner turned into one we'll always remember—for several reasons. We had more food than any of us had seen in years and it was the last Thanksgiving before the war. I'd never seen Mrs. Yother in a better mood than when we started planning everything. It had been a long time since she'd invited that many guests to her house and Elton would be coming home from Vanderbilt too. He would be bringing a girl with him as well, a Miss Spradley.

"I don't know anything about this girl," Mrs. Yother confided in me one morning. "Her family's from Indiana, just across the Kentucky line; a town called Evansville. They met at school. What kind of girl goes to an engineering school? Her father's some bigshot in the steel business and Elton says they're well off. I don't know how she'll take to us country folk. Having all of you around will make things easier. I was dreading having to entertain her by myself. Who knows, I could be meeting my new daughter-in-law for the first time and I do want to make a good impression. Mr. Yother has promised me a turkey big enough to feed everyone and I already have the vegetables we'll need. If you could ask your mother and Mrs. Leeth to make their favorite desserts, we'll have everything. I'll supply the bananas if one of them will make a pudding."

That would be Mama. She loved banana puddings more than any dessert she made, and Mrs. Leeth could make a pecan pie or two. There were plenty of pecans that year and the Platts always had a little extra syrup for a neighbor in need.

I liked Mrs. Platt, but I didn't care for her daughter, Inez at all. She was one spoiled, stuck-up girl and had been all her life, on top of being a terrible gossip. She was the first girl in sixth grade to get her period and she let all the other girls know it. I was one of the last and didn't tell anybody. All of a sudden she was grown up and we were all still children. What made it worse was that she also had the nicest clothes and made sure we all noticed when she got something new. If she'd been pretty too, she would have been absolutely unbearable. Maybe she ate too much of her father's syrup because she was fat. Well not really fat, but compared to the rest of us she was. That's why her breasts were so much bigger than ours, or that's what we told each other anyway. She would jump up and down for any reason just to make them bounce for the boys and they loved it. If we had to ask for syrup from the Platts for Mrs. Leeth's pies, at the least Hazel could go with me.

On the Sunday before Thanksgiving, I asked Hazel at church if she would meet me at home after I got off work the next day to go with me to the Platts'. We'd have to walk right back past her house, but it would give us more time together. The Platts were Methodists and went to Beulah Methodist, so Hazel didn't know the family very well. I warned her about Inez. I'd heard she had a boyfriend, but no one had ever seen him. I figured she probably started that rumor herself. She still lived at home and I hoped she wouldn't be there when we showed up. It was late afternoon when Hazel and I began walking toward their farm. It was a long walk, up the next hill past the Yothers', and the weather had turned cooler. Our walk gave us a chance to talk and when we were about halfway, Hazel stopped and looked around.

"This is it."

I knew what she was talking about, but I pretended I didn't.

"You don't remember? This is the exact spot where you first kissed me."

"That was you? I've kissed so many girls on this old dirt road."

She grabbed me and gave me one of those kisses the older girls in school always talked about getting from their boyfriends. I don't think any of them ever got kisses like the one Hazel gave me that day though; if they did, they never talked about it. When I felt her hand slide from around my waist and onto my breast, I almost collapsed. There was an instant tingle between my legs. She was for sure the one. I didn't want that kiss to end.

"I've thought about kissing you and touching you at this spot ever since that night on my couch. Now that you're my girlfriend, it's all right isn't it?"

"I don't know. When you kiss me do you get all tingly down here?"

I slipped my hand down between her legs. She jerked back a little.

Things are touchy down there right now, Otha May. I think something might be wrong. I was going to ask you about it last week at my monthly examination, but I was too embarrassed with Mrs. Yother there." I switched from girlfriend to midwife trainee in the blink of an eye.

"Things looked perfectly normal. Tell me what the problem is."

"There's this little bump that swells up sometimes for no reason and it's been swelled up all day today. It doesn't hurt, but I've never noticed it being there before. I can't bear to touch it, and then the swelling goes down on its own."

"Swells up for no reason, huh? Sounds serious. It wouldn't have anything to do with you thinking about me would it? Could it be you've been thinking about kissing me and maybe touching me in certain places all day?"

"Don't tease me, Otha May. If you know something, tell me. I've been worried sick—and maybe I have been thinking about you all day. Maybe I think about you a lot."

"The little bump that sometimes isn't so little is called your clitoris, or clit for short." I had no idea if some called it a clit, but it sure sounded like I knew what I was talking about. "If you're nice to me, I'll show you what it's good for someday. I didn't know what it was called until Mrs. Yother pointed it out on a patient, but I knew I had one—and what happens when…"

"Like your seizures on my couch."

"It's not in any of the books I've studied so far, but a lot of things aren't in those books. It's called an orgasm or climax; at least that's what it's called when men have them. During an orgasm, a man's penis squirts semen which has sperm in it for fertilizing a woman's egg."

"That slimy stuff."

"If you say so; I've never seen any."

"It's slimy. Take my word for it. So, what do we squirt?"

"Nothing as far as I can tell and that's why I'm not sure what we have is called an orgasm. Maybe it's called something else. None of the books talk about it at all. It's like it doesn't exist, but it does and the clitoris makes it happen."

"Thank you doctor, now can I have my girlfriend back? I'd like to kiss her again."

Mrs. Platt was surprised to see us and was happy to donate a quart of syrup to our Thanksgiving baking plans. Inez said hello, but that was it until we thanked Mrs. Platt and started to leave. She followed us out onto the porch.

"You know what folks are saying about the two of you. They say Otha May has a new girlfriend, a married woman, a pregnant married woman at that."

"Well, they're wrong, Inez," Hazel spoke up. "It's the married pregnant woman who has a new girlfriend and she's not only the prettiest girl in the county, she's also the best lover in the county."

We ran off the porch with the syrup and didn't stop running until we rounded the curve at the edge of the Platt's land, out of Inez's sight. We were out of breath when I took her in my arms and kissed her.

"I do love you Hazel and the better I know you, the more I love you."

That's when the rain started. We were too tired to run and got soaked to the skin.

"Now I'm wet all over," Hazel laughed, "and what I said back there's the truth. You are the prettiest girl and the best lover in the county, and that makes me the luckiest girl in the county."

"And if you catch a cold because of me, I'll be the most hated girl in the county and I'll never forgive myself. I guess I'm not thinking about you being pregnant. We've got a little baby growing inside you to worry about. When we get to your house, you're getting a hot bath if I have to heat the water myself."

Mrs. Leeth was pissed off about Hazel being out in the cold rain and she barely spoke to me while the water was heating up. In the kitchen, with just the three of us sitting at the table, she made it clear in no uncertain terms that we weren't children anymore and that she expected me to take better care of a pregnant woman who trusted me with her baby's health. I felt lower than an undertaker's shovel, but she was right, and I apologized again and again for being so unthoughtful. When Hazel got in the steaming water, I decided it was time for me to leave. Mrs. Leeth walked me to the front porch.

"It's just that Hazel hasn't come to realize that in a few months she'll be a mother. I worry about her and how she's going to handle that. You're her only friend and she listens to you more than any of us. I'm trusting you to take good care of her right now and both of them after the baby comes. You will take care of her, won't you? She's probably told you there's no husband and if she hasn't, please don't tell her I told you. As for people her own age she's close to, you're all she has. I hope you know how important you are to her. You're all she talks about and I know the two of you are close. She loves you whether she's told you herself or not. I can see it. Her father would never understand or accept such a thing. Men don't know much about women and most aren't interested in learning. Nobody has to explain to me how the two of you feel about each other. Now… I've already said more than I should've. Just take good care of my daughter and grandbaby, Otha May."

"She's told me there ain't no husband, Mrs. Leeth and I promised her I'd keep it to myself. You can rest easy that, from now on, I'll watch over her like a sister. She does love me, and I love her, and I won't ever let that get in my way of seeing that you soon have a healthy grandbaby. From now on, she's my patient first and my girlfriend second."

Then she kissed my cheek the way my own mama would have.

It rained on me all the way home, but I didn't notice. I'd threatened the health of one of my patients and her unborn child. If something happened to either of them because of me, I would never be able to live with myself. I might've been Hazel's girlfriend, but she was my patient first and that's the way it would be. I'd finished crying by the time I got my wet clothes off and my gown on. Mama wanted to know if I was sick because I didn't want any supper. All I wanted to do was go to bed.

Thanksgiving dinner was everything Mrs. Yother had planned it to be. No one noticed when I led Hazel back to the examination room before we ate and took her temperature. It was normal and she said she felt fine. I gave her a quick kiss and breathed a sigh of relief.

True to his word, Mr. Yother had bought a turkey bigger than any I'd ever seen and he'd stayed up most of the night keeping the oven at the right temperature. We also had some of his delicious bread. He would make anybody a great wife, but I kept thoughts like that to myself. His final duty before we began eating was to say the blessing.

Mama's banana pudding and Mrs. Leeth's pecan pies were eaten to the last bite. Elton and his girlfriend, her name was Elizabeth, sat directly across from Hazel and me. Mrs. Yother shouldn't have worried about what she would think of her boyfriend's country kinfolks and neighbors. She was the picture of good breeding, as Mama would say, but she wasn't uppity at all and seemed to enjoy being with us and listening to our stories. By the time dinner was finished, she was part of the family. There were a few un-Christian thoughts that ran through my head though, like if she and Elton got married and they moved close by, I wouldn't be the prettiest girl in the county anymore. She was beautiful, and her clothes just smelled of money. Her coal black hair was short and done up on top of her head by someone who knew what they were doing. Elton was a lucky man and I think he knew it even then. Mr. Yother said he noticed Elizabeth at the train station before he noticed his own son. They'd gotten to the Yothers' Wednesday afternoon before I went home. We were caught up on our work, but Mrs. Yother kept finding things for me to do. I think she wanted me to be there when they arrived. It was nice when I was introduced as Mrs. Yother's associate. Elizabeth wanted to know all about me and what I did, but I had lots more questions to ask her. It wasn't often we had a visitor from as far away as Indiana, and a rich one at that.

I insisted that Mama, Mrs. Yother, and Mrs. Leeth leave the clean-up to Hazel and me. Elizabeth didn't have to be asked to help. She might've been a proper lady from a high-society family in Evansville, but she jumped in and got her hands dirty. You can learn a lot about a woman doing dishes with her and by the time we were finished, Hazel and I both approved of Elton's girlfriend. She was smart and funny on top of being beautiful. Later Hazel and I accused each other of having eyes for her. When we were leaving, I told Elizabeth how much I enjoyed meeting her and that I looked forward to seeing her again soon. She leaned over and whispered in my ear that I would be first on her wedding invitation list. Hazel and I walked home and she made me tell her what Elizabeth had said. Elton hadn't asked her to marry him yet, but I could tell she was sure he would soon. I wondered if he'd talked about such things with Mrs. Yother.

Chapter Seven
The Best Birthday Present

On the Thursday before my nineteenth birthday, Daddy asked me what I wanted for a present. Mama had already told me she would be making me a coconut cake. That was my favorite and she only made it on my birthdays. Mostly we didn't make much of birthdays in my family, but for some reason Daddy wanted to get me something, and I had an answer for him. I wanted to borrow the truck on Saturday so Hazel and I could go into Gadsden shopping. I'd saved just about all my wages and I was ready to spend every dime. I didn't drive much, even though I'd learned how when I was fourteen and gotten my license on the first try right after turning sixteen. It wasn't often I saw Daddy smile, but he smiled when I told him what I wanted.

"As long as the two of you promise not use the truck and your money to trade for a Cadillac and head for California, I guess it'll be all right."

Hazel was on her front porch waiting for me early that Saturday morning. She was just starting her sixth month and her belly wasn't fitting into her Sunday clothes very well. Maternity clothes were already on my list. Mrs. Leeth came out on the porch as I was turning around.

"I'll take good care of her Mrs. Leeth. Don't you worry for a minute."

"I'll stop worrying when I see you pull back up to this house. You girls be careful and stay on Forrest Avenue or Broad Street. A lot of coloreds live in Gadsden, but they won't be on those streets in the daytime."

"She worries too much. You'd think she's the one who's pregnant, not me. What are we going to do first?"

"We're going to start at one end of town and stop in any store we want, all the way to the other end, then cross the street and shop on the other side."

"Mama gave me ten dollars, so my shopping might be over with pretty quick."

"I've got a hundred dollars in my purse and I don't intend to come back with any of it. You're going to take that ten dollars and buy your mama something nice and maybe buy your daddy something too. The rest of our money is going to be spent on whatever we want."

"Our money?"

"Yes, our money. What's mine is yours and what's yours is mine."

"But I don't have anything."

"That's not true. You have our baby in your belly and that's worth more than all the money in the world. I might not make much of a daddy, but I can work and make a living for the two of you. That is, if you'll have me."

"Otha May St. Clair, is this a proposal?"

"It is. We hardly ever get to be alone and I figured you might be worried I'd put you out if you said no, so I decided to ask you on the way to town."

"So you'll be my baby's daddy, but you want to be my girlfriend too?"

"Something like that. We'll figure it out."

"Pull over."

"What?"

"Just pull over for a minute."

I pulled over in the parking lot of Duck Springs Baptist Church. We had family buried there and I don't know if any of them were watching as two girls madly in love with each other kissed, but if they were, they got an eyeful.

"Does this mean you accept?"

"It depends."

"Depends on what?"

"Do you suppose we could get our shopping done a little early?"

"I suppose we could, why?"

"Do you suppose there's a hotel in town?"

"I know there is. I've seen one on Locust Avenue."

"Do you suppose it's very expensive?"

"As long as it's less than a hundred—and ten dollars, we'll have a room."

"Then I accept your proposal, Miss St. Clair."

We stopped at the Printup Hotel first thing when we got to town. It looked expensive. Neither of us had ever rented a hotel room or stayed in one, but the man at the front desk was very nice. I asked for a room for my sister and me. A room with one bed was ten dollars a night and with two beds it was twelve; both had baths. I told him one bed would be fine. After I paid him and signed in, he asked if we needed help with our luggage. I was lost for words, but Hazel spoke up and said we wouldn't be needing the room until later in the day and that we could handle our luggage. The smile on our faces as we walked out with the key to our room would have made anybody think we'd just robbed a bank.

It was Saturday and a lot of people were in town, so I really did have to park at one end of Forrest Avenue. Hazel was as giddy as a schoolgirl on her first date. "Let's go in Sears and Roebuck first. I have their catalog memorized, at least the women's clothing part."

"Do they have maternity clothes? That's the first thing we're going to buy for you and if they don't have anything we like, we'll move on until we find something."

They had maternity clothes and plenty of them, but I let her know in no uncertain terms we weren't only going to buy maternity clothes with our money. They also had something else I was looking for: bras for both of us. She needed one and I wanted one. We had no idea how to choose a size, but the salesgirl knew everything there was to know about bras and after taking our measurements, told us the sizes we should look for. She guessed that Hazel was pregnant and suggested we choose a cup one size too big to take into account how much larger her breasts would be by the time the baby came. I didn't ask what a cup was. We took six into the dressing room, three for each of us. It was fun trying on the different styles, although none of them was very comfortable. They were for sure more stylish than the one Mama wore to church on Sundays though. She only had one as far as I knew. We settled on two each, one white and one beige. The way they were made, it looked like they would last for years. When I said something to the salesgirl about how thick and stiff they were, she assured me they would get softer with washing, although she wasn't very convincing. Since we were in that part of the store, panties were next and we both agreed on one thing—anything but white.

"I saw something in the catalog yesterday that I thought would look nice on you and you have to promise me you'll get it for yourself."

She walked over to a dummy wearing a black garter belt and hose. She didn't have to beg me. I bought two garter belts, one black and one white and four pairs of hose of different shades.

"You really want to see me wearing the black one don't you?"

She blushed when I said that and then she added, "With the dark shade of hose, like I saw in the catalog."

"Well, I'll buy them, but only if you'll let me buy you the same thing."

"I wouldn't look good in something like that right now and in another month I sure won't. Next year sometime, we'll come back and I'll let you buy me whatever you want."

"Nope, I want us wearing the same thing under our new dresses tomorrow at church."

"But I'm so fat…"

"Fat? A baby's not fat. You're pregnant and you look exactly the way a pregnant woman is supposed to— and what if I like how you look; ever think of that? I like pregnant women or I wouldn't be working where I do. Maybe I'll just keep you barefoot and pregnant."

I got my way in that argument. She was just over six months and not at all fat, and I did like how she looked. I got to see her completely naked often enough, although it was with Mrs. Yother watching, and she was as beautiful a pregnant woman as I'd ever seen.

I took a collection of dresses, skirts and blouses into the changing room, but I only modeled three outfits for her; the others I didn't like once I put them on. My favorite was a grey skirt with a slit in the back and a light blue blouse. I decided I hate winter clothes and promised myself we'd come back in the spring when they had some brighter colors. Then it was her turn. The two skirt and blouse suits she picked out looked gorgeous on her even if the brown skirt was a size larger than she needed and the blue one was two; she wouldn't model any of the maternity dresses. We had to get shoes too, something that would match everything we bought. That would be black, we agreed. They weren't very comfortable, but they looked nice. We also found a scarf and a new purse for Mrs. Leeth and a new Sunday hat for Mr. Leeth. We had to guess at the size, so we went with a large one that had adjustable strips in the band in case it was too big. After paying for everything, our last stop in Sears and Roebuck was back in women's clothing. We picked out what we wanted to wear from our bags and changed in the dressing room. I chose the grey skirt and blue blouse and Hazel decided on the brown skirt and white blouse. It took a while to figure out the garter belt and hose, but we managed. When we walked back out on the street, we were two well-dressed, good-looking young women anyone would be proud to be seen with.

We had intended to stop in every store, but Sears and Roebuck had had almost everything we wanted. Skipping the rest would give us more time together in our hotel room after all. We did stop in Murphys and Grants anyway to have a look around. When I saw the jewelry counter in Grants, a thought came to me. The rings I got for us weren't expensive, but they looked nice and they were identical, each sterling silver with a tiny chip of a diamond. Hazel wore her grandmother's wedding band on her left ring finger, so we decided to wear our engagement rings, as we called them, on our right.

There was one more stop I'd thought about for a long time and when we got to the My Fair Lady beauty shop, I stopped at the picture window and we looked in at all the ladies getting their hair done.

"You ever think about maybe getting your hair cut short?"

"It's like you can read my mind sometimes Otha May. I would already have my hair short if I knew anyone who could cut it so it would look right. Mama cuts everybody's hair in the family, but I won't let her near mine anymore."

"It wouldn't hurt to go in and see what they have to say. We don't have to get anything done, but I'd like to see what they could do with my hair, and they sell makeup too. I think we should buy some lipstick, maybe some floozy red."

"You wouldn't dare wear it anywhere, except maybe to bed."

"Then I'll wear it to bed—with you."

The lady we spoke with was Mrs. Cash, the owner, and she didn't try to rush us into anything. Neither of us had ever been in a real beauty shop before so we had lots of questions. There were dozens of photos on the walls from fashion magazines showing the latest hairstyles. I had no idea there were so many.

When two chairs opened up, it was decision time. I looked at Hazel and she nodded. We were going to do it. Our chairs were back to back so neither of us could see very well, even with all the mirrors around, what the other was getting done until they were finished with us. I had settled on two styles and Hazel already knew exactly what she wanted. I let the girl cutting my hair make the final decision for me. I really liked the big curls-on-top styles, but I didn't want to spend that much time on my hair every night and sleep in curlers I'd have to buy, so I went with something Hazel and I could pin curl or finger curl when we wanted. When we were told about the permanent wave they could do for an extra five dollars, that sounded perfect for those days when I had no time to do anything to my hair but brush it out. It would look good even if I did nothing to it through the whole week. In the mirror, I saw the first foot-long strands of my hair fall to the floor. I closed my eyes until the big cuts were done. No one would recognize me. When I opened my eyes and looked in the mirror, I didn't recognize myself.

"No going back now, Hazel," I said loud enough for her to hear me over the other conversations going on.

"I'm never going back. I should've done this years ago. Do you think they'll let us in the church house door tomorrow?"

"They may not let me in for corrupting a married woman."

If there were any doubts left in the community that I had set my cap for Hazel, they would soon disappear and I didn't care. We were grown women. One of us was pregnant, and married as far as they knew, and the other had a good paying job; let them talk. I was sort of looking forward to Hazel's husband getting killed.

While we waited for the permanent wave cream to set, another woman came around and demonstrated the latest makeup on us. It was the first time we'd ever worn any makeup and it was amazing what that lady could do. We were going to be the two best looking girls in a pickup truck Gadsden had ever seen. Our stay in My Fair Lady cost more than everything we'd bought earlier. I didn't care. It was over two hours later when we emerged from the beauty shop. Short hair really suited Hazel and I thought it made her look taller. I noticed something about her right away that I'd never seen before, her beautiful long neck. Maybe that's what made her look taller and I liked it. Before we left, we got makeup, lipstick, perfume, curlers, bobby pins and new hair brushes. We got an extra brush for Glenda so she wouldn't feel left out. I had ten dollars in my purse after I paid our bill, but Hazel still had her ten so we were far from broke. I just wanted to save enough money to fill up Daddy's truck with gas and oil on the way home. I couldn't stop looking at her and I caught her looking at me several times as we walked up the sidewalk hand in hand like we owned the town.

It was well after noon and we were both a little hungry, so we stopped at the BonAire for something to eat. I'd eaten there before when the family came to town and knew it wouldn't cost much for a couple of hamburgers and Coca-Colas. We sat on opposite sides in a booth and couldn't stop staring at each other. She was gorgeous, and I couldn't get over what a haircut and style had done for her.

"You could be a movie star, Otha May and I'm the luckiest girl in the world. You were beautiful to begin with and now you're something more than that, like a living doll or something."

"And we have necks. Did you notice that? With all that hair, who would have known?"

Neither of us could believe we'd actually done it, gotten our hair cut, and we were on top of the world. Since it was after the dinnertime rush, we almost had the place to ourselves, so I leaned over the table and kissed her. It was going to be just a quick smack, but she surprised me and reached behind my neck, pulled me to her and gave me a kiss that reminded me of the hotel room we had waiting for us.

The first hamburger I ever ate was at the BonAire and I always got one whenever I came to town with the family. They were almost as big as the plate they were served on and they had a little bit of everything on them. Bill could eat two most times, but one was a meal for me. Hazel and I must have used about a dozen napkins each; we weren't going to get mustard or catsup on our new clothes.

Farther up the street, we stopped in at Frank's Drugs for ice cream cones: Borden's ice cream, made right there in Gadsden. It wouldn't have been a trip to town without ice cream, even in December. She probably wasn't thinking what I was thinking as I watched her lick the ice cream until it was almost gone and then go into the cone with her tongue for the last bit.

"Is this how you impress all your dates, Miss St. Clair; buying them expensive clothes, good food and ice cream, and treating them to a beauty shop visit? A girl might get the idea you were expecting something in return."

Then she turned serious and I could read the nervousness in her voice, which had become a whisper. "I hope you won't be disappointed in me, Otha May, and please don't expect me to know what I'm doing. You know I've only ever been with one boy and you're not a boy."

"I'm glad you noticed."

"You know what I mean. Tomorrow's your birthday. You'll be nineteen and I want things to be perfect for you this afternoon."

"It's already been a birthday I'll remember because I spent it with you. Now, let's go back to the truck, load our stuff and drive up to our room. We'll have to take everything inside with us. The doors on the truck don't lock and I wouldn't want anyone stealing our new clothes."

It was almost two when we got everything done and were able to sit down in our room. Hazel soon went exploring and yelled for me to come and see the bathroom.

"All the hot water we want, a real bathtub and a little tin of bath salts."

"Well, it's paid for and it would be a shame to let anything go to waste, but I'm building a fire in the fireplace first. It's cold in this room and it'll be even colder when we get out of the water."

I could build a fire better than anyone in our house and in a few minutes I had a good one going. There was plenty of rich pine kindling and enough firewood to last a couple of days. I thought about how nice it would be to have at least one whole night with Hazel, but an afternoon would do just fine. When the fire got going I pulled the drapes on the window together. It was dark in the room except for the light from the fireplace, just like I wanted it.

Neither of us had ever had a bath in a real bathtub before and we would probably have taken more time undressing each other if we hadn't been thinking about all that hot water already running. I undressed her first and when she finished undressing me, she sat on the bed and just looked, like she was inspecting me or something, and then she asked me to turn around for her.

"Well, you get to see my bare bones often enough, but I've only seen you naked once and I wasn't your girlfriend then, so I tried not to stare. I want a good long look now if you don't mind. It's just like I remember; you really are even prettier without your clothes."

"Quit ogling me and come over here. There's something I've been wondering about." I reached down, took her hands in mine and pulled her up off the bed. "I've been wondering if kissing you naked would be better than kissing you with clothes on." I wrapped my arms around her and pulled her body into mine, making sure our nipples touched before I kissed her. It was better without clothes. It was so much better without clothes. If the tub hadn't started overflowing, we might've forgotten about the bath altogether.

The bath salts made the water slippery and we got mountains of bubbles we weren't expecting. I drained out just enough water so we could get in without getting the floor any wetter. We were like two kids in that tub, splashing around and blowing handfuls of bubbles in each other's faces, while being careful not to mess up our hair. Her breasts seemed to float among the bubbles and I couldn't resist touching her nipples when she'd let me. Before the water cooled off, I had her stand up so I could get my soapy hands between her legs. Instead of sitting down again when I had everything down there nice and clean, she pulled me up and took the soap from me.

"This I have thought about, almost every night," she whispered and smiled.

She reached down with the soap and took her time making sure everything she could reach was clean, and then her hands were all over my breasts and stomach. It was a warm slippery feeling when she pulled me to her and everything touched, like we were mirror images of each other. Her body sliding over mine drove me crazy and if she'd kept it up, I would have fainted dead away and drowned in the tub. We sat back down in the cooling water long enough to rinse the soap off, and when she stepped out of the tub, she held out her hand for me. It was one of those picture-perfect moments. When I reached for a towel, she stopped me and pointed. I hadn't noticed the wide full-length mirror on the wall of the little dressing room adjoining the bathroom. We walked over and stood dripping in front of it. There's something about seeing yourself and someone else naked in a mirror. For a few moments we stared at our images while we touched each other all over. It's like we were peeking at two other girls through a window. As she slipped her hand down my wet stomach, chills ran over me and it had nothing to do with the cool air.

"Otha May, I still can't believe we're here, that I'm here with you, naked in our room in the most expensive hotel in town." She spoke to my reflection in the mirror instead of turning to face me. "I love everything about you: your eyes, your mouth, your angel-like body, the way you kiss me. I never thought I would fall in love with anyone and then you came along. I love you Otha May St. Clair. With all my heart, I love you."

The whole time she talked, she watched us in the mirror. She was fascinated with our reflections and I thought of something to make a memory; something she wouldn't soon forget. I wrapped my arms around her and turned the two of us slightly sideways, then dropped down on my knees. She stood there frozen, looking at us in the mirror as I parted her labia majora with my thumbs—I'd long since drilled the right words into my head; knowing the correct names for things made slang seem vulgar to me. *Maybe we should have a couple of mirrors in the examination room so our patients can see what we're doing.* I don't know why that thought ran through my head at the time. At least I didn't stop and say it out loud. If we hadn't been so cold and wet, I might have finished what I started, but there was a soft warm bed waiting for us, so I reached up and gave her nipples a final pinch. When I stood and brought our bodies together, I noticed she was shivering and it wasn't because of the chill in the air.

We grabbed towels and ran for the fire which was roaring hot with the two split oak logs I'd thrown on before our bath. The fire dried us so fast we barely needed the towels. The room was becoming nice and warm and so were we. Things look different in the light from a fireplace and that's how I wanted to see her. The image of the two of us naked and wrapped up in a kiss in front of that glowing fire was one I would've given a week's pay to have in a photograph.

When we finally stopped shivering, I took her hand, led her to the bed and turned back the covers. The sheets were ice cold but lying side by side with our legs and arms wrapped around each other, we soon warmed up. I smiled and gave her a little peck of a kiss.

"It sure has been hard getting you into bed with me."

"Promise me that someday we'll have a bed of our own. It doesn't have to be as nice as this one, so long as it's ours.

"We'll have a bed bigger than this one and a couch and we'll be naked on both whenever we want. And we'll have running water, hot and cold, and electricity. Someday we'll have it all; you wait and see." Her hand slid down my stomach, then stopped short of where I wanted it to go. The urge to push it on down was hard to resist. I told myself she would go the rest of the way on her own—maybe—if I would just wait. She'd touched me there before, but only through my clothes and this was so different. With my free hand, I caressed her back down to her waist and this time when she shivered, I knew for sure it wasn't from the cold. I hadn't told her, but she had an adorable butt, and this was my first time getting to touch it. That wasn't part of her monthly examinations and Mrs. Yother would surely have noticed if I'd gotten a feel, not that I would have, so I took my time exploring her perfect curves and smooth skin. I think women notice a woman's butt more than men do. When she lifted her leg slightly, that was an invitation I thought, so I moved my hand around to her stomach. Hoping she would follow my lead, I slipped my hand between her legs, but hers never moved; I was ready to scream.

"It's a good thing that touching me there's not part of my monthly visits or I'd jump off the table every time."

"I have one too, you know."

Her hand slowly, painfully slowly, inched downward. This was a feeling I hadn't had since Rosa visited that summer and it was enough to take my breath away. I wondered if she'd ever been this close to Donnie. I was jealous, even if I had no reason to be. It was a stupid thought. Another kiss from her and he was forgotten.

When I rolled over on top, I had other things in mind. Our bodies touched in as many places as possible without me putting much weight on her belly. That was what I'd dreamed about for months and I knew it would probably be a long time before we could be this close again. Rosa was the first and last person I'd been naked in bed with until that afternoon with Hazel and I wanted to cram everything I'd missed in those years into a few hours. In a kiss, I tried to show her how much she meant to me and just how desperate I was to make love with her. It must have worked because she wrapped her legs around me and pushed her hips up into mine long before our lips parted. The rhythm of our bodies twisting and driving into each other soon had me trying to catch my breath. That alone was almost enough to do it. The small circular rotations I began making were enough to send me over the edge. I think every muscle below my belly button contracted at the same time in a single hard convulsion, then there was a flood of spasms like quick kisses. She felt them too. I wanted to say something, but I couldn't.

We lay there hot and sweaty until she brought my face to hers and grinned. "Was that as good as I think it was?"

"You have no idea."

"You're right, I don't and we're not leaving this bed until I do." I couldn't see her smiling, but I knew she was.

"Okay, dear Hazel, the rest of the afternoon is yours, I promise.

I went to the bathroom to have a pee and get a glass of cold water. I brought one for her and sat down on the bed while she drank it.

"This is just the beginning for us. Someday we'll have our own place and we'll sleep naked together every night and we'll make love anytime we want."

She lay back, pulled me down to her and kissed me. "I'll wait for 'someday' if you'll show me now what I'll be waiting for." That Hazel wasn't even related to the shy homely girl I'd met only a few months before.

I rolled off her and turned her face sideways enough for a kiss. This was going to be something very special for her and there was no need to rush things.

"Do you think I'm pretty, Otha May, I mean, without clothes? I know I'm not much to look at in them. I'm plain as can be, and here lately I feel even plainer than that."

She was being serious, so I tried to be just as serious. Mrs. Yother had told me she secretly reminds all the husbands of her patients to tell their wives they're pretty every day. At that moment I understood why. "If I haven't told you today how pretty you are, then I'm not a very good girlfriend and I know better than most what naked girls look like. You have a beautiful body I can't stop staring at when you come to Mrs. Yother's and I know she's caught me looking. If I had breasts like yours, I'd be called a floozy for sure because I'd let anyone who asked have a look at them. Not too many girls are prettier without clothes, but you are and no one in their right mind would call you plain."

I could be the husband when one was called for.

I kissed her and then slid down in the bed just enough to find one of her nipples with my tongue. Somehow, lying next to her at that moment was different and I felt like a real lover for the first time. Maybe it was because I was thinking of her instead of myself. What I wanted to do was work my kisses down her belly and drive her crazy, but it wasn't about what I wanted anymore.

"You know just how to touch me, Otha May. You've got million-dollar fingers and a silver tongue."

Everything was perfect, and I could feel every little twitch she made and every short breath she took.

"Otha May, I think…"

She took a deep breath and then her whole body went stiff and shook. The long slow groan from her lips came with a hug that squeezed all the air out of me. The world stopped for a few seconds while she caught up on a few of life's pleasures she'd missed, and I caught up on some of the hugs and kisses I'd missed growing up curious. I lay there imagining ways we could stay the whole night and just about had it figured out when her hand went up my leg. "What do we feel like… inside? I'm sorry, Otha May, for sounding so stupid, but I thought I could ask you."

I rolled over on my back, leaned forward and shoved our pillows behind me. "Now, use two fingers and reach as far as you can." I wanted her to feel what I felt for during her exams. I don't know why I thought of that and it wasn't a very romantic thing to suggest, considering where we were and what we'd been doing up to then. When I took her other hand and pressed down on my stomach, it was so she'd remember what I'd done during her examinations.

"Feel that? It's my cervix. There's a hole in the end and very soon a baby will be pushing its way through yours."

"I feel it, but I don't see how a baby can ever get through that little hole."

"Yours is a lot bigger and it'll be plenty big by the time you go into labor."

"I'm scared, Otha May."

"I am too, but not about that. I'm scared of what your mother's going to do to me if I don't get you home before dark."

We dressed each other in the clothes we left home in, with a promise that we'd wear our favorite new clothes to church the next day. If we were late getting home, I didn't want to have to explain everything all at one time. Our hair would be enough. We had a last long kiss and a final look at our room, then went back out into the real world.

When I got the truck started and pulled away from the Printup, she slid over next to me and was quiet until I turned onto Broad Street. I could have read her mind even if she hadn't spoken up. "Promise me we'll come back someday and see a picture at the Princess." My mind reading was way off.

"I promise the next time, we'll see a picture and then spend the whole night together in our room at the Printup."

"Room 104. You sure know how to sweep a country girl off her feet, Miss St. Clair, and it wouldn't surprise me a bit if you kept that promise."

Chapter Eight
War

The roof of the High Point Baptist Church didn't collapse when Hazel and I walked in and sat down together the next morning, but there was some powerful whispering heard, and after the service I noticed our rings getting some attention. Mama and Daddy didn't have much to say about my short hair and Hazel's mama liked hers, but I think she was mostly relieved we'd gotten home before dark. We were prepared for the worst, although everybody sort-of accepted that what was done was done. Bill wanted to know what everything we bought had cost and I was proud when Mama told him it was none of his business, that it was my earned money and that it had been a long time since any of the St. Clair women had spent money on themselves. He didn't have much to say to that.

It was cold that Sunday and the sky was clear; perfect weather after dinner for a walk—and I had a plan. Right after church, I told Hazel there was something special I wanted to do that afternoon, so she was waiting for me when I got to her house. She couldn't figure out why I turned around and started walking back toward my house. She also couldn't figure out why I was still carrying my Sunday purse. After we crossed the bridge, I went over to the side of the road and lifted two strands of the barbed wire fence. She crawled through then held it for me. It wasn't a far walk and when we got to the top of the hill— my hill, I stopped.

"You see that big flat rock over there? Two years from tomorrow that'll be our rock and I want to be right here with you and little Abby or Nate." She kissed me and then ran over and climbed up onto it. It was a huge rock and I went over and sat next to her. The view was like a picture in the *Geographic*. We could see the Yother's house and my house and if it wasn't for a little patch of woods, we could've seen hers. I opened my purse and took out the pad of paper and pencil I brought. "Now, what would you like our house to look like?"

It was almost dark by the time I got her home, but we had a dozen drawings we could work on together later when the weather got bad. One thing she insisted on in all the drawings was keeping the rock where it was.

My birthday started like any other Monday, except Mama gave me a kiss and told me "Happy Birthday" when she woke me. I got dressed, ate breakfast and headed for the door, but she stopped me and gave me another kiss. "I remember where I was nineteen years ago today. I prayed for a girl and the Good Lord gave me the best daughter a mother could ever want. I hope you have a good day and remember; your last year as a teenager begins today." I hadn't thought about that. "There'll be a coconut cake waiting when you get home." Mama would also see to it that it wasn't cut until then. There might be candles if she could find them. They only burned long enough for a wish and then they were saved for the next birthday cake.

There were two appointments scheduled for that morning. Mrs. Watts would be around for a checkup for herself and little Dora May and I didn't recognize the other name. It was in Mrs. Yother's handwriting. She saw me staring at the appointment book and must have guessed the question I was about to ask. "Mrs. Edna Greene was my second-grade schoolteacher, Miss St. Clair, and one of the finest women I've ever known."

"But how…?"

"She died when I was a teenager. She and her husband Chester didn't have any children and I always thought that was a shame." The faint smile on her face only added to the mystery. "So, you see, she doesn't need her name anymore. This is our new patient's first pregnancy and her first visit to us. Her mother came by yesterday afternoon and made the appointment. She seems to think Edna's about three months along, however she's not sure.

"Now, Miss St. Clair, do you remember the discussions we've had regarding ethics? That premise extends to privacy rights of the patient as well. You already know you aren't to discuss anything specific regarding a patient with anyone outside this office, but that can go further. If the patient indicates she doesn't want anyone to know she was here, we must respect her wishes. She doesn't even have to give us her name. It's not our purpose to judge others or their motives, although for internal purposes, we have to be able to identify our patients. You may recognize Mrs. Greene or her mother when they come in, but you're to behave as if you don't. Mrs. Greene is here for our care, not our questions. I know her and her mother. I delivered Edna a little over twelve years ago and, as you may have surmised, her pregnancy isn't a planned one, and she's scared to death. She's not the youngest pregnant girl I've had, but she's close. Because you're much nearer to her age than I am, it will be your responsibility to put her at ease if you can and get as much of her medical history as possible. At least find out when her last period was. She'll talk to you. She knows you work with me now and has asked that you do her examinations. I'll be right outside if you need me."

"You're not even going to be in the room?"

"This is another test, Miss St. Clair; the final one before I make the decision to…"

"To what, Mrs. Yother?"

I didn't get an answer because there was a knock on the office door. "Mrs. Yother, Mrs. Watts is here," Mr. Yother announced.

"We'll continue this conversation later, Miss St. Clair. Right now, we have work to do."

It was good to see Virginia again and Mrs. Yother held little Dora May while I got her mother ready for her examination. I followed the usual procedure, helping her undress and helping with the gown. Her body looked like it belonged to someone twice her size. There was loose skin hanging down from her stomach and her breasts sagged with her nipples pointing toward the ground. When she was ready, I took the baby and tried to make notes while Mrs. Yother talked and Dora May squirmed. She examined Virginia's breasts as if it were her first visit and found nothing unusual.

"Breasts symmetric, full and heavy; milk easily expressed from the nipples; no abnormal tissue detected." I didn't expect to be involved in the examination, but Mrs. Yother took the baby from me and asked me to repeat every step she had made. Her breasts were like little feather pillows in my hands and milk began dripping when I squeezed them as I normally would in the procedure.

"Areolas enlarged and..." I couldn't think of the word.

"Protruding," Mrs. Yother whispered.

Dora May was handed back to me so Mrs. Yother could wash her hands and help Virginia get onto the table and put her feet in the stirrups. When she finished with the pelvic exam—I'd learned the real word for the procedure— she washed her hands again, took Dora May and indicated it was my turn. I repeated what she'd done and was glad to see everything was back where it was supposed to be, although still swollen. It was no problem getting my two fingers inside her vagina and it seemed to me her cervical opening was almost back to normal.

After the examination, I helped Virginia get dressed while Mrs. Yother took Dora May and completed some paperwork in her office. I followed Virginia to the office to sit in on the conversation Mrs. Yother would have with her, and asked if I wouldn't mind waiting outside. The closed-door meeting didn't last long, and I escorted her out of the house where her husband was waiting in the car.

"What was that all about?" I asked as soon as I got back to the office.

"Miss St. Clair, have you already forgotten the conversation we had not more than an hour ago about ethics and a patient's right to privacy?"

I felt lower than dirt—until I saw the grin on her face.

"Her husband wanted her to ask me if he might have privileges in the bedroom again and she didn't want to have that conversation with you in the room. You examined her, Miss St. Clair; what would you have told her?"

"Maybe you're asking the wrong woman," I answered with just as big a grin. "But, professionally speaking, it looked like everything was back where it should be. I would have told her to wait another two weeks and if there was any pain, wait another two weeks."

"You're close. I told her to wait a week, gave her a sample tube of K-Y and didn't specify what she—or Mr. Watts—was to do with it." There was a side of Mrs. Yother that no one saw. She had a sense of humor that took some time to understand, and then some more time to appreciate. She saw humor in the strangest things.

I was just about to ask her what she meant when she'd said earlier she was going to decide something about me when another knock came on the door. Mr. Yother had a distinctive knock and he never came into the office without knocking. "Mrs. Green and her mother are here."

"You may bring them back in ten minutes, Mr. Yother. Then she turned toward me. "Now, Miss St. Clair, you have ten minutes to go over every inch of the examination table with bleach water and get ready for our next mother-to-be." I knew the routine and went to work.

I could hear voices outside the examination room, but they weren't the voices of anyone I recognized. When Mrs. Yother opened the door, a very small colored girl and a very large colored woman came in.

"Mrs. Greene, this is Miss St. Clair, whom I think you may know already and Miss St. Clair, this is her mother, Mrs. Camp."

Mrs. Camp gave me a good looking over and I could tell she wasn't too pleased with what she saw. "You sure this girl knows what she's doing Mrs. Yother?"

"Your daughter is in capable hands Mrs. Camp. I assure you Miss St. Clair is the best assistant I've ever had and you're welcome to stay in here during the examination if you choose."

"No, I don't want you to, Mama. I'll be okay. Otha May'll take good care of me." I could tell Edna was about to cry.

"We'll be in the office, Miss St. Clair, if you need us." With that, she led Mrs. Camp out and closed the door behind her.

If this was a test, it was the hardest one I could imagine. Edna looked about eight years old and she started crying the second the door was closed.

"Now, Mrs. Greene, there's nothing to be afraid of. I promise…"

"My name's Ruby and I ain't got no husband and now I won't ever have one. The only reason I'm here is because Mama made me come. Once everybody finds out I'm pregnant, I'll be called a hussy the rest of my life, but that ain't gonna happen. I ain't gonna have this baby. I'm gonna kill it before it's borned. I know how to get rid of it with a potion and nobody'll ever know."

"You'll know. I want you to understand that anything that's said in this room or the office is private and not even a judge or the sheriff can force me or Mrs. Yother to talk. We'd go to jail first. You're our patient. Your health and your baby's health are all we care about."

"You won't tell nobody about me being here?"

"Mrs. Yother would lose her license and I'd lose my job, and I love my job. We don't even have your real name and we won't ever ask for it. You're Mrs. Greene to us and your mother is Mrs. Camp. That's the way things will stay, and you can name your baby anything you like. You can call him or her President Roosevelt if you want and that's what we'll put on the birth certificate."

She managed a little smile and almost stopped crying. "She ain't my real mama. She died when I was being born and that's why I was brung here. I was her first and only baby. Mama don't want me to die like her little sister. Mama—Mrs. Camp, is mama's sister and she took me to raise like I was her own, even though she already had three babies. She didn't have no husband so Daddy and her lived together until he died last year. My real last name is Camp and that was Daddy's name—Raymond Camp. I'm Ruby Lee Camp. Mama took our last name, but she never married my Daddy, but he was married to my real mama. I have the paper. Her name was Goldie and Mama's told me lots of stories about her.

"I told Mama I know you but I don't. I just heard from some colored girls who you are. They say you're a different kind of girl, one that likes other girls. Is that true? Are you really like that?"

We talked for almost an hour before we got down to her examination, which went perfectly. Touching a colored girl was another first, but there'd been so many firsts since I started working for Mrs. Yother, one more didn't matter. I couldn't examine her cervix very well because I couldn't get two fingers inside her vagina far enough. Her hymen was still partially intact, and I believed her when she said she'd only done it once with one boy and that he was her own age. It was a small penis that had penetrated her vagina; that was certain. She remembered only having a few periods before she got pregnant, so I had to guess about the date of conception, but I reported to Mrs. Yother my best speculation was that she was maybe three months along, as her mother had said. She didn't appear to be malnourished at all and her breasts were well developed for a girl her age. By the time the examination ended, the two of us had come to a kind of understanding. She would take care of herself and we would take care of her and her baby. There was another understanding being reached while I was busy with Edna—or Ruby. When I brought her back to the office, Mrs. Yother and Mrs. Camp were just walking out.

"Miss St. Clair, what would you say to having an assistant of your own? Mrs. Camp and I have been talking, and I've wanted for some time to have help running the house. Mr. Yother's getting up in years and he needs someone to do things he has trouble with, like cooking and cleaning, and I believe you could use some help in everything you do. Mrs. Camp has proposed that Mrs. Greene would be the perfect addition to our clinic here. It's much too far for her to drive Mrs. Greene every day, so I suggested that she stay here. There are bedrooms in this house that haven't been used in years and she would have her pick. What do you think of that idea, Miss St. Clair? Mrs. Greene?"

"It would be a lot of work," I lied. "Why, I could keep her busy myself most of the day and then there would be the housework and cooking to do…"

"I can do it. I'm a lot stronger than I look, Ma'am, and I've been cooking most of my life, and nobody keeps a house cleaner than me."

"You would…"

There was a loud knock on the office door that wasn't Mr. Yother's. "Mrs. Yother you gotta come quick. Arlene's in labor and I had to leave her by herself. She's scared half to death and her water's already broke. You gotta come now. The boys are in the truck and I'll drop them off at the Winters' house. They're expecting them."

I opened the door to find Mr. Hancock standing there looking like his house was on fire, with Mr. Yother behind him trying to explain how he got past him.

"You start right now, Mrs. Greene. See to it that Mr. Yother gets something to eat. You're the woman of the house while Miss St. Clair and I are gone. I have no idea how long we'll be. Pick out a room. Mr. Yother will show you. Miss St. Clair get my bag."

Nothing rattled her. It was like she was expecting this emergency and had seen expectant fathers in worse shape several times that day. I went for her bag and grabbed a handful of clean towels and anything else I thought we might need. As we were pulling out of the driveway, I saw Ruby and Mrs. Camp unloading things out of the truck they came in. She and Mrs. Yother had this all planned. The smile on my face must've said a lot.

"Well, I do need some help in the house and Mrs. Greene needs a place to stay, away from where she's been living. I've known Mrs. Camp most of her life and her sister might have lived if someone had come for me. Hiring her was the right thing to do. You can stop your grinning now, Miss St. Clair."

Mr. Hancock only slowed down when we got to the Winters' house and the two half-grown boys in the back of the truck jumped out. The Winters—Mrs. Hancock's sister and her husband—had a house full of kids themselves, but the boys could stay with them a few days until things got back to normal.

Little Carl Hancock arrived just after midnight. He was healthy and after the cord was cut and tied off, Mrs. Yother wrapped him in a sheet and had me put him in an open drawer of what looked like a dressing table. Mrs. Hancock was in trouble, probably because she'd started pushing long before we got there, and she was losing a lot of blood. She passed out sometime during or after the delivery. This was the first time I saw Mrs. Yother suture.

"Pay close attention Miss St. Clair and you'll learn how to save a mother's life. She is our patient and would likely die if we weren't here. This isn't her first baby and she should have known not to push too early, but then, it's probably been ten years. Find that spool of catgut in my bag and thread it into one of the smallest needles, not the smallest one. Bring that bottle of chloroform with you too and if she starts to wake up, pour some on a cloth and hold it on her face. She'll fight you but hold it there. She doesn't need to feel the pain in what we have to do. You'll have to hold my flashlight while I do this, and I want you to cut each suture as I finish. You'll also have to keep washing away the blood so I can see what I'm doing. Sewing up torn flesh and muscle isn't something to be done carelessly." I was to earn my pay that night and learn how fragile life is.

After each suture was tied, I cut the thin catgut thread close to the knot while holding the flashlight in my mouth. When Mrs. Yother ran out of thread, I rethreaded the needle for her. Twice I had to replace the pillow under Mrs. Hancock. I couldn't even stand to watch a hog butchered, but somehow my mind didn't let me think about what my eyes were seeing. Mrs. Yother was like a machine built to do what she was doing. Every move was planned and every stitch and its location was described to me as she worked. She talked the entire time. I thought that was probably to calm me. She only stopped what she was doing long enough to check Mrs. Hancock's pulse occasionally. It was almost two hours later before she finished. The stitches looked as carefully done as any quilting I'd ever seen.

"Now, Miss St. Clair, she might live. I've seen women survive a lot worse. We have to get her awake and force her to drink all the water we can. Bring that bottle of smelling salts from my bag. She'll be in a lot of pain when she wakes up, but I can't give her morphine until we get some liquids into her and give her an iron shot. Did you count the number of stitches, Miss St. Clair? It's critical that you do that. They have to come out in about a week and if we miss one, a serious infection can result." There were exactly seventeen—I had counted for some reason.

"Hold her down and talk to her when she comes to. Let her know the baby's fine. Tell her we have something to stop the pain, but that she has to drink three glasses of water first. She needs the water so her body can make blood after I give her the iron shot. We also have to make sure she can urinate and the water will help with that too."

Mrs. Hancock woke up instantly when she got a breath of the smelling salts and the scream that came from her was like nothing I'd ever heard. That brought Mr. Hancock in, but Mrs. Yother got rid of him by handing him the baby and telling him to boil some water. When I was able to get Mrs. Hancock's attention through all the screaming, I told her the things I was supposed to. She wanted to see her baby before she would do anything, so we allowed Mr. Hancock back in for a minute. Because she was in such bad shape right after the delivery, we hadn't done anything with the baby but cut the cord and tie it off. I was glad to see that Mr. Hancock had made himself useful and bathed little Carl. He hadn't forgotten how to do that. Once Mrs. Hancock was allowed to hold him, she drank the water I had waiting. After giving her the iron and morphine injections, she drifted quietly off to sleep.

"All right, Miss St. Clair, I want you to undress her, bathe her as best you can, and find a clean gown. I'm going in search of clean sheets. Pay attention and tell me if you see her urinate. We won't be leaving until she does. She'll sleep the rest of the night and we'll be back tomorrow."

I did what I could with warm water and soap and when I touched her breasts, she gave a good pee; all over herself, me and the bed. At least she didn't wait until we had the sheets changed. It was after four by the time we left. Mr. Hancock was given strict orders not to wake his wife unless the place was burning down. The baby would be fine as long as he was kept warm and dry. He had also peed and when he peed the second time, Mrs. Yother declared both mother and baby would live until we returned. I knew Mama was probably worried sick. There hadn't been time to go the other direction from Mrs. Yother's house to mine to tell her where I was going. Mrs. Yother talked continually while we drove, but I was too tired to listen until I heard her say something about an exam.

"If you're awake Miss St. Clair, I want to tell you that the decision I had to make has been made. After your performance tonight, you have passed all my tests and it's time you started studying for the midwife examination coming up next June. I have decided to sponsor you. You'll be my first and I will see to it you're well prepared. I hope you heard me because I might change my mind after I've had some sleep. I should have prepared a dozen women to take the examination over the years and now maybe I'm too old."

"You're a saint, Mrs. Yother and we'll teach those men doctors a thing or two about birthing babies."

"I've been called lots of things, Miss St. Clair— never a saint, and that's exactly what I intend us to do; and we don't birth babies, we just deliver them. We may be from the backwoods of Alabama, but they'll never see a better prepared student than you'll be. You have the gift and I'm glad I've been allowed to live long enough to find you. Be aware, however, that if you accept this offer, it means I have all your free time, Saturdays and some Sunday afternoons included until the examination. This might not make your mother or Mrs. Campbell very happy, but it's what I require, so think about it before you answer. Now if our new assistant is worth her salt, we should have breakfast waiting for us. As I recall, we missed supper last evening."

"And dinner yesterday too, as I recall."

Ruby met us at the door. Mr. Yother had long since gone to bed. "You folks all right? I was worried sick. Did Mrs. Hancock have her baby? Was it a boy or a girl? Mr. Yother had me go down to the St. Clair's and tell them what was going on so's they wouldn't worry. I know you didn't get any supper yesterday, so I'm cooking breakfast. The biscuits are about done now." She talked a mile a minute and I decided I was hungrier than I was sleepy when the smell of frying ham got to me; just like last time.

There was no mention of everything we'd gone through, only that mother and baby were doing fine, and I understood why. First, it would have been unprofessional, and second, the details would have scared Ruby to death.

We ate like wolves; everything Ruby cooked that morning was good. She and I started clearing the table while Mrs. Yother had an extra cup of coffee.

"President Roosevelt was on the radio last night," Ruby announced when we were about done, "and Mr. Yother had me listen with him. Something terrible's happened. The Japanese have bombed us—not here, somewhere at a navy base in the ocean. It was a sneak attack and a lot of our sailors have been killed. He said yesterday was a day that will live in infamy. Mr. Yother started crying and said that this would mean war with the Japs and probably with the Germans too. What's infamy?"

I didn't know either. "It means shame and dishonor," Mrs. Yother said, and I could see tears forming in her eyes. "It means our boys will be going across the Pacific to fight the Japanese and across the Atlantic again to fight the Germans. I lost two uncles in World War I and my grandfather never got over it. There were only boys in the family and two of his sons were killed. My father was wounded and for months, Mother and I didn't know if he was alive or dead. Those were terrible times and they've not been forgotten.

"Come along Miss St. Clair and I'll take you home. Don't bother coming in today. We don't have any appointments."

"I make the appointments, Mrs. Yother, so you know very well that I know that's not true. We have Mrs. Campbell at ten. I want you to go to bed. Mrs. Greene and I can take care of her just fine. I'll get a nap for a few hours and I'll be right as rain."

"That's what I would have told Grandma Yother forty years ago. All right Miss St. Clair, you take care of things, but if you need me, wake me or get Mr. Yother to. He'll be up and about in an hour or so." She seemed a little stooped as she made her way down the hall.

"All right Ruby, let's get these dishes finished and get some sleep. I bet you didn't sleep all night either."

"No, I didn't Miss St. Clair, but I did get my bed fixed."

"Then you'll have company this morning, and my name's Otha May. We only call each other Miss or Mrs. when Mrs. Yother's around and we always call a patient Mrs. regardless of who's around. Remember that or Mrs. Yother will tear your head off. The woman coming in at ten is Hazel Campbell. She's a good friend of mine, but in this house, she's Mrs. Campbell. Got it? And remember, we never talk about one patient to another. Things that happen here go with you to the grave."

"I got it and I swear I won't ever tell nobody what I see or hear, not even if they throw me in jail. Did I do okay on my first half-day?"

"Just perfect, but you'll find out every day's different around here"

Ruby let me borrow one of her gowns and the two of us went to bed. It was broad daylight and neither of us cared if the other had a look as we changed. I'd already seen her as naked as she could ever be. It was only a half-bed and things were tight, but I could have slept standing up. I took Mrs. Yother's baking timer to bed with me and set it for three and a half hours. That would give us time to get things ready for Hazel's appointment.

I woke up five minutes before the timer went off. Ruby's arm was around my waist and her head was between my shoulder and neck. She looked like a little angel.

Hazel was a little surprised when Ruby answered the door. I knew she would be, so I followed along behind.

"Mrs. Campbell, this is my new assistant, Mrs. Greene."

"Well, I'm glad Mrs. Yother has hired a little help for you. Maybe now you'll have time for other things—and other people." The smile on Hazel's face probably told Ruby that Hazel and I were more than friends.

I led both of them to the examination room and explained Ruby's duties to her. I was Mrs. Yother for the day. I watched as she helped Hazel undress and helped her with the gown.

"Do you want me to leave, Miss St. Clair?"

"That's up to our patient, Mrs. Greene. We do whatever puts her at ease."

Hazel grinned. "You're going to see a lot of naked women around here, Mrs. Greene. I might as well be the first."

The examination went by the book, beginning with scrubbed hands and arms. I explained to Ruby everything I did and had her repeat it. She wasn't shy and I'd already noticed her hands, small with long fingers. I wish I could have taken a picture of her face as she inserted two fingers into Hazel's vagina. Everything was fine up until then, but her expression at that moment looked like that of someone trying to take a hot skillet off the stove without a potholder.

I convinced myself she'd laugh about it someday and continued with instructions about what she should feel for.

After the examination, in which I found nothing abnormal, we went to the office and I made notes in her file. I wondered if Ruby could read and write. I didn't want to ask. There was a colored school in the area, but it only went to sixth grade and most children didn't go. When the paperwork was finished, I walked with Ruby and Hazel to the front door of the house.

"Thank you, Mrs. Greene. You can go and start cleaning the examination room now. Use the bottle of bleach water under the sink. I'll join you in a moment. When Mrs. Yother wakes up, she'll want to go back out to the Hancocks'. You should ask to go with her. I'm going home in a little bit." As soon as the front door closed behind me, I wrapped my arms around Hazel and gave her a kiss like I hadn't seen her in a month. "I've missed you so much. It seems like forever since Saturday."

"So, to get to see my girlfriend, I have to make an appointment—and then she gets to see me naked, but she keeps her clothes on? All right, I would like to make an appointment for tonight, say about sundown at my house. Everyone's going to church because of the Jap attack. There's a prayer meeting or something, but I can get out of it."

"I have something to tell you that can't wait. Mrs. Yother has offered to prepare me to take the midwife examination at Vanderbilt next June."

"That's wonderful, Otha May. I know…"

"But it means I'll be at her house six days a week, maybe even some Sunday afternoons. We won't get much time together, but I promise I'll study hard and pass. Then I can get my license when I turn twenty-one and we'll be set for life."

"And then I'll make sure you make up for all the times we'll have missed being together."

Her hand went up my blouse and mine went up hers—in broad daylight right there on the Yother's front porch. Her goodbye kiss took my breath away and made my knees weak.

When I opened the door to go back inside, I heard a door close in the direction of the examination room. Up to our elbows in bleach water, I stopped and looked Ruby in the eye. "Were you spying on me and Hazel?" I could see the answer in her eyes and I was furious. "You know, a lot more colored women would ask for our help if they knew a colored woman would be examining them and someday you could be that woman. I hope you're not so thoughtless that you don't see the opportunity Mrs. Yother's given you. You think you're here just to cook and clean? You're here because people are stupid. Colored women won't go to a white midwife and their babies die, and a white woman wouldn't be caught dead letting a colored midwife touch her. It's senseless, but that's the way things are and it's not gonna change anytime soon. You can make a difference.

"I should send you home right now and let you have that baby while you scream in pain for a day or longer. It might live. It might not. You might not live either. Your mother would be alive today if there'd been someone—like you could be someday—to help her. Mrs. Yother gave me a chance and now she's giving you one, but I won't have anyone working with me I can't trust with my life. Yes, I love Hazel and she loves me. I don't care who knows it and I would marry her tomorrow if people weren't so damn ignorant.

"So what's it gonna be Ruby? You're old enough to get yourself pregnant, so I figure you're old enough to swear right now you'll give this everything you have or get out. Look at me. I want to see your eyes."

She was bawling by the time I finished and I felt like I would faint, but sometimes it takes a storm to clear the skies.

"I didn't mean nothin'."

"Don't give me that field nigger answer. Talk to me like a woman."

"Yes, Ma'am, I was spying, but it wasn't so I could tell anybody else. It was because I wanted to know. People say the two of you are girlfriends and I wondered if you'd kiss her. That's all. I wanted to see you kiss. I never seen anyone kiss like that before. I know why I'm here. Mr. Yother talked a lot last night. He's worried about Mrs. Yother; that she's trying to do too much. I already swore that nothing I see or hear will ever come from my lips and I swear that again to you. Please don't send me home."

"To do what Mrs. Yother does, you get one chance and this is ours. We have to trust her and trust each other more than sisters." I hugged her and kissed her forehead. "Now if you can forgive me for my white trash language, I intend to forget we ever had this little talk."

"I'll forget what you said, but I'll never forget what you meant. I want to be like you someday."

I'd never imagined anyone saying that to me.

I left Ruby in charge and walked home. Mama had dinner fixed, but I only ate a few bites. She wanted to know all about what had happened and I wanted to know about the war.

"Your daddy left early this morning to buy batteries in town before he goes to work. He says they'll be the first things people buy up. They say thousands of our sailors were killed and that the Japs are going to attack California next. They sunk most of our ships and we've got nothing left to fight them with. Everyone's waiting, the news reporter said, to see what Hitler's going to do. There's a prayer meeting at church tonight if you want to come. They've moved the Wednesday night meeting to tonight for this week."

"It's been a busy two days, Mama; I think I'll go to bed."

"I heard you went out to the Hancocks' and you should tell that colored girl thanks again for coming last night to tell us where you were. How is Mrs. Hancock?"

"She had a hard time, but she'll probably pull through. The baby boy's fine. Mrs. Yother's likely on her way out there right now to check on them."

"All right dear, you get some rest and I'll leave supper on the table for you in case you get hungry."

No one had to rock me to sleep and it was so nice sleeping in my own bed by myself. It was almost sundown when I woke up. I needed a bath but there wasn't time. Clean panties would have to do. Hazel would be waiting, and I needed her arms around me.

Chapter Nine
Life Goes On

The next morning when I got to Mrs. Yother's, it was like any other day. There was no mention of the Japanese or the bombing. I looked at the appointment book and saw we didn't have anyone coming in the whole day. I was glad of that; we needed a break. Mrs. Yother had gone out to the Hancocks' the afternoon before and Arlene and the baby were doing fine, although we would be going back every day for a while to give the new mother iron shots.

"There's no reason both of us have to go every time and it's time you learned how to give a simple injection. Maybe tomorrow you can make the trip with me to the Hancocks'."

That morning was spent giving injections into an overripe pumpkin someone had given Mrs. Yother at Thanksgiving. The outside skin was supposed to represent muscle and the inside fleshly part was supposed to be soft tissue. My test was giving Mrs. Yother an iron injection, which she normally gave herself twice a week, and I passed.

"Mrs. Yother, can I ask you a question that's none of my business?"

"It's 'May I ask you a question that's none of my business,' Miss St. Clair, but go ahead."

"How do you make any money? You charge four dollars for a monthly visit and ten dollars for a delivery. You pay me thirty dollars a week and some days we don't have any appointments. You're losing money."

"Otha May, I have more money than I'll ever spend." She never called me Otha May. "All of this is mine and I have property in Blount County and a house in south Alabama, near Mobile. Mr. Yother has relatives there. I do this because when I was no older than you, I knew this is what I was meant to do. It's one of the reasons I married Mr. Yother. His mother was one of the best-known midwives in this part of the state and I wanted to learn from the best. My parents weren't happy with my decision to get married at such a young age and to get their blessing I had to promise to graduate college and make something of myself before having children. I was past thirty and had this practice established when Elton was born.

"Something you'll be interested to know that I just thought of: people around here don't like to remember that Grandma Yother had a sister named Fanny who sometimes would help with deliveries and examinations. She was curious like you and her lover was a beautiful woman from Atlanta named Willa. The two of them lived for years in the house the Leeth's now live in. People mostly didn't accept Fanny being the way she was, but I thought the world of her and Willa. They were together for so long, I thought of them as any other married couple. They died of pneumonia one winter when Elton was just a baby. There was a big fuss in the community because Grandma Yother insisted they be buried side by side in the Yother plot at the church cemetery, but she got her way."

I knew that grave and had wondered why two women who didn't seem to be related, were buried together.

"Now enough of your questions and ancient history; we begin today preparing you for the midwife examination if you've decided to accept my offer, and you'd be a fool not to. Early this morning Mr. Yother moved a desk from the barn into the parlor and it will be yours. It was mine when I studied under his mother. It brought me luck and I see no reason why it won't do the same for you."

"You knew I would accept, didn't you?"

"Yes, Miss St. Clair. In addition to being the best midwife in the state, I'm also an accomplished fortune teller."

Ruby and I spent the morning cleaning up the desk while Mrs. Yother put together reading assignments for me. The lessons she'd given me before were mostly about practical things I needed to know, but now I was expected to learn the hard details. After lunch, it took me the rest of the afternoon to read two pages in a book she gave me, with having to look up half the words in her medical dictionary. In school I was always pretty good with 'comprehension' they called it. I could read a story and understand the general meaning, then put it into my own words. That wasn't good enough for Mrs. Yother. She wanted the exact words with the correct pronunciation. It was dark by the time I got home and I forgot to look at the appointment book to see if we had anyone coming in the next day. I hoped we did.

***

Daddy was limited to only buying two batteries at Sears and they'd cost him twice what they should have, almost three dollars apiece. When he went back after work, there were none left and men he worked with said there were none for sale in the whole city. Bill had the bright idea of recharging the dead one Daddy took out of the radio. It blew up when he connected jumper cables from the truck's battery.

The Germans and Italians declared war on us that Thursday. It didn't seem to be a surprise to the radio news reporter, but it made Mama cry. Italy was the country shaped like a boot wasn't it? There would be a draft, Daddy said, and Bill announced he was joining up before he got his letter. The look Mama gave him would've paralyzed me. He was going to join the Navy, he said, because he heard they had better food.

War or no war, Christmas was coming and there were presents to buy. I wanted to go back to Gadsden shopping with Hazel, but that didn't work out. It was bitterly cold, and Mrs. Leeth put her foot down saying no pregnant woman should be out. She was probably right, so Hazel gave Glenda strict instructions on what she was to buy me when the rest of her family left that Saturday morning. It turned out to be perfect. Hazel and I had the whole day together and we spent a lot of it in her bed, which had been moved into the living room so she could be near the fire at night. It seemed her breasts had doubled in size since we were in Gadsden and I couldn't get enough of touching them. I went shopping with my family the next Saturday, the last Saturday before Christmas. The twenty-dollar Christmas bonus Mrs. Yother left in an envelope on my desk that Friday needed to be spent.

Before daylight Christmas morning, with everyone at my house still asleep, I slipped out the back door. My idea was to put Hazel's present under their tree without her knowing. She would be getting lots of baby things, but from me she would get something special just for her. I hoped her daddy wouldn't shoot me if their dogs started barking. The two pieces of leftover cornbread in my pocket were for them. It was a clear night at least and there was some moonlight. The fire in the fireplace was still blazing and I thought about getting out of my clothes before climbing into bed with her, but I wouldn't be staying long. I leaned over and whispered in her ear, "Merry Christmas, Hazel."

"I knew you'd do something crazy. I just knew it." She threw back the quilts and I crawled into bed with her and gave her a Christmas Day kiss. "I've been sleeping with your present, so here, open it."

When I tore open the Christmas wrappings, I recognized right away what it was even in the dim light from the fireplace.

"It's not very romantic, but I saw Mrs. Yother's and decided you should have one too." The bone handled little knife did look a lot like the one Mrs. Yother kept on her desk. I never saw her use it for anything but opening letters. One day I asked her what the odd shaped single blade knife was for and she told me Grandma Yother had given it to her, that it was called a doctor's knife. Mrs. Yother said it reminded her of how far our profession had come in the last hundred years. "Daddy got me a knife for my thirteenth birthday; it's always in my purse and I use it a lot. Do you like it Otha May? Please say you do even if you don't."

"It's perfect, Hazel. I'll put it on my desk and think of you every time I look at it." I'd never had a knife before. Bill got all of Daddy's when they were about worn out. I got up and moved close to the fire and opened the blade. The name stamped at the base was 'Cattaraugus, Little Valley, NY'. Our church was in Little Valley; not New York, but that's what the place was called by some.

"I'm afraid my gift isn't romantic at all and I should have gotten you something else, but these might not be available much longer." I continued trying to explain her present as she tore off the wrappings of the heavy box. "I happened to be in Sears and Roebuck just as one of the employees was opening a box of batteries to put on the shelf. He told me they would be the last ones for a long time and I could only buy two. I know it's not much of a Christmas present but…"

"Are you crazy? These things are like gold. No one has them. The one in our radio is about dead and Daddy's been worried sick. He's been everywhere, to every little country store around and there aren't any. Not even the big stores in Gadsden have them, he said. Now we'll be able to hear all about this war with one battery and the other one will be just for us. We'll listen to music whenever we want."

"Someday we'll laugh about the stupid Christmas present I got you, but I'm glad it was something you wanted."

"We won't laugh. We'll remember how much we cared for each other in hard times." She was right; I do remember how I spent my Christmas bonus that year. Those batteries were ten dollars apiece and Daddy said I was crazy for spending that much, but he didn't say I shouldn't have done it. There wouldn't be any more for a very long while.

The sun was almost up when I got home, and I could see a light in the window. I had some explaining to do but it would have to wait.

"Ruby was here looking for you an hour ago," Mama said as soon as I opened the door. "Mrs. Yother sent her to fetch you. There's some emergency. You'd better get up there right now."

The colored woman had walked who knows how far at night in the cold to get to the Yother's house. I felt lower than a snake's belly and couldn't look Mrs. Yother in the eye.

"Nice of you to join us, Miss St. Clair. You haven't missed anything important. Please scrub up and examine the patient. I think you will then see why I sent for you. Her name is Mrs. Washington. This is her third pregnancy. The other two babies died during childbirth and this one probably would too if she weren't here."

"Please don't let my baby die."

"Mrs. Washington, you're in good hands—now that I have my full staff in place—and we're going to do everything we can to see that this baby makes it. I'm going to give you a little shot to help ease the pain. Mrs. Greene, your help has been much appreciated, but Miss St. Clair and I can handle things from here. Why don't you start breakfast; we'll be a while with Mrs. Washington." She wanted Ruby out of the room. That scared me.

I watched as she filled the syringe with morphine and injected it; double the dose she'd given Mrs. Hancock, and Mrs. Washington was soon dead to the world.

"Have you finished your examination Miss St. Clair?" I hadn't started. "Mrs. Washington will be out a good long time. She was in the final stages of labor when she arrived and I suspect the baby's dead; I would never give morphine to a woman in labor otherwise. In any case the child has to come out or she'll die too. It's as simple as that. Get a new scalpel and that bottle of iodine. Soak some gauze in it and rub her lower belly. We're going to do a Cesarean delivery and there's no time to waste; never rush this operation, however. Remember the mother is our patient, not the baby. When I finish making all the incisions, you will reach inside and pull the baby out. I'll be busy with the mother after that, so you'll do what you can for the baby if it's alive. Are you ready?" I wasn't ready.

The vertical incision from her navel almost to her vulva still looked too small, but the skin stretched as I inserted both hands. The baby was upside down with its feet in the birth canal. I felt for the head and pulled it out through the opening without much trouble. It was a boy. Mrs. Yother cut the cord and tied it off. There was no movement when I carried him to the sink. The water was ice cold. It was too early for anyone to have built a fire under the hot water tank. The baby was dead; what difference would it make. When I dunked him under the stream, it was like I'd switched on a light. He came to life and started squirming around in my arms, and then there was the first cry; one from him and then one from me. "He's alive, Mrs. Yother. I can't believe it."

"Wrap him up in towels and put him in the other sink. I need your help here. Mrs. Washington's in trouble." She was in a lot of trouble and Mrs. Yother was trying to do everything herself. My body went on automatic and I began dousing the area with alcohol and cutting off the stitches as fast as she could make them. At least we had plenty of light. Even if it was a matter of life and death, I couldn't help but enjoy what we were doing together that morning. It was fascinating, and I would be able to do what Mrs. Yother was doing someday. She was completely relaxed and during the whole operation she spoke to me like the teacher she was. An hour later, we were done and somehow Mrs. Washington was still alive.

"What this area needs, Miss St. Clair is a clinic where women, colored and white, can come to have their babies so they can be cared for properly for a few days. The hospital in Gadsden is a fine place if you're sick, but our women don't have a disease or injury and they shouldn't be treated as if they do. Like right now; what are we going to do with Mrs. Washington? If she wakes up, I can't just hand the baby to her and send her on her way. She'll simply have to stay here a few days and Ruby will have to take care of her."

With Mrs. Washington's problems, I'd completely forgotten about the baby. When I unwrapped him, he was still kicking and started crying again.

"Give him to Ruby. She can take care of him for the time being. She'll have one of her own soon enough. Right now, we have to get some liquids into our patient. It's fortunate she's here because I have glucose we can give her intravenously. It's much better than water alone and she doesn't have to be conscious." I watched as she hooked the bottle of glucose to a stand and ran the rubber tube down to Mrs. Washington's arm. The needle was huge, and I cringed a little when she inserted it into a vein at the elbow. "Tape her arms and legs to the table. I don't want her waking up and pulling this needle out. Now tell me, Miss St. Clair, why couldn't Ruby find you at home before sunup today? Our job isn't nine to five Monday through Friday. Someone positively has to know where you are at all times, either me, your family, or Ruby. You can't have a personal life anymore if it means our patients are put in jeopardy and…"

"I was at Hazel's, giving her my Christmas present. I'm so sorry, Mrs. Yother. It won't happen again."

"I've known you long enough to believe you and that's all that needs to be said. We won't have this conversation again Miss St. Clair."

She could have sent me home and told me not to come back, but she didn't. I wouldn't need another chance.

We took shifts watching Mrs. Washington that Christmas day and after my first shift, I went home for a few hours. Ruby and Mrs. Yother would have three hours each before I had to be back. I didn't want to leave, but I was assured our patient wouldn't wake up in the meantime.

Mama had made everyone wait to open presents until I could be there, so I was a welcomed sight and there was no mention about where I was before daylight that morning. I'd spent all my regular paycheck on their gifts and I think Mama liked hers best of all. Finding a spring dress in the middle of winter wasn't easy, but I managed to get a salesgirl at a small women's store called Marie's to find me something from last year's stock. Mama hadn't had a new Decoration Day dress in a long time, but she would have one the next spring. Daddy got a new pair of Sunday shoes and I got Bill a box of shotgun shells. Mama and Daddy got me a beautiful hat. I'd never had a proper lady's hat before and Mama said it was time I started looking like a grown woman at church. It wasn't a little hat like the older women wore. It was baby blue with a floppy wide brim, just like the ones I'd seen in the magazines at the beauty shop. I loved it. When I opened Bill's present, I knew he got help from Mama picking it out, but that was okay. The leather purse matched the hat perfectly.

***

Word got around in the community, even before Christmas, that the Platts were having a New Year's dance in their barn. They hadn't had one in several years and I guess, with the war and everything, they figured everybody needed something to take their minds off what came out of the radio every evening. Maybe they just thought it would be a long time before we would have anything to celebrate again. The Japs were after what few ships of ours they hadn't already sunk.

Mrs. Washington and her new baby left the Yothers' a couple of days after Christmas. Mrs. Yother drove them home and left Ruby with them to help out as long as she was needed. We didn't have any appointments between Christmas and New Year's, so I thought I might get some time off. That wasn't to be. Every day was spent at my desk with the books and if I didn't ask Mrs. Yother a question every half-hour, she would ask me one.

The dance was all I could think about and every afternoon after work and supper, I walked to Hazel's—after telling Mama where I was going and how long I would be gone—so we could plan what we would wear and talk about who we would and would not dance with. It was fun getting to be a girl again. The blue skirt she got in Gadsden would have been much too tight on her, but she left a button undone and the pink blouse that must have been her Mama's came down over her waist, so no one would notice. She said she wanted to wear pink and blue. I decided on the grey skirt and white blouse. The garter belts were adjustable, so I insisted she wear hose. She would have to start wearing maternity clothes soon after the first of the year whether she wanted to or not, but there was no reason she couldn't wear what she wanted for one more night.

Mama declared she wasn't going to the dance and Daddy declared she was. He won and she admitted the next day she was glad he'd gotten his way.

With their sorghum business, the Platts had the biggest barn in the county. Daddy said that Mr. Platts's father and his brothers built that barn and that everybody thought they were crazy building a barn around a sorghum mill. They were always built outside in the open. The Platts had most all the sorghum business in north Alabama as soon as word got around to the farmers how the Platts did business. Before, they would have to stand around in the sun or rain while their cane was pressed and cooked out if they wanted syrup made from their own cane. They could just drop it off and take syrup already made from someone else's cane, but that didn't sit too well with most farmers. Pride usually won out and the Platts's business grew. It was a well-known secret too that you could always trade a bushel of corn for syrup at the Platts. The corn got turned into hard liquor in the winter and that was the worst kept secret in the community. The barn was a magnificent building and by the time we got there, half the county was already dancing. There were two bands, one on each end of the barn. One played square dance music and the other played more of the music Hazel and I liked to listen to on the radio. Daddy dragged Mama toward the square dancers and it wasn't long before they were on the floor.

Hazel and her family showed up and her parents joined mine on the dance floor. I'd already found a table for us that wasn't taken and was waiting for her. She looked like a princess and when she saw me and smiled, it was easy to remember why I fell in love with her. The night before, we'd done each other's hair, but we never knew exactly how it would turn out. This was one of those times it turned out right for both of us. I was sort of hoping Glenda, Bill, and James would sit somewhere else; that didn't happen. They all sat down with us. When a song was played I recognized, I stood and asked Hazel to dance. There were lots of girls our age dancing together, so no one would have anything to say about that. The Brashers were already on the floor and I remembered some of the waltz steps they'd taught me back in the early summer. I made up the rest and led Hazel like I knew what I was doing.

When the band started the next song, I didn't have any idea how to dance to it. "All right, Miss St. Clair, now that you've had me waltz with you, you have to swing with me. Glenda's been teaching me."

It was fast, really fast and she had me spinning and turning in ways I'm sure gave everyone a good look at my garters and more. It was so much fun, but I made her slow things down on the next song and show me what she was doing. Two sort-of hopping steps to the left, while leaning left, then two to the right, then a step with one foot back were the basic steps. After the fourth straight swing, I was ready to sit down for a while. Hazel pointed toward the dance floor and I saw Glenda dancing with Mr. Brasher. The two of them knew swing and put everyone else to shame. I didn't know at the time where Bill and James had wandered off to, but I was pretty sure they weren't dancing. The next day, I found out from Mama what had happened. The two of them and some other boys got into Mr. Platts's hard liquor and were falling down drunk long before we were ready to go home. Mr. Leeth loaded them in the back of his truck, took them home and came back to the dance. When we were ready to leave, I was told Bill was riding with one of his friends. I knew there was liquor there; I could smell it on a couple of the boys I danced with. Mama said Bill spent most of the next day in bed or on the back porch puking. Daddy didn't say anything to him, figuring he'd learned an important lesson.

Mrs. Brasher came over and sat with us for a while and I could tell she was working her way up to saying something.

"I heard you're working with Mrs. Yother now. That must be interesting work."

"It's a new job every day and I love it."

Finally, she got around to saying what she had wanted to all along. "I think I may be pregnant and I was wondering if I could come by sometime."

"You surely can and if I remember right, we don't have any appointments until Wednesday of next week. How about Monday morning at ten?"

"That would be perfect. I haven't told John yet."

"Well don't tell him anything until you've missed your third period. See you Monday morning."

She went back out on the dance floor and rescued her husband from Glenda.

"She's pretty. Didn't you mean 'See you naked Monday'?"

"What's this? Do my ears hear a hint of jealousy, Mrs. Campbell?"

"Well, she is pretty and you will see her naked."

"And I'll tell you all about it."

"You will not."

"You're right, I won't, and do you know why? It's because I have the prettiest, sweetest girl in the state and I'm so much in love with her, I wouldn't dream of looking sideways at another woman."

"Liar, you have to look. It's your job."

"All right, I'll look, but I won't touch."

"Double liar."

To anyone who couldn't see our faces, it would have sounded like we were having a terrible argument, but the smiles we traded with every shot were those shared between lovers who know each other's thoughts. Then she turned a little serious. "I do sometimes wonder what you're thinking when a pretty girl comes in and she's all naked right there in front of you."

"I compare every one with you and none of them come close."

"That was the right answer. I love you Otha May. It's just that after the baby's born, I might never look the same again. If I ever had a girlish figure, it'll be gone."

Mrs. Edmondson stopping by to say hello was timed perfectly. "Two kids and she's pregnant now; do you think she's lost her figure? No, she's a beautiful woman."

"In clothes."

"You forget what I do for a living. She looks just as good without them."

"You're terrible Otha May St. Clair. I don't know why I put up with you."

Chapter Ten
Twins by Different Mothers

Hazel's appointment on February 20 showed that her cervix was partially dilated, and Mrs. Yother said that she would go into labor in a week's time. The baby had partially turned, and I told Hazel it should finish turning in the next day or two. That news brought everything home and when I walked her to the front door, she began crying.

"I'm going to walk Mrs. Campbell home, Ruby. I'll be back in an hour or so."

"I'm so scared, Otha May. What if something goes wrong?"

"Nothing's going to go wrong. Yours is the very picture of what a pregnancy should be. The baby's strong and active. You're young and healthy. Besides, you've got your own personal midwife trainee watching over you."

"But I hear stories…"

"And I bet all of them are just that. I don't talk about any of the births I've helped with, but I will tell you that there's nothing tougher than babies and mothers. We haven't lost one of either since I've been working with Mrs. Yother and some births have amazed even her. I believe the will to survive comes at the moment of conception, when the egg is fertilized, and it only gets stronger as the baby grows. I shouldn't tell you this but, you know Inez Platt? Mrs. Yother told me she delivered her in a ditch during a cyclone. Their house was almost completely destroyed. Mr. Platt had gone for Mrs. Yother just as the storm was coming up and when he got back with her, they couldn't find Mrs. Platt anywhere and they were afraid the twister had taken her. She'd made her way down to the road and got in the ditch just in time. Mrs. Yother found her lying there with her knees in the air and delivered Inez on the spot."

"Maybe that's why she's the way she is now."

"You don't have anything to worry about Hazel. I'm not going to let anything happen to you or little Abby or Nate."

"You know we've gone over a hundred middle names and I've decided not to decide. It'll be up to you."

"And I'll know his or her middle name as soon as I get a look. It'll come to me. You send James or Glenda to get me if you need me anytime."

"We've already got that figured out. If the baby comes at night, James is going to Mrs. Yother's to tell her and Glenda's coming to your house to get you. If it comes during the day and you're at work, Glenda or Mama will come to the Yothers' to tell you."

We stood on her front porch and I put my arms around her—almost all the way around her and gave her a kiss that would have to do until I could do better.

"Can you come by later? The junior high basketball tournament final game is tonight at High Point and everyone but Mama will be going. We'll have some time together after she goes to bed."

"Yeah, everyone at my house is going too. I'll tell Ruby and Mrs. Yother where I'll be in case something comes up, but the only babies we're expecting are yours and Janice Redmon's. She was in yesterday. Looks like it's a race to see who'll deliver first."

I'd done Hazel's exam that day and Janice's the day before, after Mrs. Yother examined them, and I saw no problems with either. Hazel's baby had begun to turn, but Janice's hadn't, so I guessed Hazel would deliver first, but only by a few days or a week at the most. I kept trying to convince myself Hazel's would be like any other delivery, but this was Hazel and my convincing didn't work very well. I wanted to examine her every day and having some time alone with her would give me the chance, but I didn't want her to think I was examining something every time I touched her.

Everybody had already left for the game by the time I got home, and my supper was in the oven. I've always hated eating alone, so I made myself a plate, wrapped it in a dishcloth and took it with me to Hazel's. Before I left, I grabbed a can of peaches and a couple of big slices of the plain cake Mama made that day. Hazel hadn't eaten any supper, so I talked her into some of mine. Food is always better when someone else cooks it and the cake with peaches was eaten first.

"That's the first bite she's eaten all day," Mrs. Leeth said as she gave me a kiss on the forehead. "Tell your mama, I'm in her debt again."

We listened to the news for half an hour sitting on her bed together. The couch had been moved out to make room. It was mostly bad; London being bombed almost every night and the Japs attacking Australia. I didn't even know they were in the war, but they were, and on our side. Hitler's army being stuck trying to take Moscow was the only thing I heard that was close to good news. After the broadcast, Mrs. Leeth went to bed and Hazel switched batteries in the radio. "Your Christmas present, and I can't tell you how many times I've thanked you for it. With your studies taking up so much of your time, it's all I have to keep me company."

"Let's see if I can make up for how bad you've been treated." I helped her sit on the bed, which was too high off the floor, I thought, and snuggled up next to her as a slow love song started playing on the radio. My hand went up her dress with my first kiss.

"Are you sure that's okay? I mean…"

"I'm sure that if you go into labor, you won't have far to go to find a midwife trainee. We'll take it easy. I've missed touching you so much. It's been weeks."

"You touched me this morning."

"Not like this."

"Easy. That thing's even touchier than usual."

I reached my hand around her and undid her bra. "I'd wanted a bra since I started sprouting and now I hate them, but it's worse if I don't wear one. My breasts feel like a yoke around my neck. Her dress was already above her waist, so I stood up and pulled it off over her head. The bra went next and I draped both over the headboard. Her breasts were full and soft and squeezing them was like squeezing a feather pillow. Her areolas were triple their normal size and her nipples stood out like sore thumbs. She lay down and pulled me to her breasts. I knew how babies sucked and within a few minutes I had a mouthful of milk and shared it with her in a kiss.

"That's my milk isn't it? I've had a few drops in my bra, but you must have the touch."

When she rolled over onto her back, she reached for the bottom of my dress and pulled it off over my head. I couldn't have pretended I was doing some sort of follow-up examination then if her mama had decided to check on her. She pulled the cover over us, slipped her hand downward and brought my ear to her face like she had a secret to whisper to me.

"Do you think it would be okay if we…"

"If we what?"

"You know… make love… all the way. I've been feeling really…"

"Horny?"

"Yes, smart ass, horny, and you know I hate that word. Now do I have to beg?"

"Well, in my professional opinion, I think it would be perfectly okay as long as we take it easy." I wasn't sure about that. Mrs. Yother would tell women to keep their knees together the last six weeks, but I wouldn't be sticking anything inside her and that was different. There was nothing in those books about intercourse of any kind in the last weeks; I'd already looked. Not the kind of thing men would write about anyway. By the time our panties were off, I wasn't worried anymore.

Without putting any weight on her belly, I leaned over so our bodies could touch in as many places as possible, and there weren't many. It was the best feeling in the world being that close to her again and a familiar tingle started up. It was a long slow reach around her belly until I felt another hand guiding mine.

"We have to go slow and I don't want you pushing down."

Things developed slowly and without straining anything too much. I could tell she was drawing out every bit of pleasure she could. She stretched her normal ten seconds of pleasure into thirty and we both felt every little muscle contraction when it came. When they finally stopped, she pulled me back to her lips and gave me a kiss that lasted even longer. "That was amazing. It was like I was floating in air, and they just kept coming one right after another. Thank you for helping a horny girlfriend and for knowing exactly what to do." I hadn't, but I wouldn't forget that lesson. We curled up together and it was tempting to join her when she drifted off to sleep. She didn't notice when I got up, got dressed and tiptoed out the door. There was no one awake at home when I got there, so I had a nice quiet bath and went to bed. I didn't go to sleep though, not before trying to do for myself what I'd done for Hazel. It didn't work. I got frustrated and got the job over and done with.

A week later and there was still no baby from Hazel or Janice, but Hazel's had turned completely and was pointed in the right direction. Janice's decided to stay put for a while longer. I spent all day that Sunday with Hazel. She was miserable sitting or lying down, so I talked her into a walk. We made it to the rock where our house would someday sit.

"We are going to have a house here someday aren't we Otha May? And we'll have a garden where I can grow squash and hot pepper and sweet corn?"

"And you'll have supper waiting for me when I get home and when I come in, you'll kiss me like it was ages since I left that morning?"

"I promise I'll be the best lover in the county."

"And the best mother."

"What are we going to do when little Nate asks about his father? What are we going to say when the other kids at school tease him about his mother living with another woman? How're we ever gonna handle all the problems we'll cause him?"

"I've already thought about all that," I answered as I pulled her up off the rock. "We're sending him off to boarding school up north as soon as he's old enough, and who says it's going to be Nate? Maybe it'll be Abby and maybe she'll be smarter than both of us and won't let anything like that bother her."

"So if it's a boy, we ship him off to boarding school as soon as he's weaned and if it's a girl, we keep her? Is that right?"

"That's about the way I have it figured."

"Otha May St. Clair, you're the world's worst daddy-to-be."

***

Tuesday morning things started off with me almost getting run down by Darryl Redmon at Mrs. Yother's driveway. Janice was in labor and he was sure her water had broken right before he left. I jumped in the truck with him and rode up to the house, grabbed Mrs. Yother's bag and loaded it into the back seat of her car. Ruby wrapped up some leftover sausage and biscuits and handed them to me on the way out. Darryl took off with Mrs. Yother and me following on his tail. As Mrs. Yother and I rounded the sharp curve at mine and Hazel's bridge, Darryl slammed on his brakes and we almost rammed him. I couldn't see, but Glenda was standing there in the middle of the road waving her arms. She ran to our car and swung open the back door.

"You gotta come quick," she screamed as she got in. "Hazel sent me. She's hurting bad and says the baby's coming."

It was my Hazel, but I wasn't me in that car anymore. "When did the contractions start?" I asked in a dead calm.

"About two hours ago. She thought it was the kraut we had for supper last night. Daddy said it didn't taste right, but Mama said kraut didn't go bad, that she just hadn't put enough sugar in it when she made it last fall. I thought it tasted bad too, but we all ate it and it didn't bother the rest of us. She was feeling so bad this morning I told Mama I wasn't going to school."

"Has she thrown up?"

"No, she says she doesn't feel sick, but every few minutes, she has pains down there. Are they labor pains? Mama thought so right away, but Hazel said they weren't—until about half an hour ago when one really bad pain came. She sent me to get you right after that. Will she be all right?"

"She'll be fine Glenda and you did right coming to get me. It'll be a long while before the baby comes. It sounds like she's in the first stages of labor."

When we got to the Leeth's, we stopped. Darryl kept going; then I saw his brake lights. Mrs. Yother got out with her bag. "Miss St. Clair, I'm going on with Mr. Redmon. You'll have to handle things here." She raised the trunk lid and handed me a bag that looked just like hers.

She must have read the look on my face. "I'm always prepared, Miss St. Clair. Now go and see about your patient. Send Glenda back to my house for Ruby. If you don't think you'll need her, send her on to the Redmon's. I might need her small hands by the time she can get there walking." Cool as ice and in control of every situation; I would be like her someday.

I did as Mrs. Yother had asked and sent Glenda back for Ruby. I don't know who was in worse shape at the Leeth house, Hazel or her mother, but when I started talking, everything stopped, even the labor pains; maybe they listened too. Hazel wasn't my girlfriend anymore, she was my patient and she needed me. I should have noticed two nights before that the bed wasn't going to work as it was. A feather mattress might be great to sleep on, but it was too mushy for what we needed. "Bring some quilts and make a pallet for her in the floor, Mrs. Leeth; we wouldn't ever be able to find the baby in this soft bed, and put a kettle on to boil."

While she was gone, I did a quick examination of Hazel's belly. The baby was in the right position and I noticed something else. "Feel this Hazel." I took her hand and ran it across the little bump she could barely reach.

"What is it?"

"That's a nose. Your baby's going to be born face up, just like I was. Mrs. Yother says that babies that are born face up are curious—not that kind of curious—that they want a look at the world first thing. She just says that. Babies can't see very well for a week, but it's a good story." A contraction started just as she started to laugh. I held her hands and counted forty-five seconds, then looked at the clock on the mantle so I'd know how much time passed before the next one,

"Do you know what I want for my next birthday or Christmas present—a watch. I need a watch and I don't want a fancy little one to wear to church. I want a man's watch with a big dial and a second hand. Mrs. Yother has one. She bought it for Mr. Yother years ago, but she wears it. They're a funny couple."

"But can you imagine any man other than Mr. Yother who would be better suited for her?"

"That's putting it politely. I can't imagine any other man or woman who could begin to live with her."

Mrs. Leeth got the pallet made with three quilts. It still wouldn't be very comfortable, though it would serve our purpose just fine. It took the two of us to lower Hazel onto it, and as soon as we got her on the pallet, her water broke. Hazel screamed, but no one else did. She knew to expect this, but it caught her by surprise all the same. Mrs. Leeth found three more quilts and remade the pallet. Pillows under her head and bottom put things where I wanted them. I opened Mrs. Yother's spare bag she'd handed me to find an exact duplicate of hers. I knew where everything was without having to look again. Ruby and Glenda showed up and I sent Ruby on to the Redmon's. Things were going well at the Leeth's.

"Don't push, Hazel. I know you know that already, but I have to tell you or Mrs. Yother would have my head on a stick in her front yard. Let the contractions work themselves out. Things have to stretch—and I know you know that too."

It was starting to get dark before the labor pains came in earnest and I was glad Mrs. Yother's bag also had a flashlight in it; right where it was supposed to be. The coal oil lamps in the house would never have put enough light where I needed it. I took out the bottle of alcohol, poured some on a cloth and wiped the flashlight. We couldn't boil it and someone had to hold it for me. Mrs. Yother always did that, and I wondered why until I thought about it. The person holding the flashlight might be needed for something more than holding a flashlight and they would already have clean hands if they were helping. Every procedure had a purpose.

"Glenda, are you ready to help? You can if you want to. If you do, it's time for the two of us to scrub up to our elbows. I have some special soap and your mother has some water boiling. Take the water off the stove and rinse out a clean dishpan with some of it, then pour the rest of the water in and as soon as it cools enough we'll wash up. Fill the kettle again and put it back on to boil. We'll need that later. Mrs. Leeth, when your husband and James get home, tell them to go to my house for a while. I'll send Glenda to get them after it's all over. This is women's work."

"Do you want to help, Glenda? You don't have to if you don't want to. Miss St. Clair and I can do it." Mrs. Leeth called me Miss St. Clair for the first time ever. That day I wasn't the daughter of her best friend or her daughter's best friend. I was her daughter's midwife, or midwife trainee anyway.

"I want to help, Mama and I won't faint; I promise." Mrs. Leeth looked pretty relieved with Glenda's answer and I think Hazel was too.

We scrubbed up and I noticed her small hands. "Now, sit on the floor right behind me and hold the flashlight where I can see what I'm doing." After rearranging the pillows under Hazel's bottom, I pulled her dress up to her breasts. I couldn't see Glenda's eyes, but I'm sure they were big as saucers. Everything looked perfectly normal to me, but probably not to her. I held Hazel's labia major and minor back and watched as the next contraction came and went. When I inserted my fingers into her vagina, Glenda held the flashlight close. I didn't need the light for what I was doing, but she wanted to see. Hazel was dilated about two and a half inches and her cervix was thinning like it was supposed to. By eight o'clock, contractions were coming about every five minutes and they lasted a little over a minute. At the last check, she had dilated a good four inches and it was time to push. I held the flashlight and let Glenda have a look. Hazel's cervix had thinned enough you could see through it and clearly make out the shape of the baby's head.

"All right Hazel, it's time to push. When you feel the next contraction, take a deep breath and push down with those muscles you've been saving. You can do it."

I took the tube of K-Y that was right where it was supposed to be and squirted some on my fingers, then inserted them into her vagina and smeared it all around. "This slicky stuff will make things a little easier," I explained to Glenda. I hadn't said anything about Hazel's clit, which looked like it was fit to bust. And then came the question I was expecting.

"What's that?"

"It's her clitoris. Every woman has one and sometimes they swell up like that. It'll go down after the baby's born." She didn't ask any more questions and I didn't give any details. At that moment, I was glad Mrs. Leeth had found reasons to stay in the kitchen, keeping a kettle boiling or something.

After another hour, I got worried. The baby had stopped moving and the contractions had slacked off to nearly nothing. She was fully effaced, and the head was crowning, but nothing was happening.

"All right, Hazel, you've got to push this baby out now whether you feel a contraction or not."

"I can't. I don't have any more muscles." Then I thought of something Mrs. Yother had said.

"Yes you do and you're about to use all of them." With more K-Y on my fingers, I began massaging her clit with both thumbs. "This time, we're not going to take it easy. This is going to be an orgasm like you'll never have again and you're going to push that baby right out." In a minute, I had her begging me to stop, but she didn't sound in pain and I needed her contractions to start up again. I was glad I couldn't see Glenda's face and did my best to forget she was sitting right behind me. "Feel it building up inside you? Think about being in bed with me and all the things we did in our hotel room. You were such a good lover and I wanted to be the first…"

"Glenda."

"She's not here. It's just the two of us making love in our own bed in our own house. You're going to explode like you never have before, but you have to push it out this time. It's what you need and it's what I need, and then you'll take me to that same place. I'll wrap my legs around yours and I won't let go until…"

The moan that came from her shook the windows and I saw her vaginal muscles begin to spasm in huge contractions. I didn't let up with my thumbs and the spasms continued until she screamed and tried to lean forward. The baby's head pushed out of her vagina and I took hold of it and gently pulled until I saw a shoulder. Another series of spasms, another scream, and the baby was in my arms.

"You did it Hazel. The baby's out. It's a girl."

She tried to say something I thought sounded like, "Never again."

The baby girl started squirming and I watched as her mouth opened and she drew a long breath, like she was glad it was over too, and she let it out as a cry that could've been heard at my house.

"Hazel, I think this baby went to sleep halfway through being born and we had to wake her up."

"You woke us both up. I love you Otha May and I'll love you the rest of my life. You're everything in this world to me."

I gently laid the baby on the floor between Hazel's legs and reached for the special scissors and catgut. She kept up the crying while I tied off the cord and cut it. Mrs. Leeth was standing at the kitchen door and I could see tears rolling down her face. "You have a granddaughter, Mrs.

Leeth, and you have a niece, Glenda." At this point I didn't think Hazel would mind that I'd lied to her about Glenda being there before. It didn't matter to anyone then.

"Is she beautiful? Can I see her?" Hazel said in almost a whisper.

"Help me get her dress off over her head, Glenda, and let's rearrange her pillows. A mother should meet her baby naked for the first time." The baby stretched out on her stomach and stopped crying. When I saw Hazel's stomach ripple, I knew the afterbirth was being pushed out. I took care of that while everyone got to meet the new addition to the family. I felt for the bag I knew would be right where it was supposed to be, placed the afterbirth in it and told Mrs. Leeth that Mr. Leeth was to bury it the next morning. Hazel's vulva looked like a watermelon had gone through it, but there was no tearing and very little bleeding. Mrs. Leeth handed me a warm wet towel and I did my best to clean her up, then took a sanitary pad out of Mrs. Yother's bag and taped it on.

After cleaning the baby up with some more wet towels, I did a quick examination; ten fingers, ten toes, two eyes, and one nose. Her eyes were open, and she seemed to be trying to focus on what was going on around her and looking as if she were thinking, "Who are all you people"?

It took some more rearranging of pillows before Hazel was comfortable on that hard floor, but I didn't want to move her just yet. She said her pains were bearable, so I didn't give her a shot of morphine.

"Do you think my baby's hungry?"

She was, and when I helped her find a nipple, she latched on and began to suck. The expression on Hazel's face was something no artist or photographer would ever be able to capture.

"You've had a good look at her Otha May. What's Abigail's middle name?"

I had nothing, even though I'd promised to give her a middle name as soon as I saw her; my mind had been on other things. After lots of suggestions from Glenda, Mrs. Leeth spoke up. "If no one would object to it, I would like her middle name to be St. Clair. We owe a lot to Otha May."

"I don't know, Mrs. Leeth. How does it sound when you holler it?"

"Abigail St. Clair Leeth, you come here this very minute."

We all agreed it sounded pretty good, but I told Hazel she had the final say.

"It's a high class sounding name if I ever heard one and I'll be proud to call her that."

I noticed Mrs. Leeth had called the baby by the last name Leeth, not Campbell and that would be the way the birth certificate would read. There was no point in anyone pretending anymore.

I stayed the rest of the night with the Leeths, sleeping in Hazel's bed with her and Abby. Glenda helped me change the bed when Hazel peed the first time and the second. That was fine; I didn't want her up for a while and a bedpan wasn't something that would fit in Mrs. Yother's bag. Mr. Leeth and James weren't sent for until the next morning. Mrs. Yother and Ruby showed up about noon and Mrs. Leeth fixed breakfast for everybody. Janice's delivery had gone well, and she now had a new baby boy. They named him Frances and we all had a laugh about that. After breakfast, Mrs. Yother examined Abby and declared her to be the healthiest baby she'd ever seen. She told all the mothers that.

"We have other work to do, Miss St. Clair and it's time we got to it." I thought surely I would be given the day off. "Mrs. Campbell has plenty of help around here and they'll send for us if we're needed. Come along now."

It wasn't a very romantic goodbye kiss I gave Hazel, but it would have to do. My sergeant had other plans for me; paperwork had to be done and instruments had to be cleaned.

When we got back to the Yother's, Ruby and I unloaded the car and brought everything into the house. Mrs. Yother took the bags and asked me to help her clean the instruments. As I was cleaning out the bag I'd used, there was something I hadn't noticed before: a brass plate under the handle with the engraved initials O.M.S.

"It was supposed to be your present after you pass the midwife examination, but you needed it yesterday. After seeing that healthy baby at the Leeths', I want you to have it now." She was a little uncomfortable when I hugged her. Mrs. Yother wasn't the hugging kind, but she tolerated it. "You're to know where that bag is every minute for the rest of your life, Miss St. Clair and you're to check every day to make sure everything's in there and in its place."

"Yes, Mrs. Yother."

When she sat down to fill out the birth certificates, she smiled a little when I told her Abby's full name, and she had nothing to say when I said the last name Leeth. "I have to sign this as a licensed midwife, but I've left space under my name for you to sign as well. The law requires it." I knew that wasn't true and she knew it too, but I was proud to sign anyway. In the space for the father's name, she had written "unknown." The mother's name was given as Hazel Ruth Leeth. Mr. Campbell officially ceased to exist that day and he didn't have to be killed off in any war.

Chapter Eleven
Making the Grade

That spring should have been the happiest time in our lives for Hazel and me, but Mrs. Yother's sights were set on the midwife examination. Every spare minute was spent with Stockham, Playfair, Jardine, Williams, Grandin, and Jarman. They were the authors of the books I had to study. Some had been written more than fifty years earlier, but Mrs. Yother said they were the books the doctors who would be testing me learned from. The books on midwifery I could understand well enough, but there were books on surgery and physiology too. The examination would be in three parts; written, oral, and practical. If I passed two of the three, I would be allowed to retake the third at a later time, but that's not at all what I wanted. I never wanted to go through what it took to prepare again.

In early April, Mr. and Mrs. Yother took a three day trip to Nashville and left me in charge. We weren't expecting any deliveries and the examinations scheduled were to be routine checkups. The Yothers never went on vacations and three days seemed to be too short for one anyway. My curiosity got to me and I asked why they were going.

"Mr. Yother and I have appointments with our doctors. It's good to get a physical now and then and those county doctors in Gadsden aren't good for anything unless you're bleeding or have a broken bone. I want you to stay here while we're gone. If there's an emergency, this is where they'll come. Ruby can cook for the two of you while you study. I'm almost finished with the practice examination I've been writing and you can take it when I get back. I don't object to Miss Leeth coming for a short visit, but I want you here at all times—and watch Ruby. She's due in six or eight weeks and you know babies come when they want, not when we want them to."

I had my orders and Ruby wouldn't lie for me if Mrs. Yother asked her any questions later on, though a nice dinner one night wouldn't be out of line. After they left, I sat down and wrote Hazel a note. I got a little carried away with myself and spent way too much time on it, but it was better than studying.

Dear Miss Leeth,

I would be honored if you would grant me the privilege of having supper with you Tuesday evening at the home of Mr. and Mrs. Edwin Yother. It would make my imprisonment bearable if I might see you once again. Please reply as soon as possible through the messenger delivering this note. Supper will be served at seven o'clock. I am looking forward to your response and the pleasure of your company.

Yours always,
Miss Otha May St. Clair, Midwife Trainee

I put the note in an envelope, addressed it to Hazel and sealed it. "Ruby, I have a note here for Hazel. Would you deliver it to her for me? I want to invite her to supper tomorrow night and I want us to do it up right. I'll walk to my house so I can get my best clothes. Mrs. Yother has some candles and we'll fix something special to eat."

"You love her a lot don't you, Otha May?"

"More than anything in this world, Ruby."

"Don't you worry about a thing. I know what I want to cook and I'll be your servant for the evening and everything. This is gonna be fun."

I ran home and told Mama what was going on and that I would be staying at the Yothers' for a few days. She didn't ask any questions when I left with a clean uniform, my best suit of clothes and anything else I could think of to wear for Tuesday night.

I got a little worried about Ruby; she was gone a lot longer than it took to walk to the Leeths' and back. When she finally arrived, she had an envelope addressed to me.

Dear Miss St. Clair,

As it happens, I am free this Tuesday and would be happy to have supper with you. I have missed our times together and look forward to hearing about your most recent adventures. I shall arrive at seven dressed appropriately for the occasion. Until then, I am

Yours always,
Miss Hazel Ruth Leeth, Mother

"I hope she said yes. It took her nearly an hour to write that note. She said it had to be just right."

"She said yes and it is perfect. All right Ruby, you have a free hand. I have to get back to studying. Mrs. Yother's giving me a test when she gets back. Let me know if you need help."

"You just leave everything to me. I hope someday a man—or anybody—courts me the way you do Miss Hazel."

We'd just finished lighting the candles when Hazel knocked. She looked like a million dollars and the kiss I got told me how much she'd missed me. She was able to get into one of the larger skirts we'd bought before Christmas:

the blue one, and it looked good with the white blouse. I noticed the lipstick and hose too. She'd gone all out for me and it looked like she'd spent the day on her hair. Neither of us had any nice spring clothes, but I promised myself we'd both have plenty someday. I hadn't gone to nearly as much trouble prettying up, although I had chosen the nicest clothes in my closet and put on some red lipstick. My hair didn't turn out right though, even with Ruby's help. I was too nervous, and she didn't know what she was doing. None of that mattered; we were together in the same house and Ruby promised me she would find a reason to disappear at the right time.

She hadn't asked for my help making supper, so when we sat down to a table set for two, I had no idea what we would be served. I shouldn't have worried. Ruby could cook and Mr. Yother wouldn't miss that chicken—maybe a stray dog got it. Mrs. Yother told us we could have anything to eat we could find and Ruby found a lot. Baked sweet potatoes, green beans, and a peach cobbler went perfectly with the fried chicken she made better than my own Mama. It was a meal fit to be served in any sit-down restaurant.

"I don't know nothing about wine, but this says it's from France," Ruby announced as she placed the two long stemmed glasses at our plates. "Well, I heard Mrs. Yother when she said we could have anything to eat we could find and they've got a dozen more bottles. They won't miss just one." It took all of us looking before we found the corkscrew; mostly because no one knew what we were looking for exactly. None of us had ever tasted wine before, but we agreed it was delicious. Ruby filled our glasses and then disappeared with hers.

It was a wonderful evening. We talked about little Abigail St. Clair and about the test I was studying for and about our future. We also drank the rest of the bottle of wine. Neither of us had ever had much to drink, so it was pretty funny when we started to not make any sense. On Mrs. Yother's huge couch, we held each other and promised we would have our own someday and that we would make love on it until the sun came up. When the big clock in the hallway struck ten, I told her I wanted to walk her home. Her house was quiet and we had a final kiss on her front porch.

"Promise me that we'll always find time to do things like this, Otha May. I need to know you still think I'm pretty and that you like seeing me dressed up, even if we don't go out anywhere."

"We'll go out because I want everyone to see what a beautiful woman I've found. I want them all to be jealous, the men and the women, when you take my hand and walk with me. You're all I ever hoped for when I was growing up. I love you Hazel."

That was to be the last evening we had alone together for a long time. When Mrs. Yother got back, she was like a woman possessed. I did all right on her test, but not perfect and she wanted perfect. Every Tuesday and Friday there was another test and she became especially critical of my answers, watching me like a hawk while I wrote, making sure everything was by the book.

Ruby's delivery on May 28 was a nice break from the drilling I got every day. Her water broke while the two of us were doing dishes the evening before. I was expecting her to have a hard time of it because she was so small. Luckily, the baby was small too, but healthy, and she did name him Roosevelt. When none of us could think of a middle name that went with it, she decided on Franklin, so it was Roosevelt Franklin Camp and that's the way the birth certificate was filled out. Mrs. Yother and I took her and the baby in the car out to see Mrs. Camp and while we were in the area, we checked on Mrs. Washington and her baby boy. Mrs. Yother had a copy of the boy's birth certificate in her purse and handed it to her. I remembered very well when we filled that one out.

"You watch, Mrs. Yother. This boy's gonna make something of himself someday."

"With a name like Abraham Lincoln Washington, it wouldn't surprise me one bit, Mrs. Washington, not one bit."

"Someday, Miss St. Clair, when you're my age," Mrs. Yother said with a grin on the way home, "you'll tell stories about helping deliver a Roosevelt Franklin and an Abraham Lincoln."

***

The test was to be given on Friday, June 19 and Mrs. Yother mailed in her letter of recommendation on May 15 just before she and Mr. Yother left to go to Elton's graduation up in Knoxville. She was so proud of him, but scared to death he'd be drafted soon because of his college education. I got a letter in the mail on June 2 saying I was expected to be at the nursing building of Vanderbilt University at nine o'clock sharp the day of the examination. The letter went on to say that my letter of recommendation from Mrs. Yother and the fifty dollar examination fee had been received. I didn't know it cost to take the test and when I brought it up to Mrs. Yother; she told me I would have to pay her back if I failed. "But you're not going to fail, Miss St. Clair, so consider it a graduation present."

I slept at the Yothers' more than at my house those last two weeks and the last week Mrs. Yother cancelled all our regular appointments. If we'd had another two weeks to prepare, I think it would have killed us both. Mrs. Yother was as worn out as I was and it seemed she'd aged five years in five months. She looked tired every day, though she never let up on me.

We left for Nashville on Thursday morning with sandwiches packed for us by Ruby. Mrs. Yother didn't want us eating at some highway restaurant. We'd be home Saturday by dinner at the latest. There were no deliveries expected during that time and Ruby would have to handle any emergencies as best she could. She'd seen and done enough to be able to handle a simple delivery and Mr. Yother had learned a lot in his years of being married to Mrs. Yother. If they couldn't handle things, he could always drive the mother to Gadsden. On the way, I was constantly questioned, and twice we had to stop to look up something in one of the books Mrs. Yother brought along. I was as ready as I ever would be by the time I saw the Nashville city limit sign. If I hadn't been so nervous, I would've paid more attention to the buildings she pointed out as we drove past them at the university. She knew all their names and remembered the classes she'd taken in each one.

"This university is known for its medical school, Miss St. Clair—the finest in the south. There are doctors and nurses serving all over the world with diplomas from here."

There were well dressed young men and women walking everywhere and I already felt out of place in my plain uniform. Mrs. Yother insisted I wear it; that she wanted me looking like I'd just come from work. She was dressed in her finest and would be mistaken for a professor by anyone. That was the plan as well, she said. We were to look the part of professor and student so the doctors would treat us that way.

That night in our hotel room, I got my final instructions. "I know the old doctors who will have made out the written tests for you and they're the same ones who will be conducting the oral. I know what they think is important, but the doctors overseeing the practical may be new. However, they learned from the same doctors I did, so you shouldn't get many questions you haven't heard from me already. As far as the actual practical goes; follow your procedures. You'll probably be examining a nursing student and if you get one who thinks she's an actress, you might get some crazy questions. Talk to her as if she were one of our patients. Don't use any fancy medical words. Explain things like you were talking to a woman your age who had never gone beyond sixth grade and you'll be fine. In that part of the test, the doctors will be watching what you're doing, but they'll also be listening to what you say. Pretend you're back in our examination room and forget the doctors are there. They won't talk among themselves and they won't talk to you, and for goodness sake, don't talk to them either. Talk to your patient and talk to yourself. Ask the patient's name first and address her as Mrs. You have to work without an assistant, so you'll be writing yourself notes during the entire examination. Don't write as if you're writing for the doctors. You're making notes for yourself. The doctors may ask you to explain what you wrote afterward, but don't let that bother you. No one can read a doctor's handwriting either. The written test is from nine to eleven-thirty and then you'll have a lunch break. The oral part goes from one to three and the practical starts immediately afterward. There's no time limit for it. Sometimes they're over in half an hour and sometimes they run two hours if the doctors want to see you do more than one examination. That happens, so don't be concerned about it; it doesn't mean you did something wrong in the first one. They might just want to see how you would handle a different patient and by now you know they're all different."

The huge grey building looked more like a prison than a building where nurses were taught. We arrived at eight-thirty and there were already a few girls standing around in front of the room marked "Midwife Examination."

"The bathroom is just around that corner to your right. I suggest you visit it now—empty bladders and full heads are what we need this morning, Miss St. Clair."

I sat on the toilet and couldn't pee for the longest. Finally it started and my bladder must have been full because I felt so much better afterward. I was ready.

When the door opened, Mrs. Yother pulled me aside. "Otha May, you are ready for this, but some of the girls aren't; some will walk out, and some may run out crying. Don't you let them get to you. You've been trained by a woman who was trained by the best. Show these city slickers what you're made of. I should be back by the time this part of the test is over. I'm going back to see my doctor. He ran some tests when I was here last and I want to see the results for myself." She then hugged me and kissed my cheek. "Take your time. The test is designed so that most will finish early, but if you need the full two and a half hours, take it. I'm proud of you Otha May. You stuck with it as I knew you would."

The room looked like it would hold three hundred people, but there were only seven of us and we spread out everywhere. The heavy-set bald man with the white doctor's coat would be Doctor Jamison, I guessed. Mrs. Yother had described him to a T.

"Good morning ladies. I'm Doctor Jamison and I'll be proctoring your examination this morning. You have two and a half hours and we will collect your papers promptly at eleven-thirty. Make sure your name is written clearly at the top of every page. The first part of the test has fifty short answer questions and the second part consists of essay questions. You may do the test in any order. In precisely two minutes, Miss Brooks and Miss Caldwell will pass out the tests. If you need additional paper, ask one of them for it. Also, if you need to visit the ladies' room, ask one of them to escort you. If you have a question, raise your hand and I will come to you. Are there any questions before we begin?"

When it was straight up nine o'clock, Miss Brooks handed me the exam and I barely remember any details of the next two and a half hours. My brain sort of went on automatic. The questions were all familiar, but some were worded like the doctors who made out the test were trying to confuse us. At the top of every page of the exam was stated "Misspelled words will be penalized one point each." Mrs. Yother gave me spelling tests all day long, every day, so that warning didn't scare me. If they were spelled right in the book, I spelled them right on the test. I finished the short answer questions and looked at the clock. Ten past ten. Question one of the essay part was: Describe a prolapsed cervix in detail and its treatment during delivery. I decided part of that was a trick. You never do anything for a prolapsed cervix during delivery, after delivery maybe, if it didn't take care of itself. All of the questions were like that and I got the idea those who wrote the test were testing us on more than procedure. They were trying to figure out if we had our priorities in order. I finished the last question at exactly eleven o'clock and spent the rest of the time going over my answers and making changes. When time was called, I looked up to see there were only five of us left. I hadn't noticed two of the girls walk out. Maybe they finished early. I started breathing again when I saw Mrs. Yother at the door waiting for me. She didn't smile until she saw me smile and it was almost a laugh by the time I got to her.

I couldn't eat much lunch at the cafeteria and Mrs. Yother was busy giving me all the instructions again for the practical, but I was more worried about the oral coming up. "There's not much I can tell you about the oral. The doctors can ask you any question they want and if you don't know, say so. You're not expected to know everything. Students get into trouble when they start talking too much and if you say something totally wrong, they'll jump on that and give you enough rope to hang yourself. Don't fall for that. There will be three or four doctors conducting each oral and they'll all be men. Talk to them as if they were women. It's luck as to which doctors you'll get since there will be exams for the other girls going on at the same time. If you get Doctor Brainerd, watch out for him. He'll look the least like a doctor of all of them. He's from out west somewhere and looks like a cowboy; even wears a cowboy hat to lectures sometime. He'll ask you questions that don't make sense and he expects you to correct him before trying to answer. The name for a condition will be wrong or he'll point to something on a chart and call it something else. He's a clever old codger. If he's in your examination, the others will let him lead the questions and he'll interrupt theirs. If he ever smiles, it means you got something wrong—fix it before he goes to the next question. Or sometimes he smiles when you catch one of his trick questions. Watch his face."

My oral was in one of the medical laboratories. There were charts hanging on the walls and some of them I didn't recognize at all. That's when I got scared. The doctors came in and sat on the stools where students would normally sit. The one I was certain was Doctor Brainerd took off his cowboy hat and placed it on the table in front of him.

"I'm Doctor Brainerd, this is Doctor Chelsea, and this is Doctor Morse. You are?"

"Otha May St. Clair, Sir."

"I see by your paperwork that you've been trained by Lois Yother, one of our graduates. Is that correct?"

"Yes Sir."

"Then I'm certain she has taught you everything there is to know about the muscles in the vagina. Can you point out on the chart behind you the bulbococcygeus muscle and tell us about its role in childbirth?"

I looked on the chart and it wasn't there, but I knew where it should have been. "The *pubo*coccygeus isn't shown on the chart, but it's…"

"Thank you, Miss St. Clair." He tried to hide the smile, but I saw it. He intentionally got the name wrong.

There were only a couple of questions I didn't answer. I thought I knew the answers, but I decided to take Mrs. Yother's advice and say I didn't. The doctors then proceeded to tell me the answers, and I would have had them about right. The time passed quickly and toward the end, it was like I was having a conversation with them about the deliveries I'd helped with. The final question was one I wasn't expecting and it came from the doctor who hadn't said anything. "Miss St. Clair, have you ever done a delivery entirely on your own?" I knew as a trainee under a licensed midwife, I wasn't allowed to do a delivery without Mrs. Yother. She could lose her license. I froze. "Would you like for me to repeat the question, Miss St. Clair?" When the other two saw I was hesitating, they started firing questions at me so fast I wanted to run out of the room. They repeated the question and wanted to know how many deliveries I'd done alone and if I'd signed the birth certificates.

"We're more than thirty miles from the nearest hospital and people out there can't… and we have emergencies…"

"Answer the question Miss St. Clair."

"No, I've never done a delivery on my own without Mrs. Yother and I've only signed one birth certificate, under Mrs. Yother's signature." For the first time I noticed how hot that room was. They might not believe me, and I might fail, but Mrs. Yother wasn't going to get in trouble because of me and whether I passed or not, she would never know about this question or my answer.

"Thank you, Miss St. Clair. Your examination is concluded."

I walked out half blind and dizzy. Mrs. Yother wasn't around, and I had to get to the practical at three. It was a quarter to, so I walked outside and sat on a bench under a big oak tree.

"You did fine, Miss St. Clair." I turned around to see Doctor Brainerd standing there with his cowboy hat on. "Morse is a prick. He was just trying to trap you and he would have reported Mrs. Yother to the Board. He would probably even report Doctor Chelsea and me if we hadn't insisted you answer his question. Now, get back in there and finish up. You'll make a fine midwife, but I wouldn't want you testifying on my behalf in court. You're a terrible liar."

The practical was conducted by three other doctors and they looked much too young to have been Mrs. Yother's professors. After a few questions, I was asked to go with them into an examination room. It looked a lot like ours, which was a relief.

"In a moment, your patient will come in," the youngest of the three, with the name Doctor Gannon stitched on his white coat, announced. "We want to observe your examination and you should pretend we're not here. Just do what you normally would."

The knock came and I opened the door to a girl my age who was terribly overweight. No, she was fat. There were no fat girls in our community back home except for Inez Platt. "Good afternoon. My name is Miss St. Clair and you are?"

"Wilma, Wilma Ogilvie."

"All right, Mrs. Ogilvie; I will be doing a basic prenatal examination. Have you ever had one before?"

"No, and I don't see why I should have one now. I'm pregnant and I know it. I'm only here because my mother-in-law insisted I come." Lucky me; I got one of the actresses Mrs. Yother warned me about.

"It's to make sure your body's developing as it should so you'll have a healthy baby. How far along are you? When was your last period?"

"The middle of February."

"Well. We're going to say that conception occurred around the first of March. That makes you about fourteen or fifteen weeks along and you should deliver near the end of November." I could figure those dates in my sleep.

Our procedure at Mrs. Yother's was followed exactly, including helping her undress and put on the gown, which didn't fit very well. The scales said she weighed almost two hundred pounds. Her breasts were huge and sagging, but I managed to do a proper examination, then stopped and looked around for something to write on. Thankfully, the first drawer I opened had a pad and I had a pen in my uniform pocket. I recorded everything during the exam in the shorthand I'd gradually created for myself. I talked continuously, mostly about things that had nothing to do with the examination, the way Mrs. Yother would with new patients, and helped her up onto the table. "All right, Mrs. Ogilvie, I'm going to wash up and then I will insert two fingers—only two—into your vagina to examine your cervix."

"What's that?"

I shouldn't have used a medical term, so I spent a minute explaining what a cervix is. The examination had to have been uncomfortable for her because I had a lot of trouble reaching her cervix. I pressed down on her lower stomach the way I was supposed to, but I had to press a lot harder than I would have with my patients back home. By the time I got a feel, I had almost my whole hand inside her.

"What are you doing down there? It feels like you have your arm inside me. Just stop and let me up."

"Now, Mrs. Ogilvie; all women are different, and your cervix happens to be a little higher up than most and a little harder to reach. Nothing to worry about at all and I'll be done in a minute. I am sorry for the discomfort, but you can be sure that later examinations won't be this rough because your cervix will drop as the pregnancy progresses."

After the examination, I wiped the K-Y off her and myself; then helped her from the table. I was relieved when she was standing on her own two feet again. After helping her get dressed, I thanked her for coming in and asked her to wait in the office so we could go over my findings. It was all done in fifteen minutes.

"Miss St. Clair, if you don't mind, we have another patient we would like for you to examine. You may open the door and let her in when you're ready for her." That didn't upset me. Mrs. Yother said they might ask me to examine more than one woman. I got busy and cleaned everything with the bleach water I found under the sink; the same way I would have at Mrs. Yother's. When I opened the door, a very pregnant woman walked in. They wanted to see how I would examine a woman this far along and I was ready.

When I finished with Mrs. Bloemer, I asked her to wait for me in the office with Mrs. Ogilvie; that I would be in shortly. Only when the door closed behind her did I look at the doctors.

"Thank you, Miss St. Clair. You are finished for the day," the best looking of the three doctors informed me. "The results of the midwife examination will be posted later sometime this evening on the door of the room you took the written test in—after we've had a chance to meet with the other doctors and discuss everyone's performance."

Mrs. Yother was waiting for me on the sidewalk in front of the building. We sat on the bench under the oak tree for an hour while I told her about my afternoon. She listened and asked questions, but I could tell her mind was on something else. There was no way of knowing how long it would be before the results were posted, so she suggested we have supper at a good restaurant.

After changing back at the hotel, we made our way downtown to a place she knew. A smartly dressed man met us at the door and showed us to a table for two. "When I was a student here, neither I nor any of my classmates could afford this place," she whispered as we sat down. "I was on a strict budget from my parents. Now I can afford it and there aren't any restaurants to go to out where we live. Do you ever think about leaving, going to a big city and starting life all over again?"

"Why would I want to do that, Mrs. Yother? Everything and everyone I love is back home and besides, they don't need midwives in big cities."

"They need them anywhere women have babies. They don't know there's another way to give birth. They think only a doctor can deliver a healthy baby. Do you know that I can count the number of babies I've lost on one hand and the number of mothers on three fingers? I wonder how many doctors my age can say the same thing. I've delivered babies in places no doctor would go."

"Like in a ditch during a cyclone?"

"I bet Miss Leeth told you about that. It's true. I was as scared as Mr. and Mrs. Platt, but babies come when they want—Hell or high water. That night we had hail *and* high water."

The menu was full of things I'd never eaten, and I wanted to try one. I knew what lobster was and it was awfully expensive, six dollars, but I had thirty dollars in my pocket and nothing else to spend it on. When Mrs. Yother heard what I was going to order, a smile came to her face. "Celebrating a little early are we? Well, why not? We should be celebrating after all we've been through, or should I say, all I've put you through. Whatever those hifalutin doctors have to say, you'll have your job as long as I live. I can promise you that, and I think we'll have some wine with our meal as well. Mr. Yother bought a case of expensive French wine twenty years ago and I think we still have most of it left. I don't like it, but I'm willing to try something else. You're supposed to have white wine with seafood. Maybe I'll like it better."

I could have eaten another lobster I think, and we drank the whole bottle of wine. Mrs. Yother was a little tipsy by the time we left, but she still put up a fight when I tried to pay. "Miss St. Clair, do you want to hear me raise a ruckus in the finest restaurant in Nashville? They'll never let us back in. It's a long way for you to walk home, so you'd better give me that check." I did insist on driving though and she didn't complain too much about that. By the time we got back to the nursing building, she had calmed down.

"You stay in the car, Miss St. Clair. I'm going to go in and see if the results have been posted. I'm sure they have. It's Friday night and those doctors are sitting in their easy chairs smoking their pipes by now. I want to be the one to tell you the results."

I did as I was told. Even though I had to pee so bad it hurt, I stayed put. Mrs. Yother swayed a little as she walked up the steps and I was worried she might fall. The room was right inside the door, but she was gone a long time. My bladder was fit to bust by the time she came back through the door. I got out of the car and met her in the middle of the street in front of the building. She didn't say a word but reached out her hand to me. I took it in a firm handshake.

"Congratulations Miss St. Clair, you passed. Only three names are listed and yours is one of them. Go and see for yourself. Sorry I was so long. I had to visit the ladies' room." I was at the top of the stairs to the building by the time she mentioned the ladies' room. Peeing could wait. I had to see my name. There it was on the door, a typed sheet of paper with the heading: "Those Passing the June 1942 Midwife Examination" and first on the list was Otha May St. Clair. Mrs. Yother said they listed the scores from highest to lowest. I don't know if she was just saying that or not, but the names weren't in alphabetical order either. I stood there looking for a good long while, until a drop of pee made its way down my leg. I absolutely had to get to the ladies' room. Sitting on the toilet, I thought of Hazel and the life I'd now be able to make for her and little Abby.

Mrs. Yother talked continuously on the way back to our hotel, telling me things I then needed to know, having passed the examination. "You'll be getting a letter in the mail in a week or two with the official results and a form you can fill out and mail to Montgomery. They'll keep it on file and when you turn twenty-one, you can apply for a license. You can do that in Gadsden at the courthouse. Your license will come from Montgomery and it's good for five years. You have to renew it then and it costs five dollars. It's the same for doctors. If you don't renew it for another five years, you have to take the test again, but I'm not worried about that happening unless we lose this stupid war they've gotten us into."

Maybe it was the wine or maybe it was the relief of passing the test, but I slept like a baby that night. Mrs. Yother was already up and packed by the time I woke up the next morning. We drove for a while and I could tell there was something on her mind because she didn't talk much. After an hour, I asked what was bothering her.

"Otha May, there's something I have to tell you and I'm not going to make you promise not to tell Miss Leeth, but I would appreciate it if the two of you would keep it to yourselves for now. I'll tell Mr. Yother and Elton when I feel the time is right. I went to Nashville back in April for a check-up, but I knew something was wrong with me then. I couldn't put my finger on what it was and decided to get someone else's opinion. Doctor Jacobs did a physical examination just like the ones we do and wanted to run some tests on my blood and scrapings from my uterus. It'd been years since I'd had a proper pelvic examination and that's terrible for a midwife to say. I met with Jacobs again yesterday morning and went back yesterday afternoon to see a different doctor. The tests confirmed my doctor's initial diagnosis from the pelvic examination. I have cancer. It's in my uterus and has spread to my cervix and liver. They would have to do exploratory surgery to see what other organs are affected, but I know the answer already. The tests also showed that my liver function is only half what it should be, and you can't live without a liver. If I do nothing but take care of myself, I have maybe two years. If I have the surgery and they remove my uterus, that won't help much and I could die from the stress at my age. So that's it. I have two years maybe and I have a lot to do while I'm still able to work; I have a wedding to go to. Elton finally asked Elizabeth to marry him and she said yes. The date is set for September 26 in Evansville. I was against it, but things will work out."

I couldn't speak. All I could do was cry and I cried like I'd lost my own mother. "Now Miss St. Clair, I'm not dead yet and the doctors told me I'll feel pretty good up until the end, and I have plenty of morphine to help when the time comes. Even before I got this news, I had plans for you. I thought we would discuss them sometime in the future, but I guess now is as good a time as any. They depended somewhat on you passing your examination and now that's out of the way, so let me tell you what's going to happen. You can say no, but you won't.

On Monday the two of us are going to Gadsden to Mr. Saperstein's office. He's my lawyer and an honest man—for a lawyer. My will is going to be changed and I want you present. You will be willed the house where Mr. Yother and I now live and the sixty acres it sits on. You will also inherit twenty thousand dollars I put in stocks and bonds years ago. It may be worth considerably more now. We'll stop at my stock broker's after we finish with the lawyer and my account will have your named added to it, but you can't own it until you turn twenty-one. You get all this when I die if you are then twenty-one and legally considered an adult. If I die before then, the estate will be held in trust for you by my lawyer until you are twenty-one."

"But what about Mr. Yother and…"

"I'm not finished Miss St. Clair. Mr. Yother gets the house in Mobile and the money in my bank account which should allow him to live comfortably the rest of his life. Elton gets the property in Blount County and the trust fund I set up for him when he was born. Mr. Yother's will already states that his property goes to Elton when he dies if I die before him and it looks like that will be the case. Now, there is a stipulation on what you get. I know you will inherit that hill adjacent to my land when you turn twenty-one and I have a good idea you and Miss Leeth will want to build a house on it and live there. That's good, because you won't be able to live in my house. It's to be turned into a maternity clinic for colored and white women. I don't care if you have to put a wall down the middle of the house to satisfy the state; just do it. The money in the brokerage account will be enough to make whatever modifications you need. I do ask that you reserve part of the house as a living quarters for Ruby. She's a good soul and you will need her. I expect you to take the business I've built and turn it into something the area needs. Hire a new doctor from Vanderbilt if you think you need one. They'll work cheap for a few years; then hire another one to replace him. I also suggest you put Miss Leeth on the payroll to do the books. She's a bright girl and you'll need someone because you're going to be too busy. You need to know how much money's coming in and going out. I don't know if Ruby is capable of passing the midwife examination, but if you think she is, train her. You'll need a licensed colored midwife and don't let anyone tell you colored women can't get a license. They can, and they are desperately needed. As for your salary, pay yourself what you need and no more. I've always lost money doing this, but there's no reason you have to. Speak to the people in the county welfare office and go all the way to Montgomery if that fails. There's money available to help support places like the one you'll have, and you'll have to fight for it. I intend to write Senator Sparkman and ask him to help. His father and mine were good friends and I've never asked him for anything, but I will when I write. Now you can speak, Miss St. Clair. I think I've about covered everything I want to say."

"I don't know what to say."

"Yes you do. Say you'll follow my wishes exactly."

"I will follow your wishes exactly, of course, and thank you Mrs. Yother for having faith in me."

"Faith is belief in that which is unseen. I have seen your character demonstrated and I have watched you learn. I was younger than you when I was given my chance and I can think of no better legacy than to give you the same opportunity. I believe there is a Heaven, Miss St. Clair, and I believe our Creator will let me in and allow me to stay at least long enough to see what you make of yourself."

The trip from Nashville seemed to take half as long as the trip there. We were just pulling up in her driveway when everything got said. I helped Ruby unload the car and Mrs. Yother offered to drive me home but I told her I would rather walk. When I started down the driveway, Ruby came running after me with my bag. "Mrs. Yother says this is the first and last time you was to forget this." She was still thinking about me.

The weight of a hundred bushels of corn was on my heart. I was the saddest and happiest I'd ever been. Hazel would have to be told everything. It affected her as much as it did me, but I would respect Mrs. Yother's wishes and keep what I knew from anyone else. I was almost in front of Hazel's before I realized where I was. There would be a party that afternoon. They had planned it all week I was sure. There would then be a supper fit for the governor and a cake, maybe with candles, and I would have to be happy even if I wanted to cry my eyes out. What would I do without her?

My serious talk with Hazel could wait.

Chapter Twelve
The Price of Marriage

The world hadn't stopped spinning while I studied, and the war news was almost all bad when I started paying attention again. On the west and east coasts everybody was keeping an eye out for Jap and Kraut submarines. Thousands of our boys had been shipped to England in January. Some said it was to invade Europe and others said it was to fight off the German invasion of England that was surely coming. It seemed like Hitler was bombing British cities whenever he wanted, but they had given the Germans a dose of their own medicine with a thousand bomber attack on Cologne. I remembered the name of that city from geography class. Bill and James were itching to join up before the draft got them. That wouldn't happen until they turned twenty-one, but boys could join at eighteen. President Roosevelt got the draft more than a year before Pearl Harbor. I guess he figured we'd be in the war sooner or later.

***

True to her word, Mrs. Yother and I left for Gadsden the Monday morning after we got back from Nashville. Mr. Saperstein's office was next to the Etowah County courthouse and his secretary recognized Mrs. Yother as soon as we went in. The two of them talked and while we waited, I had a look around the office. Everything was wood or marble, like a fancy church, and people who came in spoke in whispers, like in a funeral home, and no one smiled. When Mr. Saperstein walked out to where we were, he didn't seem to fit in at all. He was loud and smiling and hugged Mrs. Yother like they were kinfolks. "Lois, it's good to see you again and I'm happy to say you look lovelier with every visit to my humble little office."

"Abe Saperstein, you're as good a liar as you ever were. This is my new associate, Miss St. Clair. She's just passed her midwife examination up in Nashville and we have some official business for you."

"Well, congratulations Miss St. Clair. Come in and tell me what I can do for the two of you."

We walked into the inner office and it was even nicer than the waiting room. I felt like a first-grader sitting in the principal's office. Mrs. Yother explained what she wanted done and Mr. Saperstein understood perfectly. Then she told him about the cancer. He got up from behind his desk, walked around to her and hugged her. There might have been tears in his eyes. "Mrs. Yother, your instructions will be followed to the letter. In fact, I'm not very busy right now, so why don't we just take care of it today?" He called his private secretary in from an office next to his and began dictating to her. He only stopped once so that Miss Cagle could get an original copy of Mrs. Yother's will from the files. I didn't understand much of what he said, but he said it very well, with a lot of wherefores and thereupons. He was finished in a few minutes and Miss Cagle was told to type up the new will immediately. Everything was done and signed that morning and Mr. Saperstein insisted on buying us dinner.

When we returned to the office, Mrs. Yother wrote a check and left it with the receptionist. I wasn't being nosy, but I looked. It was for a hundred dollars. She must have seen me looking because as soon as we left the office, she gave me some good advice. "Never hire a cheap lawyer. They'll cheat you and won't do what you want. When the time comes, he'll do the reading of the will. You, Mr. Yother, and Elton should be present, so right after the funeral would be the best time. I suggest you keep Mr.

Saperstein after I'm gone. In the long run he'll be worth every penny to you and the clinic."

"Yes, Mrs. Yother."

The next stop was at Mayfair Investments and I got to meet Mr. Gamble, which I thought was a funny name for a man in his line of work. She didn't say anything about her illness to him. It was a simple matter of putting my name on her account. We were back at her house by mid-afternoon and she gave me the rest of the day off.

***

Things had settled down at the Yothers' and Leeths' by the fourth of July. Little Abigail St. Clair and Roosevelt Franklin were both healthy babies and growing like grass in a fencerow. Their mothers had mostly recovered, and it was good having things back to normal. We had four new patients and one of them was a colored woman related to Mrs. Washington. Her name was Mrs. Blackwell and she'd known Ruby's real mother. Mrs. Yother was happy as she could be. "You see, Miss St. Clair, word gets around when you treat people right. Someday you'll have as many colored mothers-to-be coming to see you as white. That's why you need a colored assistant or better yet, a licensed colored midwife. Remember though, a licensed midwife has to sign all official records of examinations and birth certificates." I wouldn't forget that detail after what I'd gone through at Vanderbilt.

In our spare time, we drew up plans for the clinic. The way we had it figured, there was enough space for at least three extra rooms we could make out of the den and part of the living room. Mr. and Mrs. Yother's bedroom could also be divided for two more and there were two other spare bedrooms that could be used if needed. "That's up to seven rooms you could have without touching the kitchen, the examination room, your office, or Ruby's room and I bet when word gets around that women can come here to have their babies and recover, they'll stay full most of the time." She'd called it my office.

"And it'll be called the Lois Yother Clinic for Women," I added. I should have kept that idea to myself because tears came to her eyes. I'd never seen her cry before, no matter the situation.

"I've told Mr. Yother and Elton about everything and they've promised to help you any way they can. There are pitifully few people in this world I trust, but they are two of them." I knew I was one of them too, and succeed or fail, I would see to it that the clinic was built. She hired a builder from the community, Mr. Darnell, to look over our plans and he thought the job was something he and his sons could do. I had gone to High Point with his son Jeremy. They'd built lots of houses and barns in the area and were known for doing good work.

A week later, Mr. Darnell had a price: sixteen hundred dollars including materials. That was more than it cost to build a house the size of the one my family lived in, but Mrs. Yother didn't question his figures and wrote him a check for half. After he left, I asked her why the price was so high. "It's because he knows I have money. If it had been your daddy wanting the work done, it would have been five hundred dollars less. That's just the way things are; however, I know he'll do a good job and don't you pay him a penny more until it's done to your satisfaction, and that includes cleaning up the mess."

"Yes Mrs. Yother."

Toward the first of August, I received a wedding invitation in the mail from Colonel and Mrs. Archibald Spradley of Evansville, Indiana. I had to think a minute who that was. The invitation was elegant with double envelopes and fancy script printing inside. I could tell it had been addressed by Elizabeth because it said: Miss Otha May St. Clair and Miss Hazel Leeth. I liked the looks of that. Evansville was a long way though and I didn't expect we'd be able to go. We didn't have anything to wear to a fancy society wedding; besides someone had to be around in case of emergencies. But Hazel and I would get them a nice gift and send it by the Yothers.

This was for certain a good excuse for a trip to Gadsden for the two of us and maybe we could see a picture at the Princess theater while we were there. We hadn't had much time alone together and Abby was doing well enough that she could spend one day without her mother. Hazel was making plenty of milk and I volunteered to help her collect enough to keep the baby fed for a day. They could always use boiled milk from one of the Yothers' goats if they ran out. Mrs. Yother kept them for that very reason. Abby liked it the one time we gave her some. There was no shortage of people to watch her either. She was an adorable baby and between Mrs. Leeth and Aunt Glenda, there would be eyes on her around the clock if needed.

Glenda was becoming a very pretty girl and would be starting sixth grade in the fall. She was full of questions and had gotten a hurried education in exactly where babies come from when Abby was born. Hazel had a lot of explaining to do afterward. Finally, she sent her to me when she got tired of trying to come up with answers she'd rather have someone else give. Mostly she asked what things were and what they did. Mrs. Yother's medical books and their pictures helped me get through the basics.

"This is the thing you rubbed that helped Hazel push little Abby out." She was pointing at one of the few pictures that showed the clitoris, although it wasn't named.

"That's right. It's called a clitoris or clit for short. Massaging it can cause muscle contractions which sometime help in delivery."

"But that's not all it's good for is it?"

The smile on her face told me I didn't have to answer that question.

***

I had no idea what Hazel and I were supposed to get Elton and Elizabeth as a wedding present, so I asked Mrs. Yother. She'd been thinking about it too because she had an answer by the time I got the question out of my mouth.

"They're going to be living in Evansville in a house left to Elizabeth by her Aunt Gloria. Elton says it's completely furnished and all they have to do is move in. They won't be needing any of the usual things you would get newlyweds. I'm buying them a clock like the one in the den, if Roosevelt hasn't drafted all the clockmakers already. The perfect gift for you and Hazel to get them would be bed linen. Newlyweds shouldn't sleep on old linen. I know a place in Gadsden that can monogram the pillowcases while you wait and that would be a nice touch. Maybe they'll bring good luck and Elizabeth will get pregnant soon. They're not drafting married men with children yet."

It didn't sound like a very romantic gift, but Mrs. Yother knew best, so bed linen it would be. Hazel and I planned our trip for the last Saturday of the month. When she told her mother what we had in mind and asked if someone could watch Abby, she wasn't expecting the answer she got—why didn't the two of us spend the night there? Mrs. Leeth understood a lot more than we gave her credit for. Hazel said her mother and sister just wanted Abby all to themselves for a while. I didn't care which one was the truth; I would have a whole night with Hazel. Mama and Daddy didn't have much to say when I told them. After all, I was a responsible, almost grown woman with a good job and I helped with the bills a lot more than my brother. All he did was pester them to sign the paperwork so he could join the Army, or was it the Navy? Hazel said James was being just as big a pain at their house. They thought the war was some kind of game that would be over with before they got to play.

We left early while it was still cool that Saturday morning, and I think we both packed enough for a week's stay. I didn't know what to wear out at night and I'd heard there wouldn't be much in the way of nice clothes to buy. All the major clothing manufacturers were making uniforms, they said on the radio, and women would have to wait until the end of the war for new styles. My long-sleeved blouses we bought at Christmastime the year before had already been turned into short sleeved ones. It didn't matter; Hazel and I would have almost two whole days together and I, for one, was much more interested in seeing her out of her clothes than in them. Not since her last examination after Abby was born had I seen her naked and that was with Mrs. Yother watching. In the examination room, she was treated like any other patient and I knew any unnecessary touching on my part would be unprofessional and risk Mrs. Yother's wrath. Besides, she couldn't touch me back and that was already torture enough. Her stomach was still swollen then, but that had been months earlier and by the end of August, even with her clothes on, I could see that the swelling had gone away.

We weren't a mile from her house when her hand went up my dress. "Hazel Ruth, do you want me to drive this truck in a ditch?"

"You just keep both hands on the steering wheel. It's been a long time and I've got some catching up to do." When I lifted my leg to push the clutch in and change gears, her fingers slipped under my panties. Daddy would have died if he'd heard the grinding sound coming from the transmission as I made that shift.

Long before we reached the city limits, I was ready to pull over and rip her clothes off. I have no idea how many times I had to grab her hand and make her stop. As soon as I had to change gears with one hand and steer with the other, her fingers were back at it. "You've been practicing," I managed to get out between the little contractions that weren't going to stay little for very long.

"Maybe I have. Maybe I've missed you."

I pulled into the parking lot of the Duck Springs Baptist Church just in time to let go of the steering wheel and grab her hand with both of mine. The seizures between my legs weren't going to stop even if her fingers did. Things had already gone well beyond the stopping point. The groans could've been heard by my long dead relatives if they were listening. I wrapped my arms around her and held her as tight as I could until the spasms turned loose of my body and I was able to breathe again. This was nothing like the little twitches I could squeeze out with my skinny fingers.

"You said the last time we were here that we would figure out whether you were my husband or my girlfriend," I think she said. "And I've decided you're good at both, Otha May. Now you're a father too. I've never been so happy in my life and it's all because of you." The kiss she gave me made me want to find room in the cab of that truck to crawl all over her. She'd only made me want more.

"We're not going to make it to town if you don't get your hand out of my panties. You just wait 'til I get you alone in room 104. In case you couldn't tell, I've missed you too."

I remembered the man at the desk and he didn't question me when I asked for room 104. This time we had luggage like proper ladies and a young colored boy named Garrett carried our bags to our room. He smiled when I handed him a quarter. "The two of you picked a good time to stay with us. Monday we'll be full up. There's some big Army general coming to town and talk is, he's soon gonna have folks at the Goodyear working three shifts, seven days a week making tires for army trucks. All the Goodyear big wheels from up north are coming down and staying a week to get things going. They say the plant's gonna double in size and that means good paying jobs for whites and colored."

Our room looked like we'd just left it the day before except there was no wood stacked up for the fire and the heavy quilts we shivered under had been replaced with cotton sheets and a sheer bedspread. High ceilings and open windows with fans in them made the room quite tolerable for late August. We were sweaty from the long ride and a cool bubble bath was what we needed first, although it wasn't at all what we wanted first. Our squeaky-clean bodies wrapped together was a lot more sensible and for that we could wait long enough for a proper bath. While the tub was filling and the bubbles were rising, we started undressing each other. It was so hot we weren't wearing much—except she was wearing the largest cup size bra we'd bought. When I pulled her dress up over her head and got rid of the bra, it was like I was seeing her naked for the first time. The baby bulge was gone, replaced by a firm almost flat stomach. Her breasts were full, without hanging to her waist like those of some women when they're breastfeeding. The real change, that I would never have mentioned, was in her nipples and areolas, which had both tripled in size since her last examination. It was like her areolas were trying to spread out and cover her breasts. "I know what you're looking at. They started doing that just lately, when Abby began feeding six or eight times a day. They're horrible looking."

When Hazel was pregnant, I made a point of telling her how beautiful she was every day, but since Abby's birth, I hadn't kept it up. I thought it often enough, but I didn't say it, and when a tear crawled down her face, I felt my own eyes begin to fill. I didn't let a single tear escape as I pulled my dress over my head and hugged her. "Don't ever think such things and don't ever imagine I do. Lord, your body has gone through things that would kill a man and you still have the figure of a sixteen-year-old schoolgirl. I don't know how you did it. Any woman would trade her soul to look half as good as you and don't worry about the little things. Nature will take care of them. Right now, you share your body with your baby and that's a privilege most of us will never know. I love you Hazel Ruth and I still don't know what I did to deserve you."

She took a deep breath and the tense moment passed. Her face flushed when one of her nipples started dripping. "It's time for Abby's feeding and I guess my breasts don't know she's not here." I leaned over and took the nipple in my mouth, which started the other one dripping. The bath could wait a little while, so I shut the water off. I led her to our bed and with some pillows, propped her back up against the headboard. She stroked my hair when I curled up next to her with my head in her lap. Maybe it was her milk or maybe we were both tired, but the catnap we shared was exactly what we needed. When my eyes opened, she was looking down at me with a smile like you see in paintings of angels.

Our bath in the cool water with mountains of bubbles brought us back to life. "Do you suppose we could get something to eat around here?" Hazel asked with a grin as I dried her off. "My breakfast has run out and I'm starved."

"I don't think they're rationing food yet and I want to walk by the Princess to see what's playing, and we have to see if anyone has summer clothes that don't look like they belong at a funeral. I'm so tired of wearing the same things every Sunday and I want to buy you something pretty, something bright and... yellow, I think."

Our first stop was at Sears and Roebuck, but we didn't stay long, even though the cool, air-conditioned store was heaven-sent on that scorching August day. Everything was some shade of gray if it wasn't black or white—funeral clothes. I did buy us a couple of new bras though, and three pairs of panties each, all in white because that's all they had. Since Hazel had to wear a bra almost all the time, I decided I would too, even if I didn't need to. The clothes story was the same at every other store and I began to notice the women we met were all dressed in the same dull shades. There wasn't a yellow blouse to be found anywhere and then I got an idea. "We're going to buy three white blouses each and dye them ourselves. Mama used to dye my white blouses when I was little. She used Hedgeapple and Sumac bark to make yellow, Sassafras leaves for orange, Dogwood bark for blue, blackberry juice for purple, and Snapdragon and Black-eyed Susan flowers for green. Weeping Willow bark made a beautiful peach color and Sycamore bark worked for red. She mixed several together to get different shades. We can do that too and I know Mama will help. It'll be fun." Everyone had white blouses and we found plenty of white skirts at Mason's, the place that sold my uniforms. I asked for dye at all the stores so we wouldn't have to make our own, but I was a few months late and was told there wouldn't be any more until after the war. That was all right. We had plans for those white blouses and skirts.

In my single-minded search for something with a little color in it, I'd forgotten that Hazel was hungry. We were on Broad Street, not far from the Princess and I promised her we would find a restaurant as soon as we walked by the theater. *The Major and the Minor* was playing that night and I knew who Ginger Rogers was. They talked about her and Fred Astaire and Gene Kelly on the radio all the time. I figured the movie would have a lot of dancing in it. We were too late for dinner and too early for supper, so we had the Rainbow Restaurant to ourselves, except for a few kids without their parents. This place was a lot nicer than the BonAire, with real cloth napkins on the tables and everything. Since we couldn't find any clothes we really liked, I told Hazel we would at least eat well while we were in town and it was next door to the place where Mrs. Yother told me I could get the bed linen for Elton and Elizabeth. It only took a few minutes to stop in and pick out sheets and pillow cases. The monograms would be done in an hour. We weren't dressed nearly nice enough for the restaurant, but since we were about the only customers they had, no one cared. Hazel had never had a meal in a nice restaurant before and I'd only had one, but we knew what a steak was, although there were more kinds to choose from than we'd ever imagined. For what that dinner—or maybe it was supper—cost, we could have bought a couple more white blouses and skirts. We wouldn't have had nearly as much to talk about when we got home though.

When we walked back by the Princess after picking up the bed linen, there was a crowd of kids hanging around and buying tickets. I soon found out why. On a small sign I read that all day Saturdays, children under twelve could get in for a dime to watch cartoons and The Three Stooges. In a few minutes the doors opened and a gang of children ran out as the gang we were watching ran in. It was sweltering hot outside and neither of us had ever seen a cartoon or The Three Stooges, so when Hazel offered to buy our tickets, I didn't argue. All the children sat down front, so we had the back of the theater to ourselves. It's one thing to listen to The Three Stooges on the radio, but it's something else to be able to see what we'd only imagined—on a forty-foot screen. They weren't on the radio often, and then they were only on for a few minutes as guests on one of the comedy programs. I could see why. They were so much funnier when you could see what they were doing. After an hour, the lights came up and we were chased out. I guessed it was so they could clean the place before the evening crowd showed up for *The Major and the Minor*.

I knew where I wanted to go next. If we couldn't buy any nice clothes, we could jewelry shop, and not at

Grants either. I wanted to look around in a real jewelry store. A friendly young man at a newspaper stand said that Stenson's was the best place in town. I gave him a nickel and took a newspaper. Hazel gave me a strange look. "Well, maybe I want to read about what's going on in the city and I know Daddy would like to have a Saturday paper. He hardly ever gets one. Now, we have to go back to the hotel and change. We're not going in a fancy jewelry store looking like we've been in the field all day and I want to do something with my hair, or better yet, let's stop by My Fair Lady and let them." We were lucky in that most of the women in town came in right after dinner to get their hair done. The girl who'd cut my hair remembered me and when I told her we didn't have much time, she knew exactly what to do. We were done and looking like movie stars in half an hour; then it was a fast walk back to our room at the hotel.

It was after four by the time we got changed and found Stenson's. The sign on the door said they closed at five, but when the salesman got the idea we were going to buy something, he didn't rush us. I had our story made up long before I knew we were coming to town. We were both engaged to soldiers and were getting married as soon as the war was over. We'd been sent money to buy wedding rings and that's what we wanted to look at. Hazel let me do the talking. Before I got finished, the salesman knew he had a couple of buyers on his hands. When he walked down to the other end of the counter for wedding rings, Hazel looked at me, grinned, and whispered in my ear, "If I'm ever arrested for anything, I want you to be my lawyer."

Our rings weren't fancy, but they were real gold— the first piece of gold jewelry I'd ever owned—and I liked the way they looked on our fingers as we walked down the street. "Now, Hazel Ruth Leeth, if I could find a willing justice of the peace, I'd make an honest woman of you."

"Would I become Hazel Ruth St. Clair or would you become Otha May Leeth?"

"Doesn't matter. Neither of us has to change our name. That's done at the courthouse and Mrs. Yother says a lot of couples never do it or even file the signed marriage license and get an official marriage certificate. The women just take the name of their husbands and that's that."

"But you have to get a license, right? Do you go to the courthouse for that?"

"Yes, but either one of the people getting married can do it. It's just a piece of paper you pay two dollars for. It's not legal until someone official or the preacher who performs the ceremony signs it. Oh, and you have to have a witness; at least one."

"And just how do you know so much about all this?" The smile on her face told me I'd been found out.

"I asked Mrs. Yother. She said I was crazy for having such thoughts and that I would be throwing away two dollars… but the courthouse is just a little farther down the street and it would only take a minute for us to go in and get the license. That is, if you want to. Marriage licenses don't expire, and who knows, we might find someone who'll marry us someday."

"It's Saturday, Otha May; the courthouse is closed for sure."

"You're right, but the probate judge's license office is open until five Mrs. Yother said. We have fifteen minutes. Mostly they sell hunting and fishing licenses on Saturdays, but that's where you go to get a marriage license too. I know that don't make much sense, but Mrs. Yother's always right."

Lightning didn't strike us when we kissed and no one called the police. I don't think anyone even noticed. "Where there's a will, there's a way Miss St. Clair and I've already seen too much to doubt you'll find it. I love you more with every breath I take and tonight you're all mine."

The older lady at the probate judge's window didn't even look up when I told her I wanted to get a marriage license and I watched as she wrote Hazel Ruth Leeth and O.M. St. Clair on the form. Lots of men had initials for names, like L.J., R.C. and O.T. They were all men in our church and maybe the woman at the window knew an O.M. sometime in her life. "That'll be two dollars Miss Leeth and congratulations on your engagement." I caught myself before I corrected her. If she wanted to think I was Hazel, that was fine by me.

It was only a piece of paper, but we took turns holding it on our way to the theater. In the span of an hour we'd bought wedding rings and a marriage license. It was too much for either of us to believe.

The movie was a funny kind of love story with Ginger Rogers pretending to be a young girl so she could get a cheap train ticket. She might have fooled Ray Milland, but she wouldn't have fooled me. There weren't many people in the theater, so we sat near the back and held hands. It was my first movie and I got to see it with Hazel.

Our first night together wasn't anything like either of us had planned. An unbelievable afternoon with us getting rings and a marriage license turned into a night that neither of us would want to remember all of. It was two in the morning when we got back to our room after the party we sort-of invited ourselves to and the night was far from over. Hazel told me before we left home that we couldn't miss church Sunday or her mama would never forgive us. That turned out to be the least of my worries.

After the movie, we found Frank's Drugs still open and went in for some ice cream. They only had vanilla and we could only get one scoop. Our waitress said there wouldn't be any at all pretty soon because sugar was in short supply and the government was going to ration it. Why did the government need sugar for the war?

"If they'd allow it, I'd buy you another cone just to watch you lick the ice cream again."

"Otha May St. Clair, you're terrible, but don't think I haven't been watching you too. Do you think we could have another bath tonight? Who knows how long it'll be before we have the chance again."

"I don't see why not. No one said there was any limit on how many baths we can take and the government's not rationing water yet."

When we got back to the hotel, there was a party going on in the grand ballroom. I'd never seen so many beautiful women and handsome men all dressed up. There was a line waiting to get in. A real band was playing music like I'd never heard, and I could see couples dancing everywhere. I spotted Garrett and asked him what was going on. "It's Judge Henderson's retirement party. Monday's his last day to serve and he's invited everybody who's anybody to celebrate with him. He's already a little drunk and I imagine the rest will be soon enough. Why don't the two of you join the party? No one would notice two more pretty girls and I can get you in the back way through the kitchen. The food's good and the liquor's free." It was an adventure we couldn't turn down and it was still early. We had the rest of the night to spend together and how often would two girls from the country get to mingle with high society? I must have had that "I dare you" look in my eyes because Hazel smiled and nodded.

We barely got through the door before being dragged onto the dance floor. Our partners were just drunk enough not to care if we couldn't follow them very well and the lights were low enough nobody could see how bad we were. After two songs, we followed them to their table and sat down. They were brothers, Thomas and William, and the judge's nephews—his favorite nephews. They had both joined the Army the day before and were either celebrating or trying to forget what they'd done. While they went for our drinks, I told Hazel to be nice to William and that I was going to be nice to Thomas.

"I have a plan coming together in my head and we need these two boys to make it work."

"What if he tries to kiss me?"

"Then kiss him. I won't be jealous and if things work out, you'll be glad you did."

"What if he…"

"I hope the two of you like rum and Coca-Cola," Thomas yelled over the music, "but what girl doesn't? Drink up; there's plenty more where that came from."

I couldn't taste anything but the Coca-Cola; maybe with a little of the fizz gone out of it. Hazel and I finished our glasses in a few minutes while the boys talked about how much fun they were going to have in the Army. Our next trip to the dance floor went a lot better and after another two drinks, we were practically experts. I'd never been drunk in my life and the only hard liquor I'd ever tasted was some nasty corn made by the Platts, but rum and Coca-Cola was nothing like that stuff. It was sweeter the more I drank and it gave me a nice warm feeling inside.

I knew the hand I felt go up my leg wasn't Hazel's, but I didn't push it away, not until it went too far and then I only pushed it down a little. Shouldn't he try to kiss me first? He got a good feel of both my thighs before he leaned over to kiss me. It wasn't much of a kiss and his lips felt nothing like Hazel's. She was having her own problems with William. When he kissed her, I saw her eyes open wide and she stared helplessly at me. The way she was squirming around in her seat, I figured his hand was up her skirt as well. Now that they'd had a feel, it was time for me to put my plan in motion; it was getting late.

"So you're the judge's favorite nephews, huh? I bet he's gotten the two of you out of a lot of trouble."

"Uncle Horace would do anything for us," William answered. "He's the best uncle anyone could ever ask for."

"You think you could get him to sign something without reading it too close?"

"You kidding? He's already signed a release for Marvin Davis and he's probably the biggest thief in the county. He'd be looking at five years in state prison if he didn't have a pretty wife who wanted him out real bad. If Aunt Sarah finds out what Uncle Horace got in return there'll be Hell to pay."

"And earlier tonight," Thomas added, "he signed a divorce decree that'll never be seen by anyone in this town. Mrs. Humphrey's been trying to kill her husband for years and I think he got tired of trying to stay alive. He gets to live in the house with Mrs. Humphrey, but since they're officially divorced, he won't inherit any of her family's money if she dies before him. It all goes to their daughter Patricia, who'll never marry unless some miracle happens and she can marry that woman she's been living with for years. They're a couple of Lebanese."

"Lesbians," I corrected.

"Yeah, that's it. Everyone says it's a shame because they're both good looking women any man in town would crawl in bed with."

"Let me guess," William spoke up, "one of you has an old traffic ticket and the county sheriff has issued a warrant for you. That's easy; Sheriff Holcomb and Uncle Horace have been friends for years. They each know too much on the other to turn down a favor."

"It's a little more than that. I need him to sign a marriage license without asking too many questions."

"Secret wedding, huh? The bride's pregnant and the license has been backdated; is that it? If the happy couple managed to get old Mrs. Naylor to fix the license, it won't be any problem. We'll have the ceremony tonight. Who are they? Are they here?"

"You and your brother have your hands up their skirts at the moment." His hand slipped from its place on my thigh and the two men left the table to discuss things. I couldn't tell by the look on their faces what they had to discuss, but William was grinning like a canvassing politician when they returned. Hazel and I downed our drinks and watched the judge try to dance with two women half his age. Pretty soon he would be too drunk to sign anything, or passed out on the dance floor.

It was already well past midnight and the crowd had thinned out considerably. When our dates returned, they walked past our table and on to the judge's. They managed to drag him away from his group toward the men's room with both of them holding him up. It was half an hour later when they returned him to his seat. William still had that grin on his face and it had spread to Thomas. His hand was back up my skirt as soon as he sat down and when I stopped its advance upward with my own, he gave me a look that told me he had some news I wanted to hear—and that it was going to cost me a feel. I held my glass with both hands and let him get to what he was after. Hazel gave up trying to fight off William's roaming hand when she saw I wasn't resisting anymore. Maybe it was the first time Thomas had ever gotten that far because he sure didn't know what he was doing. At least he wasn't rough or anything. His hand wandering all over my thighs that evening must have had an effect on me too, or maybe it was the rum. Whatever it was, things were warming up down there.

"Uncle Horace says he might do it. He can perform the ceremony himself here at our table and sign the marriage license. William and I could be witnesses. There's just one little catch."

Hazel had been quiet most of the evening, but she spoke up when she heard that. "What does he want?"

William answered for both of them. "You remember my brother talking about Patricia Humphrey and her Lebanese lover?" I didn't bother correcting him. "Well they wanted to get married too, back several years ago. I didn't know any of this before tonight, but when we told Uncle Horace what the two of you had in mind, he told us the whole story in the men's room. He married them in this very hotel."

"Then he'll marry us?" Hazel barely got the question out before William answered. The way she was squirming around and the way her voice quivered, I knew his fingers were busy.

"As long as we get what he got for marrying Patricia and what's-her-name. He made sure the marriage was good and consummated that night and we want to do the same for the two of you."

It was my turn to drag Hazel toward the restrooms. We were both too drunk to walk without the other, but we had to talk. It took a while for us to convince ourselves they were too drunk to go through with the deal, with me doing most of the convincing. I knew the effect alcohol had on men and was positive they wouldn't be able to do anything. My explanation sounded like I knew what I was talking about.

"But what if you're wrong, Otha May? What if we get pregnant?"

"That's not going to happen. We'll tell them the deal's off if they don't have rubbers." Mrs. Yother and I talked to all our patients about methods for avoiding or delaying their next pregnancy, so Hazel knew what I was saying. We were betting on them being too drunk to need the rubbers and passing out peacefully. It was a chance we made up our minds to take and the kiss we shared sealed the deal. At that point neither of us cared who might've seen us.

"All right, we'll do it," I announced when we returned to our table, "but, as you would say, there's one little catch." I was in charge of things now. "You'll have to use rubbers and if you don't have any, the deal's off."

Hazel hadn't started having periods again, but I didn't want either of us taking any chances.

"Frank Mitchell's son, Howard, is sitting right over there and I'm sure he'd open up his daddy's drugstore across the street for this kind of emergency," my horny date answered with a grin on his face. "He'll do it for us. I'll be back in fifteen minutes." He was back in ten and Howard gave Hazel and me a good looking over before going back to his table.

"Let me see them." I was still in charge. Four round white plastic containers spilled onto the table and I opened all of them. There were two rubbers in each box. They were either awfully sure of themselves or terribly drunk. I'd already made up my mind to go through with it if I had to. How bad could it be? "I've got the signed license; one of you go get the judge." They both went and it took both of them to get him to our table. He had the ceremony memorized and slurred his way through it somehow. Mostly we couldn't understand what he was saying, but when he got to the "I do's", he was perfectly clear.

"Do you…" Thomas whispered my name in his ear. "Otha May St. Clair, take this woman as your lawfully wedded wife, forsaking all others, to have and hold, in sickness and in health, for better or worse, for as long as you both shall live?"

"I do."

"And do you…" William whispered Hazel's name in his ear. "Hazel Ruth Leeth, take this woman as your lawfully wedded wife—wait, didn't I already say that—forsaking all others, to have and hold, in sickness and in health, for better or worse, for as long as you both shall live?"

"I do." Those were the most wonderful words I'd ever heard come from anyone's lips.

"Then by the power vested in me by the citizens of Etowah County and the Great State of Alabama, I pronounce you… wife and wife. You may kiss… each other."

I didn't realize how loud the judge had gotten. There was a small crowd standing around by the time the ceremony was finished. We had plenty of witnesses to the kiss we shared early that Sunday morning. I don't know if they were so drunk they didn't realize what had happened, or maybe they didn't realize Hazel and I were both women, but they applauded all the same. There were two brides for everyone to kiss, but no one seemed to care, and I made certain the judge signed and dated the license and that Thomas and William signed as witnesses. We'd done it. We were married on Sunday August 30, 1942 at 2:15 a.m. and dozens of people had witnessed it. You can't get any more legal than that. The judge even led everyone in a toast to the newlyweds and that ended the party. Those who were sober enough, left. Garrett found rooms for those who weren't and after Thomas and William slipped him some money, he got them the room right next to ours.

"We have to pack now," I told Hazel as soon as our door closed. "We're leaving as soon as they pass out. It'll be Thomas knocking on our door any minute. I'll go back to their room with him and send William over here. Don't lock the door. As soon as Thomas is dead to the world, I'll come over and get you. We'll be sober and on the road before sunup. God, I hope the lights are working on Daddy's truck."

It was a good plan, a very good plan. The knock came just as I was finishing my instructions.

Chapter Thirteen
A Deal with the Devil

We didn't talk until we were halfway home. Earlier I'd been worried about Hazel's mama not ever forgiving me if I got Hazel back too late for church, but she would have hated me the rest of my life if I'd brought her home in the shape she was in. Neither of us realized how drunk we were, but we weren't drunk enough to not remember most of what happened. It was all my fault; me and my perfect plan. Thomas and William had been drinking straight Coca-Cola most of the night and were stone cold sober, just pretending to be drunk. We didn't know that until we were alone with them and then it was too late. Losing my virginity to a complete stranger was something I could have gotten over, but that's not exactly what happened.

***

The knock on the door came from Thomas and William, not just Thomas, and when I let them in, they told us the plan had changed. They spoke as if they hadn't had a drink all night, before Thomas poured the rum he brought with him into four glasses. William made it perfectly clear what they wanted.

"We've been talking and we've decided that girls everywhere love a man in uniform and there'll be plenty of pussy after we get to wherever the Army sends us, but how often are we going to get to watch two lesbians go at it?" He got the word right this time—there was no reason for him to pretend to be drunk anymore. "So what we want from you two newlyweds is a show we won't ever forget. How about it? We get to see that this new marriage is properly consummated, just like Uncle Horace did." That's not at all what I thought he'd meant earlier when he said his uncle had made sure Patricia's marriage was consummated.

"And what if we say no?" I asked, knowing he probably had an answer for that.

"Uncle Horace can sign an annulment as fast as he can sign a marriage license and don't count on anyone backing up your side of the story either. I guarantee no one saw anything if Uncle Horace says they didn't. No witnesses, no marriage."

I opened the door for them. "Give us a few minutes to talk about it. We'll let you know what we decide."

"I can't do it, Otha May. It's one thing to do it with one man alone in the dark, but to put ourselves on display for the two of them is an even worse sin. I just can't do it. I can't touch you with them watching." Her eyes welled with tears that tore at my heart. What had I gotten the two of us into? I was drunk enough to come up with another bad idea.

"After all we've gone through we can't let them win, Hazel. We're married now and we're going to stay married the rest of our lives. What if you don't have to do anything? I'll give them the show they want. You can close your eyes and pretend they're not there. We can do this and as soon as they've had their spectacle, we'll go home and forget it ever happened."

"I can't let you… What if…?"

"Don't worry about me. I love you Hazel and we're staying married. I hope they get all the pussy they want in the Army and come home with some terrible disease. I'm going next door and tell them they can come over in ten minutes. We'll get undressed ourselves. They don't get to watch us do that." She nodded and I went to tell our blackmailers what they wanted to hear. Hazel had the bottle turned up and was sucking on it hard when I returned.

"I don't want to remember any of this ever and if I have to drink this whole bottle to make sure, I will. If either of us remembers anything, let's promise not to tell the other—promise me, Otha May."

I took the bottle and kissed her. "I promise."

After I undressed myself—she was in no shape to help—I began undressing her and doing my best to let her know that everything would be okay, whether I believed it or not. I threw back the covers on the bed, our bed, and she lay down with her eyes already shut. The knock on the door came just as I got her covered with a sheet and wrapped another around myself. My final demand when I went over earlier and told them we would act out their little play, was that they couldn't make a sound or speak while they were in our room. If Hazel kept her eyes closed and only heard my voice, it would be easier for her I thought. They agreed to keep quiet. I hoped it wasn't the bulge in their pants making that promise.

When I opened the door, the two men came in without speaking a word. They placed the chairs from the desk in the room near the foot of the bed and sat down. Without looking at either of them, I pulled back the sheet covering Hazel just enough to slip into bed beside her. It was hard to wiggle out of the sheet I was wearing, but I managed and pushed it off the bed onto the floor. I closed my eyes too and wrapped my arms around my new wife. If they stayed quiet and she kept her eyes closed, things might work out. She responded to my touch as if we really were alone and her lips met mine in a long kiss that felt right. I barely noticed that the sheet covering us was slowly being pulled away. They would get their show, however I wouldn't be acting. Maybe it was the alcohol, but I began to not care if we were being watched.

The faint scent of the drops of milk at her breasts temporarily removed any thoughts of our audience and I took one of her nipples in my mouth. The sweet taste and her body next to mine created a familiar twinge in a familiar nerve that wouldn't be ignored for long. Without thinking, I squeezed her other breast and got a spray of milk on my ear. *No extra charge for that, boys.* When I slid over on top of her and her arms drew my body close, we touched in all the right places and I felt the last bit of the sheet covering us disappear. Every slight push of my hips into hers was met with a stronger one back. When she wrapped her legs around me and her hands grabbed my butt and pulled me into her, I knew her mind and body were in two entirely different places. I joined her in that dreamland, where we were all alone in our bed, in our house, on our hill, on our land. If our spectators were paying attention, maybe they learned something watching me patiently lead Hazel to a stifled scream they would probably never understand. No one heard when she turned my head and whispered in my ear, "I love you."

If it hadn't been for all the liquor, I would have been content to curl up with her and sleep 'til sunup, but instead I slid down in the bed and showed our blackmailers how second-rate men are when it comes to making love to a woman. They say liquor is liquid courage and these pigs would remember what two women could do all night that men can only do once before rolling over and going to sleep. Poor Hazel was so drunk she begged me not to stop and I was drunk enough to listen to her

I was satisfied with my arms around her and our feverish cheeks touching as she came back to her senses after finally pushing me away—but she wasn't finished, not with me anyway, When her hand slipped between us, I had no idea she was sober enough to know what she was doing. Things were aching to be touched and I was moaning even before her fingers got to where I wanted them. We'd agreed that she wouldn't have to do anything, but if she wanted to change her mind, it was more than all right with me. She had a way of knowing when I was close and I was already very close. If she'd circled that spot once more, I would have screamed, but that's not how she wanted it to happen.

When she pulled me on top of her and slid down in the bed, I leaned forward and held her face with my thighs. Without moving a muscle, I waited as she drove me closer and closer to the edge of the bluff I wanted to jump off of. My mind was fixed on squeezing that building eruption out of me and when it came, I put on a show for our bystanders sitting there with their mouths hanging open. Hazel might want to forget a lot of things about that night, but not that moment. My body shook like I was being electrocuted and I had to stifle the scream that wouldn't be kept inside me. Maybe she remembered what I'd just put her through; because she was just getting started and I don't remember anything after the third time my insides twisted and paralyzed me.

I was still trying to breathe regular when I noticed both men were up and walking toward the door.

"We got to see something tonight, big brother. The other boys in basic ain't never gonna believe this."

That was the last thing I remember until the knock on the door. The room was filled with sunlight when I opened my eyes. "Maid service. Maid service." Then I heard a key go into the lock on the door. The worst pain I'd ever experienced in my life shot through my head as I jerked myself up in the bed, bringing the sheet that was stuck to my back with me, but I got to the door naked in time to keep it from opening.

"We don't need anything this morning, thank you."

"Checkout was at noon, Ma'am and I have to clean the room."

"Can you come back in a little while?"

"I'll do the rest of my rooms and then come back, but you'll have to be out in an hour. We're booked up this week and the room's been taken."

"Thank you, we'll be out in an hour."

The clock on the nightstand said twelve-thirty. How was that possible? Hazel hadn't moved and for a second I was afraid she might be dead; then I saw she was breathing.

"Hazel you have to get up. We gotta be out of here in an hour." My head was splitting, and I couldn't keep my balance. That pain was matched when I sat on the toilet to pee. I didn't have to look down to know how swollen and sore things were down there. Somehow, I managed not to scream long enough to finish peeing and then turned on the water to fill the tub. We would have a bath even if the maid came in and watched. Hazel was moving when I got back to the bed, but the sounds she made scared me.

"Help me to the bathroom, Otha May, I'm going to throw up and I have to pee." She threw up in the toilet, then cried, then cried some more while she peed. "It burns so bad I can't stand it."

"You have to pee, Hazel, or you'll get an infection that'll be a lot worse. We both got too rough with each other last night and I'm sorry. It was my fault." I held her hand until she finished peeing and crying.

"I think I'm gonna faint. I feel lightheaded and the room's spinning."

The room was spinning, but I managed to get her into the tub and crawled in with her. The warm water soothed the burning between my legs enough for me to have a good look down there. Everything was swollen and it burned when I touched myself, although I was in good shape compared to Hazel. Nothing in Mrs. Yother's medical books said anything about this condition.

One of the bottles in the cabinet next to the tub said shampoo, I was pretty sure. Whatever it was, I poured half the bottle on my head and the other half on Hazel's. She leaned over and threw up in the toilet again when I finished shampooing her hair, but she was alive. "My head's busting," she moaned while I dried her off, "and things between my legs are on fire. Let me go back to bed, Otha May. I just want to die in my sleep."

"You're not going to die, and we have to be out of here in half an hour. We've already missed church and if we don't get home soon, your mother'll kill us both." I was hoping to get her panties on before she noticed what her clit looked like, but she must have gotten a look in the mirror. She spread her legs, looked down and began to wail.

"I've got some kind of disease, Otha May. Look at it. I deserve to die a horrible death. I wish I was already dead."

"You'll be fine in a couple of days. Things are just a little raw down there. I'll get something to put on it to stop the burning when we get back."

Somehow I got us dressed, packed, and out of the room. Hazel was white as a sheet when I dragged her downstairs to the coffee shop. I had to have something to wake me up so I could drive home. After three cups of strong coffee each, I put her in the truck. We had to stop twice on the way home for her to throw up and the second time I joined her. My whole body ached, my head throbbed and the muscles in my stomach hurt from throwing up. I didn't even think about going home. Mrs. Yother would know what to do.

***

One look at us and she must have known we'd been drinking the night before. When I told her we had some bad swelling and inflammation, she had us on the examination table right away. I went first and didn't dare look at her face as I spread my legs in the stirrups. She didn't ask what had happened except to ask if we'd been raped. Ruby mixed up vinegar and warm water and Mrs. Yother added some sulfa powder to it. When she filled the biggest enema syringe we had with it, I knew what to expect. We often douched mothers after delivery. "This is going to sting, but if I don't administer it right away, you'll have a lot worse to deal with in a few days. Hold this inside as long as you can." I gripped the rails on the table and held my breath as the warm liquid was forced into my vagina. The stinging wasn't so bad and after a few minutes, I released my muscles and filled the pan Ruby was holding under me. This was repeated four times. Poor Hazel was probably thinking I was having major surgery I was in there so long. When that treatment was over, I almost jumped off the table when Mrs. Yother rubbed some salve between my legs, but in a few seconds, the pain went away. "Take this vial with you and put some on your clitoris three times a day until the swelling goes down. It's my own formulation for this sort of inflammation: Vick's salve, sulfa powder, and cocaine. If you douche yourself with one syringe of vinegar and warm water twice a day for the next three days, you should be fine. You can get dressed and send Miss Leeth in now. I suspect she'll need the same treatment you've had, and after she leaves here you have to make sure she douches for the next three days and uses the salve too. She can come here and you can do it for her to make sure it's done right. She has a baby to take care of and we can't risk any infection in her body that might get transmitted. I'll give you both some tablets to help you sleep tonight."

Hazel still looked like a corpse when I went out to get her. She made me promise I would stay in the examination room with her and Mrs. Yother didn't object. As I undressed her, tears began flowing down her cheeks. "You're going to be all right, Hazel. Mrs. Yother knows what to do."

"No I won't. I won't ever be all right again."

It was almost dark when I pulled into the Leeths' driveway. *We lost track of the time, enjoyed our weekend, sorry if you were worried...* I didn't have a chance to make up a good story and the look Mrs. Leeth gave me I hadn't seen since I brought Hazel home soaking wet from the Platt's. She didn't have to say anything. I already felt like the Whore of Babylon.

Maybe my appearance said more than words because I didn't get any questions from anyone at my house. All I wanted to do was get into my bed and sleep for a week. Mama had supper waiting for me, but the thought of food made my stomach turn. When I reached into my purse for the vial of salve and the pills Mrs. Yother had given me, the piece of paper we'd traded our souls for was right there. I took it out and read it again. It was perfectly legal. All the signatures and dates were clear. As I gently smeared the smelly salve on anything that burned, I wondered if Hazel and I would ever think that piece of paper was worth the price we'd paid.

There was something else I had to do and whenever I woke up that night, I was thinking about it. Mama had to be told. I didn't want her finding out about the marriage from someone else and there was no way we could keep it quiet forever. It had to be done.

Next morning at the breakfast table, I ate slowly so Daddy and Bill would be gone by the time I finished. When she came back from kissing Daddy at the door, she had that look in her eye that told me she knew something was coming. "Otha, hurry up and finish your breakfast. You're not even dressed yet. You're gonna be late and you know Mrs. Yother doesn't like it when you're late."

"We're not very busy right now Mama. It'll be fine. Sit down a minute. There's something I need to tell you." She sat down and looked straight at the wedding ring on my finger. She'd never asked any questions about my engagement ring and I hadn't volunteered anything, but it was a wedding ring she was staring at and she knew it. "Mama, Saturday night in Gadsden—or really it was after midnight so it was yesterday morning—Hazel and I got married." I don't know what I was expecting to see on her face, but what I saw was something I'd never seen before. If I could have, I would have taken back everything I'd said. My getting married had hurt that dear sweet woman who gave birth to me and always told me I was special and pretty. I tried to tell her I was still her little girl and no wedding would change that, but the look on her face never changed. Without saying a word, she turned her head, got up and started clearing away the breakfast dishes. "It's all legal. We had a judge perform the ceremony—just like you and Daddy when you got married. I love her Mama, more than anything in the world. Please be happy for me, Mama." I just wanted her to say something, anything, and when she finally did, her words cut me to the bone.

"My mother was at my wedding."

Chapter Fourteen
Life and Death in Your Hands

We survived our visit to the den of iniquity more or less sane and in one piece. I went to work as if nothing had happened and neither Mrs. Yother nor Ruby ever mentioned that Sunday afternoon emergency visit. It was her core belief that it wasn't ours to judge, but only to treat those we could. Hazel and I had been her patients that afternoon. She surely guessed what had happened and Ruby either didn't have any idea or she thought of us as patients too. For the next three days Hazel came to Mrs. Yother's and I douched her vagina for her. By the last treatment, the swelled tissues had mostly gone down and the redness had been replaced by a healthy pink color. I had recovered as well and we both agreed it was nice to be able to pee again without wanting to scream.

I kept my promise not to ever talk about what happened, but she had broken hers in the truck on the way home from Gadsden that Sunday afternoon. She probably didn't know what she was saying. She'd hoped she wouldn't remember, but she did and so did I. She should have blamed me for everything and it would have been better if she had. Instead, she blamed herself.

"I'm nothing but a whore. You should have left me in that hotel room. How can you ever stand to be seen with me in public?" I thought about answering her but decided it was best to keep my mouth shut and let her talk. "I won't ask you to forgive me, but I will ask you to forget me as soon as we get home. You deserve someone better."

"Don't forget whose idea this was from the beginning. If it hadn't been for my stupid plans, none of this would have happened."

"If it hadn't been for your plans, we wouldn't be married either."

I wasn't exactly sure what she meant by that and I couldn't tell by the flat tone of her voice.

***

After her treatments at Mrs. Yother's were finished, it was a month before I saw Hazel again. When I walked to her house, her mother told me she was either sleeping with the baby or that she had gone somewhere with her brother or father. I knew she was home and just avoiding me. She didn't even come to church with the rest of her family. After the fourth time trying to see her, I stopped going to her house. September's always a lonely kind of month and this one was the loneliest of my life.

Mr. and Mrs. Yother left for Evansville early on Thursday morning. The wedding would be that Saturday the twenty-sixth. It would take them most of the day traveling and they wanted to see the town and meet all the new in-laws on Friday. Ruby and I were left in charge, but there wasn't much to be in charge of. There weren't any appointments and no babies were due. It would be a vacation for us and we had the truck if we wanted to go anywhere. I was to stay at the Yothers' in case there was an emergency and I had Ruby and baby Roosevelt to keep me company.

"Maybe I'd rather have a girlfriend than a boyfriend," Ruby announced at supper that first night. "Looks to me like you and Hazel are awfully happy together. All a man's good for is making babies anyway, and don't get me wrong now, I love the one I got, but I sure don't want no more. I've got me a good job and that's what colored women want most in a man, so I don't figure I'll have much trouble finding a good-looking woman once word gets around I'm convertin'. Maybe it runs in my family. My mama's sister and my daddy's sister have lived together for as long as I can remember and now I'm wondering if maybe they ain't a little curious. When I was little, I used to spend the night at their house and I know they slept in the same bed, 'cause often as not, I woke up in bed with them, especially if it was stormin' outside. Problem is—I ain't too sure what to do with a woman. I ain't even sure what you do with a man other than let him do what he wants, and I never got too much out of that. I've seen you and Hazel kiss plenty of times and it looks real nice, but is that all there is to it?"

"There's a whole lot more to it Ruby and you'll find out for yourself." The grin on my face brought on a slew of questions I didn't want to answer, but it was Ruby and she wouldn't let me go until I answered some of them—and she had made us a fine supper. All this talk made me miss Hazel even worse and finally I told Ruby the two of us weren't seeing each other anymore.

"That just can't be, Otha May and I won't have it. The two of you are meant for each other. Whatever the problem is, you've got to fix it. I know plenty of married folks that ain't near as happy together as the two of you."

"We are married and I think that might be the problem."

"I knew it. I just knew it. I saw the rings on your fingers first thing when you stopped here on your way home from Gadsden, and then you both had the new bride miseries."

"New bride miseries?"

"Oh, I don't know your fancy doctor's name for it, but I've heard it called that all my life. It's when things get real touchy down there and it hurts to pee. New brides get it if they let their husbands have their way with them too much right after they get married. Colored women use vinegar and warm water just like Mrs. Yother did. Camphorated oil helps with the swelling they say, but I think it's the smell keeping the husband away for a while that does the trick. You and Hazel really get married?"

"Yes we did, by a judge and in front of witnesses. I have the signed marriage license to prove it. We're legally married, but I'm afraid she doesn't love me anymore."

"She's just a new bride. She'll come 'round and figure out how lucky she is soon enough."

I leaned over the table and kissed her on the cheek. "I hope so, Ruby. I miss her so bad I can't stand it sometime."

"Don't you worry yourself for a minute. Hazel, or is she Mrs. St. Clair now—she'll work things out in her mind and the two of you will be together again just like before. So I guess Abigail St. Clair Leeth has a new name too, Abigail St. Clair St. Clair." I had to grin; I hadn't thought of that.

"Don't you ever tell anyone we're married. They'd kick us out of the church for sure and that would kill our folks. I don't care what people have to say about us, but I don't want to make trouble for our families, and Abigail is still a Leeth, unless we can figure some way I can adopt her."

"You and Hazel are patients here and I know Mrs. Yother's rule about keeping things that happen here to ourselves. I like my job and I hope you'll keep me on when…"

"When what?"

"I can't say no more, Otha May. I keep what Mrs. Yother tells me to myself too."

"It's all right, Ruby. I know Mrs. Yother's sick and I'm glad she told you. I don't know what we'll do without her."

"You and Hazel can run this place and I can help."

"That's what she told me she wants, but I can't do it without Hazel."

"I see. So the way I got it figured, for me to keep my job and the place where me and my son live, you and Hazel have to get back together."

"Ruby, don't you go talking to Hazel for me. If she wants to talk to me, she knows where I live and where I work."

"Mrs. St. Clair, I'm a free colored woman with a mind of my own and the new Mrs. St. Clair's a patient here. Maybe I want to see how she and the baby are doing so I can tell Mrs. Yother if she's having any problems. Or if I happen to pass by her house, I might just stop in to be neighborly."

"Would you? I have to hear from her and if she happens to ask about me, tell her I miss her and that I…"

"That you love her and can't live without her."

"You're the best Ruby."

"Just trying to keep my job," she answered with a smile that made me think things might be all right after all.

We kept busy the next morning seeing after the livestock and little Roosevelt. Until then I hadn't realized everything Mr. Yother did around the place. There were goats, cows, horses, and chickens to feed and we had our instruction for all of them. After dinner Ruby asked if I would watch the baby while she tended to a few things that needed tending to. She stumbled around her words until I told her I would be glad to take care of little Roosevelt the entire afternoon if she needed me to. We both knew where she was going, though neither of us wanted to come right out and say it.

Supper was almost done when she returned, and I had to bite my tongue all through our meal to keep from asking her how Hazel was. She deliberately tortured me talking about nothing in particular until she stood up to clear the table. She walked around me then stopped, leaned over and whispered in my ear. "She misses you too."

A pounding on the front door kept me from asking any questions. It wasn't completely dark outside, and I could make out the figure of a lone woman through the window, but not her face. When I opened the door, she fell into my arms begging me to help her. I didn't know every colored woman in the surrounding communities, but I knew most of the families, so when Ruby called her by name, I knew who she was or at least who she was related to. "Mrs. Webster, what kind of shape have you got yourself in?"

"The pains come on me quick, Ruby. I didn't know what to do. Everybody's pulling corn somewhere over in Marshall County and they don't get home 'til late. I've been staying home to fix supper for the last week. The baby's not due 'til the middle of next month so I thought I'd be fine staying by myself. I left Cecil a note and started walking an hour ago. Thank the Good Lord Mr. and Mrs. Platt picked me up and brought me here. I would never have made it. The pains are coming every few minutes now and they're getting worse." Ruby and I held her up and started toward the examination room.

"Do you have any other children, Mrs. Webster?"

"Two grown boys; didn't think I could have no more." The pain that came before we could get her back to the examination room made her double over. Mrs. Webster was a big woman and it took all of us to get her up on the table after Ruby helped her undress. I stayed calm on the outside after doing my initial examination, but inside I knew my patient was in a lot of trouble. The baby was breech and had already started down the birth canal. It was too late to try and turn it. What would Mrs. Yother do? She'd give her a shot of morphine and do a Cesarean—simple as that—except I'd only ever seen one done and at the time I was busy helping with everything else that had to be taken care of. I made my decision.

"Ruby if you're not doing anything right now, would you walk down to the Leeths' and ask Hazel to come and sit with us for a while? It's been ages since I've seen her, and I've got something for you to take to her mama. I'll be right back, Mrs. Webster." Ruby looked at me like I was crazy, but I motioned for her to follow me out of the examination room, then I walked with her to the front door to make sure I was out of earshot of Mrs. Webster.

"You run like you've never run before, Ruby. Mrs. Webster's in trouble. Tell Hazel I need her here right now. Don't ask me any questions. The two of you come back in her daddy's truck; it'll be faster. Now go." On the way back to the examination room, I wished I'd taught Ruby how to drive when she asked me to back in the spring.

"All right Mrs. Webster, I'm going to give you a little shot now to help with the pain. Try not to push. We'll take good care of you."

"Where's Mrs. Yother?"

"She's at her son's wedding up in Evansville, Indiana, but don't you worry, she's taught me everything there is to know about delivering babies." I was surprised at how calm my voice was; something I'd learned from Mrs. Yother without realizing it. The morphine took effect as soon as I got it injected. I added a little more to make sure she would be in no pain for at least an hour. When Hazel and Ruby arrived, I was waiting on the front porch for them. It was good to see her again, but there was no time for private words between us.

"Mrs. Webster's in the examination room. Her baby's breech and already too far down to turn. We have to get her to a hospital right now or they'll both die."

"I'm here, Otha May; just tell me what to do."

"Ruby, strip one of the beds and put the quilts in the back of the truck. Hazel, you can drive and I'll ride in the back with Mrs. Webster. I've already given her morphine to delay labor, but that won't work for long. She'll deliver that baby or die trying."

It took all three of us to carry Mrs. Webster out and load her into the bed of the Yother's truck. I left instructions with Ruby that if Mr. Webster showed up to tell him what had happened as best she could and that we were doing everything possible for her and the baby. *The mother is our patient, Miss St. Clair… Can you cut a dead woman's belly open and deliver a live baby, then walk out of the room with that baby, hand it to its father and tell him his wife's dead?* Mrs. Yother's words came back to me all the way to the Holy Name of Jesus Catholic Hospital in Gadsden. Mrs. Yother hated hospitals, but she hated this one a little less. With all the wind, the chloroform kept evaporating off the gauze I held over Mrs. Webster's face and by the time we made the city limits, the bottle was empty. The morphine was wearing off too and that meant the urge for her to push with every contraction would be coming back. There was no doubt in my mind that the baby was dead. Too many things can go wrong in a breech birth and I'd studied all of them for my examination.

Mrs. Webster was screaming at the top of her lungs and I tried my best to tell her where we were when Hazel pulled into the brightly lit emergency room entrance, though she wasn't paying any attention to me. Hazel jumped out of the truck and in no time had a nurse and two men with a gurney running toward us. Mrs. Webster's knees were in the air and I was sitting between her legs; the baby was coming and there was no time to move her. Her vagina was pouring blood and I could feel a foot when I tried to do an examination. If I could find the other one, I could help her deliver the baby. The nurse climbed into the truck bed and between screams from Mrs. Webster, I told her what I knew while still feeling for the other foot. "The baby's breech and she's already effaced. I can feel one foot, but not the other."

She ordered one of the men to find the doctor on duty and bring him to us. "Tell him to hurry; there's a pregnant woman about to deliver at the emergency room entrance." She wasn't as calm as Mrs. Yother would have been. "You wait until the doctor gets here. He'll know what to do." Well, I could wait, but Mrs. Webster couldn't. I felt the other foot push down into the birth canal just as a strong contraction started. Could the baby be alive, or was I imagining things. That contraction was enough to cause her to lose consciousness, or maybe it was the blood loss. Holding my breath and without stopping, I pulled the baby out. *Can you hold a baby as it takes its first and last breath?* Mrs. Yother was in my head as I brought the blood covered baby to my chest. There was one rattling breath. I prayed. Another breath and I was screaming at Hazel for the pocket knife she always carried in her purse. I cut the cord and wrapped it around my finger, climbed out of the truck bed and ran into the doctor as he was coming out the emergency room door. He didn't say a word but pointed in the direction I should go. Two nurses ran in front of me opening doors until I was in an operating room.

"Run some cold water in that sink," I ordered. I wasn't sure the baby was still breathing until I dunked it head-first under the flood of water coming from the oversized faucet. Tears streamed down my face when I felt a shiver run through the tiny body in my hands. "Now, warm water, warm water." There was life in the tiny eyes that looked up at me when I lowered the baby into the filling sink. I watched as the little chest heaved, and lungs filled with air. It might have been a scream of terror for someone so new to the world, but for everyone in that room, it was life itself. One of the nurses unwrapped my finger from the umbilical cord and did a proper cutting and tying. It was only then that I noticed the new baby was a girl.

My patient was Mrs. Webster and I had to get back to her, so I left the baby with the nurses and ran back to the truck. I'd only been gone a few minutes and the doctor was in the bed of the truck yelling instruction to the nurse there beside him. "I've stopped the bleeding, but we have to get her inside now. She needs blood and lots of it. Mrs. Webster was still unconscious when she was wheeled into the operating room next to the one her baby was in.

"They'll take good care of her, Otha May," Hazel whispered.

"No, she's my patient. I should be in there with her to tell her she has to live, that her baby's alive."

"You've done all you can possibly do for her and the baby. Be still a minute and…"

She was about to kiss me when a smiling nurse I hadn't seen before stepped around the corner. "There are showers down the hall and we have clean uniforms you can change into. My name's Amelia and just let me know if there's anything else you need. The two of you look like you've had a rough night."

Hazel and I were out of our clothes and under the shower before Amelia finished explaining where we would find the uniforms. It was a very tired, very naked kiss we shared as the warm water washed away the blood and tears. Neither of us cared that we had an audience. I needed to touch something real. The last hour and a half had been worse than any bad dream.

The uniforms didn't fit very well, but they were clean and when Amelia found us wandering around in the emergency room area she showed us to the nurses' lounge. "You can wait in here and I'll go and see how they're doing with the lady you brought in. Doctor Barnes is the best emergency room doctor in the area and if anyone can help her, he can."

"Thank you. My name's Otha May and this is Hazel. I'm Mrs. Yother's assistant—she's a midwife about thirty miles out in the county. We weren't expecting any deliveries and she's away at her son's wedding. I didn't know what else to do but bring Mrs. Webster here. I've passed the midwife examination and I'll be getting my license a little over a year from now, but I've only ever seen one Cesarean delivery and I was afraid I couldn't do it myself."

"You did the right thing. If something had happened to either the mother or the baby, you might never get your license. I've heard Mrs. Yother's name mentioned around here—she sounds good, but even if she'd been at home, she would probably have wanted to bring Mrs. Webster in. You saved the baby's life and maybe hers too."

Another nurse stuck her head in the door of the lounge and asked if one of us was Otha May St. Clair. "You have a phone call at the desk. A woman named Yother wants to talk to you." How had she tracked us down?

Mrs. Yother had called home and Ruby told her what had happened and where we were. I was afraid she would be upset with me for not taking care of Mrs. Webster myself and I was crying before I got to the phone. "Miss St. Clair get hold of yourself this minute. You can cry when you get home. How is Mrs. Webster? I assume she's doing well or she has died, otherwise you would be with her and too busy to talk to me. Were you able to save the baby?" I gave her the bare facts—that I had panicked and that Mrs. Webster was probably dead already. There was no other way of putting it.

"I delivered the baby in the back of the Leeth's truck after we got here. She's alive and I think she'll make it. They took Mrs. Webster and I haven't heard any news. She's dead; she has to be. With all the blood she lost, she can't possibly still be alive. I'm so sorry, Mrs. Yother. I didn't know what else to do." Then I started crying again.

"Stop crying, Miss St. Clair; that's my fault, not yours. I should have trained you better in Cesarean deliveries. You reacted as you saw fit and that's all any of us can do. Now, get me a nurse on the phone and you stand right there while I talk to her. Mrs. Webster's your patient and you should be with her." I handed the phone to the nurse at the desk. She hardly spoke and when she hung up she looked as if she'd been talking to her mother.

"Come with me."

I followed her into a small room with surgical gowns hanging in rows along a wall.

"Find something that fits you. When you're dressed, go through that door into the operating room. Stand in the back, don't say a word, and if Doctor Barnes asks you to leave; you leave. The nurses won't know or care who you are." And with that, she left and closed the door behind her. The gown and mask were new to me, but I knew enough to scrub up and put on a pair of gloves. I opened the door carefully and stood in the back. It was like watching a play or something. Everyone knew what to do and the doctor spoke in a low voice, giving orders that I only understood a little of.

She was alive.

Chapter Fifteen
The War Comes Home

Hazel never mentioned our month-long separation and neither did I. It was an understood thing between us that no explanation would ever be needed or asked for. We loved each other, and we were glad to be married; that was enough. Mrs. Yother never did talk much about Elton's wedding either. I got the feeling she and Mr. Yother weren't exactly treated as equals by Colonel and Mrs. Archibald Spradley. Elton was roped and there was no way in Hell he would ever be moving back to DeKalb County Alabama. I liked Elizabeth, but she grew up with money and she was used to being treated like a princess by her parents. She wouldn't get that from Mrs. Yother or anyone else around here.

Bill would be twenty-one in December and he'd finally convinced Mama and Daddy to sign so he could join the Navy before being drafted. James wanted to quit school so he could join with Bill and he worried the Leeths so much they finally agreed. At least with them joining, they had some choice, and the Navy was better than the Army. It was noon Thursday, November 12, the day after Armistice Day, when we said goodbye to them at the Gadsden train depot and everybody we knew was there to see them off. Mama and Mrs. Leeth cried and I think I saw a tear roll down Daddy's cheek too. When I was little, he would take all of us into town to the Armistice Day parade, but for years, even before the war, there hadn't been one. Old soldiers die off and the young ones don't know anything about war, or that's what Mrs. Yother said when I asked her about it. Lots of parents were at the station seeing their sons off too and I wondered how many of their boys wouldn't be coming home. Hazel noticed that it was a good thing they weren't leaving the next day. It would've been a Friday the 13th.

Bill promised to send us a postcard from San Diego when they arrived. It would take them three days by train. He'd never even been out of Alabama and now he was on his way to who knows where—maybe on a ship. In his life he'd never been on a boat that held more than three men with fishing poles. I should have been worried about his joining up, but I knew if he didn't join, they'd get him all the same. It was something no one could do anything about. Daddy said he knew men with sons who had gotten their boys deferred by saying their jobs were important for the war effort. He could probably have said that about Bill with him working at the Goodyear plant, but he never told Mama. He said that those healthy boys who got the deferment would always be looked down on for not joining and no son of his would ever be looked down on.

Mrs. Webster had a long hospital stay, but she and baby Georgia survived and recovered. On her first check-up visit to us, Mrs. Webster brought her husband with her. That was unusual, for the husband to come along, but I soon found out why. After the examination, he had me come out with him to his truck. The young calf he brought with him was payment for all we'd done for his wife and daughter. I tried to convince him to take it back home, but he was determined. "Joseph Webster pays his bills, Miss St. Clair, and if this ain't enough, they'll be more coming. If it hadn't been for you and Miss Leeth, I could have lost everything I love in this world. I don't have no money to pay you with, but I'd appreciate it if you'd take this calf. She's a Guernsey from good stock and she'll make a fine milk cow I know. We've got six of them at home and Mrs. Webster milks them every day. Sometimes she makes more money from milk and butter than I do working in the fields."

"This is more than payment enough, Mr. Webster. She'll be the beginning of our herd and her milk will feed lots of babies and us for years to come." We shook hands and I knew Hazel and I had a friend in the future. After our last appointment of the day, I led the calf to Hazel's to show her.

"Your husband—or wife—has been busy today, Mrs. St. Clair. Mrs. Yother says we can keep her in their pasture. Isn't she beautiful?" We had decided we'd both be Mrs. St. Clair since the marriage license had listed me as the groom to be. I liked that arrangement and declared that when we had our own mailbox, it would say "Mrs. and Mrs. St. Clair".

"I'd say she's the best-looking heifer I've ever seen, Mrs. St. Clair." I loved it when she called me that. "We have to name her. When I was little, Mama used to read me a story that had a cow named Sue in it. How's that for a name?" So the first cow in our herd had a name, and it wasn't the name of anyone we knew in the community. You didn't name cows mostly, but if you did, you never gave them the same name as somebody you knew.

The next morning, Ruby told me we had a new patient coming in, a Mrs. Wade. Every day was different. She wasn't pregnant, but she had some problems she hoped we could help with. Mrs. Yother mentioned that her new husband, who was in the Army, had been home on leave from Camp Polk in Louisiana a month earlier. I suspected what Ruby had called the new bride miseries. Mrs. Wade turned out to be Leona Bradley back when I knew her. She was a year older than me and one of those girls who didn't mind practice kissing when we were in school at High Point. She and her family moved out of the community when I was in eighth grade and I didn't see her again until high school. The Bradley family was poor even by our thinking and Leona dropped out of school in the eleventh grade. I lost track of her, but we recognized each other as soon as I opened the door at Mrs. Yother's and we had to hug before walking back to the office. I didn't even know she'd gotten married.

"Otha May St. Clair—I was hoping I'd see a familiar face today. You're as pretty as ever. Are you working with Mrs. Yother now?"

"I don't just work here; Mrs. Yother's been training me and as soon as I turn twenty-one, I'll be able to get my midwife license. I've already passed the examination up at Vanderbilt."

"I always knew you'd amount to something; that is if you didn't find somebody as curious as you and run off with her."

"Didn't have to run off; her name is Hazel and she lives right here in the community. She's the love of my life and don't tell anyone, but we even found a judge in Gadsden to marry us. We've been married almost three months now."

"If it was anybody but you, I wouldn't believe it. She's a lucky girl and I bet you're still the prettiest girl in the county."

"Where're you living now, Leona?"

"I'm living with Jacob's family down in Reece City while he's in the Army. They only have one other child at home—a girl, Ester. She's a junior in high school and we've become real close friends. They had plenty of room and I couldn't stay at home. Mama and Daddy have enough to worry about with four kids still to feed. Mrs. Wade seems to like me, and I help out with whatever needs doing."

"Well it's really good to see you again, but I have to ask why you came all the way here when you could have gone to a doctor in Gadsden."

"Mrs. Yother's a female doctor and I have a female problem I couldn't bear telling a man about, so last week I called her from Fant's grocery store and made an appointment. I didn't tell Mrs. Wade about it. She thinks I borrowed their truck to…"

"I thought the two of you might know each other," Mrs. Yother said with a smile as she opened the office door.

"Yes Ma'am. Otha May and I went to school together, but we haven't seen each other in years."

"Well, Mrs. Wade, tell us what brings you in today." The socializing part was over.

"Like I told you last week, I have a problem down between my legs. It itches, and I feel this burning when I pee. Lately I've noticed some kind of yellow smelly stuff in my panties every night. And I don't know if this has anything to do with it, but I've been having some aching pains down there that won't go away. My last period was a week ago, so I don't think I'm pregnant. I just don't know what's wrong."

I took down all her information while they talked and put my notes in the folder Ruby had already prepared. From everything Leona said, it didn't sound much like the new bride miseries to me.

"Miss St. Clair will help you undress and then we'll have a look. I'm sure we can find out what's wrong and fix you right up, Mrs. Wade." I'd long since gotten used to her changing the way she talked to fit the patient. I could do it too, but it didn't come as natural for me.

With that, Mrs. Yother led us out of the office and opened the door to the examination room. Leona walked in and I started to follow her, but Mrs. Yother pulled me back for a second and spoke to me in a whisper. "Regardless of what you see, Miss St. Clair; don't say a word to Mrs. Wade. There's no reason to alarm her." There was no time to ask any questions, so I put a smile back on my face and walked into the examination room.

Leona talked as I helped her undress. It was a nervous kind of talk about nothing and I could tell she was uneasy; not so much about me though. Without saying anything, I noticed the yellow stain in her panties while the two of us kept up the conversation about people we once knew. "All right Leona, you're ready. There's not much to the examination, but I want you to know what we're going to do before we do it."

"Will it hurt?"

"I can promise it won't hurt. It might not be the most comfortable thing in the world, but it won't hurt. First, I'll have a general look at you to see that everything's where it's supposed to be and then I'll take your height, weight and temperature. When I examine your breasts for any lumps or discharge, I'll have to squeeze them pretty hard and I apologize for that."

"No harder than Jacob has, I bet. Sometimes I think he believes they're there just for him to play with." The bright red flush in her face told me she wished she hadn't said that.

"And then you'll lie down on the most uncomfortable table in the world and put your feet in stirrups with your legs spread wide apart so I can have a look. I'll insert these two fingers into your vagina to examine things inside." Then I thought of something else I should probably tell her—just in case. "Mrs. Yother might want a closer look for herself, and if she does, I'll insert a thin metal tube-like thing called a speculum that we can adjust so your vagina is open enough for her to see inside. That won't be very comfortable either, but it won't hurt. Everything will be slippery, and I'll warm all the instruments first. That's all there is to it."

Mrs. Yother had a smile on her face as always and talked continuously in her best southern accent while taking notes as I did my usual look-over of a new patient. Everything appeared perfectly normal. Her skin was smooth, and her posture was good. There were no lumps in her breasts and I ignored earlier memories that went through my head as soon as I touched them. When I got her into the stirrups, things changed. Her vulva was red and a tiny thread of yellowish mucous trailed from it. I'd never seen anything like it and I stopped dictating to Mrs. Yother for a few seconds. When I turned around, she was opening a new box of surgical gloves. Without saying a word, she slipped a pair on my hands. We always scrubbed our hands thoroughly, but we never wore gloves. I then helped her put a pair on her hands.

"Continue Miss St. Clair."

I stumbled as I tried to describe what I was looking at. She came over and had a look for herself, returned to her chair and continued writing. The smile was gone, but Leona couldn't see that. Her cervix felt bumpy and when I described it, Mrs. Yother took over. I sat and took notes while she continued the examination. "Miss St. Clair, would you warm the Hartz speculum for me and fetch the flashlight. I want to have a closer look."

"What is it? What's wrong?" There was a tremble in Leona's voice.

"I don't know just yet, Mrs. Wade, but I'd say you have an infection of some sort. I want to have a closer look and I'll take a swab sample of what I see. We'll find out for sure what it is later. Whatever it is, we can treat it; don't you worry a bit."

I coated the warmed speculum with K-Y and watched as it slipped easily inside Leona's vagina. With a squeeze of the device's handle, her vagina was spread open wide enough to have a look inside. Mrs. Yother took the flashlight and it was several minutes with no one talking before she handed the light to me. Her cervix was covered in white splotches. I hadn't seen anything like that even in Mrs. Yother's medical books.

"Miss St. Clair, please bring me a new one hundred milliliter test tube and a long swab from a new package." I watched as she swabbed Leona's cervix with two swabs, broke the wood parts off, placed everything in the test tube and put a new rubber stopper in the end. "You can remove the speculum now and help Mrs. Wade get dressed. We're finished."

I was shaking a little as I helped her dress, though I tried not to let it show. Something was very wrong, but there was no hint of it in Mrs. Yother's voice while she talked to Leona after the examination. "Can you come back tomorrow afternoon, Mrs. Wade. We should have the results by then and we'll know how best to treat your problem. Don't you worry; these things come from nowhere and we know how to take care of them. You'll be fine." I walked Leona to the door and tried to make small talk on the way. She was in tears as she hugged me on the porch.

"I'm scared Otha May. What if it's something bad? What if I can't ever have children? What am I going to tell Jacob?"

"Now Leona, don't go worrying yourself over nothing. Mrs. Yother is the smartest woman in the state when it comes to female problems and if she says we can fix you, we can. Come back tomorrow afternoon and we'll know what needs to be done. Jacob doesn't need to hear about any of this. It would just worry him for no reason and by the time he gets your letter, you'll be well anyway. Now go home and think up a reason why you need to borrow the truck again tomorrow."

"Thank you Otha May. I don't know what I would've done without you." The little kiss she gave me on my cheek was thanks enough.

When I went back inside, Mrs. Yother had her coat on. "Let's go Miss St. Clair. We have to get this sample to the lab at Holy Name right now." She handed me a gallon jug that felt heavy. "Wrap the test tube and this gallon of warm water in a couple of towels. It's a bacterial infection and we have to keep the bacteria alive until we can get it tested. I know what it is, but I want it tested to be sure." I recognized the tone of her voice and knew not to ask questions at the moment. We were within a mile of the hospital when I got up my courage.

"You said you knew what it was. What is it? Her cervix looked terrible. Is she going to be okay?"

"It's gonorrhea, Miss St. Clair. The Gram test will tell us for sure. That son of a bitch husband of hers was screwing whores in Louisiana while he was stationed there. The Army doctors will take care of him, but we have to take care of Mrs. Wade. I knew this would come to us sooner or later. Men just can't keep their pricks in their pants when there's a willing woman anywhere around, and there's always plenty of them around Army bases."

I'd never heard Mrs. Yother talk like that before and the closer we got to the hospital, the madder she got. "I ought to just tell Mrs. Wade what her husband's been doing. It would serve him right if she left him. If he were here, I'd castrate him myself."

I learned a lot about venereal diseases in that last mile and she told me there was a whole book she wanted me to read. She hadn't given it to me before because she thought my brain was full enough with all the preparation I'd gone through getting ready for my examination at Vanderbilt. I knew some of the names of the diseases, but that was about it. "It's time you learned the ugly side of what we do, Miss St. Clair. It's not all about delivering healthy babies to grateful parents. Sometimes we have to deal with human weaknesses and it's never pleasant."

We were lucky that Amelia was working that evening. She took us straight back to the lab and I got to watch while the technician did the test. I introduced her to Mrs. Yother as we walked. "I could have guessed who you are, Mrs. Yother. The hospital's administrator, Doctor Cash has told the entire staff about you and that you are to be given full hospital privileges whenever you come in."

"Did Lowell also tell you what a bitch I can be?"

"Only when someone gets in your way, Mrs. Yother, and he advised us against it."

The bright purple color on the microscope slide left no doubt that Mrs. Yother had been right.

"We've had a lot of new cases since the war started," Amelia said when we left the lab. "I can give you enough Sulfathiazol to treat this case and I'd give you more but it's hard to get. The Army takes about all that's made."

"Can you also spare some crystal violet and Safranin or Carbol Fuchsin? I'd like to be able to do this test myself without bothering everyone here."

"That we have plenty of."

"How do you know the Holy Name's administrator?" I asked on the way home.

"Lowell Cash and I went to school at Vanderbilt together. We were in a lot of the same classes and it drove him crazy whenever I got a higher test score than him. That didn't happen very often though. He's a brilliant doctor— and they've turned him into a worthless administrator; what a waste. Now, Miss St. Clair, your patient will be coming in tomorrow afternoon to find out the results of the test. What are you going to tell her?"

"Me?"

"Yes, Miss St. Clair; from now on all our patients are yours and I'm your assistant. It's one thing to train a woman to be a midwife and quite another to teach her how to run things on her own. You'll have to do that soon enough and I want to make sure you can handle it." I didn't like it when she talked like that. I couldn't imagine being without her to look over my shoulder. "Now, what are you going to tell Mrs. Wade?"

"I'm going to tell her she has a bacterial infection and that we have the medicine to treat it. We do, don't we? If she asks me how she got it, I'll tell her it's an infection that comes and goes and that it's making a comeback now. She won't ask any other questions. If she does, I'll lie. That lie won't be a health risk to her because I'm going to write her husband a letter tomorrow and tell him exactly what's happened and that if he doesn't get himself treated, I'll tell Leona everything."

"It's too dark for you to see me smiling Miss St. Clair, but be assured I am—and how are you going to get his address?"

"He's at Camp Polk. The Army'll get my letter to him."

"You're a devious woman after my own heart, Miss St. Clair."

The medicine worked well and in two weeks, Leona's symptoms disappeared. On her last visit, she asked the questions I'd been dreading.

"Do you think Jacob could have gotten it from me when he was home on leave? In his last letter he said he wasn't feeling well. That would be terrible. Should I write him and tell him that if he's still sick, he should tell the doctor it's a bacterial infection?"

"I can guarantee he didn't get it from you Leona and Army doctors take good care of our soldiers." I'd already mailed the letter.

***

Bill and James made it safely to San Diego and we got a letter from them every week while they were in basic training. Daddy said they had to write home at least once a week; that they were obligated to. I worried about my brother even though he wasn't in much danger of being killed by the Japs or Krauts in San Diego. I worried about what he would do if there were loose women around the base, and whatever Bill did, James would have to do too. Neither of them had ever had a real girlfriend and the only girl Bill had seen naked was Cousin Rosa, and I wasn't even sure he'd seen her. If he got some disease while still in training, the Navy might send him home and that would kill Mama and Daddy. Even though Hazel and I talked about everything else, she knew there were things about my job I couldn't talk about. Besides, there was no reason to worry her about some disease James might catch. The only person I could talk to about such things was Mrs. Yother and someday I wouldn't have her. It hurt my soul to think about her being gone.

***

It was cold, dark and rainy that last Sunday in November. The day looked like I felt while getting ready for church that morning, but I was going to have dinner with Hazel and her family after the service and that would be nice. Everybody had surely noticed our wedding bands we'd been wearing for two months, but only Glenda mentioned it and she waited until we were doing the dishes while Hazel fed Abigail. It was sort of a tradition for Glenda and me to do the dishes when I had dinner or supper at their house. I didn't mind helping and it gave the two of us a chance to talk. She'd just turned thirteen back during the early summer and was just as pretty as her sister.

"I wish I could have been at the wedding." Hazel had already told me she'd told Glenda, so what she said didn't come as a surprise. "I bet it was wonderful."

"It was just a simple ceremony in front of a judge; not much to see."

"But it's all legal, right?"

"It's as legal as any other marriage, but I doubt anyone around here would say we were properly married."

"Well, I don't care what anyone says, I have a new sister. Hazel says you're Mrs. and Mrs. St. Clair now, but I say it's not official until I get to kiss the bride. I've already kissed Hazel, but she's my sister and that doesn't count."

"Then I guess we'd better make it official." I shouldn't have done it, but I turned, took her face in my hands and kissed her square on the lips; nothing Hazel would have objected to. Maybe she was a little surprised, but she didn't back away and when our lips parted, I caught a little smile on her face.

"I guess now if anyone asks me I'll have to say that I have been kissed before, and I might just say it was a girl that kissed me too. I'm so glad you're my new sister, Otha May. I hope you and Hazel will always be happy together."

Hazel walked into the kitchen at the end of that conversation—with little Abigail still firmly attached to one of her nipples. "What's this, Mrs. St. Clair? You've only been married two months and you're already looking for a younger woman?"

"Mama and Daddy know too," Glenda said in a whisper. "Mama noticed the ring and asked me. I'm sorry, but I couldn't lie to her and people at church are talking as well. I hope they don't cause trouble."

"Did you know that Mrs. Yother's mother-in-law, Grandma Yother, got kicked out of the High Point Baptist Church for holding dances in her house?" I'd never told anyone that story, but I didn't think Mrs. Yother would mind if I repeated what she'd told me. "It's true. She had three daughters and made it known that she would rather have her daughters dancing in her living room than doing who knows what somewhere else. The deacons and pastor sent her a letter saying that if she didn't stop having the dances, she would no longer receive the fellowship of the church, which was their way of saying she was going to be kicked out. She sent them a letter inviting them to the next dance. They kicked her out and it was twenty years before she set foot in that church again—but she and her husband are both buried in the cemetery."

That was the first time Glenda saw us kiss. "And if they want to kick us out," Hazel added when she caught her breath, "they can, but they'll have to have someone with a gun at the church door keeping us from being in our pew every Sunday and I don't think anyone would want to see that happen. Anyway, what's all this talk about things that could happen? I want to talk about something that's definitely going to happen a week from next Tuesday. It's somebody's twentieth birthday, her graduation from being a teenager, and I know two sisters who have something planned for the Saturday after." I hadn't done anything for Hazel's birthday back in July, except I did help Mrs. Leeth make her cake. Birthdays were never a big event in our community unless it was your first or eightieth, but we did always have a cake even after they started rationing sugar. They were syrup cakes, but they were good. "I can't take credit for this. It was all my baby sister's idea, but when I heard what she was planning, I thought it was perfect."

"You see, Otha May," Glenda explained with a smile, "it's not really a birthday party for you. It's a bridal shower for both of you. It was my idea to call it a birthday party and that's what some of the invitations say, but those that were sent to girls you know say bridal shower. I was going to reserve the High Point Community Center for it, but when Hazel told Mrs. Yother what we had in mind, she insisted on having it at her house. Your mother knows, and she helped with the names and addresses. She and Mama are making three cakes—enough to feed everybody. It'll be the biggest all-girls party ever seen around here."

There was no holding back the tears. A gloomy discouraging sort of day had been turned upside down in a few minutes. "I don't know what to say. You two are the best wife and sister in the world and if this don't get us all run out of the church and community, I don't know what would. I love you both more than you'll ever imagine." I also thought that maybe Mama had forgiven me a little for not inviting her to our wedding.

Mrs. Yother outdid herself for that shower. We had fifteen women and girls show up and Denise Rowell came all the way from Glencoe. I hadn't seen her since ninth grade, though I surely remembered the kisses we'd shared, and at the time they hadn't seemed like she was just practicing on me. Mama and Mrs. Leeth had no idea their daughters were so well liked. I almost cried when every single baby I'd helped deliver was introduced to us by their mothers.

"When I got that invitation, I told Mr. Webster that little Otha Jean and I were coming if I had to walk every step of the way." Mrs. Webster had completely recovered from the scariest birth I'd ever been a part of and by some miracle, the baby was healthy. She had told me when she came for her first checkup after getting out of the hospital that her husband didn't much care for the name. He said it wasn't very fitting for a colored baby, but Mrs. Webster wouldn't have it any other way. Two babies at the shower had been named after me; one white and one colored. Little Dora May Watts wasn't so little anymore. It was hard for me to imagine it had been a year already. It was like a reunion with every girl there I'd ever been good friends with and some I'd only met since starting with Mrs. Yother. Mama and Mrs. Leeth had invited a few of their friends from church and Glenda invited two of her friends from school. Some probably wondered what a bridal shower for two girls would be like and showed up just to find out. A stranger showing up wouldn't have thought it different from any other shower. Everyone had fun and Hazel and I appreciated the gifts, although after the last girl left, I could tell something was bothering her. It was freezing outside as I walked her home.

"When will we ever be able to live together like a real married couple? We went through Hell to get married and now we're still living in two separate houses—with our families. I don't even feel married, Otha May and now this shower has me thinking none of it means anything. When will you come home to our house so I can meet you at the door and kiss you like a proper wife? When are we going to start acting like a married couple? I want Abigail to have a real home and not be dragged from pillar to post. Are we rightly married or not?"

She wasn't the only one who had such thoughts. We hadn't slept in the same bed since our wedding and we were both, as would be said in a polite way, on edge. What we needed was some time together away from work and families. I don't know if Mrs. Yother had a sixth sense about such things, but a week after the shower, she gave me an envelope with a hundred dollars in it, saying it was my Christmas bonus. "This is your money Mrs. St. Clair." She called me Mrs. St. Clair after the shower. "You can spend it any way you choose, but I suggest you buy two train tickets for somewhere south where it's warm. There's nothing like a little warm weather to make a body feel better. Besides, you owe your new bride a honeymoon, don't you?" That thought hadn't crossed my mind. People in our community generally didn't take honeymoons. There was no money for such things and always work to be done, but when I told Hazel about the money and what Mrs. Yother said, I was smothered with kisses and tears. So there would be a honeymoon, the first for anybody in our families, but where would we go?

Chapter Sixteen
Florida

Halfway through their eight weeks of basic training, we got letters from Bill and James saying they were being sent to Fort Pierce in Florida for more training when they were done in San Diego. That would put them a lot closer to home, but still too far away to visit when they got leave. They would have two weeks leave before having to report though and would be home sometime toward the middle of January. Daddy said that Fort Pierce is where the Navy trains men to do underwater demolition. That sounded awfully dangerous, but he said they would be a lot safer under the water than above it. Were they going to blow up submarines? That was the only thing I could imagine the Navy needing underwater demolition men for. As long as Bill and James were together though, whatever they were doing, we wouldn't be as worried about them.

It was a peculiarly warm day when Hazel and I left for Gadsden to do our Christmas shopping. There was a war on, although that didn't keep the town from decorating for the season. It was only a week before Christmas and the stores were pretty bare. According to the salesgirls, all the stores in town were that way long before the holidays. It was hard finding presents for anyone, even babies. I had money, but there wasn't much to buy. By lunchtime we'd bought billfolds for our daddies and hats for our mamas. They never wore hats except on Sundays and it had been forever since they'd had new ones. Sitting in a booth at the BonAire, I noticed our waitress paying particular attention to us. When she brought our hamburgers, she just stood there looking at us.

"I know you. I was at your so-called wedding a few months ago. Judge Henderson married you at his retirement party. My name's Henna O'Dell and I was Thomas's date until the two of you showed up. He left me on the dance floor and ignored me the rest of the evening. I guess he and his brother recognized a couple of girls who would put out for them. We heard all about that night. I'm surprised the two of you would show your faces around here after that, but I guess some girls have no self-respect."

"What we do have Miss O'Dell," Hazel spoke up, "is a legally signed marriage certificate—something you'll never see and by the way, your boyfriend's a wonderful lover. Both boys were, but I guess you wouldn't know anything about that." We took our own sweet time eating our hamburgers and didn't leave her a tip before walking out the door arm in arm.

"Do you really think everybody in town knows?" There was something special about the kiss I gave her in broad daylight on Broad Street, and after that I don't think she worried so much about what we might hear the rest of the day.

We'd already decided that the honeymoon would be our Christmas presents to each other, though we still didn't know where we were going. After finding a few more gifts for the family, we wound up at the train station, across the street from the Printup. "You think our room's vacant this afternoon?" The smile on her face told me what she had in mind. "We can at least have a cup of coffee in the coffee shop, can't we?"

"Yes we can and I hope Mrs. Kroelinger's working today. She likes us, remember?" She didn't remember the name, but sort of knew who I was talking about; the nice lady who had tried to sober us up the day after our wedding. Mrs. Kroelinger was indeed working and wanted to know all about the Judge's party the night before we dragged ourselves into her shop and as long as she kept filling our cups, I kept talking. That day after our wedding I'd felt worse inside and out than I'd ever felt in my life and she'd made things a little better.

At that time of day, we were the only customers in the place and Mrs. Kroelinger wanted to talk. "The two of you look better than the last time I saw you. How's married life? Tell me, is living with another woman any easier than living with a man? I think it has to be." I'd forgotten what all I'd told her that day, but I figured out pretty quick I must have told her everything there was to tell. "Your wedding's the best kept and most widely known secret in the whole city. Hell, I hear that everybody who's anybody was there. Edward Cline, the photographer for *The Gadsden Times*, even got some pictures." Photographer? I didn't remember any pictures. "The judge didn't know about them and if he had, he would've made Edward give him the film. There was only one set of prints made, 8 by 10's, and guess who has them? Edward's my husband's nephew and I made him give them to me." She disappeared back into what looked like an office for a few minutes, then came out and handed me a large envelope. "I told myself I'd give you these if I ever saw you again. Think of it as a late wedding present."

My eyes filled up when I saw the first picture and by the time we got to the last one, we were all three wiping tears. They were perfect. The photographer caught all the best moments and my favorite was the one of us kissing at the end. When I was able to speak, I hugged Mrs. Kroelinger and thanked her for making our Christmas the best ever. Our coffee and apple pie that day was on the house, so I left her a tip that was probably too much, but I didn't care. That woman had turned an already good day into one I would never forget.

Those twelve photographs meant more to us than all the shower gifts put together. Before we left the coffee shop, we picked out two to give to our parents and bought frames for them later at Grants. We thought maybe this would make up some for us not having any of them at the wedding. Glenda especially would like seeing the photographs and I picked out one to give to her. Daddy and I never talked about the wedding, but he didn't object a week later when Mama hung the picture I gave her above the mantle next to the one of Bill in uniform. Hazel declared that the one of us kissing would hang in our bedroom when we got a bedroom.

At the train station, we didn't exactly know how to ask for what we wanted, so I waited until there weren't any people around and walked up to the window. "Suppose two girls had a hundred dollars to spend on round-trip tickets south, somewhere warm, how far could we get?"

"And it has to be where we can walk to the ocean," Hazel yelled from her seat.

"Well, let me see. If you two are looking for someplace really warm, you'll have to wait a month. If you do that, I can get you all the way to Clearwater and back. On a nice day, it'll be in the nineties. Is that warm enough for you?"

"Is that in Florida?"

"Yes Ma'am, halfway down the state; a beautiful place with white sand beaches and it's not terribly expensive, not like Daytona Beach or Miami. My wife and I went there on our honeymoon years ago and she's wanted to go back ever since."

"That's perfect. It'll be our honeymoon too." Those words came out before I thought what I was saying.

"Say, I know you. You're the couple that got married by Judge Henderson at his retirement party, aren't you? My wife and I were there; first time I'd ever seen two women get married. I didn't know such a thing was possible, but it sure looked like a proper wedding to me. The judge married me and Gladys thirty years ago and from what I remember, your wedding wasn't no different." The grin on his face told me there was more coming. "I bet you didn't know there's a special deal for newlyweds taking the train for a honeymoon destination, and Clearwater's one of 'em. You get a first-class ticket for the regular price. That includes a sleeper car, which means you don't have to sit up all night and I'm giving you ten dollars off as a wedding present. We're allowed to do that for honeymooners— company policy."

I don't know if it was a lady-like thing to do, but I leaned over through the ticket window and gave him a kiss. For ninety dollars, we had first class tickets round-trip to Clearwater, Florida, leaving on Friday morning, the 29th of January and we wouldn't be back 'til Friday afternoon February the 12th. That was perfect. We would be home for our brothers' visit on their way to Fort Pierce. To catch the train on the 29th, we could ride with Daddy to work and ride home with him too on the 12th. I hadn't gotten up the nerve to ask to borrow the truck since bringing it home too late for everyone to go to church after my and Hazel's wedding. What we needed was a car of our own.

"Was everybody in town at our wedding?" Hazel whispered as we walked out of the depot.

Every day after our trip to Gadsden was nothing but waiting and getting ready, packing and repacking and then waiting some more. Not even Christmas and New Years and presents took our minds off the honeymoon for very long, but there was one present from Mama and Daddy that was special. Hazel must have told them I needed a watch and wanted a man's size, not one of those tiny women's you can't read. It wasn't a cheap dime store watch either. I knew the name Hamilton. Grandpa St. Clair had a Hamilton pocket watch he left to Daddy and it was his most prized possession. He only carried it to church on Sundays and always found a reason to take it out to look at the time when church was over.

Thinking about our trip was making both of us crazy and that's probably what led to the plan we put together the first Saturday afternoon after Christmas. It was too cold to be out walking, but that's the only time alone we had to talk, so we bundled up and went anyway.

"I'm not going to church tomorrow, Otha May. I feel a terrible cold coming on." She didn't seem sick to me. She wasn't hoarse or sneezing or anything. When I turned to look at her, she was smiling from ear to ear.

"You know, I don't feel so well myself. I think I'd better not go either."

The hour and a half we had together in my bedroom with the curtains drawn tight that Sunday morning was just what the doctor ordered. I thought several times about asking Mama if Hazel could stay overnight at our house sometime, since we were a married couple, but I knew that wouldn't sit well with Daddy. The idea wouldn't have gone over any better at Hazel's, so until we could have a place of our own, we were stuck. There was no mention of our sudden illness or our sudden recovery by anyone but Glenda. Hazel said she was grinning when she asked that afternoon if the two of us felt better.

Every Leeth and St. Clair was waiting at the depot on Saturday afternoon, the 16th of January when Bill and James arrived. They looked like different boys. They were strong and muscular looking, or maybe it was the uniforms. Whatever it was, they looked different and they didn't talk like the young boys we'd said goodbye to at the same depot two months before. They'd grown into young men.

Mama and Mrs. Leeth had been cooking for days and the two sailors said they hadn't eaten in a week just waiting for some good home-cooked food. The way they ate, I believed them. It was like another Thanksgiving supper, complete with pork chops from Mrs. Yother. January was always hog-killing month at their house and anyone who helped got plenty to take home with them.

Hazel and I mostly kept the fire going under the two big cast iron pots. Boiling water-soaked tow sacks loosened the hair on the hogs so it could be scraped off with a sharp knife. Bill usually had that job, but Hazel and I had it to do that year.

After Mama and Daddy went to bed, I had a chance to talk to Bill. I wanted to know how he was really doing and about the war. He wanted to know about me and Hazel. For a while it was like we were both talking to strangers. Mama had written him some about the wedding and after supper she showed him the picture I gave her, so he already knew most of what I had to say. "So I have a sister-in-law now? I knew I'd never have a brother-in-law, but I never expected a sister-in-law." We talked past midnight and I learned something about what we were facing in the war. At first, he talked like he believed the whole thing would be over in months, though the more we talked, the more I was convinced he was only saying things like that to make me feel better. I knew about Guadalcanal from the radio and kept asking him until he told me what he knew. We lost a lot of ships and men, he said, but he believed things had turned in our favor lately.

"The hardest thing for me so far was when Captain Stewart came into our barracks late one night two weeks ago and spoke with my bunkmate, Frankie. I'd never even seen the captain up close and there he was. There was no one with him and we were all asleep. I woke up when I heard talking close by, which ain't allowed after lights-out. I didn't know whether to jump up and salute or pretend to be asleep. The captain sat on the lower bunk and talked to Frankie in a low calm voice, but I could hear what he said. His brother had been killed at Guadalcanal just after Christmas. After the captain left, I heard Frankie crying. Word of what had happened spread through the barracks in minutes. No one came in to yell at us when we went to Frankie's bunk one at a time to say how sorry we were."

Hazel and I had never slept at each other's houses, even though we were properly married, but she did sleep at our house on Thursday night before we left for Florida, and it was Mama's idea. Wednesday afternoon after I got off work, Hazel was at my house waiting for me and after we had a couple of slices of plain cake, Mama told us what she was thinking. "There's no sense in Mrs. Leeth having to get up and make your breakfast and probably waking Mr. Leeth up too. When the husband works second, the wife has to too. I know what I'm talking about." Mr. Leeth had just started working second shift. It paid a nickel more an hour. "You just stay here Hazel. Our couch makes a good bed and you can eat breakfast with us before you leave. You and Otha go collect your things and bring them here. Tell Mrs. Leeth what I said, that there's no sense in her having to get up early tomorrow morning." I was sorry Mr. Leeth was working second, though that meant extra room in the cab of the truck for Hazel and me. I was really sorry too that Mama had mentioned the couch. Later on, I offered to give Hazel my bed, but she wouldn't hear of it.

At Hazel's house, Glenda got a repeat of the instructions for Abigail I'd heard her give a dozen times in the last week. "Don't you worry about a thing," Glenda said for the hundredth time. We can take care of little Abby. She's no trouble. Mama and I have it all worked out. She takes care of her during the day and I see to her at night."

"Call Mrs. Yother as soon as you get there so we'll know you're all right. You two take care of each other," were Mrs. Leeth's final instructions from the front porch.

I told Hazel she could sneak into my room after everyone went to bed. She didn't like the idea after Mama being so nice in letting her stay the night. She was probably right, but I did give her a goodnight kiss before going to bed.

It was freezing cold and raining when we left at dawn. I prayed that wasn't a bad sign. Hazel and I curled up under one of Mama's quilts until the truck's heater started working, and by that time we were almost there. Daddy gave us both a hug and a kiss after I handed the man in uniform at the station our tickets for a double sleeping berth car—with the honeymoon discount. He didn't say anything, but it wasn't because he didn't want to. I knew that look. I figured he didn't even know the right name for what he was thinking about calling us. We waved as the train pulled out and I saw Daddy wipe a tear away. He never talked much and often what he didn't say meant more. He'd always accepted the way I was and just didn't see the point in talking about it. He never talked unless he had something to say he wanted everyone to hear. I was his little girl leaving on her honeymoon, maybe not a normal honeymoon to anybody else, but nobody would ever dare say anything out of turn about his daughter where my daddy could hear them.

We spent most of the day looking out the window. Neither of us had ever been on a train before and there was so much to see. Mama told me they would feed us, and we were treated to meals in the dining car like we would never get at home; you wouldn't think there was a war on. It was like living in a fine restaurant where you could have just about anything you wanted to eat. At supper, we decided to order things we'd never eaten before. The spaghetti with meatballs was good we both decided. Neither of us particularly cared for the ravioli, but we ate it all the same. It was Italian food night, we found out from the nice couple we sat with, and the colored lady serving us said every night the food would be something different. She laughed when I asked if there'd be a Japanese food night. Well, we were at war with them too, just like the Italians. Norman and Linda—those were their names—had taken this train several times and were on their way from Chattanooga to

Savannah to see their daughter and son-in-law and new grandson.

The clicking of the train wheels and the swaying of the cars took some getting used to, especially at night. We had an upper double berth and our nights together on the train were my favorite part of the ride. We didn't dare sleep naked—what if one of us fell out during the night—but that didn't matter, there were still smiles on our faces every morning at breakfast. I guess some people thought that with all the noise from the train, a little more wouldn't be noticed, because that first night the couple below us moaned and groaned like they were the only passengers aboard.

"Do I sound like that?" Hazel whispered after one particularly long, sort of high-pitched squeal from the woman.

"Just like that… maybe. It's been so long, I don't remember."

"Well you're even louder, though I'm too much of a lady to say so."

Hazel was asleep the next morning when I peeked out through our curtains to see who crawled from the berth below us and I made sure we sat with them at breakfast. They had entertained us so well the night before, I had to meet them. Alice and J.C. were newlyweds, just married the day before, and I recognized his uniform as Navy. He'd finished basic training in San Diego and was on his way to Orlando for more. He didn't have leave, but managed to get his train trip routed through Birmingham, close to Alice's hometown. They got married at the depot. It must have been a quick ceremony because we only stopped long enough to take on passengers. They would have two nights together—on a train—and then Alice would ride back home. It didn't seem like much of a honeymoon to me. We asked if he'd run into Bill and James while he was in basic training, but that was too much to hope for with thousands of boys there at the same time.

After breakfast, I told Hazel they were the couple in the berth below ours. "Well, it might be their honeymoon, but judging from what all we heard last night, she's either a mighty quick learner or it wasn't their first time under the covers together. It's hard to believe those sounds came from that sweet girl."

"It's the sweet ones that'll surprise you."

"And I won't ask my wife how she knows that, unless of course she's talking about me."

It wasn't quite daylight when we pulled into Clearwater that Tuesday morning. We would have made better time if it hadn't been for all the stops in every two-horse town along the way. The first thing I noticed was the air; it smelled different. I'd never smelled ocean air before and it had a cleanliness to it that makes you feel good. We pulled our coats off and stuffed them into our bags as soon as we collected them alongside the train. I didn't know if we were supposed to tip the colored porter who fetched them for us after giving him our tickets, but I handed him a dollar anyway. He smiled when he thanked me and wished us a happy honeymoon. *Was he at our wedding too?* Maybe he noticed from our tickets that we had the honeymoon discount and didn't care that we were both girls. Ruby had told me that colored folks didn't bother so much about such things and maybe she was right.

It felt like home in mid-June without the swelter. We had no idea where we were going to stay, but we had money and all day long to find out. In the depot there were brochures advertising all the hotels and I let Hazel pick one. When I asked the man at the ticket counter how to get to the Moritz, he sent for two porters who picked up our bags and asked us to follow them. They got fifty cents apiece. The taxi driver loaded our bags in the trunk of his car and opened our doors for us. I told Hazel I could get used to this kind of treatment. When we started moving, she leaned over and gave me a little kiss.

"My first honeymoon, my first train ride, and my first taxi ride; if I didn't know better Otha May St. Clair, I'd say you were up to something—again." The taxi driver pretended he didn't hear that. I thought three dollars for a fifteen minute ride was too much, even if he did unload our bags and take them into the hotel for us. That was worth a fifty cent tip. We took our own bags up to our room on the third floor. This tipping was getting out of hand. The room was fifteen dollars a night, and that was because I asked for a bath. The man at the desk must have seen the look on my face when he told me how much it was because he said we could have a king-sized bed at no extra charge. I didn't know beds came in but two sizes, singles and doubles.

After having a look at our room, I stopped complaining about how much it was costing us. We even had our own phone. Before I could suggest a bath, Hazel had her clothes off and the water running. Seeing her bent over the tub like that, I had to get a feel. "No you don't; not until we get a bath and wash that train smell out of our hair. Don't put the clothes you have on back in your suitcase either or everything you brought will smell like diesel smoke."

"What would I do without you?"

"The way we smell right now, nobody would have anything to do with either of us."

After nearly an hour in the tub, draining and refilling it twice and washing each other's hair, we felt like ourselves again. With towels around us, we walked out of the bathroom and I went to the window to close the curtains. "Leave them open Otha May. We're three floors up and we're facing the ocean. I don't want to miss a minute of this sunshine."

While sitting cross-legged behind her on the bed combing out her hair, I asked if she wanted to find something to eat. We hadn't gotten breakfast on the train and it was already dinnertime—and I wanted to get my feet wet in the ocean.

"This is our honeymoon and what I want right now is for you to turn back the cover on this wonderful bed that's big enough for four people and show me how much you've missed me."

I might not be the most romantic person at times, but when she turned completely around to face me, reached for my hand and squeezed it, I got the idea. It had been so long since I'd seen her naked and been able to touch her at the same time—it was, I don't know, beginning to feel like a real honeymoon I guess. It's one thing to be naked under the covers at night with the lights out, but it's something else to be sitting naked on a huge bed and able to look into the eyes of the person you're touching, who happens to be just as naked as you are. We could get reacquainted with little details we never got to see in the dark. She pulled my face to hers and the kiss she gave me was enough to stop the war. She was everything in the world to me again. The way she smiled as her areolas scrunched up when I lightly circled them with a single finger, and the way her nipples slowly went from being slightly inverted to stiff little knobs any baby would cry for were things I'd almost forgotten. I caught the drops of milk with my tongue before they had a chance to fall. Looking up from her breasts, the changing expressions on her face, with her eyes closed like that, was enough to make me warm in all the right places. I couldn't resist teasing her a little. "Tell me how much you want me to make love to you right now Mrs. St. Clair. Anything you want, I'll do."

"Anything, Mrs. St. Clair? You might be surprised what I think of late at night all alone in my room without my wife." She pushed me back onto the bed, but instead of crawling on top or rolling over pulling me on top of her, she had something altogether different in mind; something

I'd thought of as well. From being face to face, she turned half way around and threw one leg over me. She wasn't the only one who'd had such thoughts late at night. Everything she did, I did, but we soon figured out we weren't nearly coordinated enough to make things that complicated work right. It was impossible to keep my mind on what I was supposed to be doing when the rest of my body only cared about what she was doing. Hazel must have been having the same problem because it wasn't long before she twisted around and gave me a wet slippery kiss. "I'm sorry Otha May; it seemed like a good idea, but it's harder to do than I thought it would be."

"Someday we'll have all the time in the world to practice, but right now I have a lover who needs something I can help with." I bit her nipple, not too hard, on my way down her stomach and soon I had a very happy wife. An hour later we were sweaty and in need of another bath. I hadn't forgotten about getting a bite to eat either, but then Hazel reminded me of something important we had to do.

"We'd better call Mrs. Yother and let her know we got here okay. Mama will be asking if she's heard from us." She was right about that and after figuring out how to work the telephone to get to the hotel operator, she made the call for me. I wasn't surprised when Mr. Yother answered, but when he told me Mrs. Yother wasn't feeling well and hadn't gotten up yet, I got worried. She was always up at the crack of dawn and had half a day's work done by the time I got there. I could hear it in Mr. Yother's voice that he was more concerned than he let on.

After we ate supper, I convinced Hazel that the weather was warm enough to splash around in the ocean. We waded out in our clothes as far as we could and decided we had to buy swimming suits the next day and do it right. It was almost a full moon and even though there were a few people around, I had to get a kiss on the beach in the moonlight to remember when we got back to freezing

North Alabama. She must have been thinking the same thing because it wasn't just any kiss.

What we knew about swimming suits would fit in a thimble, but the lady at the first shop we went into helped us pick out something. We didn't care much for them. There were no bright colors, of course, and we were warned about getting a white suit wet; that it would be see-through until it dried, even with the sewn in bra. We settled on black and white striped ones that made us look like convicts. At least there was no stiff bra, only an extra layer of black cloth across our breasts. The suits were six dollars each, which I thought was robbery for that tiny amount of cloth and elastic, but we did get a couple of beach towels for free.

After putting our suits on back in the hotel room, we felt more naked than we had trying them on in the shop. "Otha May, we can't just walk out in broad daylight looking like this; we're practically naked. What if someone sees us?"

"Plenty of people are going to see us and let 'em look." It took a few minutes to get her out the door, even with a beach towel wrapped around her. There were lots more people on the beach than when we'd waded the evening before, people of every age and shape imaginable. When Hazel finally decided no one was looking at anyone in particular, she unwrapped the towel. There were some girls as white as we were, and others were dark tanned. We decided we should get a tan to show off when we got home, so we spread our towels out on the sand and stretched out. The sun was hot, but the cool breeze from the ocean felt nice.

"You're gonna fry in a few minutes if you don't get some oil on you." I looked up to see a pretty blonde girl wearing a white two-piece swimming suit standing over us. The little top didn't come close to covering her breasts and I had to force myself not to stare. Her skin was tanned so dark she could almost have passed for colored—except for the hair. "My name's Susan and whenever I see girls as white as you two on the beach, I figure they're from up north and don't know how burned you can get in only half an hour. I have suntan oil if you want to borrow some."

"That's awfully kind of you. I'm Otha May and this is Hazel. We're from North Alabama where it's still freezing cold and we've never been to the beach before. We don't really know what we're doing."

"You sit behind Hazel and I'll sit behind you and we'll get you everyone covered in oil right now." She poured some of the clear oil in my hands and I rubbed it all over Hazel's back while Susan did the same for me. The oil had a nice smell. She said it was coconut oil. I didn't know you could get oil from a coconut, but it smelled good enough to eat. "Okay, now down and on your stomachs. It's the backs of the legs that burn the fastest it seems like, but it's probably because everyone forgets to oil that part." She wasn't shy about making sure everything got covered and when her hands went up my thighs, I probably jumped a little. I know Hazel did.

After being oiled from head to foot, we sat in a little circle and talked. "Are your husbands on the beach too? They should get some oil on as well. Even though most men think they won't burn, I've seen a lot of them this week red as a fire truck." Hazel had the same expression on her face I probably had. "It's just that I noticed your wedding rings and…"

"We don't have husbands," Hazel blurted out.

"That's right. We thought the rings might keep horny boys away." I was pretty proud of myself for thinking up that lie so fast.

"For girls as pretty as you two, it won't make much difference. Boys know that a lot of girls try that trick. I think both of you have been out in the sun long enough for your first day. Are you hungry? There's a hotdog stand just up the beach and a place we can shop for hats and sunglasses. You need a hat to keep the sun off your face and I want a new one too."

The hotdog stand was bigger than I imagined it would be and there were all kinds of little shops attached. We spent the rest of the afternoon shopping. The only color hats they had were white and beige, but there were lots of styles to choose from. "I'll be so glad when this war's over and we can get clothes in bright colors again." Susan was saying what I was thinking. "Maybe the tourists will come back too. Right now, things are tight around here. My boss at the Pearl has already cut some girls back to three nights a week and I don't know how I can make it on that."

"Oh, what do you do?" Hazel asked.

"I'm a stripper at the only kiki club in Clearwater. The Pink Pearl is the best kept secret in town that everyone knows about, but nobody talks about. Before the war, we got lots of young men who came in just to see a woman strip and middle-aged tourists from up north who were curious to see what a Florida lesbian looks like. Then we had the local crowd as well, mostly older bulldykes who've lived here for years. Now the young men are getting drafted or joining and the tourists are staying home because they're afraid to travel, or they don't have ration cards for tires. It's tough all over."

"Are you working tonight?" Hazel would never admit it, but I know I took the words right out of her mouth. Any place called the Pink Pearl had to be worth seeing.

"This week I'm working tomorrow night, Friday night and Saturday night. Would you like to drop by? It might be fun and I can get you in without a cover charge. Normally it's five dollars just to get in the door. Please say you'll come."

"We'll think about it," Hazel answered for both of us.

Late that afternoon, when the sun was about to set, Susan suggested we go for a walk down the beach later. "There'll be lots of people out walking. I'll bring a bottle of something. I just love rum and Coca-Cola, don't you?"

"Anything but rum and Coca-Cola," we answered at the same time.

"Then screwdrivers it is—meet you back here at ten. I need to take Mom grocery shopping, but we'll be done by then."

Even before we got back to our room, I knew Hazel would have questions I would have to answer carefully. As soon as we got inside, she let me have it. "You see naked girls every day. Why on earth would you want to go to a striptease show? You don't know what kind of people will be there—and what's a kiki? What's a bulldyke? You just want to see her naked, don't you? I thought this was supposed to be our honeymoon and all of a sudden you want us to share it with a pretty girl? Three's a crowd, Otha May. If you want to go, then go, but it'll be without me."

"I won't be going anywhere without you. I just thought it might be fun and she seems like a sweet girl. She wouldn't let anything happen to us. I don't know what a kiki or a bulldyke is either, but I'm sure they're nice people."

"And you'll get to see Susan naked."

"That's her job."

"Our daddies have jobs and you have a job. Taking your clothes off in front of strangers ain't a real job. What kind of girl could do that?"

"Let's go on the walk with her tonight—we sort of promised, and if you still feel the same way tomorrow, we won't go."

"And you'll be mad at me for not going. I can't help being jealous, Otha May. I know how pretty you are and what every boy and half the girls are thinking about when they see you. I bet Susan's one of them too."

"You mean one of us don't you?"

"I am not a lesbian." She didn't exactly scream it, but she made sure I heard her. "Being in love with you does not make me a lesbian. I don't ever look at another girl that way. I never have and I never will." I'd only seen her cry a few times, and I hadn't been the cause of it, so when the tears came, I felt lower than a sow's belly. She didn't want me to, but I took her in my arms and held her close.

"Nothing and no one in this world will ever turn my head. It's been turned already and I'm so sorry for acting like such a fool with Susan. We do things *together* and we always will. If one of us says no, it's no for both of us; simple as that. Now, how about a long bath together and let's forget about my crazy ideas." That must have been the right thing to say because she kissed me and after our bath, we spent more time together in that giant bed.

That night we walked for miles and drank orange juice, the first fresh orange juice I'd ever tasted. I'd've liked it even without the vodka. Susan drank more than anyone and she talked more than anyone. It was like she'd been waiting for us to come along. It had been a rough life for her so far. Her father left when she was a baby and her mother had to work in the orange groves while Susan stayed with a woman who kept children for a dozen families in the same shape. This woman was good to her, but there were eleven other children she had to watch all day. She grew up barely knowing her mother and not knowing her father at all. When her mother's legs were crushed by a falling scaffold, Susan had to quit school at sixteen and take her place in the groves. She worked there for two years until she was old enough to work in a strip club; there were dozens of them in the area. She worked seven days a week until the war came. It was good money and her mother thought she had a second shift job at the orange juice canning plant. Now she only had work occasionally at the Pink Pearl and the Sand Castle, which she described as an old man's strip club. Most of the girls her age wouldn't work there because the tips were always small, and tips were all she got paid at either place. She also tended bar at the Oasis hotel when they needed her. She and her mother were getting by, but just barely.

"We're going to the Pink Pearl tomorrow night," Hazel announced when we got back to our hotel after our walk with Susan. "She's such a sweet girl and we're going to tip her like we have money to burn... if it's all right with you." I didn't know if it was the booze talking or not and it didn't matter at the time. "She's not a lesbian either. I asked her when you ran out into the ocean to pee. Remind me, I want to do that before we leave. I needed to go too, but I wanted to talk to her a minute without you around. It's not really talking behind your back if I tell you about it afterwards, is it? I'm sorry if it is, but I couldn't ask with you right there. What was I talking about? It doesn't matter. You know, you would make a great stripper. I bet you could make a lot of money. You have a beautiful body any man or woman would pay to see. Forget I said that—not the part about you having a beautiful body—the part about you making a great stripper, but you would. So, can we go tomorrow night? I figure it would be rude if we went and didn't watch, so I won't be upset if you happen to look at the naked girls occasionally. We have to really applaud when it's Susan's turn to strip. I wonder if that's what you're supposed to do." She kept talking while I undressed her for bed and she was asleep the instant her head hit the pillow. I lay there next to her and thought again how lucky I was to have found her.

We went to the Pink Pearl and had the time of our lives. If Susan hadn't been with us, we would never have found the place. There were no signs, only a door and you had to be let in. We tipped all the girls that night and Susan a lot. We didn't pay for anything because Susan said that good tippers never had to pay for drinks. I don't think there was much alcohol in any of them we tried because I had five and didn't feel woozy at all, neither did Hazel. Susan said they watered them down, but I think ours were all water and some kind of fruit juice. There was a lot to learn about how to act in a strip club, so we sat and watched a while after Susan found us a table and went to get changed. The first thing I figured out was how to tip. You don't just throw money at the girl on the low stage. You walk over and stand there until you're noticed; then the girl comes over and shows you where you can put the money. Sometimes it goes in her garter, but if the tip is big, there are other places she lets you put it—while getting a little feel if you want. There were as many women in the place as men and even a few couples. Some were girl couples— but they were couples. I'd never seen two girls kiss before, but after their dance, each girl went around to the big tippers and gave them a kiss, whether they were men or women. Some of the kisses were on the lips and lasted a good long while. Hazel and I got lots of kisses that night and those from Susan were special. She sat with us after she finished her dance in the rotation of six girls, and then the other girls began sitting with us after they finished. We met all of the dancers and every one of them was as nice as any girl you'd meet at church on Sundays. Susan said that all the girls who worked weeknights were nice, but that the ones who only worked the weekends were a rough bunch.

After the place closed, Susan walked with us back to our hotel and Hazel asked her to stay, that it was too late for her to be walking home alone. "This town's as safe as they come and there's a certain cop who just happens to know when and where I'm working. He drives back and forth from the club to my house while I'm walking until I get home. He's asked me out a couple of times and maybe I'll say yes the next time. Thank you both again for coming. It was a lot of fun." The kisses she gave us before she left were hot enough to start a fire in wet kindling.

Watching her kiss Hazel set things to tingling even more than when she kissed me.

"Are you sure you're not..." Hazel was breathless when her kiss ended and it was hard for her to get the words out.

"Yep, I'm sure. I just like kissing girls and always have. They're better than boys, but I don't have to tell you that. I have a stretch for the next two weeks where I'm working the bar at the Oasis beginning at noon and dancing at night whenever I can. I won't get much time off, but I really need the money. You can come by while I'm working and see me for a few minutes, can't you? I do get breaks whenever I want."

We saw a lot of her while we were there, but we never had more than a few minutes at a time to talk after that first night. It wouldn't have surprised me if Hazel had offered to sneak her onto the train and take her back to DeKalb County with us. For a girl who said she didn't like girls—except for me, Hazel sure liked Susan a lot and so did I.

For the first time since our wedding, Hazel and I got to live like a married couple—maybe a married couple on vacation, but a married couple all the same. We talked a lot and we had the chance to talk things through all at one time, not splitting up the conversation when one of us had to go do something at home or at work. There was so much about her I hadn't known until then. Her grandfather, Riley Leeth, arranged her daddy's marriage to her mother. Her mother's father was a man named Percy Oliver, a worthless drunk who treated his wife and Hazel's mother worse than slaves. Hazel said he killed her grandmother Oliver because she didn't have supper waiting for him when he got home drunk late one night. Hazel's mother was twelve years old at the time and an only child. The Leeths lived just down the road and saw what was going on and didn't think Uldean, Hazel's mother, should be living alone with a man like Percy after what he'd done. That's when Riley came up with the idea of his sixteen-year-old son, Emmitt, marrying her. Percy didn't like the idea, but for twenty dollars he would consider it. Everything was arranged, and the marriage was set. It wasn't like Emmitt and Uldean didn't know each other, Hazel told me. They were three grades apart in school, but it was a small school and everybody knew everybody, and they did see each other at church when Uldean would go with her mother, and she went by herself after her mother died. When Percy had spent the twenty dollars, probably on liquor, Riley was told it would take another twenty for him to consider signing for Uldean to marry Emmitt. There wasn't another twenty dollars in the Leeth's house, or anyone else's. The wedding was called off, but that wasn't the end of it. A few months later, after having Uldean come to their house in the middle of the night several times when her daddy would come home drunk, Riley and some of the other men of the community decided to pay Percy a visit. More than a dozen men in white robes showed up late one night to put a stop to things. One of the men happened to be a judge and brought along the marriage consent form. Percy signed. Riley took Uldean back to his house with him that night and the judge performed the marriage in their living room with all the Klansmen as witnesses. It was an upright marriage. Emmitt and Uldean were good people and anyone could see they were good parents to their kids.

I also didn't know Hazel had almost died when she was three, from whooping cough, and that her daddy sold his truck to get enough money to take her all the way to Evanston, Illinois for treatment. He was that kind of man: the kind that would do anything for his family. The medicine was no guarantee she would get better, but it was their only hope back then. Hazel remembered the doctor's name, Doctor Sauer, because her mother sent him a card every year on Hazel's birthday, thanking him for saving her little girl. That was easy for me to believe because that's the kind of woman Mrs. Leeth was.

I didn't have any good stories to tell Hazel about me. I had good parents and good grandparents and if Daddy was ever in the Klan, I never knew about it. We eventually got around to talking about how I could adopt Abigail and we decided that finding another retiring judge with two horny nephews was out of the question. We still didn't laugh about that night, but bringing it up wasn't so painful anymore.

"We're legally married, so I don't see why you couldn't just adopt her like anybody else would do."

"I could try to do that, but Mrs. Yother says we would have to appear before a judge. That would be a problem right off the bat. It's not like he wouldn't notice we're both women. If we managed to get past that, you would have to swear that the daddy's dead or that he's run off—or you'd have to get the daddy to give up all rights. Do you think Donnie would do that? He wouldn't have to go before a judge. All he has to do is sign a paper and have it notarized. Mrs. Yother knows what to write and she said she'd do it. You'd just have to get Donnie to sign it."

We decided there had to be a way and that we would find it. Mrs. Yother would do what she could, but I couldn't help thinking she might not be around much longer.

Chapter Seventeen
Seeing Things Clearly

It seemed like the train that took us home traveled a lot faster than the one we rode going the other direction. I thought we'd get homesick after a week, but that didn't happen, although Hazel had to have thought about little Abigail when I did my part in keeping her breasts from getting too full and aching. I thought I should help out a couple of times a day just to keep her milk coming—that's what I told her anyway. For months she said she was going to wean Abby right after her first birthday, though I didn't believe her. She liked breastfeeding too much and I liked having a taste when we had time alone. Soon we wouldn't have much of that, so her milk would dry up on its own when she did decide to wean Abby.

It was a wonderful trip and we didn't want it to end. Then again, we knew we had people who depended on us. I thought a lot about Mrs. Yother on the way back and hoped she'd like the little Florida souvenir I got her. They called them snow globes and we saw them for sale everywhere. We had two pasteboard boxes full of things we bought everybody, although most of it was for Abby.

Daddy was waiting at the depot when we pulled in and, even though he was never a hugging kind of man, he grabbed us when we stepped off the train like we'd been gone a year. Hazel and I talked so much on the way home, he barely had a chance to get in a word edgewise. When we slowed down a hundred yards from the Yothers', he interrupted me talking about seeing a shark—that turned out to be a dolphin.

"All this was your mother's idea and when she told Mrs. Leeth, the two of them went a little crazy. Truth be told, it was the Yothers' idea in the first place and Mrs. Yother told your mother what they had in mind right after the two of you left. The rest of us just helped. I hope you won't be aggravated at them. They thought they were doing the right thing and you know Mrs. Yother's a strong-willed woman. If you, and I mean either of you, hate what's been done, please don't show it. They worked so hard on getting everything ready and they're waiting for us." He then turned into the Yothers' driveway. "They made me promise not to say anything, but I know how you can be, Otha May, and that's why I waited until now to speak up. You would have gotten it out of me and your mother wouldn't have been happy about that. Now, that's all I'm gonna say, other than enjoy your supper. Your mothers have been working on it all day I'm sure. Don't ask me any questions. We're here and you two can get out and go on in. The women can do the rest of the talking. I'm going on home. They have a lot to talk about that I don't need to be around for and Mr. Leeth's probably thinking the same thing."

I was expecting a little "welcome home" supper, but with all Daddy said, it sounded like something serious had happened and I'm sure Hazel could see in my eyes what I was seeing in hers. We were both a little shaky as we climbed out of the truck and walked up to the front door. Mrs. Yother must have been looking out one of the side windows because she opened the door before I had a chance to knock. She looked fine and hugged us both and then it was a hug from Mama and Mrs. Leeth. Glenda handed little Abigail to Hazel and she got a hug too. Nothing seemed wrong and when Ruby announced that supper was ready, we followed her into the dining room. It was a great supper they'd made for us, but Hazel and I kept looking at each other as if we were expecting them to tell us something awful had happened while we were gone.

"Dessert can wait." Mrs. Yother announced when we had our fill of catfish, mashed potatoes and green beans. "We've been busy while the two of you have been off honeymooning and we'd like to get your opinion of our work." She stood up and motioned for us to follow her. I had no idea where we were going when she started for the front of the house. When we got to the stairs, Mr. Yother took her hand. "I can make it just fine Mr. Yother. You watch yourself." I'd never been upstairs in the Yothers' house and didn't even know how many rooms were up there. "You see, Mrs. St. Clair, these stairs have become troublesome for Mr. Yother and we've discussed what to do about it." She stopped halfway up, and I could tell she was using talking to us as an excuse to rest a spell. "I guess I have to be careful when I say Mrs. St. Clair now since at the moment there are three of you in the house."

She was out of breath when she finished the long flight of stairs, but she continued talking. "Your families were nice enough to help us move my and Mr. Yother's bedroom and things downstairs into two of the spare bedrooms that haven't been used since Elton moved out. It was a shame to keep those rooms closed off and Mr. Yother and I decided we would be happy using them ourselves. So you see, we then had all this space up here that wouldn't be used. There's a full bathroom, a study, and another room that was never used for anything but storage. All of that's gone now and thanks to your mothers, everything is clean. I don't know what Mr. Yother and I would have done without their help. Your fathers moved the heavy furniture and set it up for us downstairs. Ruby and Glenda moved some of my books and all our clothes. They also fed us every day we worked. This is the bedroom."

When she opened the door, we followed her in. I recognized the quilt on the bed and Hazel recognized the curtains on the window. We looked around and found other things we recognized. When I opened the double closet, there hung my clothes on one side and Hazel's on the other.

"What is all this, Mrs. Yother?" I managed to get out before being given the answer.

"It's yours Mrs. and Mrs. St. Clair—that is if you want it and you'd be damn fools not to."

"We moved everything while you were gone," Mrs. Leeth said with a tear rolling down her cheek while hugging Hazel. "All your things are here, plus a few more Mrs. St. Clair and I decided we could do without. It's not proper for a married couple with a baby to have to live in separate houses. The bed is new. Mrs. Yother bought it for you and Hazel. She made me promise I wouldn't tell you and now I have."

"Rent is twenty dollars a month and I will be taking it out of your pay. Now, say 'Thank you, Mrs. Yother', and shake my hand. That will be good enough for me; besides, I have witnesses." She finally smiled. "I know it's just temporary until you get your house built, but we thought it would do until then."

"I don't know what to say. It's too much. You didn't have to do this—all of you. Thank you Mrs. Yother and I promise you won't even know we're here."

The room next door was empty except for a mailbox leaning in a corner, which looked completely out of place. "This is Mr. Yother's housewarming present," Mrs. Yother explained. "He wanted to put it up last week, but I wouldn't let him until we heard whether you wanted the rooms or not."

"And I had to paint it three times before Mrs. Yother would approve the color and then I had to paint ours the same color. I hope you like it."

It was the most beautiful mailbox in the world, not because of the color, but because Mr. Yother had painted Mrs. and Mrs. St. Clair on both sides in big red block letters that stood out from the yellow that was the same color as the house. The study still had two bookcases full of medical books in it that Mrs. Yother said I might want to read. She said they didn't move them because they were so heavy. It was her way of saying she was leaving them to me. While Hazel and I were gone she'd started getting ready for what was to come. Letting us move in was Mrs. Yother's way of telling me she wanted me nearby in case she needed me. I knew that, and she knew that, so there was no reason for either of us to say anything.

After our tour of our new home, we went back downstairs for dessert. Ruby had made a blackberry pie and while we were having seconds, I asked what had been going on with our patients while I was gone.

"We delivered Mrs. Amberson's baby boy and cured a stranger of the yellow fever."

"Ruby, I told you it wasn't yellow fever. Just because a woman has a yellow discharge from her vagina and a temperature, it doesn't mean she has yellow fever." Mrs. Yother was clear in what she had to say, as always, and Mr. Yother found a reason to excuse himself from the table.

"Well that's what colored folks call it. I've seen what it can do. That's what killed Opal Johnson when I was just a young'un. I heard the older women talking about it. She went crazy just before she died and tried to cut her own head off with a butcher knife. Some of the men had to tie her to the bed."

It wasn't the kind of conversation most folks would have at the table, but we weren't most folks. I was glad that Daddy and Mr. Leeth weren't there though.

Our first night in our new home Hazel and I settled into what would become a nightly routine. We cleaned up the table and helped Ruby with the dishes, fed the babies and listened to the radio with Mr. and Mrs. Yother. I had to be caught up on the war news that first night. I was a little ashamed about how little I knew with me having a brother in the Navy—and a brother-in-law too. The Germans were tied up at a place called Stalingrad somewhere in Russia and Mr. Yother said the Russians weren't giving up so easy this time. There wasn't much good news about the war in the Pacific and Atlantic. The German U-boats were sinking anything afloat, and even though we were taking islands on the way to Japan, their navy shelled the islands as soon as we landed. The good news on that front was that we would soon have dozens of air bases we could reach Japan from.

***

That spring I learned more about Mrs. Yother's cancer. She said it was a part of my continuing education from her that would never end as long as she was alive. She had started morphine injections while Hazel and I were in Florida, but she preferred that I give them so I could keep up with how much she was getting. It hurt me to my soul seeing her getting weaker by the day, but I never heard her mention anything about how she felt. Hazel was a happy housewife with a one year old. She and Ruby kept the house running and the babies happy while Mrs. Yother and I saw patients. I worked harder than ever to make sure she wouldn't have our patients to worry about when she could no longer help. She insisted that I do all the examinations while she took notes. In early April we had a new patient, Mrs. Eloise Cochran. She and her husband had just moved into the community and when she told a few of the women that she thought she might be pregnant, they referred her to us. She'd only missed one period, but I failed to tell her not to get her hopes up like I would normally have done, and Mrs. Yother noticed. She was so excited, I didn't want to spoil the mood for her. It was a routine examination. She didn't know me, and I didn't know her, but when it was all over and done with, she said she would be back. That was the kind of patient I liked. After the examination, Mrs. Yother left me with her to finish up. All I had to do was wipe away the K-Y and help her get dressed. After that was done, I led her into the office to find Mrs. Yother sitting in my chair in front of her oak desk. I didn't want to say anything right then, with Mrs. Cochran there, so I walked around the desk and sat down in her seat. We talked with her and I explained what I had observed—nothing to be concerned about and Mrs. Yother entered the additional information in her file; the way I'd always done. When I finished, I walked Mrs. Cochran to the front door and reminded her of the next appointment we scheduled for her on June 5. I also told her not to tell her husband she might be pregnant until after that visit. Mrs. Yother was still sitting in my chair when I returned to the office.

"Mrs. St. Clair, I think you have somehow learned a great deal about bedside manners in your training. Lord knows you didn't learn it from me."

"You are mistaken, Mrs. Yother. Everything I know, I learned from you." The new office seating arrangement with patients was never mentioned. That's just the way things would be from then on.

Besides worrying about Mrs. Yother, I was worried about Bill and James. We heard from them at least once a week while they were in training at Fort Pierce, though no one had heard anything since early March. We guessed they'd been shipped overseas and couldn't write, but Mama said Bill wouldn't have left the country without letting us know—unless it was on short notice. When we finally did get a letter, it was so cut up we couldn't read it. He didn't say where he was or where he was going. All we knew was that he was alive. His letter was dated March 28, but it was postmarked April 12 and we didn't get it until the 20th. With all the letters being read before they could be delivered to anyone, it was amazing we got it that soon. The Leeths got a letter from James the day before and we compared what they'd written and still didn't learn much. We had just finished supper the day after we got the letter from Bill when we heard over the radio that the Japs were executing prisoners. The reporter said that President Roosevelt released the news in a speech earlier that day. Mr. Yother said they would pay for that, but all Hazel and I wanted was to go home and be with our families for a little while. I knew Mama and Daddy heard the same broadcast on WLW out of Cincinnati. It was about the clearest station on the radio after dark and Daddy always listened to the news when supper was finished. I wanted to make sure they knew the soldiers killed were pilots, not regular Navy men. Mama was already in bed when I got to the house and Daddy said she'd been crying ever since the news went off. I went in the bedroom and lay down next to her. "Bill's okay, Mama and this war will be over with before he has to fight. He's probably on a ship somewhere a long way from the war, and the radio announcer said it was airmen the Japs killed. You know he's afraid of airplanes."

"You don't know how much I wished you were here a while ago. I hoped you would come and be with me a little bit and you have. Have you eaten supper?" I never visited her without being asked if I'd eaten.

"Yes, Mama. Ruby made a good supper for us tonight and I had plenty."

"Well, you've been looking too skinny lately. Has work been hard?"

"No harder than usual. You know I always get skinny before the garden comes in. I'll fatten up when we start getting fresh corn." I hadn't lost weight and could tell she was just making conversation; she didn't want to talk about Bill or the war, so we just talked about whatever came to mind until Daddy came in and said he needed to get to bed so he could get up the next morning for work. I gave her a kiss and started to get up.

"I pray for him every night."

"I do too Mama."

***

The first Sunday in May was coming, Decoration Day at High Point Baptist and everyone we knew above ground and below would be there. Mrs. Yother had a surprise announcement at breakfast that Monday morning after Easter. We always ate breakfast together early; as soon as Ruby got it done.

"I'm not going next Sunday."

"Yes, you are Mrs. Yother."

"I don't feel well."

"You just don't want anyone seeing you walking with your cane; admit it. Elton and Elizabeth will be in on Friday and everyone will be expecting to see them in the graveyard on Sunday morning with you. Missing church yesterday was bad enough."

"I don't have anything to wear. I've lost so much weight; everything I own just hangs on me like a scarecrow."

"Tomorrow morning you can sign a check and Hazel and I will drive to town and buy you something that fits. We don't have any appointments all day and it'll be a good trip for us. Besides, I want to get Hazel something new; she deserves it. She's down to her weight before Abby was born and I'm going to buy her something pretty whether she wants me to or not."

"Where did you learn to be so hard-headed?"

"I learned from the best, Mrs. Yother."

That night at supper, plans were made. By then I didn't like for both Hazel and me to be away at the same time, but it would only be for a day and Ruby could help Mrs. Yother if any emergency came up. Between the two of them, they could do about anything. Ruby was strong and Mrs. Yother's mind was still sharp as a fish hook even if her body was becoming frail.

"Do you remember what happened here?" We were about a mile from the Duck Springs Baptist Church and I knew what she was talking about, though I didn't let on.

"Here? It's not even a wide spot in the road. I can't imagine anything ever happening here, not anything important anyway." If I hadn't been grinning from ear to ear, she would probably have punched me.

"If you had it all to do over, would you still ask me? I'd still say yes if you did." My dead and buried relatives of the Duck Springs Cemetery had another chance to see us kiss that Tuesday morning. Yes, I would ask her again. The things we had to go through to be married were all worth it and we were beginning to only remember the good parts.

The salespeople were glad to see us in every store we went in and I found Hazel a beautiful yellow dress at Sears and Roebuck. There were a few colors to choose from and that was a nice surprise. I wasn't satisfied with just a dress though; I had to buy her everything from her skin out. She wasn't pleased with me spending so much money, but getting to see her in new clothes that weren't black or brown was worth every penny. When it came to a bra, she chose one of those bullet ones like she'd seen in a magazine—but she wouldn't let me buy her one unless I bought one for myself. They were stiff as pasteboard, but I liked how they made us look. "Everybody will sure think we've filled out since last spring, Otha May."

"They'll certainly think I have."

It being a weekday, there weren't many shoppers, and besides, there still wasn't too much to buy, although it was a lot better than it had been the last time we were in town. I didn't bother going in any of the discount stores for Mrs. Yother's dress; she wouldn't care how much we spent on it. We headed straight for Mildred's. I'd only ever window shopped at that store, but I saw some boxes at Mrs. Yother's, so I knew she'd been there. It was like walking into a different world. There were colors everywhere. It seemed that not every clothing store was suffering, and when I asked one of the salesgirls, she told me that Mrs. McGee had connections in New York. After looking around, I figured out the catch. Unless you were skin and bones or big as a cow, there wasn't anything in your size, but half the dresses in the store would fit Mrs. Yother. We settled on a light pink dress and a cute little yellow hat to go with it. They had bullet bras too, but we figured that would be going too far for her.

Things were busy in the Yother house that Wednesday and Thursday. Between our regular appointments, we cleaned, and Mrs. Yother saw cleaning the same way she saw everything else. It had to be done right, and if she couldn't do it, she would make sure everyone else did. Hazel and I weren't exactly model housekeepers and it took us most of the time with the upstairs. Ruby kept the downstairs in good shape, but Mrs. Yother made it clear she wasn't to clean for us. We didn't finish until nearly noon on Friday, just before Elton and Elizabeth arrived. It didn't take long before we figured out how pussy whipped Elton had become, but some of that was overlooked when Elizabeth announced at supper she was three months pregnant. She also made a point in saying she had the best doctor in Evansville.

"Do you have a man doctor or a woman?" Mrs. Yother asked before even congratulating her. I expected that question and Elizabeth should have.

"It's Doctor Moorehouse and he's the best. All the girls in our neighborhood go to him."

"Walter Moorehouse?"

"Yes, that's his name. Do you know him?"

"Well enough to know he's not delivering my grandbaby. I'll bet he didn't do any of your examinations himself. He had a nurse do them. Tell me if I'm wrong. Walter Moorehouse hasn't seen a woman naked since he graduated Vanderbilt."

I could tell by the expression on Elizabeth's face that Mrs. Yother wasn't wrong. Elton changed the subject and Elizabeth's pregnancy wasn't mentioned again. There was no doubt in my mind though that someone else would be delivering her baby when the time came.

Mrs. Yother looked like she was ready to walk out onto a stage when she arrived at the graveyard that Sunday morning—and there was no cane in her hand. Mr. Yother stood close to her as she walked with a purpose among the graves of long lost friends. Hazel and I walked with her and listened as she told us stories at every gravestone of someone she knew. We'd always made a point of saying hello to the Yothers at Decoration and talking a while, but this was the first time for me to spend the morning with her. I barely said hello to my own family and Hazel's. Something told me this would be my only chance to hear the stories she was telling. They were all good until we came to a grave with no flowers and a name on the headstone I didn't recognize. I thought I knew all the family names, but Hagerty wasn't one I remembered. The tombstone read "Mary Ellen Hagerty and infant daughter". "That wasn't her real name," Mrs. Yother said loud enough for anyone around to hear. "Her parents didn't want her buried in the family plot. She was just a child herself." Mr. Yother took the flowers from his wife's hand and placed them in a vase on the barren grave as the rest of the story came out. "Grandma Yother and I did everything we could to save this child and her baby. That's her vase on the grave. I hadn't even started school at Vanderbilt, but I thought I knew everything about delivering babies after watching and helping her for a few months. I didn't know anything about real life. Her name was Roxie. She was an only child. Her parents are buried at the other end of the cemetery. I hope wherever they are, they see me when I put flowers on their daughter and granddaughter's grave and know how much I despise them. That's the same thing

Grandma Yother would say every year when she put flowers in that vase; you'll put flowers in it every year when I'm gone."

"Yes, Mrs. Yother." She wasn't asking me, she was telling me.

"She was such a beautiful girl, not more than thirteen and it was her uncle Grady that got her pregnant, although I'm pretty sure only he, Grandma Yother, and I ever knew. He's buried in this graveyard with the rest of the family. Damn your soul, Grady Hubbard. Damn the whole Hubbard family for what you did to this poor girl. They never had a pot to piss in, but they had their pride and they kept that girl at home when she started showing so much they couldn't hide it. She walked four miles alone in labor that night to come to us. With a simple examination even a month earlier, we would have known the baby was breech. We could have saved her life at least and maybe the baby's. Stupid proud people killed them both."

Mrs. Yother was getting loud, so Mr. Yother took her hand and led her away from the grave. I knew the Hubbards and would never look at any member of that family again without thinking about what Mrs. Yother told me that Decoration Sunday.

***

We had several new patients that May. Mrs. Yother said that men didn't realize that sometimes when their wives scooched up close to them on a cold winter's night, it was only because they were cold. The women were all about four or five months along, so maybe she was right. On June 5 Mrs. Cochran showed up for her appointment and I could tell right away that something was wrong. It was a ten o'clock appointment and Mrs. Yother was just getting her bath, so I asked Ruby to assist me. Eloise had been perfectly healthy a month earlier, so I didn't expect anything out of the ordinary, but something had her at the point of tears. "I'm not pregnant. My cycle came back two weeks ago. I'm so glad I didn't tell Claude I thought I was pregnant. It would kill him to find out I'm not. We've been married two years now and I think he's beginning to wonder if something's wrong." I had Ruby find her file, so I could see what Mrs. Yother had written down at Eloise's last examination. There was nothing out of the ordinary except for a high cervix and I didn't remember anything else unusual either.

"All right, Mrs. Cochran; don't you worry. I'll have another look and see if there's anything I missed before. I'm sure whatever the problem is, we can fix it and if we can't, we'll find somebody who can. Ruby, would you help Mrs. Cochran get undressed and into a gown? I'll be in as soon as I can speak to Mrs. Yother."

Mrs. Yother was in the tub when I knocked on the bathroom door. "If the house isn't on fire and you're not Mrs. St. Clair, come back in half an hour. I'm fine and the water's still warm."

"It's me, Mrs. Yother. Mrs. Cochran's here and I'd like to talk to you about her."

"All right then, come in Mrs. St. Clair."

I told her what Eloise had told me and I felt a little ashamed having to ask what I should do, but this hadn't come up before. Our patients were usually well along in their pregnancies, so there were no doubts about things having gone right for them up to that point.

"Do the examination just like you normally would and then have a look with the speculum. Don't forget to warm it up first and tell her what you're doing. If you don't feel or see anything unusual, you're going to have to ask her some questions. Don't be shy about it. Ask how she and her husband have intercourse and how often. Most women don't have any idea how they get pregnant, not really. It's not as easy as everyone thinks. You know all the details, so explain them to her in a way she can understand. Don't leave out anything and set up another appointment for her in early October. If she's still not pregnant, we'll deal with it then. Mrs. Cochran won't be the only woman you will have this talk with, so remember what I said. Now, leave an old woman to enjoy her bath until the water gets cold."

"Thank you, Mrs. Yother."

Mrs. Cochran was standing in the short gown looking like she was expecting me to say what was wrong without ever having touched her. After removing it, I did the usual visual examination while Ruby took notes. I'd taught her the words I would be using and given her regular spelling tests so I could read what she'd written. She learned quickly. Mrs. Cochran looked like a healthy twenty-four-year-old woman. Her breasts were small but symmetrical and there was no discharge from either nipple. I saw nothing out of the ordinary anywhere in my visual examination. There were no lumps in either breast and I felt nothing out of place in her lower abdomen.

"All right Mrs. Cochran, if you would lie down on the table and put your feet in the stirrups, we'll check everything else." There were no external abnormalities. Her labia major and minor were pink and her clitoris appeared normal when I used both thumbs to push back the loose skin covering it. Ruby had the warmed K-Y ready for me and I took my time examining her cervix. It was smooth and symmetrical, but it was much higher up than normal and I understood why Mrs. Yother had made a note of that in her file. I had to push down on her lower abdomen hard to get my fingers all the way around it. A high cervix isn't so unusual and I knew there was nothing indicated by it, though this got me to thinking. The inspection with the speculum and flashlight didn't tell me anything new, but I took my time and had a close look while rehearsing in my head what I was going to say. When I had it down as well as possible, I wiped the K-Y off Mrs. Cochran and asked Ruby to bring her gown.

"Ruby, would you leave Mrs. Cochran and me alone for a few minutes. There are some things we need to discuss." Ruby left without asking any questions and I was grateful for that. Mrs. Cochran didn't bother getting up and putting the gown back on before coming apart at the seams.

"It's bad news isn't it? I have cancer don't I? I'll never be able to have children." Tears streamed down Eloise's face and I realized I should have found another way of getting Ruby out of the room.

"I'm so sorry if I've upset you, Eloise. I didn't mean to. No, you don't have cancer. In fact, you're healthy as a horse. Everything looks perfectly normal inside and out."

"Then why can't I get pregnant? Something's wrong and you don't want to tell me."

"No, I swear, nothing's wrong. I just thought the conversation we're about to have should be between us. Ruby's as trustworthy as the day is long, but I thought you might be more comfortable talking about the things we have to talk about with her out of the room. Truth be told, I'd be more comfortable too. I'm your midwife and I've heard and seen it all, so don't think anything you say today is going to surprise me."

"I don't have much to tell. I just can't get pregnant and I do know how women get pregnant."

"It's not as easy as you think. A lot of things have to happen at just the right time. So, I'm going to be very direct with my questions and I need you to be honest in your answers, okay? Now, how often do you and your husband have intercourse?"

"That is a pretty direct question... About once a week; usually on Sunday mornings. I know that sounds terrible—to do it before going to church, but that's the only time Claude feels up to it. He works twelve-hour days, sometimes six days a week. I'm lucky if he stays awake through supper. Mama said I was marrying an old man and that I shouldn't expect too much if I went through with the wedding, but I love him and I want to give him a baby." The tears came back and I stumbled for something to say.

"And what kind of work does your husband do?"

"He loads railroad cars at the depot now, though he's got to get a different job. His back hurts him something terrible."

"And when you and your husband have intercourse, are you usually on top, or is he?"

"Really, Mrs. St. Clair—that's not a question you should be asking. I'm not some two-bit floozy looking to get his money. I'm Mr. Cochran's wife and a respectable woman in the community." The tears were all gone and I realized I had a problem on my hands.

"I know you are, Mrs. Cochran, and I would never ask such questions if I didn't have to. Like I said, it's not as easy getting pregnant as you might think and we have to give you the best possible chance."

"You'll never breathe a word of this to anyone? You'll take this to your grave—promise me with your right hand to God."

"I've worked awfully hard to be where I am, and I'd lose everything if I ever talked about a patient to anyone other than a doctor or a midwife. The law is plain on this and I like what I do, so yes, I promise with my right hand to God."

"I'm always on top, for as long as we've been married. It's the only way Claude's back doesn't hurt him when we do it."

"And when the two of you finish, you get up and get ready for church?"

"I get a bath and get ready for church, that's right, but I don't see…"

"What that has to do with anything? Well, we might have found the problem."

"We should do it on a different day?"

I didn't mean to laugh, but I did and so did she. We made it through the hard part and I then got to the details of exactly how pregnancy occurs. She had lots of questions and I did my best to answer them in words she understood. Her high cervix and the way they had intercourse made it almost impossible for sperm to get to where they needed to be. That story made perfect sense to me anyway.

"So, I'm supposed to just lay there on my back with my knees in the air and a pillow under my butt for half an hour. Claude's gonna think I'm crazy."

"Tell him it's doctor's orders. Now lie back down and I'll show you a trick." I ran my finger the length of her labia and showed her how to tell if she's ovulating by how far she can stretch the mucous between her thumb and forefinger."

"And what if it's not wet down there, then what?"

"We both know how to make it wet down there, now don't we?"

That got another laugh and by the time she left the office, she was one determined woman. I made her an appointment for the first day of October and hoped she'd want to see me earlier than that with some good news.

***

Later in the summer, Hazel decided Mrs. Yother was going to have some help. "She won't let Mr. Yother help her get dressed in the mornings or with her bath and I'm afraid she's gonna fall and hurt herself. I have to tell her she's getting my help whether she likes it or not."

"You know that nobody tells Mrs. Yother anything, but if you talk to Mr. Yother and let him bring it up to her, she might listen." That sort of worked, but for a month, Hazel's help was not welcomed. Eventually though, it became part of the morning routine.

***

I could always tell when Ruby was hiding something and after a couple of days trying to imagine what it was, I just asked her what was on her mind. "I was just wondering, if it wouldn't be too much trouble, if you and Mrs. Hazel could maybe watch little Roosevelt some Sunday afternoon if I needed to go out for a while by myself. I know he's a handful and you already take care of Abby and Mrs. Yother and…"

"Why Ruby, you have a boyfriend don't you?"

"No Ma'am. I ain't got no boyfriend and don't want one. You remember me telling you once that every colored girl dreams of meeting a man with a job who'll be good to her? Well, it turns out that some colored girls dream of meeting a woman with a job."

"And one's met you, or you've met one?" The smile on her face gave me the answer to that question, but it wasn't exactly what I was expecting.

"To tell the truth, I've met half a dozen fine looking women at church, and several have asked me out. I've spent time with three of them Sunday afternoons at Mama's house and she said she'd watch Roosevelt if I wanted to go out somewhere with any of them, but I'd sure feel better if he was here. Mama already watches three children six days a week and I don't want to bother her on Sunday with mine. It would only be for a little while. There's a social at the church every third Sunday afternoon and I'd like to go to one sometime. I could bring the baby back here after church so you wouldn't have to watch him the whole day."

"So, who is the lucky girl? Is she pretty?"

"It's me that's lucky. Her name is Estelle Baker. She was married, but her husband ran off a year ago and nobody's heard from him since. She's got a proper divorce now. She showed me the paper."

"Just how old is this woman?"

"She's seventeen. She got married when she was fifteen and she don't have no children. She's the prettiest girl in church and all the boys are after her, but she says she's done with them for good. I was afraid to even talk to her and then one Sunday after church, she came up and started talking to me. Pretty soon talk got around to you and Hazel and she asked what it was like working and living with two women married to each other. I told her it wasn't no different than if you was married to a man, except I liked Hazel more than I ever could a man. One thing led to another and she asked if she could come to Mama's some Sunday afternoon. Of course, word got around and pretty soon, I had other girls asking if they could come over, but I like Estelle best of all of them. Last Sunday she asked me to the next social and I told her I'd give her an answer this Sunday. If it's too much trouble for you, I'll get Mama to watch Roosevelt. I really do want to go. I never been asked on a date before. She's from a good family too. The Bakers are hard workers and her daddy's held a job at the Ferguson's saw mill for the past eight years. Mama likes her and that means a lot to me. She and Mrs. Baker have known each other since they was kids. I didn't tell her that I might have more in mind than just being friends with Estelle, but I think she's figured that out."

"Well, you can tell Miss Estelle Baker you'd be proud to go to the social with her, and that if she has anything more serious in mind later on, she'll have to meet all of us before proposing." I couldn't help but grin when I said that last part.

Chapter Eighteen
When Everything's Said and Done

In early September one night after supper, Mr. Yother called me downstairs for a phone call. No one ever called me. I didn't know anyone with a phone. Mr. Yother had a funny look on his face and when I said hello, I knew why. It was Elton. "Elizabeth's not doing well, Otha May and I'm worried sick about her. She has horrible pain in her lower back and leg cramps that are so bad she cries, and she sometimes wakes up in the middle of the night with a fever. Her doctor told her it was nothing to worry about and gave her some medicine that hasn't done anything. I don't want to worry Mama, so I thought I'd ask you if you might know what's wrong with her."

"You should talk to your mother anyhow. She's probably seen this before."

"Who should talk to their mother?" Mrs. Yother said as she walked into the living room with Hazel hanging onto her arm. I handed the receiver to her and got up so she could sit down. I only got one side of the conversation, but I could tell Mrs. Yother was concerned, although she was trying her best not to upset Elton. When she hung up, she was no longer Elton's mother. "Ruby, go upstairs and pack my suitcase, then pack the car tonight with anything else you think we might need. Mrs. St. Clair and I are leaving for Evansville at sunup tomorrow morning. Make breakfast for us early and we'll eat it on the way. Mrs. St. Clair, go to my office and find the home phone number for a Doctor Theodore Blankenship." Neither of us questioned our orders. Mrs. Yother asked me to stay while she made the call. "Doctor Blankenship, my name is Lois Yother and I'm calling from near Gadsden, Alabama. I'm a licensed midwife and I got your name and number from Doctor Henry Gillespie at Holy Name of Jesus. I understand you interned under him in Lexington years ago." She talked for a few minutes and listened a few more and seemed pleased when she hung up the phone.

"Henry's a good man and he gave me the name of this doctor in Evansville when I called him last month. Blankenship sounds like he knows his business. He'll be meeting Elton and Elizabeth at the Deaconess Hospital tonight. I'm calling Elton back and he'll have Elizabeth there if he values her and his baby's life. I'm concerned that Elizabeth may have Toxemia if he described her symptoms correctly. If that's the case, the baby will have to be delivered now if there's to be any hope for it or Elizabeth. I've only seen a few cases and there were no survivors, but in a hospital, they have a chance. We have two appointments scheduled for tomorrow; they can wait and none of our other patients are near the end of their terms. If there are any emergencies, Hazel can drive them to Gadsden. I want you with me."

"Yes, Mrs. Yother. I'll be ready tomorrow morning."

"And I'll be up early in case you need me," Hazel added.

"Thank you, both of you. Now go to bed. We have a long day ahead of us."

***

"Have I told you today how much I love you Otha May?" It was late when we got to bed, but when Hazel's fingers started tickling my nipple through my gown, I knew she wasn't sleepy. "Sometimes I think about the crazy odds of us ever finding each other. I was ready to give up on any hope of finding a man to love me, and then you came along and gave me a different kind of hope. Without you, I would never have had a future, and now, together, the two of us have the world on a string. You're smart and pretty and I make you happy. I think all the time about how lucky I am and how many girls in this world would kill to have what I've got. You have a purpose Otha May, and my purpose is to see that you fulfill yours. I love you more than you can imagine. You're the reason I get up every morning and the reason I'm content when I can lay down beside you at night." Hazel told me once that she writes down things and practices what she wants to say to me. This was one of those times and her whispered words touched my soul.

"Sometimes I'm too pulled in different directions to realize how much you mean to me. Without you, none of this would be possible. You're the anchor in my world that reminds me of the things that're important. Make love with me tonight, Hazel. I'm yours and only yours, today and forever."

I surprised myself being able to say the right romantic thing at the right time. It must have been the right thing because the kiss I got was enough to make everything that had happened that day disappear for a while. When she slipped over on top of me, pulled down the top of my gown and began circling my nipples with her tongue, I felt a tingle that turned into a quick little spasm I wasn't expecting and that she probably didn't notice. "All you have to do is touch me sometimes Hazel and crazy things happen inside that I'll never be able to explain."

"Maybe you love me; ever think of that? Maybe you do the same thing to me when I can get you to pay me some attention. Maybe I lay awake sometimes wanting you to wake up and make love to me."

I reached down and pulled her gown up and off over her head. "And maybe I'm dreaming about you waking me up; ever think of that?" I said that a little too loud and we both listened for any sound from Abigail. She was down for the night I hoped. When I pulled Hazel to me and threw off the single sheet covering us, she slid up a little so I could have her breasts at my lips. Her nipples and areolas were almost back to their normal size. She was worried about that because they got so big while she was breastfeeding. I kept telling her they would shrink, but I knew that for some women, the change is permanent. A lot of the sensitivity had also come back and a simple touch would make her jump. She couldn't hide the little ripples running through her stomach muscles whenever my fingers found the right spot. She was enjoying every minute, but she did make me stop long enough to pull my gown off for me. In August, no woman wore panties to bed, so when my gown was taken care of, we were as close as two people can get. Even with both windows open and a little breeze stirring, we were soon sweaty and slippery all over.

"If you want me to beg, you know I will." I knew what she wanted and decided to play along.

"Beg for what? What is it you want me to do more than anything in the world right now?"

"I want you to move down a little so I can wrap my legs..."

"Why would you want me to do that? Don't you like what I'm doing now?"

"And I like what you can do with that charmed tongue of yours too. Okay, please, pretty please." I decided my little game had gone on long enough and slid farther down in the bed. She grabbed onto the headboard and held on for dear life. A few minutes later the vaginal muscles, the pubococcygeus and bulbospongiosus muscles to be precise, contracted in a rhythm I knew so well. I lay there motionless, still amazed by how our bodies work, and wondering why I remembered the names of those muscles right then.

"You'll be the death of me, Otha May St. Clair and as soon as I can move again, you're going to get what you gave."

That didn't happen. She didn't move until the alarm clock went off and Abigail began to cry. "I'll take care of her, Hazel; go and see to Mrs. Yother."

"I'm so sorry I fell asleep last night, but you wore me out quick."

"Kiss me and promise to do better when we get back. Say a prayer for Elizabeth and the baby today. Mrs. Yother's really worried and she never worries."

***

"When we get to Evansville, Mrs. St. Clair, we're going directly to the hospital. I think I put the fear of God in Elton last night and I'm sure he took Elizabeth in whether she wanted to go or not. Her blood pressure will be high if it is Toxemia and they won't try to deliver the baby until they get it stabilized. We should be there by then if you don't kill us on the way." I hadn't realized how fast I was driving and I didn't slow down. It was early morning and there wasn't much traffic until we got to Nashville. It took almost an hour to get through that mess, but we made good time afterward and arrived in Evansville well before sundown. The sandwiches Ruby made for us were enough to get us through breakfast and dinner, though we were starving by the time we arrived at the hospital.

Mrs. Yother asked to speak to the hospital's administrator at the receptionist's desk and the way she asked, the young girl knew not to question why. In a few minutes, we were led back to the office of Doctor Samuel Wainwright.

"Mrs. Yother, I was told by Doctor Blankenship to expect you; that you'd probably come looking for me first."

"It's best to start at the top when time is of the essence, Doctor Wainwright. I assume my daughter-in-law was brought in last night as per my instructions to my son."

"Yes, she's here and your son can thank you for saving her life. You probably guessed it was Toxemia.

Doctor Blankenship has been here all night trying to stabilize her blood pressure so we can deliver the baby. Nurse Carson will take you to him… and I took the liberty of notifying the hospital staff that you have full privileges while you're here. That goes for any assistant…"

"This is Mrs. St. Clair and she will accompany me. She's a fully trained midwife and I trust her to help whenever she's needed." The two of them talked for a few minutes and I could tell they had a mutual respect for each other's medical knowledge.

"Now there's a hospital administrator who's worth a damn; one of the few I've ever met." The heavy office door hadn't quite closed behind us before Mrs. Yother expressed her opinion and when I turned around to finish closing it, I saw a smile come to Doctor Wainwright's face. He knew who would be in charge of Elizabeth's care.

Nurse Carson looked to be about Mrs. Yother's age and it was plain to see that she was the one who really ran the hospital. The two women struck up a conversation as we walked toward the obstetrics wing and by the time we arrived at Doctor Blankenship's office, they were talking like they'd been friends for years.

"I'm so glad you could come Mrs. Yother." Doctor Blankenship looked to be not much older than me and I thought that would be a problem, but the more he talked, the more I realized how things would be. "I have Mrs. Yother—Mrs. Elton Yother—under sedation right now and her blood pressure has improved, but I wanted to wait until you got here before doing anything else. She and Elton have requested that you be her primary physician and I'm happy to assist you in any way I can. Of course, if we had been able to stabilize her blood pressure last night, I would have done a Cesarean, however in her condition, it was too dangerous in my opinion."

"And mine too Doctor Blankenship. Tell me, have you treated many Toxemia patients?"

"Yes, I've had three since medical school and I'm glad Henry—Doctor Gillespie—gave my phone number to you. I don't think any of the other doctors here have seen a single case. They're mostly specialists in other fields. I'm one of only two trained obstetricians at the hospital right now."

I thought it strange that Mrs. Yother hadn't asked about Elton or the baby at all and hadn't even asked if Elton was still at the hospital. Then I remembered what she told me so many times my first week working for her: the mother is the patient.

"I'll take you to her room and you can do your examination."

"Doctor Blankenship, this is Mrs. St. Clair and she will be assisting me if that's all right."

"Certainly. We've been told you have full hospital privileges and I'm sure that goes for anyone you would like to assist you."

Elizabeth looked terrible and the first thing Mrs. Yother did was order Elton out of the room. She was nice about it, but he knew not to argue with her. Elizabeth's blood pressure was still 170/110, but that was down from 190/140 according to her chart Mrs. Yother was reading to me.

"Mrs. St. Clair, it appears Doctor Blankenship has been successful in stabilizing Elizabeth's blood pressure by sedating her. It has been high but level all day. If she wakes up, it's likely to go right back up and we can't chance that. We would lose the baby for sure and probably Elizabeth too. The baby seems to have experienced periods of tachycardia and bradycardia corresponding to the mother's blood pressure." I knew those words—high and low heart rates. "That doesn't surprise me and the fact that it's still alive after what it's been through tells me we have a chance for a live delivery. Now, Mrs. St. Clair, I want you to climb up on the bed, do an external examination and get the current heart rate of the mother and baby."

The baby seemed large to me, active and turned the right way for a face-up vaginal delivery even though there wouldn't be one. Elizabeth's legs were blue, and I knew that wasn't good. Her heart rate was 50 and the baby's was 120. When I told Mrs. Yother, she asked me to take the baby's heart rate again. It was still 120. "The baby's waking up. Half an hour ago it was 90. We're going to deliver this baby now. We have to get it out so we can give Elizabeth an injection of sodium sulphocyanide if her blood pressure doesn't come down on its own. It's a dangerous drug, but it's been known to work. Scrub up Mrs. St. Clair and do a quick pelvic exam just to make sure we don't have any surprises in the delivery room."

Elizabeth wasn't in labor, so the exam went by the book for any late term pregnancy and I didn't find anything abnormal. I could feel the baby's head easily through the thinned cervical wall, and the baby felt me. There was a lot of movement and for a normal pregnancy that would have been good news for the mother, but in this case, it meant we had to act fast.

Things went on automatic for the delivery room nurses when they were informed we were to do an emergency Caesarean. They knew their jobs and when they came for Elizabeth, they only slowed down long enough for Elton to give her cheek a kiss. He was a wreck, but Mrs. Yother hardly spoke to him. I tried to tell him things would be okay, even if I wasn't too sure about that. Other nurses found gowns and masks for us after we scrubbed up and while Elizabeth was being prepped. Doctor Blankenship was right there with Mrs. Yother in case he was needed. In the delivery room no one would have ever guessed that Mrs. Yother was much sicker than her patient that day. Her vertical incision was sure and the others followed quickly. In less than a minute, she was through the uterine wall and

I could see the baby's nose. "Now I need those long fingers of yours, Mrs. St. Clair." There were forceps on the table, but I knew she wouldn't use them unless she had to. Mrs. Yother stepped out of the way and I forced my hands around the baby's head. One more small cut in the uterine wall and the baby was out. I held the squirming baby boy while Mrs. Yother tied off and cut the cord. A nurse then used a bulb syringe to suck the mucous out of his nose. Babies hate that and he screamed his head off, but it was music to everyone's ears. Mrs. Yother could have handed everything else off to the doctor, but she removed the placenta herself and placed it in a glass bowl held by another nurse. "Doctor Blankenship, your eyes are better than mine and if you would, I'd like for you to suture for me, but don't get in any hurry. I want her to bleed plenty. That will temporarily lower her blood pressure and maybe it won't go back up now that the baby's out."

A nurse and I washed the baby and sucked the mucous out of his nose again.

"Mrs. St. Clair, I…"

I turned away from the sink just as she was closing her eyes. A nurse caught her before she hit the floor. Another went for a wheelchair. I helped the nurse who caught her take Mrs. Yother out of the delivery room and sit her in a chair in the operating room next door. There was an oxygen line available and the nurse hooked up a mask and placed it over Mrs. Yother's nose and mouth while I took her pulse. It was 140, but her breathing was regular. She looked pale and her pupils were dilated. That scared me. My first thought was a stroke. The nurse that went for the wheelchair came back with a doctor from the emergency room. He did the same quick examination I'd done and ordered a gurney to take her back with him. She would be very disappointed in me if I left our patient, but I now had two patients and decided Elizabeth had enough help at the time. Poor Elton didn't know what to think when his mother came out of the surgical suite on a gurney while his wife was still in the delivery room. "The baby's fine. It's a boy. Elizabeth won't be out for a while. Your mother's going to be all right. We're just taking her to the ER for now." That's about all I could tell him as we went past and it was about all I knew.

They didn't find anything specifically wrong with Mrs. Yother in the ER; she hadn't had a stroke, so they put her in a room for observation. A nurse and I stayed with her the rest of the night. About midnight, Elton found us and told me Elizabeth was doing fine, that her blood pressure hadn't gone back up and that she was awake. He'd seen the baby and said he looked like Elizabeth's father. I hoped he was wrong, having seen pictures of the colonel. Doctor Blankenship had done a thorough examination and said the baby was quite healthy considering what he'd been through. Sometime around sunup, I heard Mrs. Yother trying to speak through the mask. When I took it off, the first words out of her mouth were, "Did Elizabeth make it?"

"Yes, Mrs. Yother, your patient is fine and so is the baby. I'm more concerned about you."

"I'm fine. We didn't eat anything much yesterday and I didn't take my injections because I wanted to be alert enough to deliver that baby if I had the opportunity. If you'll find my bag, we'll get this tired old body back in working shape." I could tell she was in a lot of pain and how she'd been able to stand it as long as she did, I'll never know. She had finally fainted, but only after finishing the job she came to do.

An hour after giving her the morphine injection, Mrs. Yother discharged herself and told Doctor Blankenship she'd better not get a bill in the mail for her visit to the ER. He was all smiles as he led us to Elizabeth's room. Both mother and baby were awake and we spent the rest of the day with them. Of course we had to inspect

Doctor Blankenship's sutures and make sure Elizabeth's breasts were producing milk. Mrs. Yother was satisfied her work was done and wanted to start back home that night, but for once Elton put his foot down and said he wouldn't hear of it. We did start back early the next morning though after staying the night at his house.

"Lewis—what kind of name is that? There's never been a Lewis in my family. Lewis—I hope he changes it when he grows up. How do people come up with such names?"

"I don't think he'll be changing his name, Mrs. Yother. They named him Lewis because it sounds like Lois. They named your grandson after you."

She had to ponder that and she was quiet all the way to Nashville, but after we got through the traffic, she wanted to talk. "When it's time, Mrs. St. Clair, and if I need you, I expect you to help me leave this world. You'll see it in my eyes if I'm not able to speak and the sight of you crying is not the last thing I want to see either. I've had a good life and I have no regrets, so follow your heart and my last request. No tears. You know what to do and I expect you to do it without any second thoughts. Is that understood, Mrs. St. Clair?"

I'm glad she turned her head and began looking out the side window so she wouldn't see the tears running down my face. "Yes, Mrs. Yother."

When we got back, everything was fine; no emergencies and our patients understood why we'd been gone. After a very late supper, I helped Ruby with the dishes and I could tell she wanted to talk. "Mrs. Otha, there's something I have to tell you and I'm supposed to tell you when Hazel's not around. I don't like keeping secrets, but I promised. Hazel's sister, Glenda came by and she asked me to set an appointment for her and she told me not to tell her sister. I didn't know what to do, so I made the appointment. She's Mrs. Smith in the book and she'll be by tomorrow afternoon. I know Hazel always visits with her mama on Wednesday afternoons so she won't be here. Seeing as how she's a patient now, I figured I had no choice but to do what she wanted."

"You did right Ruby. Our patients are our patients, even if they're kin. I'll see her tomorrow and I won't tell anyone she was here." With a soapy hand, I wiped a wayward strand of hair from her forehead and gave her a kiss. "You're one in a million Ruby and I hope Miss Estelle Baker realizes that." Hazel and I had watched little Roosevelt a few times so she could spend time with her new girlfriend and we cooked supper for the two of them one evening. Estelle was just as nice and pretty as Ruby had described her. Even Mrs. Yother seemed to like her.

"Estelle's a fine woman, Mrs. Otha." I'd become Mrs. Otha lately for some reason. "And I think she's hung the moon. To tell it all, we're as close as we can be and I'd say yes if she asked me to marry her. Am I supposed to ask her or is she supposed to ask me?"

I shouldn't have laughed, but I did. "I don't think it makes any difference, Ruby. Ask her yourself if you want to and if she says yes, then twenty years from now it surely won't matter who did the asking."

"I already know a preacher that'll marry us. Mama's cousin down in Lowndes County's a preacher. We don't need no piece of paper from a judge saying it's legal."

Glenda showed up the next Wednesday for her appointment and Ruby brought her back to the office. I was more than a little nervous, but I'd already decided I would treat her like any other new patient. I did tell Ruby that if an examination was in order, I expected her to assist me.

"Mrs. Smith, I'm happy to meet you and I'm glad you chose to come in today." Glenda caught on to our story right away and went along with it. "Now what can we do for you?"

It was some time before she got around to why she had come. "They say you know a lot about girl things, not just about delivering babies, and I thought maybe…"

For the next hour we talked about how our bodies work, everything from menstruation to pregnancy to childbirth. She got all the facts in words she could understand, although I could tell there was something more she wanted to know. I was simply remembering my experiences and repeating things I'd learned from a book. That was fine and good, but when I finally got out of her that what she really wanted to know about was what a woman feels and why, I got to the details she'd come for.

"It shouldn't be a deep dark secret that women have sexual needs and desires, although you won't find many men or even women who want to know anything about them. They certainly don't want to know how those needs and desires are satisfied. Maybe I should just show you what you look like down there first of all and I'll explain things along the way."

"Can you do that? I've tried to look, even with a mirror, but I couldn't see much and I didn't know what I was looking at anyway."

"Yes, I can. You're going to get our first-class examination, Mrs. Smith and today it's on the house. I'll ask Ruby to help you get ready."

"And you won't tell anyone I was here, will you? I'm not sure how my mother and sister would feel about me seeing a doctor without them, especially a woman doctor that delivers babies."

"Mrs. Smith, your visit is completely confidential; it's the law. Ruby and I like our jobs here and the women of our community trust us."

The examination went like any other, except for the large mirror I had Ruby hold up so Glenda could see what I saw. "And this little bump?"

"That's your clitoris, Mrs. Smith. When it's stimulated during sexual intercourse or in other ways, you'll get a pleasurable sensation that can lead to an orgasm; an involuntary contraction of the muscles around and inside the vagina."

"Sometimes it feels like my insides are gonna bust out when that happens." I don't think she meant to say that because her face turned beet red.

After the examination, we went back to the office and talked some more. She was still Mrs. Smith and during our talk I hadn't reminded her of what she'd seen when she helped me deliver little Abigail or the things we'd discussed in any of our other little talks. Maybe she didn't remember much of those conversations or just wanted me to explain some things again. Whatever it was, I pretended it was the first time the two of us had spoken at all. I sure wasn't expecting her last question though.

"How can a woman keep from getting pregnant and still do it?" She wasn't holding back any questions by that time. I knew she was still a virgin from the examination I'd done, but I wanted to give her the facts in case she had other plans.

"The sperm has to be stopped from reaching the cervix and the best way right now is for the man to use a prophylactic." That got a questioning look. We kept a supply for our patients who wanted to postpone becoming pregnant again, so I handed her one, then demonstrated how it worked. "Men call them rubbers and if they put one on their erect penis before sexual intercourse, then remove it directly after, they're very effective in preventing pregnancies." Then I smiled. "And the only way to make sure he has it on is to put it on him yourself."

"Where do you get them?"

"Drugstores have them, but you have to ask the pharmacist. They don't have them on the shelf next to the aspirin. We get them free from several manufacturers and give them to our patients for free when they ask for them."

"Am I one of your patients now?"

Hazel would never hear about any of our conversation even if Glenda hadn't been my patient. I didn't ask if she had a boyfriend and maybe she didn't at the time, but I sent her home with a handful of rubbers and a promise to give her more. Maybe having had an unmarried pregnant sister taught her something.

***

Finally we got letters from Bill and James—the day before Thanksgiving. They were serving on PT boats they said, though they didn't say where. The censors would've cut that out anyway. After their letters came we listened to the radio every night for any news about PT boats. Both letters said they were in good spirits and that our boys had the Japs on the run for sure. Bill said he missed Mama's cooking and from the looks of the picture he sent, she believed him. It looked like he'd lost weight and that worried her, but I thought he looked healthy. He was wearing shorts and no shirt and he had muscles where he'd never had them before. The Navy had leaned him up all right and there would be local girls to fight off when he got home. Neither letter mentioned anything about getting the letters we'd been sending. Mama wrote at least once a week and I'm sure Mrs. Leeth did too.

Every Sunday at church just before the benediction, Pastor Bouldin always asked the parents of boys in the military to stand up; then he would ask if any of them had any news they wanted to share. Mama was full up that next Sunday. Shouting's not something most people understand, but if you grew up in our Baptist church, you knew when someone was filled with the Holy Ghost, because they could be heard praising God a mile away. It had been a long time since Mama took off like that, but she had a lot to be thankful for that Sunday.

**

Mrs. Yother lived to see Elton married, deliver her own grandbaby, and wish me a happy twenty-first birthday, but not much longer. She died in her sleep—as far as anyone will ever know—two days before Christmas 1943 and was buried on Christmas Day. Some said it wasn't fitting to have a funeral on Christmas Day, but Mrs. Yother wasn't just any woman who happened to die when she did. By the crowd of people at the church that day, I'd say it didn't matter to most folks. She'd been too sick to go with me to Gadsden to apply for my midwife's license and that bothered her. Hazel and I went, but neither of us felt like making a day of it.

Mr. Yother took good care of all the arrangements for Mrs. Yother's funeral and I was glad that Elton and Elizabeth stayed for a few days afterward. We all wanted to get to know little Lewis better. There was something else that had to be taken care of as well. The Friday after the funeral we went to Mr. Saperstein's office for the reading of Mrs. Yother's will. It was exactly as she had told me. Hazel and I got the house and the sixty acres it sits on and all of Mrs. Yother's stocks and bonds, which Mr. Saperstein said were worth probably thirty-five thousand dollars. Mr. Yother got the money in her bank accounts, about fifteen thousand dollars, and the house in Mobile. Elton got the land in Blount County and sole ownership of the trust fund Mrs. Yother set up for him when he was born. Neither Elton nor Mr. Yother knew about the trust fund and Mr. Saperstein said there was some fifty thousand dollars in it. There was one addition I didn't know about. Five thousand dollars was left to Ruby to be used in her training to be a midwife. She'd thought of everything and everyone.

"There is a clear stipulation on what you get, Mrs. St. Clair, and Lois had me write it exactly the way she wanted. You are to use her money to turn the house into a maternity clinic that will be open to colored as well as white women, with part of the house reserved as a residence for Ruby Lee Camp, a colored woman currently in your employ. The remaining money may be used if needed to keep the clinic operational and pay salaries of anyone you choose to hire. Is that understood, and do you agree with the terms Mrs. Yother specified?"

"Yes, I understand what Mrs. Yother wanted and we intend to get started in the spring."

After the reading of the will, I asked Mr. Saperstein if Hazel and I could have a few more minutes of his time. Hazel didn't know what I had in mind, but I'd been thinking about something. When the three of us were alone, I asked how I would go about adopting Abigail. He wasn't as surprised as I thought he might be. "There's nothing specific in the law that says it can't be done and there's a judge or two I'm on good terms with. I have the forms you need to fill out and you can do that right now if you want. Every lawyer in town was at your wedding, but I'll need to verify that I've seen the signed marriage license. You can bring it by…"

"I just happen to have it with me."

***

My midwife's license arrived in the mail on January 17, but that wasn't the only good news that day. The license was wrapped around a personal letter from Senator Sparkman. He had known Mrs. Yother a lot better than she'd ever let on and he had nothing but good things to say about the work she'd done in the county. At the end, he wrote that he looked forward to receiving my proposal for assistance in continuing the work she had started.

"We're going back to Mr. Saperstein's and getting him to help us write this proposal," I told Hazel. "Senator Sparkman will make sure the Lois Yother Clinic for Women stays in good shape once he sees what we've built."

Groundbreaking for mine and Hazel's house was on March 10, the same day work started on the clinic. I got a good price from Mr. Darnell to do both jobs at the same time. He hired some extra help and for a while, he was the biggest employer around. The clinic stayed open during the entire job with examinations being done while sawing and hammering went on in the next room and one baby was delivered while the men were having dinner. Ruby became my assistant and with her new job, I told her we would be needing someone else to help around the house to do her old job. Estelle moved in a week later and the two of them got married the last Sunday in April. Hazel and I drove them and Ruby's mama down to a little church in Lowndes County for the ceremony. I was expecting it to be a private wedding, but when we got there, the church was full. Everyone made us feel right at home even though Hazel and I sort of stuck out, being the only white people there. That didn't seem to make any difference to anybody though. For a wedding present, we bought them matching wedding dresses and made an appointment with a real photographer in Gadsden. It was the first time either of them had ever had their pictures taken and the four of us made a day of it.

The next Sunday was Decoration and I walked through the graveyard with Hazel, Abigail, Mr. Yother, Elton, Elizabeth, and little Lewis while repeating the stories Mrs. Yother had told me the year before. We placed our flowers on her grave last and turned to walk toward the church. "There's one more bunch of flowers here," Mr. Yother said. Do you remember where they go?" I did and walked straight to the grave that had a tombstone with the wrong name on it. I said a prayer for Roxie and her baby, then put the fresh flowers in Grandma Yother's vase.

"Damn your soul, Grady Hubbard. Damn the whole Hubbard family for what you did to this poor girl." I was sure Mrs. Yother was listening.

Also from d.a. gregory and Solstice Publishing:

Jenny B.

Your grandparents and your great-grandparents weren't always old.

A diary found in 2008 by a seventy-nine year old widow in Evansville, Indiana provides a distinctly non-Hollywood look into what life was like during World War II in this racially divided war-economy driven small town. Our diarist is eleven when the story begins in the fall of 1940 and that's about all we know about the young writer; not even a name is given. It's a personal account after all and not written to ever be read by anyone else.

Virginia Lee Brewster's the prettiest girl in fifth grade and our storyteller's soon head over heels for her. The next five years see the two friends growing up fast and experiencing infatuation turning into a love that's never questioned, although it's not quite what either of them had always imagined love to be.

Some of the stories told in this diary would not have been spoken of in 1940s heartland America, not in polite company anyway, and they certainly would not have been committed to paper, even in magazines kept behind the counter at the local drug store.

https://bookgoodies.com/a/B079T85XPQ